TAMING PREHISTORIC

THIRD IN THE WEST OF PREHISTORIC SERIES.

ERIK 'TRACER' TESTERMAN

SEVERED PRESS

TAMING PREHISTORIC

For my parents, thanks for everything.

SEPTEMBER 1885
SMITH RANCH, STATE OF WYOMING.

It was dark when I reached my ranch on Lieutenant Daniels' borrowed horse. Just enough snow was falling to cover the ground with a thin layer, but still enough to tease a hard winter to come.

I was glad to be home.

It'd been an eventful couple of weeks since I was here last.

During that time, I was briefly jailed for murder, narrowly evaded a hanging, then returned to Prehistoria to fight at the fall of Fort Jipson. There I was left for dead, in an explosion of my own doing, blocking a tunnel that the survivors of the fort were escaping through. It took me three days to crawl out of the prehistoric forest filled with angry apes and savage dinosaurs to reach the Shimmer and make my way back to our side. Then, after executing our crooked Sheriff, I headed home to where my beloved mourned my untimely death. A bit pre-emptive if you asked me, but you couldn't blame her for figuring I was dead.

I was pleased to see during my absence that the barn had been mostly completed, except for trim and some windows, and from the looks of things the little, sheep-sized Protoceratops were still being kept inside. Hopefully, they were staying warm and laying lots of eggs for my little herd of dinosaurs to grow with.

Thin tendrils of smoke rose from the bunkhouse, where my lone hired hand, Bo, would be sleeping inside. I'd check on him later, but first things first.

Carbine, my dun mustang, stood with his front half sticking outside of his pole shed, pawing at the ground. Seeing me, he stopped, ears flicking, then he bounced forward. Sprinting across the corral, he jumped the fence, narrowly clearing the top rail.

I chuckled as he reached me and leaned over in the saddle to give his ears a scratch while he gave my borrowed horse the stink eye. He didn't seem to appreciate me riding another horse. Dismounting, I grabbed the reins in one hand and patted Carbine's neck as he shoved his head against me.

"Good boy," I rested my forehead against his shoulder. "Thanks for taking care of Skyla. I owe you a bushel of apples."

Carbine neighed and stamped his feet in agreement.

Giving him a final pat, I crossed the yard and turned Lieutenant Daniels' horse loose inside the corral. With some coaching and a few muttered threats, I managed to get Carbine to go back in as well.

Hearing a door open, I turned and saw Skyla standing on the porch, her trim outline framed in lantern light. Sara, our adopted baby triceratops, peeked her horned head around my favorite paleontologist and bellowed lightly.

I grinned and waved a hand like an idiot.

Skyla rushed across the yard and threw herself at me. I could only catch her and fall. The sound we made landing awkwardly was one of laughter and a grunt of pain from my battered body. She kissed my dirty, stubbled face passionately.

Kissing her back, I pushed myself upright only to be knocked down again as Sara butted her bone shield into me. Laughing, I gave the little triceratops a hug around her leathery neck.

"You're alive," Skyla said softly, tears trickling down her pretty face and wetting the snow sticking to her shirt. As happy as she was to see me, I got the sense that something was wrong.

"Sorry that I'm late." I apologized while looking behind her at a pair of shadows stretching towards us in the light of the house.

Charles stood just inside the doorway, a slight smile playing across his lips. Stitches ran along the gash in his face from the battle. Beside him was Elizabeth Stratten, Skyla's mother. She pushed past the Brit and stalked across the moonlit snow-covered yard. Her face was twisted in fury.

Dusting myself off, I stood, helped Skyla up and grimaced in anticipation of a tongue lashing for allowing her daughter to go into harm's way once again. "Good evening, Mrs. Stra-"

The unexpected force of her open palm slapping against my face made me stumble.

She held up an old, faded piece of paper with her other hand. On it, a terrible likeness of myself stared back. My wanted poster.

"Explain this, Orville!"

***

I frowned as I looked from the poor sketching to Skyla and then to her mother. My name wasn't on the wanted poster, Skyla must have told Elizabeth about my past over the few days I was missing.

Damn the luck of being thought dead.

Holding my hands up to placate her anger, I started, "Well, Mrs. Stratten, about that-"

Thundering hoofbeats came from the forested wagon trail behind us.

In surprise, we all turned to see a shadowy group on horseback barreling towards us. A gun blossomed fire from the lead rider followed by the sharp crack of a bullet as it passed by overhead.

More flashes came as the other riders opened fire.

Without thinking, I shoved Skyla away from me, towards the house, and drew my twin Colt Peacemakers.

It was too dark to use the sights, so I didn't. I just pointed in the bad guy's general direction and began side stepping towards the barn as I lit the group up by pulling triggers. Horses, men, whoever. It didn't matter who or what got hit, just so long as they stopped shooting.

A rider slid from the saddle and crumpled into a heap on the ground. The man behind him leapt his horse over the body.

There was a loud cry to my right, and from the corner of my eye, I saw Elizabeth stagger as she rushed with her daughter towards the house.

Gritting my teeth, I fired as fast as I could work the brace of pistols.

A rider fell, then another. From the house came a muffled boom as a rifle returned fire from inside. It was probably Charles getting into the fight.

I didn't know who these people were coming towards us, but I was desperate to draw their fire away from the unarmed ladies.

The riders rushed between the barn and the house, firing in both directions.

I hit a horse with a bullet, and it tumbled, going down with its rider in a terrible crashing of limbs and flesh. The surviving attackers raced across the remainder of the yard, into the tree line, and out of sight.

Then they were gone in the dead of night with a lone boom from Charles' rifle fired after them.

The door to the bunkhouse burst open and Bo appeared in his underwear and socked feet, pistol in hand, looking around wild-eyed and confused.

"What in the hell is going on? Wait... Jed, is that you?" he shouted while quickly stepping into a pair of boots.

"It's me," I called back as I began dumping cartridges from my pistols and reloading. At the same time, I was keeping an eye on the forest and walking to the rider who had gone down with his horse. Reaching the man, I stood over him with a loaded pistol pointed at his head. The downed horse screamed in pain and thrashed side to side as it tried to rise. Seeing that its front leg was twisted and shattered, I finished the unlucky animal off with a shot through the skull then jerked the gun back to cover the rider.

"Who sent you?" I asked the motionless man.

Silence.

3

I kicked him with the toe of my boot.

Nothing.

Dropping to a knee, I felt his chest for any movement. There was none.

Too bad. I could have used some answers.

"Jed!" Skyla cried out.

Leaving the corpse where it lay, I rushed over, watching the misshapen lumps at the far end of the yard to see if the other downed riders were still alive. No one moved.

Skyla was crouched over her mother on the porch, Charles beside her, and Sara nudged Elizabeth with her hooked beak. "She's hit!" Charles shouted as he pressed a hand against her wound.

In the lantern light, I could see a spreading dark mass staining her dress around her abdomen. Sara bellowed lightly, and I shoved the young trike out of the way. Bo rushed over, gun still in hand as he watched the darkened tree line for any returning riders.

"Give me a hand, Charles." I grabbed her under the arms and hoisted her up with the Brit's help. Between the two of us we moved her into the house. She screamed in pain as we set her down on the bed. In the lantern light her face was pale, her eyes wide and fearful, and she trembled as shock set in.

Charles ripped a handkerchief from his pocket and pressed it against the wound, staunching the flow of blood.

"Bo! Get the doc!" I shouted out the door as he peeked into the room. The hired cowboy spun around and sprinted towards the barn without a word. I knew he'd do his best to get the Doc here, come hell or high water.

***

Charles was better at rendering first aid than I was and stayed in the house watching over Elizabeth with Skyla. Leaving Sara in the building with them, I quickly crossed the yard, jerked my rifle out of the borrowed horse's scabbard and ducked into the barn.

If the riders came back, we'd be fortified and ready to hit them from both buildings.

I sat for hours on a cold metal bucket, waiting and listening to the noises of the little dinosaurs shuffling around behind me in the barn as I peeked out through one of the stall windows. Thin bits of lantern light strayed from cracks in the shutters bolted shut on my house, and I knew inside Elizabeth was fighting for her life with her daughter by her side.

Small bellows and the rustling of straw behind me made me glance at my dinosaurs before shifting in position to ease the numbing in my butt cheeks.

The Protoceratops were about the size of large sheep. But they looked like small, colorful triceratops with dirty white bodies and large red spots. Blue dabs dotted the frill that extended behind their skull, and their heads were adorned with a single small, raised horn bump between their nostrils, and a hawk-like beak used for ripping up plants from the ground. A mane of thick brown hairs rose vertically from their stout little tails. The dinosaurs were my ranches future, each one probably worth their weight in gold, and wore my brand of a circle with a horned trike in the center on their rump.

At a shout from the forest, I shifted my rifle barrel and watched over the iron sights as Doc and Bo came racing down the trail. They skidded their lathered horses to a stop by the corral and slid down from the saddles. Bo had thrown on a thick coat but was still in just his long johns and boots and had to be freezing by now.

Stepping out of the warmth of the barn, I shivered in my coat and followed Doc as he ran into the house.

Doc was hunched over Elizabeth when I closed the door behind me. Skyla's eyes were red rimmed from crying, and Charles was squeezing water from a handkerchief onto Elizabeth's chapped lips.

"She's lost a lot of blood..." Doc muttered as he tore part of the dress to get a better look at the wound. "I'm going to have to remove this." He gave Charles and me a wave with his blood smeared hand. "You both need to get out of the house while I work. I won't have this poor lady's dignity ruined because of you two standing around gawking."

"Yes, sir," I muttered and hugged Skyla tightly. "She'll be okay," I whispered into her ear.

"I hope so," she whispered back. Her face was tear streaked and I knew that as much as she and her mother fought, there was still love there. I patted her on the back gently and let her go before turning to the Stratten family butler.

"Charles, get Sir Lancelot. It's time to go hunting."

"Damn straight," the British family butler replied as he picked up his rifle and followed me outside.

"Jed!" Skyla called.

Stopping halfway through the door, I turned back.

"Be careful." She blinked back more tears, and I could see she was barely holding it all together.

"Yes ma'am," I said softly before closing the door behind me.

Bo was sitting in the rocking chair on the porch with a rifle across his lap. He'd managed to get some pants on and saw the looks of grim determination on our faces. "You're going after them, aren't you?" he asked, obviously already knowing the answer.

"I need you to stay here and hold down the fort. They may circle back to hit us again."

He patted the stock of his rifle fondly. "I'll give them hell if they do."

"Thanks, Bo." Stepping off the deck, we crossed the yard to where Carbine and Sir Lancelot stood waiting by the corral fence. It was as if our horses knew what we had in mind.

***

After a couple of hours of tracking the raiders in freshly fallen snow through sparse forests and across patches of open prairie, we found where they had turned suddenly and headed into a large stand of trees and dense undergrowth. Suspecting this was where they'd set up a camp, we dismounted and tied off our horses.

Charles looked at me strangely as I removed my boots and set them to the side. At my insistence he followed suit. His socks looked worse than mine, with a pair of toes sticking out of the gray fabric on his left foot. I guess butlering for the wealthy Strattens didn't pay well.

Not enjoying the feeling of cold melted snow soaking my socks, I slipped through the trees, carefully stepping to make sure I didn't break a stick or roll a stone to give away the fact that the raiders weren't alone in these darkened woods. This was where walking in sock feet gave you an advantage. Moccasins would have worked, but I didn't think to grab a pair from the house. And I doubted Charles had ever worn a set, much less owned one.

A stick broke behind me, and I heard a muffled swear from the Brit. I also doubted he had ever done anything like this before. But this was where my past came in handy.

We smelled the acrid scent of wood smoke and heard a soft nicker from one of their horses before we saw the flicker of flames in the darkness. I didn't see anything resembling a look out. Whoever these gunmen were, they were lazy and assumed we wouldn't be out for blood tonight.

They were wrong.

Laughter drifted to us as we approached, and I began to make out bits and pieces of the conversation. Once I was close enough to make out full sentences, I held up a hand and Charles crouched down beside me.

From between the trees, I watched a man take a swig from a bottle and belch before asking, "How much you think them dinosaurs are worth?"

"A lot. He's got the only ones this side of the Shimmer that can be kept in a herd," said another.

I gritted my teeth. Was that what the attack was all about? Stealing my Protos? If so, they were the first dinosaur rustlers in existence. But I had more enemies than friends, and my paranoid side doubted it was as simple as that.

"We'll catch a little sleep, then get set up outside the ranch before dawn. When they come out in the morning, we'll kill them and torch the house and bodies. Then we'll take the dinosaurs."

"How many of them do you think there are?"

Something sizzled in a pan on the fire. Bacon from the smell of it.

"Jed, and a couple others. We got at least one of them."

"Hell, they got three of ours. And surprise was on our side!" The man who spoke spat into the fire angrily.

"Yeah, Henry. Great plan," another man spoke as he jerked a thumb towards the picketed horses. "Rush the house and kill everyone inside as they sleep, huh?"

"Shut it. It wasn't supposed to go this way. Jed walked back through the Shimmer around noon, looking more dead than alive. What were they doing outside like that in the middle of the night?" The man I assumed to be Henry swore bitterly from where he sat between the two others.

Luck appeared to have been on my side. Had I not ridden into town and kidnapped the Sheriff to execute on the prairie, I'd have been home earlier and sleeping by the time they attacked. It seemed killing Sheriff Beauford Johnson righted many wrongs and possibly saved all our lives at the same time. I silently congratulated myself on a good move.

"That Jed's a tough one. But he can die like any man with a well-placed bullet. And the reward for his death is more than enough. That herd of dinosaurs would be worth a fortune to any buyer."

I'd heard enough. Apparently, they wanted me dead. No surprise there, a lot of people did. But who sent them? That was the question I needed an answer to. Was it my father? I doubted it, he was never one for harming a woman and we'd just made something of amends.

Nodding over my shoulder to Charles, I carefully moved forward, stalking through the trees with silent determination.

It was Henry I wanted alive. The other men didn't matter.

I slowly shifted around until I was just outside the firelight and had a good view of the remaining three gunmen. Drawing both pistols, I lined up the dark sights on two of the men who helped attack my ranch.

Gently squeezing the triggers to keep the guns on target, I fired. Both bullets hit, and the men toppled backwards over the log they sat on.

Henry sat in the center, mouth open, startled at the sudden burst of gunfire from the darkness.

I shifted both guns to him and called out, "Twitch and you're dead."

His hands trembled a bit in his lap, but I let that slide.

Taking a few steps forward, I eased myself into the firelight. Charles followed me, his nickel-plated Schofield revolver shining from the dancing flames.

"Where are your boots?" Henry asked suddenly, as if that was the most important question to ask someone after having your buddies blown away beside you.

"None of your damned business. Now, take off your gun belt. Slowly," I told the raider as I inched closer to the fire to warm my cold wet feet.

The bearded man obliged and held it up by the buckle, gun hanging low in its holster.

"Toss it away," I commanded.

He did.

I holstered my left Colt Peacemaker but kept the right one trained on the gunman. I may have carried two pistols, but I was vastly better with my right hand than my left at using them.

"Charles, check on his friends."

The Brit edged around me, making sure not to get between my gun barrel and the man sitting across the fire. With his foot, Charles nudged one, then the other. The second one moaned slightly and curled up in pain.

"This one is still alive." Reaching down, Charles drew the pistol from the wounded man's gun belt and tossed it across the fire where it slid beside my socked feet.

"Will he die?" I asked while keeping my eyes and gun barrel on the remaining seated raider.

"If untreated… certainly."

Still staring at Henry, I arched an eyebrow. "Well, let's not get between a man and his fate."

Charles shot me a dark look that I caught from the corner of my eye, and I shrugged. "He earned this death. If it'd make you feel better, I can either shoot him again, or we can hang him."

The Brit was silent as the wounded man moaned again faintly.

I took in Henry sitting across from me.

He had a scraggly beard and wore a dirty red shirt with tan pants. Stepping over to him, I knocked the hat off his head to get a better look at his face. I didn't recognize him.

"Who are you, Henry?"

He spat into the fire. "No one."

"Then who sent you and your friends to my ranch?"

He grunted but remained silent.

I glared at him as menacingly as possible. "You're not making a very compelling argument for me to keep you alive."

He squinted, confused. "What's compelling mean?"

I sighed. That was my higher education coming out again. "Do you want to live?"

He cautiously tugged at his pitiful beard. "Yes."

"Then answer my damn questions before I shoot you."

"Okay!" He raised his hands defensively. "I don't know who hired us. Someone left a note under the door at the hotel for me to meet them in the stables for a job. I went there… it was dark, I couldn't make out who it was. I didn't even recognize the voice! They said I should kill you and take your dinosaurs as payment. They said you also had a little trike that would be worth a fortune to the right buyer!"

"Did the mystery man have a cane? Or was he wearing a badge?" That'd at least narrow it down to my mortal enemy and railroad tycoon, Reydan White, or one of the Pinkerton detectives that worked for him.

"No, sir. He stood in the shadows, and I couldn't see his face beneath his hat. But when I left, he had a real ragged cough and was holding a red handkerchief, like he was a lunger or something."

I stood still, thinking. It certainly sounded like Tuberculosis. The red handkerchief would help hide spots of blood coughed up. That wasn't much to go on, but it was something. The wounded man to Henry's right thrashed once, then went limp.

Charles bent over, poked him a few times, then shook his head signaling the raider was dead.

I stared back at Henry, "So, you know nothing else about who hired you?"

"No! Promise I don't!"

"Then what good are you to me alive?"

"Wait, wha-"

My bullet thumped through his chest. He toppled forward, narrowly missing falling face first into the fire.

Charles jumped up from where he crouched over the other dead raider. "What the hell, Jed? He was unarmed!" he shouted.

"He tried to kill me and shot a woman who may very well be dead now for all we know," I snapped back. "And I already have to look over my shoulder for enough threats as it is. He was never going to walk out of here alive."

"I wouldn't have come along if I'd known you were going to murder everyone who crossed you!"

"Oh, shut it, Charles. You fought in the Indian Wars with the East British Trading Company. Don't tell me you didn't get your hands dirty when it needed to be done," I told him angrily.

He frowned then quickly grimaced from the row of stitches that covered the side of his face. "That's not who I am now."

"Well, this is who I am. You saw the wanted poster. I reckon Skyla told you about my past while she thought I was dead too." I kicked a stick into the fire and sparks shot up. "I'm a bad man trying to be good. And now I'm up a shit creek because of it."

The night was silent except for the crackle of flames.

"This will pass, Jed," Charles said quietly as he holstered his Schofield.

"Pass? Hell!" I gestured with my pistol at the corpses around the campfire angrily. "I'm just getting warmed up."

I walked over to Henry and kicked him in the face to make sure he was dead. He didn't even twitch.

"You need to calm down, and think with a clear head, Jed. You accused me of fighting in the Indian Wars... well I did. I did some awfully bad things, and I know what it's like trying to make good afterwards. So far, I've accomplished it by protecting the people who mean the most to me. That includes Elizabeth, along with Skyla, and her father. You can too. Let's check on Elizabeth and we'll figure things out from there."

"Fine," I grumbled before bending over and patting down Henry's pockets. I fished a handful of coins and some folded bills out from one and a handful of .44-40 cartridges from the other.

"What are you doing?" Charles asked in surprise.

"Robbing the dead. They were going to do it to me, but to the winner go the spoils."

"Oh hell, Jed. You really are a bad man."

***

When we got back to the ranch, the sun was edging up over the mountains and I had a saddle bag full of pistols and three more rifles strapped across the back of Carbine. None of them seemed worth keeping, but a man never knew when he might need an arsenal. Besides, most rifles cost a month's wages anyways. The bodies we left by the doused fire with the raider's horses. We could have brought them with us, but I was in a hurry to get back to Skyla and check on Elizabeth. We'd go back out to get the horses and corpses later.

Doc was passed out in one of the chairs on my porch with a small brown bottle of what I assumed was whiskey resting by his foot.

We rode to the corral and tied off Carbine and Sir Lancelot. Charles' beautiful chestnut Arabian stallion whinnied and nipped at my mustang playfully who snorted and tossed his head.

"Doc! Hey, Doc!" I called to the man as I walked across the yard to the ranch house. "Wake up."

He stirred, leaning forward in the chair and rubbing his eyes with hands coated in dried blood.

"Jed, hello. Charles, I hope you're taking it easy with those stitches."

The Brit gently touched the side of his face where an ape had sliced it open. The puckered skin was tied together with bruising and swelling all around it. It had to be painful to even talk. "I am, Doc."

"How's Elizabeth?" I asked, ignoring the pleasantries.

"She'll live. But she lost a lot of blood," he raised his hands as if to show us how much. "We got the bullet out and patched her up. She was sleeping soundly with Skyla and Bo watchin' over her."

The door opened, and Bo stepped out with rifle in hand. "Did you find them?" the ranch hand asked.

"Found and dealt with," I told him grimly.

"Good. Sorry sons of bitches, shooting a real lady like Elizabeth."

I rested a boot on the porch step. "Well, lucky for them. If it'd been Skyla, I'd have skinned them alive over a fire."

"What?" Skyla stepped out, a cup of steaming coffee in her hands. Her eyes had bags under them from a lack of sleep. From behind her dress, the horned beak and bone shield of Sara peeked around to see what was going on.

"Nothing, dear."

"Oh, okay," she muttered as Doc got up and offered her the chair. Sitting, she sipped the coffee and Sara butted her head against my legs. I gave her pebbled hide a scratch.

"Who's a good trike?" I murmured to her, and her thick stubby tail swung side to side like a dog's. The little triceratops had grown frightfully fast and was almost too large to go through the doorway.

Skyla sighed wearily. "What was this all about, Jed?"

I shrugged as I looked around the yard. I'd need to do something with the raider bodies and horse corpse that still lay in the snow before they got too stiff to move easily. "Someone saw me come back through the

Shimmer and told this group to kill me and take Sara and the Protos as payment." Hearing her name, the little trike bumped up against me again with a low bellow.

"Who?" Skyla asked.

"No idea. But I'm going to find out."

She blinked rapidly as her eyes suddenly moistened. "Jed, men tried to kill us. Not apes, not dinosaurs... but men." She looked down at her coffee miserably. "Human beings."

"Yes." I didn't know what to say, or how to comfort her. But I tried anyways by stepping closer and squatting down to look her in the eyes. Reaching out, I placed my hands around hers. "I'm sorry we had to do that. But they were going to kill us... we had no choice. We did the right thing."

"It's still hard." She wiped a tear away with the back of her hand. "Jed, I know you haven't slept in, well... who knows how long. But could you take me into town please? I need to telegraph my father."

"Certainly."

"No," Charles cut in while putting a hand on my shoulder. "Jed needs to rest. I'll take you, Skyla."

I nodded up at him, suddenly aware of how tired I was. I hadn't even had a chance to sleep since crossing the Shimmer, and it was already the day after my return. "Thanks, Charles, please do. I'm beat."

"Not a problem."

Doc stood. "I'm going to check on our patient again. But I have a feeling she'll be better in a couple weeks. She just needs rest... and a lot of it. I'd recommend keeping her here for now, no sense in moving her and risking more damage."

I held my hand out and shook his blood smeared one. "Thanks, Doc."

***

Two days and a lot of sleep later, I was in Granite Falls to meet Skyla's father.

But first, I needed to return Lieutenant Daniels' horse and dispose of some bodies.

I was tempted to simply dump them into a pile by the cemetery, but I figured it'd look better if I played the part of the good guy who defended himself.

Thus, I rumbled my wagon along through the crowds of people and stopped it outside the Sheriff's office. The man was dead, of course. But as far as I knew, no one else knew he was dead yet. So, I had to keep up the pretenses of the man being alive.

Carbine snorted and gave me a disapproving look as I locked the wheel brake and stepped off the wagon onto the hard-packed dirt and gravel street. My horse hated pulling the wagon, especially when Daniels' horse walked along behind.

My boots thumped along the boardwalk as I moved to the Sheriff's door and peeked through the iron barred windows. It was dark and empty. No deputies were in yet and Sheriff Beauford was in hell.

I hammered my closed fist against the door anyways. In for a dime, in for a dollar.

No answer.

"Jedidiah."

I spun around to see the Reverend watching me with an amused look on his face. Tall and thin, he tipped his flat brimmed black hat before jerking a thumb towards my wagon where the boots of six men jutted from the back. "See you brought in some dead."

"Yes, sir. They attacked my ranch a couple nights ago... Shot Skyla's mother."

He frowned. "I heard about the attack from Doc. How is she doing?"

"She's recovering." I looked back at the closed door and knocked once again. "But she'll be laid up for a while. I'm here to drop these raider bodies off and pick up her husband at the railroad station."

"That's good to hear," he spun around and rested his forearms on the side boards of the wagon, his worn Bible dangling from one hand as he looked over the pile of corpses. "So, the question is why'd they attack?" He glanced around and lowered his voice. "Are they your father's men?"

My father led a gang that I'd been part of for nearly two decades before I finally ran off and went into hiding here for a couple of years. My old man didn't take it well, and just a few weeks ago he located me and several of his men tried to kill me in retaliation for an old feud. After that, and a failed jail escape involving the misuse of some dynamite, my father and I had entered an uneasy peace for the time being. But I was still plenty mad at him.

"I don't think so. All I know is that this one," I pointed at the blood splattered and bloated corpse on top of the pile, "His name is Henry, and someone slipped a note under his door at the hotel to meet them in the stables. An unseen man that he met there told him to kill me and take my dinosaur herd as payment. If it'd been my old man, he'd have led the attack himself."

"Who do you figure then? The mystery man was Reydan White?"

"No. Henry said he didn't have a cane, so that rules him out. Probably one of Reydan's Pinkerton detective thugs. He basically owns a private army with them on his payroll," I growled.

Reverend spat at the ground in obvious disgust. "I heard about the Pinkertons massacring that ape village."

I gritted my teeth as I recalled watching the attack on the village to rescue one of my companions. "The Pinkertons wiped them out. Even the defenseless little ones. Every single ape there… then they torched the village to make an example of them. It figures the apes would hit Fort Jipson right afterwards, with everything they had… including a dragon."

"I heard about the dragon. They are in the Bible you know," he lifted his old, battered book and waved it at me. "Just like the leviathan and behemoth."

"Yeah, well, I don't know if it's dead or not. I know we winged it. It disappeared at the end of the battle."

"If it bleeds, you can kill it."

"That's a fact."

Reverend looked back up at me, his gaze intense. "You thinkin' about leaving town for a while?"

"No, should I be?"

"There's a lot of death surrounding you these days."

"Yes, there is. And I haven't been looking for most of it. It just seems to follow me. Seems like ever since this Shimmer opened a tunnel to this lost world, Prehistoria, or whatever they are calling it… it's been a blood bath ever since."

"Big changes are usually bloody affairs." He nodded his head at the Sheriff's door. "I guess Beauford Johnson and his deputies aren't in yet."

"Apparently not," I kept a poker face on. The Reverend knew my secret past, and he looked the other way so long as I stayed on the right side of the law. I wasn't sure how me leading the Sheriff out onto the prairie in his long johns in the dead of night then executing him for being a bad guy would work out if the Reverend knew the truth of the matter. I walked back to the front of the wagon, uneasy with the conversation. "Guess I'll go by the Army's Command Post and turn these corpses over to them."

The Reverend stepped away from the wagon, his Bible clutched to his chest in both hands. "Oh, Jed… I was sorry to hear of Captain Brandthorn's passing at the Battle of Fort Jipson. He was a good man."

I nodded slowly. Brandthorn had been a good man and a good friend. Seemed like I was losing a lot of those lately. "Thanks, Reverend. I'm sorry we couldn't bring his body back for burying." It'd been left behind, with all the others who died.

The Reverend looked down at the corpses. "Once a soul is gone, a body is just a bag of blood and meat. The person has gone on. Captain Brandthorn would have understood."

"That's pretty morbid."

"Yes, well… I keep that part out of my funeral sermons."

Shaking my head, I climbed into the bench seat of the wagon. "Good to see you, Reverend."

"You too, Jedidiah."

***

Disposing of the bodies at the Army Command Post turned out to be easier than I thought; it seemed several of them were well known troublemakers, including Henry who had a small bounty. They were also willing to take Lieutenant Daniels' horse off my hands and return it to him next time he came back from the other side.

After that, I still had a little time before Skyla's father's train arrived, so I went by the store and spent the bounty on all the .45-70 ammunition they had in stock for my rifle then ordered more, and a few boxes of .45 colt for my pistols. I'd burned through just about everything I'd had the last few weeks on the Prehistoria side. It was a good bit of ammo and while I didn't know what the future might hold, I figured it probably involved some form of violence.

Having spent entirely too much money on cartridges, I laid the bag of bullets in the back of the wagon and eased Carbine through the crowded streets towards the rail station at the southern end of town.

Granite Falls had grown from a small five-hundred-person town to a few thousand within a couple of short months. Where there had only been thirteen buildings during the Battle of the Apes, there were now close to fifty spread out along the valley. There were still many, many tents scattered around the town operating as homes, rentals, or small businesses as new slap board sided housings and buildings were completed almost daily on divided land lots. A man with a hammer could make a good living here.

Several stands had been hastily built along the ends of Main Street, offering jerked trike meat at unreasonable prices. It was possible that it was real, there were still a bunch of triceratops running loose around the area after the battle. But most likely it was sheep, cow, pig, or dog meat being played off as authentic dinosaur jerky. I passed on all the hawkers' offers to try a piece.

"Jed! Hey, Jed!"

The shout brought me back from my reminiscing and I swore under my breath. Not paying attention gets people killed by people who are.

A man came running down the boardwalk towards me, waving a newspaper in the air, and wearing a dark brown suit and bowler hat. Recognizing him, I slowed Carbine down and gave a small smile. It was

John Parsons, reporter for the New York Times. A nice enough man, but I was the sort who had a lot to hide, and he had a lot of questions.

John skidded to a stop beside Carbine and gave me a confused look. "I thought you were dead!"

"Maybe tomorrow."

He chuckled. "Well, I'm glad you're alive! And you're not going to believe this. But I just got the latest edition of the New York Times, and my story about you is on the front page!" He thrust the folded paper at me.

My stomach sank like a rock as I opened it up. The headline screamed, "HEART EATER OF GRANITE FALLS." Beneath the large print was the picture of Skyla and me standing in front of the captured trikes at Fort Jipson before it fell. That was the only picture of me in existence, other than my wanted poster sketch. Part of me felt betrayed, but I should have known the photographer would share it with the journalist.

I knew John was going to do an article on me, but I had partially hoped he'd be eaten by something before it went to print or it'd just be a small piece in the back of the paper. Either way, I was intentionally vague when talking to the man, so hopefully it wouldn't be too revealing of my past. Sighing, I folded it back up and tried to hand it back to him.

"No, no. You keep it. That's fresh from New York! There's a whole pile of them getting sold around town right now! Everyone within a thousand miles will know who you are!"

Inwardly, I groaned. For an outlaw in hiding, I was doing a terrible job at it.

He must have misunderstood the face I made. "Don't worry, Jed. This is just the first article of many. By the time I'm done, you'll be more famous than your friends Wolverine Wade or Fredrick von Holsak!"

This time I groaned out loud and laid the folded paper on the wagon seat beside me. I'd probably start a fire with it later.

"Oh, and thanks, Jed." The reporter frowned and became serious. "For saving me at Fort Jipson when it fell, and for holding the line as we escaped. We probably all would have died if it weren't for you collapsing the tunnel behind us."

"You're welcome, John. Now if you'll excuse me, I've got to get going."

The reporter grinned and took a step back. "Good seeing you, Jed. Keep an eye on the papers for the next article!"

Sighing, I flicked the reins across Carbine's back and the wagon rolled down the street and away from the reporter.

***

The train had already arrived by the time I reached the station. Standing to the side, alone amongst the crowd of travelers loading and unloading the passenger cars, was a bear of a man in a nice black suit looking at a gold pocket watch and wearing a fashionable top hat.

Rolling the wagon to a stop in front of him, I pulled the brake and hopped down.

"Mr. Stratten?" I guessed as I patted Carbine's neck.

"Yes?" The bear of a man flicked his watch shut and looked up.

I stuck out my hand. "I'm Jedidiah Smith."

He looked me over from top to bottom and I was glad I was wearing clean clothes this trip. Skyla had insisted I try to make a good impression. As good of an impression as a man wearing two tied down pistols could make, that is.

Tucking the watch back into his pocket, the Regent of the Smithsonian shook my hand. His grip was strong and firm, not at all what I expected of a man who worked in a museum. "Call me Morgan."

"Morgan, your wife is still at my ranch, along with Skyla. Doc thought it best to let Elizabeth rest a while before risking moving her back into town."

He nodded curtly. "Take me there, please."

"Yes, sir." I started grabbing his baggage and setting them over the side of my wagon, trying to avoid the scattered smears of dried blood on the boards from the corpses.

With his help we quickly got his luggage in the back and climbed onto the buckboard. A flick of my wrists got the reins to slap on Carbine's back and my horse glared back at me for a moment before leaning into the harness, pulling us away from the train station as the locomotive vented steam with an ear-piercing whistle.

"So, you are Jedidiah Huckleberry Smith," Morgan said. It was a statement, not a question.

I nodded. "I usually go by Jed."

"While my daughter has been strangely quiet about you in her letters, my wife has made it very clear that she is not a fan of yours." He picked up the folded newspaper on the seat between us, glanced at the cover, and closed it. "I read this on the way here; interesting article about you, Jed."

I tried to hide my cringe. I'd known that Skyla hadn't spoken a lot about me to her father, and that Elizabeth Stratten absolutely hated me. For a multitude of reasons, I supposed. Probably the largest being that I'd turned her sweet, naïve, protected paleontologist daughter into something of a confident and armed woman who was constantly in harm's way.

And now Elizabeth knew about my true history and identity.

Great. Just… great.

Morgan continued, waving the folded newspaper. "I've been paying sharp attention to the events unraveling around this discovery of yours of the Shimmer and Prehistoria. You seem to have been in the thick of things."

We rolled past the Bucket O' Blood saloon and then the local bank as I thought of how to answer.

After a moment, I admitted, "Not always by choice. Usually, I'm just in the wrong place at the wrong time."

Out of the corner of my eye, I saw him glance over at the *Eighty-Six* leaning against the seat, then the Colt Peacemaker pistols strapped to my waist.

"You're lucky to have lived through both the Battle of the Apes and the Fall of Fort Jipson," he fixed me with a hard stare. "As is my daughter."

"Your daughter wanted to stay. I tried to get her to leave both Granite Falls and Jipson, repeatedly. But she was determined to see the battles through. You should be proud of her, sir. She kept her wits about her and was invaluable to us all."

"Skyla always was hardheaded at times. For years she insisted I allow her to visit a dig site, I finally relented and that's how she ended up at your ranch." His voice hardened, "Now tell me about that scoundrel, Oscar."

I grimaced as I thought about Skyla's former boss and Morgan's former employee. "He's a piece of work. He's linked up with Reydan White and scheming to get gold from the other side."

"He always was something of a pain in my ass. But his knowledge was especially useful to the Smithsonian."

"Do you know Reydan White?" I glanced out of the corner of my eye at the Regent as I asked. If he were one of the former union raider's allies, I would have to tread very carefully.

The big man shook his head and eased my fears. "Not really. Met him at a dinner party once several years ago. He didn't leave a favorable impression and he had zero interest in the Smithsonian. But his father is a long-serving Senator, so I was pleasant to him just the same."

I didn't mention my run in with him either, or the unfavorable impression he'd left on my scar covered backside with a whip. Some things just weren't some folk's business.

Morgan looked at me curiously. "Why do you ask?"

I flicked the reins, pretending to be nonchalant. "Just wondering, he's been around… overseeing his railroad running through the Shimmer."

Morgan didn't reply, and we rode in silence as we passed another wagon with a broken wheel being replaced at the blacksmith shop. I thought of the blacksmith we had during the battle, beating away at the trike that impaled him with his big hammer and Colt Dragoon revolver. This new man was nowhere near as good with shaping steel.

"Are you armed?" I asked, changing the subject as we began rolling up the valley that Granite Falls resided in and towards the open plains that led to my ranch. There were still apes about and some dinosaurs that'd managed to cross through the Shimmer before we'd closed it off. You never knew what you might run into these days.

"I am," he said simply.

"You need to stay that way. The Old West was dangerous, the New West, even more so."

"Yes," he shifted in the seat to stare at me. "Now, tell me how it is my wife ended up being shot at your ranch."

"I don't know yet. I'd just returned from the other side when the raiders struck. After we fetched the Doc, Charles and I tracked them down. They said they were told to kill me and take my herd of dinosaurs. But they didn't know by who."

"Where are these men? I wish to speak with them." He said it in a manner that implied he had no interest in speaking with them, but rather committing righteous violence.

"Dead."

He twisted back around in the seat, facing towards the rear end of Carbine who plodded along unhappily. "Good."

***

When we reached the cabin, Morgan leaped down from the wagon and quickly walked to the house without a word. The door cracked open and a second later was thrown wide open. From inside the house stepped Charles with a rifle in hand and Skyla bounded out behind him. She ran across the yard and wrapped her father up in a hug.

"Skyla!" He held her tight and patted her back gently.

After several long moments, Skyla pulled away, and looked her father over. "You've lost weight."

"Stress over the new dinosaur exhibits we are building, darling. How's your mother?"

"She's doing better. She's awake." Shooting me a worried smile, the paleontologist grabbed her father by the arm and led him into the house. "C'mon, Father, you can meet Sara also!"

I watched them walk inside as Charles came over to the wagon. "You know Elizabeth's going to tell Morgan who you are," he said.

"Yes. I figure so."

"If things go badly, what will you do?"

"I guess I'll cut the shit and start stacking bodies."

Charles' eyes narrowed. "And what do you mean by that?"

I looped the reins around the brake and stepped down. "What I mean is, once all this blows up in my face, I'm going to ride out of here, kill Reydan, Cato, and any of his damned Pinkertons that get in my way. Which is what I should have done months ago. Every day that wretched man spends alive is a gift that he took from numerous others. If I'm to have my life ruined by him once again, I'll burn the world to the ground around me on my way out of town."

The butler held a hand up to stop me from beginning my rampage. "Let me talk to the Strattens. Skyla and I've already been working on Elizabeth. She's starting to come around."

"No, she's not."

"Okay, not really. But maybe a little. Give us a chance."

I looked at the house then back to Carbine. He stomped his hooves and shoved his head into my chest. I desperately didn't want to leave Skyla behind. If there was a chance that we could work this out and I didn't take it, I'd regret it for the rest of my life. "Alright. Fine."

Nodding, he turned and walked towards the house as I began unhitching my dun horse from the wagon.

Bo walked out of the barn with a shovel in hand. The old ranch hand seemed to have aged since I'd seen him last in a prison cell in Granite Falls a week ago. He looked at the closed door to the house and whistled low. "I'd hate to be you right now."

"So, you know about my past as well, huh?"

"Yup, overheard the ladies talking about it."

I turned to him, watching his face for any signs of what he might be thinking. "How's that make you feel?"

He looked at his dinosaur poop covered boots, as if suddenly embarrassed. "We've all done things we regret. Don't mean we are all bad."

"Good, now shuddup and give me a hand."

He jabbed the shovel into the ground and reached for the tack. "So, you ain't gonna start runnin'?"

I glanced at him. "What's it to you? Do you want a new employer?"

"No… just Sheriff Beauford's still out there. And you swore he'd get what was coming to him."

I looked around to make sure we were alone before lowering my voice. "He's dead," I said simply.

"Good." It was quiet for a minute as Bo helped remove the rest of the tack from Carbine. "Was it you?"

I looked at him blankly.

"Good," he repeated.

"You bury Jim where I asked?" He'd been the young kid that'd been goaded into a card game by Beauford, and then called a cheat and gunned down after winning all the Sheriff's lunch money.

"I did."

Swatting Carbine on the rump with my hat, he pranced into the corral. I sighed, "Reckon I'll go pay my respects to him then."

***

Jim was buried on a gentle hilltop overlooking the plains of my ranch. Before me stretched a field of light brown grass and scrub trees, dotted with cattle in the distance. It was a good place to be laid to rest.

Looking down at the lone cross, I took my hat off and rested a calloused hand on it.

I hesitated, unsure of what to say. He'd been a good kid and had the makings of being an even better man under Bo's guidance. He worked hard, rarely swore, ate twice as much as any man should, and never complained. It felt like it was my fault, for sending him and Bo in to pick up lumber, for not realizing the danger that Sheriff Beauford was, for not seeing what was going to happen… For knowing that if I'd been there, instead of running around on the other side of the Shimmer, things would have worked out differently.

It was a shame that I couldn't save everyone.

I patted the top of the cross, looking down at the stretch of rocks that were piled over the grave to keep critters from getting at him.

"I'm sorry," I said before turning and walking back to the ranch.

***

After visiting Jim's grave, I went into the barn to feed the dinosaurs. The building was smaller than the original that I had, but better laid out and better insulated against the hard Wyoming winters. Jim and Bo had done a good job on it, and Bo was putting the final touches on the trim work. The barn doors didn't even stick this time.

"Jed!" I heard Morgan Stratten calling from outside the barn as I forked hay to the Protos. The small dinosaurs ate greedily, scooping beakfuls off the floor with little snorts and soft bellows.

"In here!" I shouted back as I jabbed the pitchfork into another lump of hay. There was a large knot in my belly. I wondered how the discussion had gone in the house about me between Skyla and her parents. I wished it was Skyla who was coming out here to tell me how it went.

The Stratten family patriarch entered and rested a polished black boot on the lower rail of the small corral Bo had built to keep the protos confined inside the barn. One of the little dinosaurs came up and tried to nip the toe of his boot with its hooked beak.

Morgan chuckled and shifted his foot away. The proto bellowed unhappily and went back to eating. "Magnificent creatures."

"Yes sir, they are."

He coughed, and his eyes met mine. "First things first, I owe you thanks, for saving my wife's life."

I flung another mound of hay into the pen. "You're welcome," I told him. Personally, I didn't like the woman a single bit. But she was Skyla's mother, so I had to play nice as much as possible and just because I was cold blooded at times didn't mean I was about to let an innocent woman die.

"Skyla told me the rest of your story. About how Reydan White and his Union soldiers raided your home and had you whipped as a child... and how your father formed a gang and went after the men who did it. Then how you continued for two decades trying to fight for the South against northern transgressions while searching for Reydan.... It's noble in a sense... fighting for a lost cause."

I looked at him out of the corner of my eye, wondering what direction this dreaded talk was going to go. "In Skyla's defense, she thought I was dead when she told your wife. Otherwise, you'd never have known anything about it."

Reaching between the horizontal boards, Morgan gently scratched one of the Proto's heads. "Seems you've had a hard life."

"Most people have." I grunted with effort as I flung another large forkful of hay into the pen. I wondered where all of this was leading.

He straightened, towering to his full height, and looking me in the eye. "Even though it was you who put them in danger... you've saved my daughter's life several times, and now my wife's. I owe you."

I stared at him in shock. "You do?"

He nodded curtly. "Yes. So, if you're interested, I'm willing to push for a full pardon for you. You won't have to run and hide anymore. You can even go back to your original name, Orville."

I blanched. "No thanks on the name, Jedidiah is who I am now."

"Very well. The choice is yours. Of course, it comes with risks. If the President denies the pardon, the law and everyone else will come after you. Probably the U.S. Marshals, the Pinkertons, bounty hunters, you name it and they're gunning for you. You'll be exposed."

Nodding slowly, I glanced down at the little dinosaurs below me. Was the risk worth it? Absolutely. It would give Skyla and me a chance at a life together, one where I didn't have to look over my shoulder for the lawman... just the bad guys in my past life.

"Okay," I thrust the pitchfork into the mound of hay. Sticking out my hand, I looked him in the eye. "A pardon it is..." As he shook my hand, I held it firmly as he tried to withdraw. He looked at me, puzzled. "Also, I'd like your permission to court your daughter."

"No," he said while pulling his hand away. "Not until the pardon comes through. If it does, then you may court her. But I'll not have her name dragged through the mud over a fling with a gunman with a lengthy criminal background any more than it already will be... no offense."

Chastised, I could only nod and agree. "Deal."

"Jed, I'll do everything in my power to get you that pardon." I could tell the man meant every bit of it, and for the first time, I dared to feel hope at a future with Skyla.

"And Elizabeth?" I asked. "Your wife knows as much as you do now."

"She'll listen to me," he grinned conspiringly. "I'll just tell her that our daughter's reputation, as well as our family's good name, is now at stake."

"Sorry to put you in this position, sir."

"Nonsense, you've shaken the pillars of heaven with your discovery, and you've kept my daughter safe. It's the least I could do in return. And it'll sound better in the history books if you've been pardoned. But hopefully, no one will ever know your background, unless you want them to."

I laughed humorlessly, "I'd prefer to stay out of history books. History is rarely kind to men like me."

***

A couple of weeks passed, and with the extra hands of Charles and Morgan, I managed to get a lot done around the ranch. Skyla was right about her father being a workaholic, I had a hard time keeping up with him. From sunup until sundown, he was working. Then at night he was up late reading from the small library of books I had. He was rather dismayed when he found out my dime novel on Wyatt Earp had been hollowed out to hide a key to my chest where my wanted poster had been kept.

Skyla and I refrained from kissing. At least where anyone could see us. We didn't even hold hands, which, from a gunman's point of view, made it worthwhile to wear two guns. I could still draw one or the other. And speaking of guns, I started practicing religiously.

Drawing and firing, drawing and firing and moving.

Nothing motivates like the knowledge that there were men out there that wanted me dead bad enough to hire a group of men to raid my home.

Charles and Morgan even joined me for a few sessions.

With a little practice, Skyla's father was getting pretty good at drawing from the pocket of his coat. The man carried a Remington Double Derringer in .41. A neat little gun, and very much like the one his daughter carried. After a week or so he was hitting fence posts at ten paces without even aiming.

We even practiced quick drawing against each other, standing side by side as Skyla shouted 'Go!' from behind us. We'd both draw and fire against a stump. Morgan wasn't too keen on it, or very good since he had a crummy pocket derringer, but I figured it never hurt to practice fast and accurate shooting.

The extra weapons that I'd taken from the dead raiders, I shipped off to Cheyenne. There was nothing special about any of them, nothing to merit their keeping, and my family friend and gun store owner, Carson Skinner, could use them or sell them off as he saw fit. I also returned the nickel-plated Colt Peacemaker that he'd loaned me. It was far too flashy for my tastes. I owed the Liberty Arms gun store owner a good bit, since he'd given me one of my Colt Peacemakers and the *Eighty-Six*, a prototype 1886 Winchester Repeater in .45-70… a fantastic rifle with a hard-hitting round that wouldn't be put into mass production until sometime next year.

As for the raiders' horses, I occasionally put them to work and waited for the Army to decide what to do with them. As I'd been needing another horse or two, it was nice to use them for hauling the wagon and giving Carbine a break from the unpleasant task.

Morgan Stratten sent off some letters to some friendly Congressmen to get a feel for starting a petition to pardon an 'unknown man' for some questionable actions that originated from the aftermath of the War Between the States. Skyla's father was no slouch, he was sharp as a tack, and knew better than to give my name up or location without any reassurances. And he figured my chances were good, as pardons had been trickling out for former Confederates and such over the past decade. Of course, they also still hanged some folks for war crimes as they found them. So, it was kind of a tossup on your chances.

Then, as Elizabeth was getting well enough to start moving slowly around inside the house, Lieutenant Daniels showed up with an entourage of mounted soldiers and a member of the Shayana tribe, Henon.

Henon was dressed typical of his culture, with leather pants and moccasins, a metal breastplate across his chest, and a sword strapped to his hip. He'd borrowed someone's coat, as the Shayana had no need on their side of the Shimmer for cold weather gear, and carried a US issued Springfield rifle slung over his shoulder. To say he was a strange sight would be accurate.

Sergeant Gibbons was among the group and dismounted with Daniels to speak with me as Charles, Skyla, and Morgan watched from the porch. I wondered if they figured the troops were there to arrest me.

"Jed," Daniels said as he clasped my hand in his. "It's good to see you again."

"You too, sir," I gestured at his other arm. "Seems like you're healing well; last time I saw you it was in a sling."

"T'was but a scratch," he grinned. "Thanks for returning my horse."

"Thanks for letting me borrow him."

The big black Sergeant walked over with Henon and shook my hand as well. "Good to see you made it back alive."

"Thanks, Gibbons…" I turned to the tall Shayana native. "Henon, how are you?"

He nodded to me, "All fares well… on our side." It was then I realized that this was the first time I'd seen a Shayana tribesman on this side of the Shimmer.

"What do you think about all of this?" I waved my hand around at my ranch.

"Living here… easy," he grinned toothily.

Compared to living amongst hundred-foot-tall, long neck dinosaurs, savage seven-foot-tall apes, and all manner of other beasts that would eat you given the chance, life did seem easy on our side. After growing up surrounded by that, what was an occasional grizzly, rattlesnake, or ornery Indian war party?

"It is," I agreed.

Skyla walked up behind me, put an arm around my waist protectively and looked at Daniels with suspicion. "What can we do for you?"

"Hello, Skyla," Daniels bit his lip thoughtfully. "I have come with a job offer."

"Figures," I said.

He held his hand up, "Hear me out first. Sergeant Gibbons?"

The black Sergeant handed me a folded newspaper. "Here's this week's newspaper."

"Thanks, we've almost used the last one I was given up in the outhouse."

Opening it, I saw the headline, "TAMING OF PREHISTORIA BEGINS!" across the top of the paper. Skimming the article quickly, I read that the East-West railroad had reached the coast and was establishing a fortified town named Whitesberg and that soon the other side would be opened for settlement. I was shocked. I supposed I shouldn't have been, it was inevitable that people would want to cross over to the other side. But there were some big damn dinosaurs over there, and an entire race of savage prehistoric apes that wanted us dead. Prehistoria made the American western expansion look like child's play.

I handed the paper to Skyla, and we waited silently while she read.

"Settlement?" she finally said with a frown. "You're going to allow settlers to cross through the Shimmer?"

"Yes. But first, we'd like Jed to help scout for us. On the other side."

"No," I said.

"Jed," the Lieutenant began again, raising his hands in a pleading manner.

"That's what you have him for," I pointed at Henon as the big Prehistoria native wandered over towards the open doors of the barn.

The Shayana peeked inside at the Protos, then looked back at us with a wide grin. "These are fine eating!" He mimicked eating out of a bowl.

"Don't you dare," Bo said as he came around the side of the barn, rifle in hand and a look on his face like he expected there was going to be trouble.

"It's okay, Bo, they just want Jed for a job," Skyla said to ease the hired hand's fears.

Grunting, the older man walked into the barn and shut the doors behind him. Henon looked put out.

The Lieutenant lowered his voice. "Yes, well, we don't exactly trust the Shayana yet. There was that thing with the Pinkertons and all, you recall, where they killed several of the tribesmen."

"But you're using him," I tilted my head towards the big Shayana who was now watching the horses feeding in the corral.

"It's a start. We're also giving them some more rifles, but mostly our older Springfields for now."

"That's real useful," I said sarcastically, recalling how the soldiers at the Battle of the Apes had carried the single-shot guns to a disadvantage against the apes. Now any soldier crossing through to the other side was issued a brand-new Winchester Repeater. It seemed someone up the chain of military command learned shooting lots of bullets, real fast, helped against massive prehistoric beasts and aggressive monkeys.

He shrugged. "It's better than what they have. Their crummy black powder muskets are still slower and less accurate than almost anything we can provide. But we aren't giving them any Gatling guns."

"Yeah, if they had a couple of those and plenty of ammunition, they could defend that mountaintop home of theirs pretty easily…. You think we may go to war with them?" I said doubtfully.

"No." He shook his head. "But my superiors are uneasy about going all in on trusting strangers from a lost world. They want us to feel each other out some more first."

Skyla spoke up suddenly, "If Jed goes, I'm going as well."

"And we'd love to have you, Skyla," Daniels grinned. "I've a job offer for you as well. To be our main paleontologist in helping us navigate through the lost world. You'd still get to work for the Smithsonian, but you'd give us your expertise on anything we come across. Pretty much what you've been doing, except now we pay you."

"Absolutely!" she beamed.

I half turned to her. "Skyla, we narrowly missed dying several times already over there. You really want to risk it?" I asked, knowing the answer already. All she'd spoken of since we came home was our adventures in Prehistoria and her desire to return to study it.

"Of course. It's where I'm meant to be."

I sighed. "Look, the Army doesn't need us. Even with the Shayana, the route between here and Fort Jipson is well laid. It should be easy to march on the canyon." I looked at the Lieutenant and his Sergeant standing before us. "You DO mean to attack the apes, correct?"

"Damn straight we do," Gibbons rumbled as his eyes narrowed in anger. I was willing to bet he'd lost a lot of friends during our defeat and was ready to get even.

Daniels kicked a clump of grass with his boot. "Yes, but we don't want to go that way. You survived while working your way from the canyon of Fort Jipson to the Shimmer, through the forest… the long way. You've the most experience in that area and we need you to lead us."

"If the apes are watching the tunnel on the other side, they'll see an army come through the Shimmer," Skyla protested.

Daniels gestured towards Henon. "On the day we cross, the Shayana have promised to take care of any ape scouts that are watching. And trust me, they've been watching."

Charles and Morgan left the porch and walked across the yard to join us.

"Charles, good to see you again," the Lieutenant said with a nod. "It looks like that is healing well," he gestured with a hand at the butler's face. The stitches had been removed, but the wound was scabbed over and would leave an inevitably ugly scar.

"Thanks. Lieutenant Daniels, Sergeant Gibbons… this is Morgan Stratten, Skyla's father and my employer." The tough Brit made the introductions.

"You're going back to the other side, aren't you?" Morgan guessed, looking at his daughter unpleasantly.

"Yes," Skyla said firmly.

"Then I'm coming with you," he said, tucking his hands into his pocket and jutting his chest out.

"No, you need to stay here and keep an eye on mother," she said softly while laying a hand on her father's arm. "She needs you."

Morgan appeared to sag slightly, and after a moment nodded, clearly torn between supporting his daughter or his wife. He looked at me, fixing me with his piercing gaze, "If she goes, you go."

I couldn't think of any other answer under his withering stare than a solid affirmative. "Yes, sir."

"Then keep her safe."

"I will," I said, feeling as though I'd just been boxed into going whether I wanted to or not.

"Shall I go as well, sir?" Charles spoke up from behind us.

Morgan turned to face him. "No, as tempting as it is, Skyla should be as safe as possible with Jed and the Army, but Elizabeth will be needing your help now more than ever as she recuperates."

"Yes, sir." The British butler frowned, obviously unhappy at the rejection to his suggestion. I'd come to realize during our adventures together that Charles cared deeply for Skyla, almost as a second father, and I knew he didn't like her going into harm's way without being by her side.

I faced Daniels, voicing my suspicion. "The Army isn't going alone… are they?"

The Lieutenant hanged his head and sighed. "The Pinkertons are coming too. Congress has decided to contract them, through Reydan White, to help bolster our numbers. The military simply doesn't exist in numbers large enough for a small-scale war anymore. Especially with our current dealings with the Apache down South. They're causing all kinds of chaos. We've got almost 5,000 troops chasing after Geronimo.

Unless the apes breach the Shimmer, they're considered a minor threat, and only to those on the other side."

"A minor threat?" Skyla raised her voice. "They wiped out two hundred men at Fort Jipson!"

"I know. But the military is slow to mobilize, and if we can hold the Shimmer, they aren't concerned about another ape incursion to our side. And we've already got five companies tied up in just that and supporting operations with the other side."

"So, we're using the Pinkertons and hitting the apes..." I sighed, hating the thought of having to deal with Pinkerton Detective Thompson and his men again.

"Before the big monkeys get a wild hair and come after us, yes. Everyone would feel better having some breathing room on the other side instead of an army of apes sitting in our old fort waiting to attack either the settlers, Whitesberg, or this side again."

I opened my mouth to speak, but Daniels lifted a hand to stop me. "A couple more things, in effort to... bolster our forces... we're taking on some Shaynees and I would like you to lead them."

"Lead them? The Shaynee?" I blurted, incredulous. "Why are they joining?"

"Yes, lead them. And I don't know what all happened in their teepees, but a few days back, their Chief rode into town, demanding to speak with our leaders. Made a heckuva sight. Next thing I know, they're with us."

"How many?"

"Two dozen."

"What for? You don't need them as scouts. You've got the Shayana for that and they don't know anything about the other side anyways."

He shrugged. "The Shaynee are fearsome fighters. And we could use that right now... And they're cheap."

"Cheap, huh? They bein' paid in firewater and glass beads?" I guessed sarcastically.

"No. Land... and freedom." He frowned at me. "Jed, you know the Shaynee best. And if you don't go, most likely it will be Sergeant Gibbons taking your place."

"And I'd rather not," the big black man raised both his hands to plead with me.

I looked at Skyla and Morgan to see if they had anything to say. Skyla gave me a pleading look to agree, and Morgan just raised an eyebrow.

"Alright, I'll lead you and them. On a few conditions."

"Such as?" Daniels asked hesitantly.

"The Indians get the same Repeaters the soldiers get. Winchesters. I'll train with the Shaynee, and lead them, but I won't have them tagging along with a bunch of ragtag worn-out brass tacked and feathered junk weapons that will get them killed."

"That can be done."

"Also, they are not to be messed with. I want that clear with both the Pinkertons and the soldiers. If there's an altercation, it needs to be fairly dealt with. I won't have one of the Shaynee punished unfairly just because he's an Indian, because the last thing any of us wants is the Shaynee on the warpath."

"Agreed, and I'll talk to Thompson. But you know how he and his men are."

"I do," I growled, the distaste for the Pinkertons thick in my mouth.

"And one more thing…" Daniels said.

"Now what?"

"After we take back Fort Jipson, we're going to search out these 'axemen' the Shayana told us about and try to make peaceful contact. Should just be a few days north of where Whitesberg is being built on the coast."

Henon appeared by Daniels' side. "Thou axemen are not friends, but neither thine enemy." He shrugged with one shoulder. "They are different from us."

"What do these 'axemen' have to do with me?" I asked.

Morgan coughed to get my attention. "Jed, can I speak with you a moment?"

"Certainly."

Patting his daughter on the back, he jerked his head towards the corral, and we walked out of earshot from the others.

"Jed, I hate to say this, because it's not only your life, but most likely my daughters as well, but you need to do whatever you can for the Army."

"Why?"

"For your pardon's sake, which apparently, also means my daughter's reputation now. You're already a hero of sorts, that will get you far, but the more atonement you do for your crimes, the better it will look when we lay out all the cards on the table as to your past and who you are now."

"A pardon doesn't do me much good if I'm dead."

"True. And my daughter's life is on the line as well," he growled. "We both know she's going to go to the other side whether I like it or not, because some damned outlaw rancher filled her head with all these notions of self-reliance and independence, and now I seem to have lost control over her."

I looked back at Skyla as she stood with the others. Her father was right; no matter what I did or said, she'd be going with them to attack the ape's canyon and to find these axemen. All I could do was buckle up for the ride and try to keep her alive.

"Alright," I called out to Lieutenant Daniels. "I'll do it. I'll lead the Shaynee and help you find these axe folks."

Skyla squealed with excitement and Daniels nodded his head solemnly. Gibbons looked visibly relieved to not have to deal with the Indians himself.

"Morgan," I turned to Skyla's father. "I need you to do me a favor then, keep an eye on the ranch as long as you can. I'd hate to have Bo here alone if more rustlers or raiders come by again. I've already had one ranch hand buried on my property; I don't want another."

"Certainly, Jed."

"And then there's Sara." I chewed on the inside of my lip, trying to figure out what to say about her. The little trike had become close to all of us.

He clasped my shoulder under his firm hand. "I'll take care of her. Don't worry, I suspect it will be another few weeks before Elizabeth is ready to leave."

"We should be back well before then." I didn't tell him that if we weren't, we'd be dead. He already looked concerned enough for his wife and daughter, I didn't want any more dreadful thoughts weighing on his mind.

Sighing in resignation, I walked towards Daniels to find out what the plan was.

***

I spent the evening getting my saddle bags packed. Then, by lantern light, I sat inside the bunkhouse across from Bo and meticulously cleaned each of my pistols, the *Eighty-Six*, and the sawed-off shotgun I kept wrapped in my bedroll.

After cleaning and caring for my guns, I carefully honed the nine-and-a-half-inch blade on my Bowie knife. I kept it razor sharp to shave with, but the action was methodical, and calming, especially considering we were about to go back to the other side and attack the apes at the site of our biggest defeat.

And a man never knew when he might need a sharp knife to poke people with.

Bo looked up from feeding small sticks into the metal box fireplace and watched me run the blade down a leather strap. "May want to hire some more hands, boss."

"I got you, who else do I need?" I teased.

He grew quiet for a minute. "Without Jim, we're shorthanded. Morgan is a boon to have around. For a suited man, he's a hard worker and helpful as can be. And of course, we've Charles. But neither of them is ranchers. And soon, Mrs. Elizabeth will be healed, and they'll leave. Then it will be just me. If we get attacked again, I'll be up a creek without a paddle and only one rifle."

"Yeah," I sighed, thinking of Jim. He'd been a good kid. It was his former bunk I was sitting on now. His things were still beneath it, and I didn't have the heart to go through them yet. "I don't know if they'll try to attack us again; whoever sent the raiders may try something else next time. But we do need more men. Morgan will still be here by the time we get back from the other side, I'll try to figure out something in the meantime."

"Yes, sir."

"And Bo, keep an eye on Sara. That little trike is worth more to me and Skyla than all the proto's combined."

He smiled broadly. "Absolutely, she's dear to me as well."

Completing my cleaning, I put my kit away. Shrugging into a coat, I stepped out of the warm bunkhouse and into the cold darkness of the night.

Walking across the yard, I tugged the coat tighter around my waist. The weather kept teasing a bad winter and even with the wagon loads of hay we'd bought, I worried we wouldn't have enough to keep the cattle herd and protos alive until spring. Glancing into the barn, I saw Charles brushing Sir Lancelot. The big Arabian horse seemed to be enjoying the attention. I gave them both a wave.

Stepping onto the porch, I knocked gently and waited for a 'come in' before opening the door. Quickly stepping into the warm room, I pulled the thick slab door shut behind me.

A fire crackled in the fireplace, and Elizabeth looked up at me from the bed beside the door. Morgan sat in my chair, one of my books in his lap, and Skyla stirred a pot over the fire.

"Evening, Stratten family," I said in partial jest.

"Jed!" Skyla exclaimed as she crossed the room and slipped an arm around my waist.

From the corner of my eyes, I saw an unhappy look cross Elizabeth's face, but Morgan barely glanced up from his book. "Evening, Jed," he said. I'd spent a lot of time working side by side with the Smithsonian Regent and was pleased at the sort of man he'd turned out to be.

The door opened behind me again and Charles knocked his boots then entered the room, followed by a gust of cold air.

"Jed, you ready to leave tomorrow?" the Brit asked as he closed the door and shrugged out of his heavy coat.

"All packed, weapons cleaned, and ready to go."

Elizabeth frowned at me and her daughter, "I don't approve of this. At all."

"Oh, Mother, it will be fine. I've Jed and an entire army of soldiers and Pinkertons to keep me safe."

"Perhaps, but not when you go to see these savage Indians."

I dipped my head at Skyla. "She's right, you know. You don't need to go with us tomorrow. I can get the Shaynee and deal with the attack on the canyon. Afterwards, when we leave for the axemen, you could meet up with us."

"No." She pulled my arm tighter against her. "We're a team and we go together. Everywhere. And that's final."

"Yes, ma'am."

Morgan laid a strip of leather in the book to mark his place and folded it shut before gazing across the room at his wife. "Don't worry, dear. Jed is more than capable enough of protecting Skyla. As he has proven so far."

Elizabeth harrumphed. "And yet I'm the one who was shot."

I grimaced, "Yeah, about that. Morgan, we've a few pistols that Charles and I took off the raiders. Might be worthwhile to give Elizabeth one in case more raiders return while we're gone."

"I shall have no such thing!" she shouted, grimacing as she pushed herself up on one elbow in the bed.

"Or not," I said sarcastically while rolling my eyes.

"I believe Charles, myself, and Bo can handle any raiders that may return," Morgan said firmly. "But we'll take the guns and stash them around the house and barn. They'll be quicker to use than a reload."

"I'll see to that, sir," Charles said, already looking around the house for places to put them.

"Okay." I glanced down at Skyla, "Will you be ready at dawn then?"

"You bet. Wouldn't miss this trip for the world."

***

A couple of hours later, I was sitting in the barn, twirling the allosaurus claw on the leather thong around my neck, when the barn door opened slightly, and a figure slipped inside.

"Well, well. Sneaking out of the house, are we?" I chuckled and patted the top of the wooden bench beside me. Bo had just made it the other day, and it was still rough on top from the sawing. It'd take years of use to wear smooth.

Skyla slid beside me. "How'd you know it was me?"

"Well, it was either you or an Indian. I can't think of anyone else who is light enough to move that quietly. So, I really hoped it was you."

"Guess you couldn't sleep, huh?"

"Nope. You neither it seems."

"Too eager. I can't stop thinking about crossing the Shimmer and what we might find." She smiled and rested her head against me. "Are you ready for another adventure?"

"Darlin', I don't think our adventure has ended yet. It seems to just keep going and going."

"One day it will be over, and you'll miss it."

"Miss getting shot at? Stabbed? Battered, beaten, blown up... I don't know. I might be okay when it's over."

Skyla smirked. "What will you do once this is all over?"

"When Prehistoria is tamed? Hopefully, if your father is right, I'll have a pardon in my hand, and I can do whatever I want. No more hiding."

"No more hiding," she repeated. "You've done a terrible job of hiding so far," she teased. "Our picture was on the front page of the most read newspaper in America, along with an article about you saving the day in Granite Falls."

"Yeah, I'm doing a horrible job of laying low."

We were silent for a few minutes, watching the sleeping protos make noises through their beaks as they lay curled into balls on the floor of the barn.

"What are you worried about more? The Shaynee, the attack, or the axemen?"

"Axemen. I dislike the unknown. The Shaynee, I get what drives them, what they want. The attack, I understand our part in it and what we are trying to accomplish... but the axemen? There ain't no telling what they are like. The Shayana say they aren't exactly friendly, but they aren't a foe either. We'll have to make sure to get on their good side."

"The scientist in me is awed by the chance to meet another culture, but do we really need them?" Skyla asked.

"I suppose the more allies we have the better. The apes whooped us pretty good at Fort Jipson, and there's a lot we don't know about Prehistoria. I figure anyone who's survived there long enough to have a civilization ought to be of help to us."

Skyla leaned against me. "I wonder what we'll find?"

"I don't know. I just hope we survive it."

"We will."

***

The next morning, famed Westerner Wolverine Wade and his sharpshooter fiancé Ashley James met us outside the stable when we rode into Granite Falls.

Wade was wearing his usual Western attire, fringed leather jacket, fringed leather pants, and a fashionable hat cocked at an angle on his head with a revolver on his hip and a heavy octagonal barreled rifle slung over his shoulder. Ashley was dressed much plainer, her blond braid hanging over a coat that covered her dress and her famous *One of a Thousand* rifle carried in hand.

Wade tipped his hat in greetings as Ashley and Skyla embraced each other with a hug.

"What are you two doing here?" I asked after Ashley hugged me as well.

"Trying to make a living," Wade grumbled as we shook hands.

"I take it you're having a hard time getting your New West dinosaur show off the ground?"

"Damnable apes are making it that way."

"I reckon you never got permission to cross the Shimmer then?" I asked as I began to pull the saddle and tack off Carbine.

"Not after Fort Jipson fell. No."

"What are your plans now?" Skyla asked as she entangled her arm in mine.

"Lieutenant Daniels has offered us the opportunity to come along on your attack," Ashley said with a big smile.

"Into harm's way... Why?"

She shrugged, "It's our only chance to see the other side again and get some feel for the area and what we'll need to capture more dinosaurs."

"Shame we didn't get that raptor to you the Pinkertons caught before the fort fell. You'd have enjoyed that little bugger. It was as vicious as all get out. Be a big draw for your show."

"Yes, we would have! Maybe we'll get a chance to catch another one." Wade pointed at the rope attached to Carbine's saddle. "Maybe you can lasso us one."

I laughed. "I'm not very good with a rope, but maybe."

"Jed! Skyla!" The voice boomed from the darkened interior of the stable.

Turning, I saw a powerfully built man with a thick mustache and spectacles perched on top of his nose approaching us. He grinned broadly.

"Fredrick!" I called back. The others turned to see the newcomer. Fredrick von Holsack was a famous Western hunter and adventurer. His travels had taken him around the world to many exotic places where he'd promptly shot everything he could and had mounted and stuffed for his personal collection or the Smithsonian's. Between him and Wolverine Wade, our small group was practically Western Mythology in terms of reputation.

Hugging the ladies, he shook my hand, then Wade's. "Wade, Ashley … by golly it's good to see you two again. And I hear you're engaged! Congratulations are in order! That's far more important than simple Jed here turning out to be alive!"

The group laughed, and I joined them. Narrowly defeating death was becoming second nature for me it seemed.

"Thank you, Fredrick. We're pretty tickled ourselves," the sharpshooter replied as she grabbed her fiancé's arm and tugged him close. "Both about 'Simple Jed' being alive and us being engaged, that is," she laughed.

Wade grinned boyishly for a moment before his face fell. "Sorry to hear about Captain Brandthorn. He was a good man and a wise leader. He'll be missed."

I looked down at the ground and kicked the toe of my boot against the corral post, "Yes, he will. He went out magnificently though. You should have seen him; he had his sword out and was slicing apes up left and right before they finally got him. He gave his life defending the palisade to buy more time for the defenders to regroup," I spoke sorrowfully, remembering the Captain's final moments.

The group grew silent for a moment as we all thought of our friend and leader.

"Jed, I know we laugh, but we had given up on you as well," Ashley said quietly.

"How did you survive that tunnel collapse?" Fredrick asked. "Lieutenant Daniels said the last he saw you, you were running right behind him."

"His dynamite didn't collapse the tunnel completely, so I used some I had and collapsed the stinking thing on top of myself. It was really luck that I made it out alive." I thought back to the charging apes running down the hewn rock tunnel, dodging their spear thrusts and grappling with them in the darkness, stabbing away with my Bowie and trying to stick it in anything hairy and fleshy. It'd been wild and terrifying.

Wade slapped me on the back, "You gave us quite the scare."

Skyla hugged my waist and pulled me close. I grinned down at her. "Nothing to it. Just crawled out of a collapsed tunnel and made my way to the Shimmer. Only took three days, one day of which was just me trying to dig my way out of my own doing."

"Still, it was a close thing. And here we are, going off again on another adventure," she said back.

"A wonderful thing," Fredrick mused. "An adventure is just what we need, and an attack on the apes! How grand! Time to get some revenge on those blood thirsty monkeys."

"So, you'll be coming as well?" Wade asked the hunter.

"I've already been invited and wouldn't miss it for the world." He smiled mischievously. "Besides, I still have that Tyrannosaurus to kill."

***

Leaving the group behind, I walked down the street to the Bucket O' Blood.

I left them under the guise of running a few quick errands. But really, I wanted to try and get a feel for the goings on in town. Plus, the Sheriff's body may have been found by now. And I wanted to see if I could find any leads as to who the mysterious man was that sent raiders to my home.

Pushing the batwing doors open, I stopped for a moment and waited for my eyes to adjust to the darkened interior. This was a moment I habitually hated, seemed like a good time for somebody with an intense dislike in their heart to plug you with bullets.

But nothing happened and after several seconds I could see well enough to make my way to the bar.

Reverend was there, perched on a stool and leaning against the counter near the giant triceratops skull with Wolverine Wade's bullet hole punched between the upper two horns. A glass of milk was in front of the man of cloth, beside it, his worn and tattered Bible. Not a big surprise to see him, he often visited places of ill reputation to try and bring wayward folks into his fold.

Skimming the room, I looked over everyone in sight. They'd replaced the piano player since I'd been here last, and a joyful melody trickled from the beaten old piano across the room. Beside him lounged several working girls, while others sat in the laps of potential clients, and a handful of men were scattered through the room. It was still too early for the high rollers and gamblers to be up and about, but Granite Falls had boomed enough to keep a steady line of customers in the bar through most of the day by serving decent food and female company.

No one seemed to be paying me any attention, and I didn't recognize any of them.

Nodding to Left Arm O'Malley, who owned and operated the bar, I grabbed a stool and slid it beside the Reverend and sat.

"Afternoon, Jedidiah," the Reverend said simply, taking up his glass for a sip. A thin white line was left on his upper lip as he placed the milk back down on the counter.

"Hello, Reverend," I said while waving at Left Arm to come to us.

The bar owner ambled down, a dishrag in hand. "You're not going to cause any trouble today, are ye, Jed?" he asked in his thick Irish accent. I reckon he had good call to be concerned; I'd had a fist fight and a gun fight in this very bar. Only thing missing was to be involved in a knifing.

"No sir, just here to see what's going on," I replied and glanced at the Reverend's milk. That looked good right now. It was a bit too early for me to be drinking any sort of alcohol. "I'll take what he's having," I gestured with my chin towards the glass beside the Bible.

Left Arm fetched me a glass, slid it in front of me, and I slipped several coins across the bar. It was enough to pay for many, many glasses of milk.

He arched an eyebrow at me.

"That's for the milk and any information you or the girls come across regarding the raiders who attacked my ranch."

With his lone hand, he swept them off the counter and pocketed the coins. Nodding, he turned and walked down the bar towards the piano where a group of ladies lounged and nursed their hangovers.

"Sheriff was found dead the other day," Reverend said quietly, as he twirled his glass on top of the bar slowly, thoughtfully.

I put on my best poker face. "That's not exactly a shame."

"Seems whoever did it, walked him out into the prairie in his underwear, then shot him through the chest. Critters had already gotten to him; his body was a mess."

"Couldn't have happened to a nicer man," I said sarcastically, before taking a sip of my drink.

Reverend lowered his voice, tilting his head towards mine conspiringly. "I don't suppose you know anything about that, would you?"

I looked the man of faith in his trusting eyes and lied. "No."

"Good. Because that would be crossing a line that shouldn't be crossed. We've judges and jurors to handle things like a Sheriff's corruption."

I snorted with disdain. "You know better than that. Judges and jurors can be bought or frightened. Especially when the guilty is protected by

Reydan White. It seems to me that someone got tired of the corruption and decided to handle it."

"At some point, you've got to have faith in the system."

"No thanks. If you'll recall, most of my adult life was spent NOT having faith in it."

He shook his head sadly. "At some point, Jed, you've got to have faith in something."

I patted the pistols on either side of my hips. "I've faith in God and my weapons. That's about it."

Glancing at my pistols, he commented wryly, "At least God will never run out of ammunition."

"I'll drink to that." I raised my glass of milk.

He brought his to mine and we clinked them before taking a gulp.

I ran my finger along the rough opening of a bullet hole punched into the edge of the counter and wondered who put it there. "Other than the Sheriff's demise, any other news around here?"

Reverend nodded, "It seems Simon and his men have gone missing."

"Who?" The name sounded familiar.

"The ape bounty hunters."

"Oh, yes. Them." They'd been responsible for hunting down any apes that survived the Battle of the Apes when their army attacked our town. They were under orders to find them, kill them, and return with their severed right thumbs for payment. I'd only met them once before in Captain Brandthorn's office across the street; they seemed like a capable bunch of men. Not the sort you'd invite to your wedding or anywhere respectable mind you, but capable of killing apes and other degenerates with a bounty on their head. Which meant if Morgan Stratten's plan for a pardon didn't work, I might end up in their sights one day.

"They went out after a band of apes a few days ago and never came back."

I sipped my milk and shook my head slightly. "Dangerous job."

"It is and Mr. Simon was rather sweet on the young dark-haired lady by the piano." He nodded in her direction without turning his head.

I glanced over my shoulder at her.

She grinned invitingly with a gap-toothed smile. I recognized her. She'd evacuated town just before the Battle of the Apes. Apparently, she was back. I tipped my hat in greeting then turned away before she got the wrong idea.

"She seems to be okay with him missing," I mused.

"Notice any black eyes?" he said quietly.

I looked at the Reverend in puzzlement. "No."

"Then you know why she seems okay with him missing."

I grunted angrily, "Simon sounds like an asshole. Good riddance."

"He may still be alive. Or the apes may have killed him. Either way, you asked what was new in town. That's about it. I suppose you already heard about the Chinese protests over labor and pay with the East-West railroad?"

"Yeah," I drawled, "I heard Reydan sent in the Pinkertons, and they killed a bunch of the Chinese workers. Lieutenant Daniels told me when I last crossed through the Shimmer."

"The Chinese are pretty upset about it still. Understandably. And being a white man, you may want to steer clear of them for a while."

"Too bad, they cook some mighty fine food." Every time I rode past into the eastern town entrance, past makeshift China Town, I was tempted by their chicken and noodles. I couldn't pronounce it, but I could eat it.

Reverend drained the last of his milk, and I followed suit, sensing he was about to leave.

He grabbed his Bible off the bar and shook it at me. "Jedidiah, be careful out there. You've powerful enemies. But, also, powerful allies. Do try and stay on this side of the grass."

I grinned and got up to follow him out of the saloon. "Yes, sir."

"Jed," I heard Left Arm call softly from behind the bar.

Bidding the Reverend goodbye as he pushed open the batwing doors, I turned back.

Left Arm was wiping down the bar where our drinks had been. He whispered quietly, without looking up, "It seems your money has loosened some lips."

"Whose? On second thought, it doesn't matter. What'd they have to say?" I figured Left Arm wouldn't tell me anyways, he wouldn't risk any of his girls getting caught up in anything he couldn't get them out of.

"Seems the new mayor was asking around about some rough characters a few days before your place was attacked. He was interested in one man in particular... some fellow named Henry."

I thought about this. The old mayor had been dead for some time and a new one had just been appointed, with substantial backing from Reydan White from what I had gathered. I'd yet to meet him so I wasn't sure why he'd be gunning for me except for his connection to Reydan. But it was unlikely a coincidence that he was interested in the same man that led the failed raid on my ranch.

"Where might I find this new mayor?"

Left Arm tilted his head slightly, pointing to my right side discretely. "Behind you. Big guy, at the table with Corine, eating breakfast."

"Corine?"

"The busty redhead."

I didn't turn to look. "Thanks."

"Don't do anything in here," he pleaded, tapping his fingers by the bullet hole in the bar. "It may just be a coincidence; he seems like a good man."

"Yes, sir." I promised him, but I didn't believe in coincidences.

After Left Arm left me alone, I turned my back to the bar and leaned back against it, surveying the room again. I'd seen a handful of men when I'd entered, scattered around the saloon. But this time I looked at the man I now knew was the freshly appointed mayor.

He didn't look like much. A large man with a thick mustache and goatee, big around the belly, wearing a suit coat that did nothing to hide his size. Beside him rested a hat on the table, next to his partially eaten breakfast. He didn't appear armed, but with his waist size and coat, he could have hidden a revolver easily enough.

Across from him sat the woman I assumed to be Corine, red haired all right, in a blue dress revealing way too much. Not very reputable for a mayor, but politicians are usually a scuzzy bunch.

But hell, who was I to talk about being reputable?

Pushing off the bar, I walked amongst the tables and chairs until I towered over Corine and the mayor at their table. They both looked up. I tipped my hat at Corine, then turned to the large man.

"Yes, can I help you?" the mayor asked as though he didn't know me, but I thought I saw something that may have been recognition in his eyes.

"Well, sir, I figured I'd come over and meet you, Mayor....?"

"Gentry," he smiled thinly. "That's my name."

"Well, Gentry, a pleasure." I stared at him, wondering if this was the sort of man who would send others to kill someone he'd never met before.

"Mayor Gentry," he corrected me quickly.

I didn't say anything, just kept my eyes on him.

He coughed, and quickly pulled a red handkerchief from his pocket. Coughing again, he turned his head away. I could hear the deep rattle inside his chest as he hacked and spat unceremoniously into the cloth.

Wiping his face, he turned back to me.

There was a thin smear of blood running from the corner of his mouth across his cheek.

A lunger.

Henry said he'd been hired by one.

I knew I needed to deal with this now. If this was the man, I needed to handle it before I left for Prehistoria. Gritting my teeth, I decided to check what I thought I already knew. "Henry talked," I said softly.

The mayor's face paled, his eyes widened in shock and understanding.

That told me everything I needed to know. This was the man who sent the raiders after me, who'd tried to kill me, almost killed Skyla, and shot Elizabeth.

Rage flashed through me, and I shook as I fought to keep from shooting the man where he sat.

"Corine, I need a moment with Gentry. Alone."

She looked from him to me, confusion etched across her face.

"No, stay," the mayor demanded, a small bead of sweat running down his temple.

"No. Go," I said firmly, fixing her with a glare so she didn't dare argue.

She got up and quickly walked to the other girls by the piano.

Without warning, I slapped Gentry across the face with an open hand. The sound reverberated through the room.

He gasped in pain and shock, and the entire building went quiet as they turned to watch us. I heard Left Arm mutter an expletive from behind the bar.

Speaking loudly, I made sure the entire barroom could hear me. "Gentry, you are a cowardly sonuva bitch. You sent gunmen and rustlers to my home. You tried to kill me in my sleep and steal my animals. And I mean to put an end to it."

"I'm unarmed, sir. And how dare you-" he stammered, his face flushing red from rage, embarrassment, and the force of my palm.

I slapped him again. Harder this time.

His head spun around on his thick neck, and his large body almost toppled out of the chair.

Reaching for my left pistol, I drew it fluidly and shoved the gun against his chest. Shocked, he grabbed it with both hands and stared down at the blued Colt.

"Outside. Now," I barked, before spinning on my heel and walking away.

I was wagering he wouldn't shoot me. But just the same, the scarred skin on my back itched as the thought of getting shot in the back crawled through my head.

"Jed…" Left Arm pleaded.

"I'm taking it outside," I growled back as I stepped around the trike skull and knocked open the batwing doors.

Stepping through, my boots thumped on the boardwalk, then onto the frozen mud and gravel of the street. Turning back to face the saloon, I waited.

After several long moments, the mayor walked out of the diner. Anger and hatred blazed across his reddened face. He opened the cylinder gate on my pistol and spun the cylinder to see if it was loaded. I reckon that meant he knew how to use it.

Satisfied that it was, he snapped the gate shut, glared at me, then stalked down the street in the opposite direction.

I followed suit, turning my back on him again and shoving between people with a look that showed I wasn't interested in hearing any complaints about my rude behavior.

John Parsons appeared before me, started to speak, then realized what was taking place. The journalist quickly ducked down behind a parked wagon and peeked around the seat; his eyes wide with excitement at what was about to happen.

As we walked apart from each other, shouts arose, and men began pulling their wives and children out of the street and hustling them into the nearby buildings for protection. It was as if the town could sense the looming shootout, and as people began to clear the streets, I could feel myself shaking with wrath and anticipation of the fight.

I relished the feeling.

After reaching the center of the street, I turned in time to see Mayor Gentry do the same to face me.

He held my Colt Peacemaker in hand, while mine was holstered. A clear advantage to him, but one I was in no shape to contemplate or care about.

"It doesn't have to be this way, Jedidiah," he shouted towards me. "No one needs to be hurt today."

That just proved my theory because I'd never told him my name.

"Shut up and shoot, chickenshit," I shouted back at him.

For a moment, everything seemed to go quiet and still. From the corners of my eyes, I could see people huddled behind barrels, water troughs, doors, windows and alleyways and parked wagons. All of them wanting to see someone die, but not wanting to die themselves.

Gentry jerked the pistol up.

I drew.

As the mayor's gun hand rose, I felt my own grab the polished grip of my pistol. I willed myself to be smooth as the weapon slid from the leather tooled holster, up my side, and forward as I thrust the barrel before me.

My eyes fell on the pistol's iron sights, and without thinking, I took a step to the left as I'd practiced with Morgan Stratten all those times back at the ranch.

Gentry's barrel burst forth flame, and a bullet cracked past where I'd stood a moment before.

Squeezing the trigger, the hammer fell on the primer of a loaded cartridge, and the gun bucked in my hand.

The mayor abruptly twisted to the side and dropped.

I stood still, gun raised, watching Gentry over the sights to see if he'd get back up.

He didn't.

Lowering my weapon, I stalked forward as people carefully left their hiding places and stepped onto the boardwalk or into the street to see the carnage of a gun fight firsthand. Parsons peeked around the wagon, seeing if it was safe.

Reaching Gentry, I saw that he'd dropped my pistol and it'd fallen several feet from his body. He gasped, and his feet kicked slightly as he stared up at me. Blood slowly stained across his shirt from where my bullet had struck him in the center of his chest.

"Was it Reydan?" I asked simply.

The mayor grimaced, nodded, and slid his hand to the wound beneath his suit coat.

"Figures." I began to holster my pistol.

Gentry's bloodied hand darted out from under his coat, pulled with force, as his face twisted in fury.

The silver derringer in his hand barked a shot as I threw myself backwards and fired the Colt downwards into his body again.

Gentry's hand went limp, and the small pistol fell away.

"Sonuva bitch!" I shouted and held my hand to my ear. Gingerly touching it, my fingers felt a small notch missing from the edge, and pulling my hand away, there was bright red blood smeared across my fingertips.

I kicked the mayor in the side. The dead man didn't feel it.

"Damn, Jed. What was that for?" someone called out cautiously behind me.

The voice sounded vaguely familiar, but I couldn't place it. Holstering my weapon, I turned and saw Sergeant Mayhew stepping towards me slowly, his hands held out and empty.

"That was for him sending rustlers after my herd." Nodding in greeting at the soldier, I dropped to a knee and retrieved the Colt Peacemaker that I'd loaned the now deceased mayor.

"Uh-huh. Well, I need you to come with me," the Sergeant said as he stepped beside me and looked down at the bloodied corpse.

"It was a fair fight." I opened the gate, ejected the fired cartridge, and slid a fresh one in.

"I know... We all saw. But Governor Hale sent me to fetch you."

"Well," I looked around at the crowd gathered. They all seemed curious, with no hostility. Apparently, the mayor hadn't had time yet to become popular and there was no sign of a deputy anywhere nearby. "I reckon if anyone needs to talk to me over this, they can find me later."

Parsons called out to me as he approached the body. "Jed, can I get a statement?"

"No!" I shouted over a shoulder to the journalist as I followed the Sergeant.

***

An inch of snow was on the ground as I rode to the top of the grassed plateau with my escort. The shouts and commands of an army camp and the ragged fire of a volley as target practice commenced echoed from below. Spitting on my blue handkerchief, I dabbed at the painful spot on my ear that'd been nicked. It'd stopped bleeding finally and clotted, but I suspected it'd take a while to stop aching. At least it was hard to see when I was wearing my hat, but I knew I'd catch hell from Skyla when she found out about the shooting.

Sergeant Mayhew nodded towards the group of men at the crest and bid me goodbye before returning to his duties.

Gritting my teeth at who I saw there, I touched my heels to Carbine, and he plodded along to the top of the snow churned hill.

"Congratulations on surviving a hanging, Mr. Smith," Reydan White said with a fake, easy-going smile as I reached the small group. Cato simply stared, his dark face blank and unrevealing. They both rode a pair of beautiful appaloosa horses. It was fitting, I supposed; Reydan had ridden an appaloosa when he raided my home decades ago.

I thought about what color the rail tycoon's intestines would be on the blade of my Bowie and grinned back with my most charming smile. "I also survived a raid on my ranch orchestrated by Mayor Gentry, seems I'm mighty hard to kill."

Governor Hale growled, "I assume you have proof, Jed?"

"No," I admitted.

Reydan White barked a short laugh. "Another baseless accusation, like the one he leveraged against me."

"Unlike you, he's dead though," I told them casually, watching Reydan for his reaction.

The tycoon raised an eyebrow in surprise, but otherwise concealed his thoughts. I suspected Gentry had been nothing more than a tool to him, as the gunman Henry had been to the former mayor.

"What?" Hale demanded, rising in his saddle in anger. "You killed him?"

"He tried to outdraw me, high noon style."

Cato looked at me with renewed interest. His nickname of the Black Plague came from killing several men who tried to rob his boss and others who challenged him to a gunfight. It was an aptly given name, as he killed everyone with incredible quickness and skill.

The Governor sighed. "Well, that was foolish of him. I swear, Jed, trouble follows you everywhere."

"Yes, sir. Seems like."

"I assume it was a fair fight?"

"It was, Sergeant Mayhew and a bunch of others witnessed it, including John Parsons."

"Good. Then it shouldn't change our plans for you. Jedidiah, this is Colonel Carver." He pointed at the third man on the hilltop, a tall, thin, uniformed gentleman sitting on the back of a black horse with an extended brass telescope held to his right eye. So far, he'd remained out of the conversation.

Lowering the telescope, he took me in with a glance. "Mr. Smith. I'm pleased you accepted our invitation to join us."

I could only nod. I hadn't realized at the time that it was something I could turn down when Mayhew escorted me here.

Distant booms from cannons reached my ears. I watched the belches of gun smoke erupt down the line as each one fired after the other down the row. There must have been almost five hundred men in the valley below me, at least half were Pinkertons.

"An impressive sight, sir," I said, holding back a shiver under my thick coat. The temperatures had steadily dropped even as the sun rose towards its highest point in the sky.

"Yes, it is." He turned to face me. "As Lieutenant Daniels no doubt told you, we're going to hit the apes. Hit them hard. Losing Fort Jipson lit a fire beneath Congress, and President Grover means to see a war in return. Most of Congress was on the fence about the excessiveness of spending money on Prehistoria, but that's changed. That tunnel you found, with the Shimmer in it leading to a lost world, is unexplainable by even the most brilliant minds sent from Europe. We don't know how it opened or how long it will be open. Every time troops are sent across, lives are being risked on just the possibility of returning. But the resources on that side have vast potential, and the word has gotten out that the Shayana have large quantities of gold and are willing to part with it for our advanced weaponry. As your friend, Sergeant Gibbons, can attest, they've herbal medicines over there that both the Shayana and apes use to quickly heal wounds. These are things we want, and there is more over there that we don't know of yet. Also, because of the relentless petitions, Congress is opening Prehistoria up to settlers." He laughed humorlessly. "Even the damned Shaynee want to go back, claiming it as their ancestral heritage and birth right. I don't know about that, but heaven knows we'd like to get rid of the heathen Indians. What better place to dump them?"

"And most likely, a new territory will be established on the other side as well," Governor Hale added as he twisted on an end of his graying mustache.

I looked at Reydan White expectantly. "Let me guess, you'll be the Governor of the new territory?"

The former Union raider glared back. "No, Mr. Smith. I will not. My duties running the railroad, establishing Whitesberg, and helping the Army with Prehistoria keeps me busy as it is."

"And wealthy, I'm sure," I snarked back. "Who then?"

"That's still to be determined. I've told President Grover of several candidates he could appoint until the eventual elections as we open Prehistoria up for homesteading." Hale shrugged with a wave of his hand, dismissing the topic as if it had no bearing on our discussion.

"Sir, about allowing settlers to cross... there's an army of apes over there, giant dinosaurs, and who knows what else. We've barely scratched the surface of what exists!"

"Welcome to the New West, Mr. Smith," the Colonel said with a sideways grin. The New West was a term that was catching on, it meant the Second Age of Dinosaurs that came with my discovery of the Shimmer and the lost world on the other side. "And the New West, like the Old West, will be tamed and brought to heel with sweat, courage, and gunfire."

I sighed. "I miss the Old West."

"I don't. It was becoming entirely too civilized for me," the Army officer grimaced.

Our group sat in silence for several moments, watching the troops train below. It was easy to tell who the Pinkertons were, they had no real military discipline to them. They moved about in small groups, freely practicing shooting, while others simply sat and jawed. In contrast, on the opposite side of the valley, the soldiers moved with cohesion, even on the individual firing line.

"Colonel, I'm a bit sketchy on the part where we work with the Pinkertons. You said the fall of Fort Jipson lit a fire beneath Congress, so why are we using a private military?"

"The Pinkertons are not a private military force-" Reydan started, turning angrily in his saddle to face me.

"Looks like it to me," I cut him off and pointed towards the multitude of so-called Detectives in the valley below us.

Colonel Carver raised his hand, silencing us so he could speak. "We simply don't have the right troops in the right places yet. Don't get me wrong, we will pacify this lost world with the United States military. But it will take time to train up a force large enough to do so. As for the Pinkertons... They are able bodies that Reydan has been nice enough to arrange for our use. But they are, like your Shaynee Indian friends, a temporary arrangement."

Reydan chuckled humorlessly. "And Mr. Smith will lead them... a savage leading savages."

"I disagree, Mr. White," Governor Hale said as he lit a thin black cigar. He took a puff before continuing. "Jedidiah here is one of the bravest men I've known. He didn't have to be at the Battle of the Apes, but he was invaluable in that fight. As was his participation in saving lives at the fall of Fort Jipson."

"So, he's brave, but stupid," the rail tycoon chortled.

"Call me stupid again, you Yankee bastard," I dared him, twisting in my saddle to glare as I felt the familiar urge to gun him down rise like bile in my throat.

Cato casually moved his right hand onto the butt of his gun and glanced at his boss as if for permission to shoot me down for the insult.

Reydan shook his head slightly at his gun hand while his bearded face flushed red with anger.

"As you were, Mr. Smith... There is no need for insults." Colonel Carver glared at me with a frown. "Back to your job, using your knowledge of the area, you're to take us in a roundabout way to the canyon where Fort Jipson was. There we are going to assault the apes with overwhelming firepower. We're going to slaughter those damn monkeys down to the last hairy savage."

"You sound like you've been talking to Thompson," I muttered. Pinkerton Detective Thompson had led the small Pinkerton Army that had been stationed at Fort Jipson. He'd been the most vocal about wiping out every single ape and favored a bloody scorched earth policy when dealing with them.

"He isn't wrong," Reydan muttered back, disdain dripping in his voice.

Narrowing my eyes, I turned in the saddle to face the Colonel. "Why did you call me here?"

"You're leading the Shaynee attachment, and I want to make sure you're on the right side of history. And that's white man history, not Indian... or ape. You butted heads with Detective Thompson when he rescued Fredrick von Holsack and Oscar Ellis. Then you caused quite a stir afterwards with Captain Brandthorn complaining about Thompson's methods. I don't want a repeat of that."

"Thompson and his men murdered defenseless apes! Apes that didn't attack us. His men shot them like they were rabid dogs, regardless of if they were fighting back or not." I ground my teeth. "They executed baby apes in their huts. Then torched the entire village."

"Yes. He did." He looked down the valley and in silence we watched the cannons being reloaded below. He sighed. "This will be different."

"Will it?"

Before he could answer, a rider raced along the crest of the hill, his coat flapping in the wind as he rode. We watched as he pulled back on the reins and his horse skidded to a stop beside us. The man swept his hat off. He was probably about my age, wearing a tan suit, and the beginnings of a mustache forming on his upper lip.

"A glorious morning to you, gentlemen," he said in a slight accent with a partial bow at the waist.

Colonel Carver dipped his head in greetings to the newcomer. "Mr. Smith, this is Arthur Donahue, a writer from Scotland. He'll be traveling with us to the other side to chronicle our travels for Europe. Arthur, you've already met the others, but this," he gestured towards me, "is Jedidiah Smith. The rancher who first discovered the Shimmer and Prehistoria."

Leaning over in the saddle, I shook hands with him. "Nice to meet you, Arthur."

"Likewise." He leaned back and studied me intensely for a few moments before speaking. "So, you are the legendary hero of Granite Falls? How did that ape's heart taste?"

Reydan White laughed without humor and shook his head while staring at the troops below us training.

I rolled my eyes. That one deed would forever haunt me it seemed. "It was chewy. And legendary, huh? I take it you saw Parson's article on me?"

"I did indeed, a fine writer. I need to make his acquaintance while I'm in town."

"He's nice enough. If a bit over the top with his writing," I snarked.

Governor Hale puffed on his cigar and blew a ring of smoke. "Arthur, did you know that Fredrick von Holsak will be traveling with you also?"

"Ah yes! My father and I are quite the avid reader of his daring exploits; he's the reason I decided to become an author myself as a boy."

"Jed will have to introduce you then."

"Excellent!"

The writer looked at Cato, puzzled. "And you sir, I take it that you are the notorious Black Plague?"

Cato looked at Arthur blankly. Reydan answered for him. "He is."

I glared at my former childhood friend. The black gunman felt my stare and turned in the saddle to face me. "No… Cato's more like a pet. A raider's pet."

Cato's left eye twitched, but other than that, he remained motionless.

Reydan ground his teeth and pointed the end of his silver handled black cane at me. "I'll not have you insulting myself or my associate with these accusations again! I was a decorated quartermaster during the War Between the States, and nothing else I assure you. You are mistaken and offending me once again."

I tapped Carbine's flanks with my heels and moved him around until I was looking straight at Reydan. My hand was loosely holding the reins, and I knew I was once again on the ragged edge of getting killed by Cato.

"Jed. Knock it off," Governor Hale warned. "We've been down this road before."

"Mayor Gentry told me you had him send men to my house." I moved Carbine closer and lowered my voice. "And one day, I'm going to come to yours."

"Mr. Smith! That's enough! There'll be no threats given before me without the law becoming involved," Colonel Carver warned. "To be frank, I don't have time for your petty shit. We've a battle coming, one I do not intend to lose. You will avoid Mr. Reydan and Cato from now on or I'll have you arrested."

"Good luck with that." I twisted Carbine around. "By the way, I hear the Sheriff is dead too," I called over my shoulder to the railroad tycoon. "Wasn't he a friend of yours?"

Tapping heels to my horse's sides, I rode away before I could listen to more of Reydan's bullshit.

***

It had been an eventful morning, I thought while taking Carbine from the stable and fighting my pain in the ass horse to get a saddle back on him. Meanwhile, Skyla easily readied her dapple-grey horse, aptly named Smoke.

I'd already received a somewhat justified berating from Skyla over an early lunch about how I foolishly risked my life to kill the man responsible for sending dinosaur rustlers to our ranch. But she seemed pleased that I'd done so well and came out of the gun fight with only a little nick on my ear, as she put it, "That's my man." Which was rather ironic, considering how much of a chewing out she'd given me before that, you would have thought she was done with me.

My horse twisted his head around, grabbed the blanket with his teeth, and dropped it to the ground at my feet. For the third time.

"Confound it, Carbine!" I shouted and slapped his back end with my battered brown hat.

"Jed, you know he just does it for the attention." Skyla smiled as she pulled a withered apple from a bin and offered to it my mustang. He shook his black mane and tail and took the fruit from her eagerly.

I picked the blanket off the ground, beat the dust and bits of straw off with my other hand and placed it on his back again. "Yeah, well, I'd love to have him turned into glue." I only half meant it.

She cupped his ears as if to save him from my verbal threats and glared at me. "Hush now, he can hear you."

"Good!" I hefted my heavy saddle and glared at my horse, daring him to pull the blanket off again.

He munched contentedly on the apple and ignored me while Skyla rubbed his neck.

I dropped the saddle onto him and slid it backwards into place. "Good boy," I muttered, knowing full well that my compliments meant next to nothing to the troublesome horse.

A pair of mules pulled a wagon into sight of the stable doors with Wolverine Wade driving and Ashley James with a broad smile on her face. Skyla waved as I worked the cinch tight below Carbine's chest and belly.

Playing with her dirty blond braid of hair tossed over a shoulder, I could hear Ashley teasing the wolverine slayer. "I told you I could get a better deal. I don't have a terrible reputation around these parts like you!"

I snickered, strapped my bedroll onto the back of the saddle, and led Carbine out into the sunlight. "Let me guess, they heard about Wade's earlier rental wagon?" We'd taken it to see the Shimmer and ended up getting chased by apes, trikes, and raptors. The poor battered wagon had barely made it into town, shot up with ape arrows, horn damage from angry triceratops, and blood from raptors, apes, and people alike spilled in the back of it.

He snorted. "Happens once and this town will never let me live it down."

"Yeah, it's pretty bad when even the newcomers have heard not to let you borrow a wagon," Skyla laughed.

"Yeah, yeah. Being famous doesn't seem to help me any," Wade grumbled. "You ready to get this show on the road? We've some Indians waiting on us."

I helped Skyla into the saddle then mounted Carbine. "Let's ride."

"What about Fredrick? Are we not waiting on him?" Ashley asked as she shifted her rifle in the seat beside her.

"We probably won't see him again until we cross the Shimmer tomorrow. He's good friends with the Governor, so I expect they'll be swapping tall tales for most of the day and downing strong drinks for most of the night." I touched my heels to Carbine's sides. "Let's get moving, before the Indians get too ornery waiting."

***

It was well past noon by the time we reached the Shaynee village.

The tribe of Indians had returned to their location prior to the ape army crossing through the Shimmer. I didn't blame them. As we crested the grassy hill and rode through the wide-open plains beside the river, I couldn't help but think of how pretty this place would be with a few hundred head of cattle grazing on it. I guessed the Indians were probably having a hard time finding places to move to, what with all the barbwire fencing going up, and taking of their land. I knew there was talk of a relocation treaty for the Shaynee, although it seemed like the Federal Government learned their lesson the hard way with the Apache resisting them. I reckoned if the government saw the opportunity to kick them off this land into Prehistoria, they'd take it over another Indian war.

The village itself was bustling with activity. Dogs were running around and barking. The women were working and cooking, while children laughed and played. Men fished in the river with spears while others rode ponies out to hunt or scout around the area for any white invaders. I was pleased to not see any slabs of beef in sight; they'd poached more than a few head of my cattle last time I was here.

A pair of Indians on ponies rode out to greet us as we began to ride down the hill towards the village.

One, an older man with a barreled chest and a craggy face full of wrinkles, smiled as the two men approached. White eagle and red raptor feathers decorated his braided hair, and a necklace of white beads circled his throat. A rifle was slung across his back, the sling decorated with small feathers, shiny brass beads and trinkets. Tucked into his waist was an old single shot flintlock pistol, one I knew to be an heirloom of his tribe and symbol of his position as leader.

The other Indian was younger, and I knew him well. He was thin but stout, with horrific scarring from shoulder to waist hidden beneath a leather shirt. This one grinned crookedly as he stopped his horse in front of us. From his horse's neck hung a belt of scalps, among them I saw a patch of white ape hair. That had come from the albino monkey he had saved me from during the Battle of the Apes. There was also a good bit of what looked like human scalps on the belt as well.

The older man's paint pony pranced to a stop, and he beamed at us. "Huck Berry," he said in greeting.

I tipped my hat towards him, "Chief."

No introductions were needed for the rest of the party, we'd all met each other before.

The scarred Indian slid from his unsaddled pony and sauntered towards the wagon with a cocky walk.

I tensed, and wondered what Otto was going to do. Wade had the same reaction. Without being subtle about it, he placed his hand on the butt of the Remington New Model Army revolver at his waist and stared at the Shaynee as he approached.

The ugly brave stepped close to Ashley, paused for a moment, then pulled a decorated tomahawk from his belt. There was a neatly punched bullet hole in the center of the hatchet-shaped blade, a memento from the time he almost caved my head in with it and Ashley shot it out of his hands with her *One of a Thousand* Winchester rifle.

Flipping the tomahawk around in his hand, Otto extended it to her handle first.

I glanced at Chief in surprise, and he winked. "Think of... peace offering," he told us in his broken English.

"For shooting hairy man off my back," Otto said.

I grunted in disgust. I saved the brave's life years ago and started a blood feud between us by slighting his honor in doing so. And apparently Ashley saved his life at the Battle of the Apes and gets a fancy weapon. It figured.

Ashley accepted the tomahawk with a gracious smile. "Thank you," she said reverently as she took it from his hands and twisted it about in hers, inspecting the decorated weapon closely. I wondered how many skulls the Indian had split open with it.

"We will have to get you a sheath made, so you can carry that on your belt," Wade said as he slowly released the butt of his pistol.

"See? We friends now," Chief Toko chuckled and slapped his belly happily.

"Right..." I said as Otto stalked back to his horse without a backwards glance. The Indian brave moved like a mountain lion with a chip on its shoulder.

I looked past the two Indians towards their village beyond. Two dozen braves were gathering weapons, lashing equipment on pole sleds, and preparing their ponies. I recognized a few of them and was heartened because I knew they were fighters. But hell, they were all fighters. The Shaynee certainly weren't left alone for their tribe's size, they didn't number all that many, but other rival tribes had learned to leave them alone the hard way.

"Chief, for those braves joining us, I bring gifts." Dismounting, I passed Carbine's reins to Skyla and walked to the back of Wade and Ashley's wagon.

Chief Toko slipped off the back of his horse and followed me.

Reaching the back of the wagon, Wade passed me a crowbar. Slipping it between the wooden panels, I broke the top of the first crate open. Inside gleamed the polished wood and oiled steel of brand-new Winchester repeating rifles. "And plenty of bullets," I added.

The Chief oohed and awed as he pulled one of the rifles from the crate. Otto led his horse behind the wagon, and the Chief passed him the rifle. With a wicked grin, the brave worked the action and brought the rifle to his shoulder to look down the sights. They both seemed well pleased at the unexpected gifts.

The Shaynee had a few repeating arms amongst them already. After the Battle of the Apes, they had made off with plenty of US military equipment, including lots of single action Springfields and the occasional dead civilian weapon. So, they had an idea as to how to work and use them.

But since the attack on Granite Falls by the ape army, every soldier crossing through the Shimmer carried a Winchester Repeater, which was why I demanded that the Shaynee be equally armed. I knew that a rifle such as this would make a big man of the Indian carrying it in his village, but I also knew that it could make the tribe harder to deal with later if it came to white and red man violence. If it came to that, the price of any white man blood spilled would be on my hands for better arming the reds.

Personally, I just hoped like hell the Indians wouldn't trade them away on horses or squaws before we departed.

"This is goodwill. Between two peoples. White and Shaynee," I told them, reverting my speech to words I figured Chief Toko would know.

Otto spoke pretty good English, but I didn't want to offend the Indian Chief by using big words.

Chief nodded and winked at me while raising the rifle up. "Good for us to push white men off land."

I shook my head. "Good luck. We're as many as stars in sky."

"But white men shit fighters," Otto said with a frown as he looked over the rifle barrel towards a puffy cloud floating on the horizon. "Without guns, white men nothing."

Wade and Ashley shared a disgusted look and I winced. If Otto was to be my liaison between the military and his braves, we were in for a rough time together.

"That ain't true," I said to him, feeling the need to defend my race of explorers, conquerors, and subjugators of lesser civilizations.

Otto passed the rifle back to the Chief and made a 'come at me' motion with his hands and a smirk. "Show me."

I slid the crowbar back into the back of the wagon, even though the temptation to bash the brave's head in with the steel bar was strong. This Indian asshole had been asking for a beating for a long time. I stepped towards him.

Chief stepped between us with hands held out. "No. We do this Shaynee way."

"Fine," I growled, misunderstanding and unbuckling my gun belt.

"No! Shaynee way where everyone can see!" he insisted.

"Even better," I grunted and passed my heavy gun belt to Wade.

"Ohh, a fight!" the famous Westerner said as he set my guns on the bench seat between himself and Ashley. "I knew this trip would be entertaining."

***

True to Shaynee tradition, we relieved ourselves of any weapons and stripped our shirts off.

For a moment, I closed my eyes as I pulled my red checkered shirt off, even knowing that most of the people present had seen my disfigured back already. Hiding the scars had been a habit I'd kept since Reydan White's whip wounds healed as a child. A white man with whip scars tended to draw a lot of attention.

Around my neck dangled a black Allosaurus claw on a leather thong, a gift from Skyla from the first dinosaur I killed that had brought us together. I promised her to never take it off and hoped the Indian wouldn't choke me to death with it. The dinosaur claw nearly touched the diagonal scar across my chest from where the beast had tried to rip me open.

As for Otto, he pulled his leather stitched shirt off and strutted around the crowd. The awful scarring from a grizzly that'd almost killed him was exposed proudly across his chest. It was really impressive looking. But it was also really nasty looking from the way the ragged strips of flesh had been stitched back together by the Shaynee's medicine man.

Rolling my shoulders and arching my back, I stretched and tried to loosen up.

While I wasn't exactly trained in the ways of hand-to-hand combat, I'd pissed some folks off before and had picked up a few things over the years. But I knew the Shaynee brave standing opposite of me had wrestled and fought since childhood, as was their custom, and this would be a tough fight.

I was ready to cheat in whatever way made me win.

Chief Toko spoke in Shaynee to the crowd, and with my limited knowledge of the language, I could only pick up bits and pieces of it. Basically, he was telling them that today we'd see Otto beat the shit out of me, but if by some miracle I won, no harm would be allowed to come to me or my group.

That last part was kind of nice I thought as I surveyed the Indians. Many of them I recognized by sight if not by name, and more than a few watched me with almost disgust. I was going up against their champion, how dare I think I was better?

Then, as I felt the familiar fearful yet excited trembling in my body that always happened before a brawl, Chief Toko stepped into the group of Indians that circled us and grinned broadly while gesturing at us to get at it.

The two of us circled each other inside the ring of Indian braves, women, and children who shouted for Otto and whooped insults at me.

I didn't take it personally. We were on Otto's home turf, and as much as the Shaynee might respect me, they weren't about to want a white man to beat one of their own.

And I had to.

I had to beat Otto into the ground as mercilessly as possible.

If I didn't, I'd never have his or the other braves' respect. They'd never listen to me. And bad things would happen to them on the other side of the Shimmer if they didn't.

This fight was for their own good. And to settle an old grudge.

Circling the scarred brave, looking for an opening to attack, I glimpsed Skyla behind Otto. Her eyes were wide, and her small fists clenched at her sides. I knew she didn't like this.

Wolverine Wade and Ashley, meanwhile, were having the time of their lives.

"Yeah! Get him, Jed!" Wade shouted as he waved his flat brimmed hat overhead. "Bust him in the mouth!"

"Kick him in the groin!" Ashley offered in way of fist fighting tips.

It's nice to have the support of your friends.

Otto, sensing that I was distracted, lunged forward quicker than a snake. Grabbing me about the waist, he fought against my larger size to throw me down.

Dropping a hammer fist on his back, I felt the solid thump as it struck him above the spine.

He twisted about, letting go of my waist, and punched me in the mouth with a savage uppercut that split my lips.

Startled, I took a pair of steps back, spat blood, and he took the opportunity to dive forward again.

Catching me off balance, he drove his shoulder into my stomach and lifted me off the ground. Taking two quick steps forward, he slammed me down into the trampled grass.

Air left my lungs with a painful oof.

Otto grappled his way on top of me, his heavily calloused hands wrapping around my throat. His fingers dug into the sides of my neck as his palms threatened to crush my windpipe.

Thrashing from side to side, I punched him in the side several times to no effect.

Desperate for air, I grabbed the Allosaurus claw between my fingers, and ground the point of it into the back of his hand.

The Indian growled in pain, and I felt his grip tighten while I dug deeper with the claw tip.

Suddenly, he let go.

Rising, he dropped a fist down on my face so hard I thought something broke. Then he hit me again, right on my bullet clipped ear.

I threw myself to the side, eyes tearing in pain, lungs screaming for air. It was a mad scrabble to get some distance. In the struggle I managed to rake my boot down his shin, scraping off a stretch of skin.

He howled and jumped up.

Gasping for air on all fours, I reached for him.

He swatted my hand away and kicked me in the side. Even with just a moccasin on, it hurt like I'd been kicked with riding boots.

Toppling over, I rolled onto my back and looked up at Skyla's frightened face.

"Ugggh," I managed to utter before shifting to dodge another kick to the head by Otto.

I didn't move fast enough and felt hair tear away as the underside of his leather shoe scraped my scalp. Seeing red, I rolled over again, leapt to my feet, and met Otto's incoming charge with a hay maker.

My fist cracked against the side of his face, splitting open the skin on his high cheekbones.

He stumbled backwards and wiped the blood away with the back of his hand.

I spat blood, laughed, and raised my fists up.

It was on now.

I was warmed up.

He took Ashley's advice and kicked me in the groin.

Excruciating pain flashed through my entire body as tears welled to my eyes. Falling aside, holding myself, I unceremoniously vomited up the steak, eggs, and coffee I'd had for lunch.

Through the excruciating pain, I heard Wade uncharacteristically utter a swear word and Skyla let out a scream.

The Indians in the crowd went wild as Otto raised his arms and sauntered around me in a circle.

Curled into the fetal position, the throbbing pain between my legs dulled to a background ache as hatred and rage filled my body. What an asshole move.

Pushing myself up, I willed myself to grab Otto from behind.

Struggling, the Indian flailed and kicked, but I wasn't having it as I picked him off the ground.

With as much force as I could muster, I slammed him down onto his back.

Scrambling, we broke and pulled away from each other, and reaching my feet first, I kicked dirt into his face.

Red was the only color I saw as Otto frantically clawed at his eyes.

Leaping onto the brave's back, I wrapped an arm around his neck and clenched my two hands together. Squeezing my elbow towards my chest, he struggled violently beneath me as I cut off his breathing.

With a great burst of strength, he pushed himself up and launched us backwards.

Miraculously, my grip held, and lying on my back with Otto on my chest, I felt the brave's struggle begin to weaken. He thrashed side to side, clawing at my arm around his throat. Skin ripped and scratched away under his fingernails. Ignoring the pain, I clenched harder while wrapping my legs around his to hold the slippery bastard in place while I choked the life out of him.

After several long moments, I felt him becoming weaker and weaker, and finally his arms dropped lifelessly to the side.

Shoving him off me, I took in deep lungsful of air and realized the circle of Indians had grown quiet.

Their champion had been defeated.

A group of braves, among them Squatting Bull and Runs With Dogs, pushed forward, rage across their faces as they reached for me. But Chief Toko shouted and stopped their advance with the help of his new Winchester rifle barrel.

I struggled to my feet, then crouched and slapped Otto across the face several times to wake him.

His dark eyes popped open, and I could tell he was disorientated and unsure of what was going on.

I held out my hand.

After a long moment, he took it and I pulled him to his feet. Groggily, he stood, shaking his head and looking around in bewilderment.

I slapped him on his bare back and held out my hand again.

This was a tense moment. Either Otto submitted to his defeat and accepted our mutual respect for each other's battle prowess, or we would be enemies again.

After several deep breaths, the Indian clasped my hand tightly.

Cheers erupted around us as Otto pointed at me, laughed, and said something in Shaynee that roughly translated to, "Lucky white asshole."

I looked at Skyla and winked, even though my face felt puffy and battered. She grinned happily, and I was glad she didn't have to see me lose. Wade laughed as Ashley cheered, and they both looked as pleased as could be.

Immediately, Chief Toko was in the center of the circle, grabbing us both by the shoulder and shouting at the crowd to shut up.

As he was going on about how I was worthy of their respect, and of my prowess in battle both with guns and fists, I gingerly touched my busted lips and there was blood on the tips of my fingers. Looking at Otto, I was pleased to see a puffy knot forming beneath one of his eyes and a trickle of blood from the gash in his cheek.

He must have felt my stare, because he turned to me and nodded briefly before turning back to face the main portion of the crowd that gathered before Chief Toko.

I started to pay attention again when Toko drew a knife from his belt.

He passed it to Otto, who took the blade and swiftly cut across the palm of his hand. Then Otto handed the blood smeared knife back to me.

I kept the frown off my face, because I didn't dare let it show. Respect was everything with these people. But I personally didn't care to become blood brother or whatever the Shaynee equivalent was with

Otto. The wiry Indian was an asshole. But maybe, just maybe, I thought as I sliced the flesh across my palm, this would work out for the best.

Otto held his hand up, and I clasped mine to his, feeling the smearing of our warm blood beneath our grip. It was kind of gross.

The crowd roared their approval, and my small group cheered enthusiastically as well.

Then Otto looked at me. And for the first time, I saw a twinkle in his eyes. Grinning toothily, he said, "We brothers now. You die, I get her," and nodded towards where Skyla stood.

This time I let my frown show and he laughed.

***

Carbine chased Smoke around the makeshift Indian corral while Skyla bandaged the cut on my hand. I'd taken quite the beating from Otto, and now had a sliced hand, a nicked ear, split lips, and probably a black eye coming on. That didn't bode well since we were just getting warmed up on this little adventure.

"Does this blood brother business mean you're an honorary Shaynee now?" she teased.

"I don't think so… Well, maybe? I'm not sure how it works. But they ought to treat us a little better now."

Chief Toko ambled up to us, a big grin on his face. "Ready for sweat lodge?" he asked me.

I groaned. Last time I did a sweat lodge with him, I had a pair of visions. One of my past when I was tortured by Reydan White as a kid, and one of us losing the Battle of the Apes. Luckily, as Chief Toko put it, the 'maybe-soon' vision hadn't come true. But it'd worried me something awful.

"You may learn something," he said as he rested his forearms on the top brace of the corral.

"Didn't learn nothing last time, Chief."

"Ah, but you learned why you needed to fight, and to fight harder. Probably would have learned more had you been naked," he winked at Skyla, and she blushed. Last time, we'd just stripped down to our britches and that'd been enough for me.

"Chief," I said, growing serious. "What are you doing trusting the government?"

He frowned, the creases in his face deepening. "Chance we take."

"Lieutenant Daniels told me they will give you land and freedom in return for your service."

Chief laughed bitterly. "We have freedom so long as we not on reservation. And land? There was plenty before white men kill all buffalo and claim land for themselves."

"Yeah, I know."

"I'm sorry, Chief," Skyla said as she tied off the bandage around my hand. I made a fist, testing my grip. I could still shoot, but it might be a little more difficult and certainly more painful than before.

"One day, we take land back from whites. Drive them into big water far away. Then buffalo come back."

I'd noticed he hadn't said that as cheerfully as usual.

"What's wrong, Chief?"

He frowned. "Shaynee lost many braves fighting hairy men for your town. Many women cry long into night. Many sons left without fathers. These braves that go with you, they cannot be..." he paused, searching for the right word.

"Replaced?" Skyla offered.

"Yes. Replaced. We lose many braves. Cannot lose more without losing ourselves."

"Then why are you risking them?"

"You laugh. But we want to go to other side. Live with these other people, like us."

"The Shayana... they aren't a lot like you. They've lived with whites for so long, that they are as one."

"Then maybe one day we will be one as well. But until then, I want my daughters to grow up strong in new lands with strong husbands."

"So, the government told you they'd give you land on the other side of the Shimmer?"

"Yes."

Figured. Instead of giving them land on this side, the federal government saw Prehistoria as a chance to get rid of a perpetual thorn in their side. I suspected the Shaynee weren't the only ones that would end up in that dangerous land. The other Indians and the Irish were probably next. But the Colonel mentioned they were opening it up for homesteading, so I supposed everyone would get an equal chance to be eaten.

"It's hard living over there. Many big beasts. Many hairy men," I told him.

He shrugged. "Hard living, make hard Indian. Hard Indian better than weak Indian drunk on firewater living at whim of white man," he spat to the side angrily.

"Ok, Chief. I understand. I'll do what I can to keep your braves alive."

61

"Good. You and Otto. Brothers now. You make Shaynee proud," he fixed me with a stare, "or you not come back."

I nodded. "Deal." It was an easy agreement, because chances were either we'd make the Shaynee proud, or we'd all be dead.

"Jed! Jed!" The shouting of my name came from among the teepees, and between them came Wade and Ashley, obviously excited about something.

"You've got to come see this!" Wade shouted. "It's incredible!"

The Chief shrugged with a sly grin and made shooing sign with his hand. "Go. See."

Grabbing Skyla's hand, we high tailed it at a trot to where Ashley and Wade stood waiting.

"What is it?"

"C'mon!" Wade said with a wide grin, and they ran through the throng of Indians that'd gathered around to see what the white people were all excited about.

Pushing through them, we quickly followed the famed Westerner and his fiancé until we reached the far side of the village. Coming around a pair of painted teepees, we were greeted by the sight of a trike rearing up on its back legs, shaking black horns at the sky, and bellowing fearsomely.

It was an impressive prehistoric display of the power and might of the dinosaur.

But even more impressive was that an Indian was mounted behind the bone shield, firmly pulling back on the leather braided reins with one hand while shaking his new Winchester rifle in the air dramatically with the other.

Slamming back to the ground, the trike took a pair of steps and stopped in front of us.

"By golly, I want one," Wade whispered.

Squinting up at the rider from under my hat, I realized it was Squatting Bull, one of the younger and more ballsy braves of the Shaynee tribe.

"Nice trike," I told him sincerely.

He said something in Shaynee I couldn't make out, something about a name. "What?"

"He says three horns name is Horny Devil," Chief Toko said, having approached unseen behind us.

Ashley laughed while Skyla hid her smile.

"I like it," Wade said. "Chief, if that brave ever wants a job, I'll give him one. I'd love to have him in my show."

"About that… That brave is Squatting Bull, he pretty much hates all white folks," I told him.

The young Indian nodded in agreement and sneered down at us from his dinosaur mount.

"Well, is there anyone in this tribe that doesn't hate us who can ride?" Wade asked, obviously put off. "The crowds would go nuts to see that exact same thing we just saw."

Chief chuckled. "Twin Moons rides."

"Twin Moons? Where's he at? Does he have a trike?"

"She."

"She? Even better," Ashley said, poking Wade in the side with a grin. "Women will draw more men into the show… especially if they are young and pretty."

The Chief stuck his fingers in his mount and whistled loudly. From around the teepees to our right came a familiar rumbling as heavy feet stomped the ground, and another trike and rider came walking into view.

Wade turned away in disgust. "I'm leaving."

Chief Toko was belly laughing so hard that he gasped for breath, his face turning a bright red. The other Indians around us began to snicker and laugh.

"C'mon Wade, she's not so bad," I said, watching the ancient, weathered old woman awkwardly ride the three-legged trike towards us.

"It's a three-legged dinosaur!"

"Probably from a cannon ball," Skyla told him.

"That doesn't make me feel any better. I can't use that! I want Horny Devil and Squatting Bull!" Wolverine Wade shouted, throwing his arms up in despair. "Not old woman and broken trike!"

The woman shook her stick at our group angrily then used it to swat the wounded trike to turn it around.

"Psst, Wade…" I leaned in close to the aggravated man. "That old woman is the Chief's first wife."

"Well, hell. How was I supposed to know?"

Chief Toko straightened and slapped Wade on the back repeatedly as he drew lungs full of air to catch his breath. "She not go with you." He pointed the barrel of his rifle at Squatting Bull and his trike. "They go with you."

I grinned happily. "Now we're talking."

***

It was amazing, but by the time we rode out of the village with a couple dozen Shaynee braves and Otto, they'd already managed to start decorating their new Winchesters. Runs With Dogs had the best looking one in my opinion. A nice leather beaded sling, a pair of red raptor feathers hanging from the barrel, and an intricate pattern beaten into the stock. The pattern matched the yellow and white paint on his pony that ambled along behind our mismatched column of white folks, Indians, horses, ponies, and lone dinosaur.

I knew I'd catch hell for the mutilation of the weapons from Colonel Carver and the likes, but it didn't matter. Whatever helped the Indians fight best worked for me. If decorating their rifles with beads, brass tacks, and feathers made them kill more apes then I was all for it. I may even slap a few on my fancy *Eighty-Six* if it worked.

With the Shaynee braves, we rode together to Fort York and the Shimmer it surrounded, a day earlier than Fredrick and the army of soldiers and Pinkertons would.

Wade and Ashley wanted to see the progress of the railroad through to the other side firsthand and I wanted the Indians to start getting used to being around a bunch of white men. If there were problems between the two groups, which there were bound to be, I wanted to deal with them as quickly as possible, and preferably on this side of the Shimmer.

But as we rode through the open plains towards the fort in the shadow of the cliff face of the Granite Mountains, I was shocked to see that Fort York hadn't grown any since I'd come through a few weeks ago.

It was still the same small encampment as before. I guess the wiping out of Fort Jipson hadn't been enough of a warning that we were not adequately prepared to stop an army of apes from breaching into our side again. But I supposed, considering what I saw on the other side of the Shimmer when I came back through, there wasn't much need. The other side had the main defenses in place to protect the railroad, this side was just a stopping point on the way over.

The Fort consisted of several wooden buildings housing troops, a corral, blacksmith, plus a bunch of empty tents for temporary housing of troops waiting to cycle through to Prehistoria. There was a palisade with a large wooden gate that blocked the entrance into our side. It was built to control access to and through the Shimmer, and to keep any dinosaurs on their own side. And, if things went to pot, to defend the tunnel from apes crossing over to our side again. Circling around the entire fort from cliff face to cliff face, was a split rail fence, about four feet tall. Really more of a garden fence than anything to keep random riders, deer, or the occasional pronghorn from pestering anyone.

Steel rails of the East-West railroad ran straight through the fort, through the Shimmer, and out to the other side where construction continued running the line towards the prehistoric coast and where

Reydan was establishing the first town in Prehistoria. Which of course the arrogant bastard had named after himself. Whitesberg.

Heavy wooden beam gates swung on massive iron hinges to secure the tunnel with just enough room beneath to clear the train tracks. A fellow, or an ape, I supposed, could try to climb over it with a ladder. But there'd be an awful lot of eyes and gun barrels on you as you did.

We rode up and the first thing I noticed was Reydan White's private car sitting on the tracks near the fort. It was off on a spur of railroad, as if waiting for a locomotive to come and haul it to the railroad tycoon's next location. Gleaming in the sun, the giant armor-plated behemoth had several Pinkertons sitting alongside the rail car on small folding stools and a makeshift bench. On top of the car, a canvas tarp covered an odd protrusion mounted in the center of the roof. An attached metal ladder on the side allowed access to the top.

Pulling back on the reins, I slowed Carbine to a stop at the edge of the fort.

Since the fence on this side was more for show than anything else, I could easily see over it. The little garden fence wouldn't stand up to an Indian or bandit attack for nothing, but I guess there was nothing to fear on our side compared to the horrors on the other.

Behind me, the Indians moved their ponies into a line parallel to the fence with Horny Devil in the center, as though showing a sign of force before attacking.

I guess old habits took a while to burn out.

Wade, Otto, and the ladies stopped their horses beside Carbine, and we waited for someone to notice us.

The soldiers within view looked angry at the line of Indians, and I saw more than a few collect their weapons and shift around as if unsure of how to act. A pair of guards heading our way looked nervous as could be, and I noticed Otto smirking at the showing of fear.

Once the two guards were close, they slowed to a stop. I shouted out who we were, and that Colonel Carver was expecting us.

They shouted back for us to follow them in.

Wade looked back at the line of Shaynee behind us. Horny Devil was ripping great beakfuls of grass up to munch on while the ponies stamped their feet impatiently. "Otto, it may be best if we keep your braves out here until we get a feel for things," the famed Westerner mused.

The scarred Indian warrior dipped his head in agreement and passed the command to his braves, then our small group of whites plus Otto headed into the fort with me in the lead.

Soldiers gathered and lined the way in small clumps, watching us with a combination of suspicion and open hostility, and I could see many of them muttering angrily to each other as they eyeballed Otto. The US soldier and Indian had been mortal enemies for a long time, and it was obvious that neither trusted the other.

But, giving credit to Otto, he acted as though he was superior, and rode his painted mount in with a haughty look, ignoring the hostile stares and jeers of the uniformed men.

Captain Hawney stepped out from one of the buildings and approached us as we came to a stop inside the fort. With him came Arthur Donahue, the writer from Europe.

The Captain took his time crossing the dozen yards to us, surveying the row of Indians outside the palisade with a look as if they were going to jump off their horses and begin pillaging the place. I'm sure they were quite the sight. Even with the new Winchesters, many of them brought other weapons, spears, bows, clubs, etc. And Squatting Bull on the trike was something that seemed to gather a lot of whispered attention.

Arthur appeared positively giddy with interest, and quickly outpaced Hawney to reach us first.

"Evening, Arthur," I said.

"Good evening, Jedidiah! And my goodness, look at them." He stared at the Indians. "They are magnificent. A much grander indigenous people than anything I've seen in my travels. I do hope they can fight."

"They've been fighting us for decades, so yeah," I retorted. I liked the fellow, but he needed to get more acquainted with the American West.

"And a trike, I must find out how they captured and trained it!"

"Me too," Wade grumbled, obviously still sore about the whole three-legged trike thing.

Hawney reached us a few seconds later, thinly concealed disgust etched across his face as he took in the line of Shaynee braves.

"Captain," I said in greetings. Otto just stared at the man with a blank expression while the rest of my companions waited silently. Skyla waved a hand.

"Jed, Skyla," he said simply and without introduction to the others beside me.

"Reporting with two dozen Shaynee… as requested."

He arched an eyebrow. "You mean ordered?"

"No, sir. I'm still a civilian, not a soldier. I'm only here because I want to be."

He shrugged as if it made no difference to him. But I wanted it to be clear that I could come and go as I pleased. I preferred keeping some sort of individual freedom during this arrangement.

Lifting a hand, Hawney pointed towards a barren patch of ground by the corner of the fort, far from where the soldiers stayed in their wooden framed barracks and neat rows of tents. It looked like there had been a corral there recently from the amount of packed bare ground and mounds of horse dung scattered across the area. "The Indians can set up teepees or sleep in the dirt or whatever they want over there. But the trike stays outside the fence; I won't have that dinosaur in here raising havoc if it decides to go for a trot."

I glanced at Otto to see how this suited him because it certainly didn't suit me. The brave looked back with a face that may as well have been made of stone. I turned back to the Captain. "And where will Colonel Carver's men be staying when they arrive tomorrow?"

"Outside the fort."

"Then we'll do that as well. I know a good place."

The Captain looked at Skyla, Ashley, and Wade while pointedly ignoring Otto. "You three can stay here if you'd like. There are better accommodations I can give you than the ground."

"Because we're white?" Ashley said bitterly.

"Oh, get off your high horse, woman. There are only a few of you, so I can easily put you up. I can't house two dozen savages though."

Otto's stone face gave way to a smirk.

Wolverine Wade leaned forward, tipping his hat back with a hand to fully expose the barely concealed anger on his face. "Captain, you are insulting your guests."

"Really? And who might you be?" he snapped back.

Wade drew up in his saddle for full effect and gripped the pommel of his saddle. "I'm Wolverine Wade Mackin. Explorer, hunter, adventurer, and generally all-around likeable fellow. But when my companions... or my fiancé is slighted," his voice hardened as he tipped his hat towards Ashley, "I am no longer likeable."

"Sorry, Mr. Mackin, I didn't realize it was you," the Captain apologized, red creeping across his face in embarrassment.

Wade stepped his horse forward a pace to get closer to the officer. "Mistakes happen and are generally forgiven... so long as they don't reoccur."

Hawney took a half step back. "Well, had I known I was in the presence of Western royalty, I'd have offered my room to you and your fiancé."

"That will not be necessary, Captain. We'll sleep alongside the savages tonight," Ashley quipped back, tossing her thick blonde braid over a shoulder.

"Very well, have it your way," Hawney said as he about faced and walked back to his building.

Arthur lingered behind, obviously contemplating something.

Otto drew a knife from his braided belt and raised an eyebrow at me quizzically, as if asking if he had permission to slit the officer's throat.

"No," I told him. "He'll get eaten eventually. Most fools around here do."

The Indian slipped the knife back into his belt.

I looked down at the writer who still stood before us. "What is it, Arthur?"

"I'd like to go with you," he said.

"You certain? There is no comfort out there. We'll be sleeping in the cold."

The Scot grinned at the mention of discomfort. "I'm here to write about adventure. And where else shall I find it then with a group of noble American Indians and the famous Wolverine Wade!"

I pointed a finger at Ashley. "And that there is Ashley James. Sharpshooter extraordinaire. She saved all of our lives from the church tower during the Battle of the Apes."

Ashley blushed.

'Oh my goodness, I've certainly got to accompany you and hear all about it firsthand."

"Saddle up then, Arthur," Wade said. "A friend of Jed's is a friend of ours."

"Thank you! I'll be back momentarily."

As we watched the Scot stroll away to gather his gear, I twisted about in the saddle to face Wade. "You should know he's not a friend of mine. I just met him."

"Yeah, well, he seems to think he's a friend of yours. And you need friends."

I sat silent for a moment, looking at their mischievous grins.

"Fine," I admitted.

***

Once Arthur was saddled and ready, I led our little entourage back to where the Shaynee braves impatiently waited and onto the plains.

The place I had picked to sleep was about a mile from the cliff face. I'd seen it before riding to and from the Shimmer and figured it would fit a couple dozen Indians and ourselves just fine.

After reaching the small stand of trees, Wade and I worked with the Indians to roll some large rocks and pull some downed trees around us into something of a fighting position. An old habit for all of us. But that was where our friendly group of cowboys and Indians split into two. The Indians made several small fires off by themselves and left the five of us white folks sitting around our own. The scent of venison wafted over us, a meal secured by one of the Shaynee who was good with a bow and a deer who was unlucky with life.

"I'll take first watch," Wade said quietly as we gnawed on beef jerky and hardtack biscuits around our fire.

"You don't trust our friends yet?" I said teasingly.

He looked towards the nearest group of Indians where Runs With Dogs sat slicing off a chunk of meat.

"Not all of them, no. Strangely, I think we're safest with Otto right now since you two are blood brothers. Normally, he'd be the one I'm most worried about."

"Only took a butt kicking to make it happen," Ashley said with a grin before biting into a piece of hardtack biscuit. Wiping the crumbs off her face, she swallowed and patted the decorated tomahawk tucked into her belt. "I do like this thing though. It's got a great feel to it."

"That is a superb looking weapon; may I?" Arthur asked with an outstretched hand.

"You think we could get Otto to join our show?" Wade asked his fiancé as she passed over the Shaynee tomahawk.

"I think he has far too much pride for that," I answered for her.

"Yeah, but all the Indians we've been able to get so far haven't been nearly as ferocious looking as him. We need to give all the pale faces back East something to fret over!" she responded.

Skyla laughed and grabbed my hand. I squeezed it and gave her a wink. She'd been a full-fledged Easterner not too long ago. Now, she carried a Merwin-Hulbert Pocket revolver on her hip and a chipped obsidian sacrificial ape knife on the other.

"This is magnificent," Arthur quipped as he took a few short swings with the tomahawk. "I do hope I can trade for one from the Shaynee before I return home."

"Where is your home?" Wade asked, being more traveled than the rest of us combined.

"I hail from Edinburgh, Scotland, originally, but I've moved around a good bit of Europe over the years."

"Oh, lord. I figured you were a Scot from your accent, but now that I know for certain, I'll try to keep you away from the drink." Wade chuckled as he made himself more comfortable leaning against a fallen tree trunk.

"Nonsense, the best of fights and literature often comes after a bit of drink. If Fredrick von Holsak were here, I'm certain he could attest to that."

I nodded and stirred the fire with the charred end of a stick. Small sparks rose into the air. "I'm pretty certain he could."

"I can't wait to meet him," Arthur said giddily.

"Tomorrow," Skyla sipped from her canteen. "Tomorrow," she repeated, "we'll meet up with him and the army back at the fort."

"Outstanding. In the meantime, I would be delighted to take the second watch."

"What are you armed with?" Ashley asked, pointing at the scabbard leaning on the saddle the Scot was resting against.

"Ah, yes. I heard Americans love their weapons. Thus, when I began my adventure to this New West, I made certain to properly arm myself before leaving London." Reaching over, he pulled the scabbard to him and untied the end. From inside, he drew a long rifle out.

The steel on the rifle was a dark blue, and the wooden stock ran almost the entire length of the barrel. Beneath it, slid into a hole bored into the length of the stock, was a cleaning rod that jutted out slightly. It was a long, but rather sleek looking weapon.

"Oh, great. It's a single shot," Ashley muttered in thinly veiled disgust.

"An excellent choice!" Wade chortled as he patted the heavy Ballard rifle that lay beside him. The famous wolverine slayer had a special attachment to his single shot rife. "That's a Martini-Henry, is it not?" he asked.

"It is, sir. A Mark Two variation."

"I've heard of them, but never seen one in person. In what caliber is it?"

The Scot worked the lever below the action and popped out the loaded round. ".577/450," he said proudly as he held the monster of a cartridge aloft. It was massive. Compared to the straight-walled .45-70 that my *Eighty-Six* used, the necked cartridge he held was a good inch longer.

"My goodness!" Wade exclaimed, leaning forward in interest. "That almost puts my sweet Ballard here to shame. We shall have to try a friendly competition sometime and see how the two compare."

"What's that there? A cleaning kit?" I guessed while pointing at the long leather flap stitched to the side of the rifle scabbard. It seemed like a neat place to keep one but seemed rather large, and there was already a cleaning rod attached to the rifle under the barrel.

Arthur passed the gun across the fire to Wade, flipped open the flap, and with a scraping noise, pulled a long, nasty looking bayonet out of a metal sheath that was concealed inside. One side of the spiked blade was ridged with saw teeth, and the other straight and sharp, the two different sides widening slightly into a curved blade before combining into a point. Almost two feet long, it looked like an odd short sword.

"What in the Prehistoria is that?" I asked, baffled.

"A Lord Elcho." He shrugged, and the big bayonet rose and fell with the movement. "At least, that's what they told me it's called. Named after the British Whig politician who designed it. Apparently, it never caught on, something about being too expensive to manufacture and too frightening to use."

"Fearsome looking," Skyla said, noticeably impressed with the big bayonet.

"I'd hate to be stabbed with it," Ashley agreed.

Wade held the rifle up and looked down the barrel at the flip up rear sight. "That short sword is neat and all, but this has got a sight you can set to 1,800 yards. Must be for volley fire."

"It is, sir. From what I understand, it was used to great effect against the Zulu tribes of South Africa by the Brit Army," Arthur said.

"You'll need to meet Charles," Skyla said, leaning over to look at the rifle. "He's British and served in their military for a while. I think he'd love to see this rifle. He may have used one when he was in the service."

"Well then, I look forward to meeting him. Will he be joining us?"

"No, he's.... keeping an eye on my ranch," I said as the group grew quiet. I think we all liked the newcomer, but we weren't exactly ready to share all our troubles with him yet.

Out of the silence, Wade pointed at the tear dropped shape of metal on the right side of the Scot's rifle's action. "What is this? A safety?"

"A cocking indicator, letting you know by both feel and sight that the rifle is loaded," Arthur replied.

His curiosity satisfied, Wade passed the weapon back to its owner. "A fine rifle."

"Thank you." The writer worked the lever underneath the rifle, inserted the long cartridge, closed the breech and slid it back into the scabbard. The bayonet he turned for a moment, watching the reflection of the fire in the steel, before eventually returning the blade to its own scabbard as well.

"No pistol?" Ashley asked.

"Ah, no." The Scot looked embarrassed. "I wasn't aware that I'd need one, though I'm a decent pistol shot."

"What's your background, Arthur? Ever fired a rifle in anger before?" I asked, curious.

He rose slightly from where he sat, undignified by my questioning. "I am a trained surgeon, and well received author. Of shooting... no. I have never fired a rifle in anger. But I have done my fair share of hunting."

I nodded. "Good, that's a start. We'll get you sorted out with a pistol and belt tomorrow, if possible."

"Maybe Fredrick has a spare one, he's always armed to the teeth," Skyla suggested as she pulled another cut log into the fire. Her Winchester carbine was one of Fredrick's customized guns, he'd given it to her before the Battle of the Apes, and she'd carried it ever since.

I glanced around the group; everyone seemed to be growing tired and ready to nod off.

"Let's get some sleep. Tomorrow is going to be a long day," I suggested as I stood and stretched. "Arthur, wake me for the third watch."

***

My eyes cracked open, and I lay motionless. Only the slight crackle of sticks burning in the small firepit broke the quiet of the night. But something woke me.

Then I heard it.

Faint popping noises.

Gunfire in the distance.

Grabbing the sawed-off shotgun that was normally wrapped in my bedroll, I flipped my blanket off and looked towards where the Indians had been sleeping. Most of them were moving to grab weapons, and several were pacing back and forth restlessly by their small fires as they watched through the trees at the surrounding prairie.

Arthur, who was still on watch, stood still with his rifle in hand and a foot propped on a log, looking into the dark of the prairie towards the direction from where the gunfire seemed to come.

"It comes from fort." The whispered words startled me. Twisting around, I found Otto kneeling beside me with the stock of his decorated Winchester braced on the ground and the barrel gripped tightly in his hand. The scarred Indian really did move like a mountain lion.

"We'd best go see what's happening," I told him.

Wade was awake now and gently jostling Ashley awake beside him. I tossed a couple small rocks onto Skyla's still form until she began to shift beneath her blankets. Like most folks who grew up in the relative safety of civilization, she was a sound sleeper.

"Let's go. We travel light. Weapons only," I spoke loudly enough for everyone to hear. Otto leapt up and ran towards his braves to spur them on. Arthur grabbed his saddle and headed for the horses.

"Ashley, Skyla… stay here," I commanded, knowing that it wouldn't go over well.

They both immediately started to protest.

"Ain't got time to argue." With heavy saddle in hand, I moved for where Carbine was picketed with the other horses. "If we're not back by dawn, go get the Army," I told the pair over my shoulder.

"Jed, we are not-" Ashley said, checking the chamber of her rifle.

"He's right," Wade cut her off as he pushed a few more sticks into our small fire. "We're running into a fight in the dark, it's going to be chaos and I don't want to worry about where you are and who is shooting at who. And if an ape army is breeching the Shimmer, we need to send warning to Granite Falls."

"This is bullshit, Wade!" she shouted back, startling a couple of nearby Indians. Seeing the anger on her face, they turned away and went around our group to get to their ponies.

"Woman! Do as I ask, just this one time."

She stomped her foot. "Fine. But you'd better not get hurt."

"Yes, ma'am." He nodded in thanks, quickly slung a blanket over the back of his horse, then reached for his saddle.

Skyla smiled at me bravely as I mounted Carbine and hung the sawed-off shotgun from a lanyard off the pommel. In the dark, things might get close and nasty, and the shotgun would be a boon to have ready.

I wasn't sure what was going on, but we were only a mile or so away. And the shooting didn't seem to be stopping. Strangely, I did not hear the continued firing of any Gatling guns, which was odd. If anything was trying to get through the Shimmer to our side, those weapons should have been going like mad.

Whatever was occurring at the Fort, it wasn't good.

***

We rode like hell across the moonlit prairie.

The smaller Indian ponies kept up easily with our larger horses and I knew from experience that the trike, Horny Devil, would be able to keep up with us for some time. I patted Carbine on the neck and kicked my heels against him again, needlessly reminding him to hurry. Wade rode beside me with his Remington New Model Army black powder revolver in hand. Arthur was behind us both, his rifle still in its scabbard.

The crackle of gunfire grew louder as we closed the distance between us and Fort York. There were several large glows in the darkness ahead. Fires. Big ones.

A hundred yards further, and we could hear battle over the thunder of our horses' hoofbeats.

Among the sporadic gunfire came the loud bellows of triceratops and the harsh guttural roars of apes.

Moments later, we could make out the shapes of the mounted trikes in the distance roving around the short palisade on *this* side of the fort.

My jaw dropped. That was why there was no firing coming from the Gatlings.

The apes had attacked from our own side.

Suddenly, I recalled Reverend mentioning that the bounty hunters had gone missing. I knew now what they found. I reckon it didn't go so well for them.

"Arthur! Stay with me!" Wade shouted, as he peeled off to the train tracks to the right followed by the Scot. I suspected he'd find somewhere nice and comfy and the two of them would start blasting apes with their single shot rifles while the rest of us entered the fray. That worked fine for me. Always nice to have someone watching your back.

Lifting the sawed-off double-barreled shotgun from its leather thong wrapped around the pommel of the saddle, I dropped the reins on Carbine. He ran straight at the burning fort while I thumbed back the first hammer of the shotgun.

Otto shouted something that I couldn't make out, then let out a terrific Shaynee war whoop. The two dozen Indians behind him began shouting as well as they thrust their weapons into the air, and then we were amongst the attackers.

Strangely, none of the apes were painted. That was new. Instead of standing out with bright swirls of color across their faces and chests, the apes were all just darkened shadows in the flickering flames of the burning fort, launching spears and arrows at the defenders while their mounted buddies stomped the split rail fence flat and raced amongst the buildings on their horned dinosaurs.

A pair of apes on foot faced our charge boldly. One launched an arrow at me from a range close enough that I could see the glimmer on his eyes and the shine on his canines. The arrow missed, zipping past my shoulder and into the darkness behind me.

Jerking the shotgun stock into the pocket of my shoulder, I fired the first barrel, letting the recoil push me backwards while blood blossomed from the ape's neck and torso as buck shot peppered the hairy monkey.

A moment later, from the back of his pony, one of the Shaynee braves drove a feathered lance through the other ape's guts.

The big monkey doubled over in half at the force of the weapon and toppled backwards with a horrific bellow of pain onto the trampled ground.

With a leap of his pony, the brave jumped over the dying ape, leaving the lance impaled behind him, and raced after a mounted trike whose rider had just chucked a spear at Otto.

As the braves scattered, I raced Carbine between the apes, keeping low to his neck, and shouting at the top of my voice, "Friendlies! Friendlies!" At the same time, I was praying like crazy to not get caught between opposing forces and killed by either side.

A female ape loomed in the firelight with a flaming brand held in one hand and a stone axe in the other.

I fired the second barrel. She spasmed and dropped, thrashing and bellowing in pain. In the background I could hear the heavy, slow, methodical boom of Arthur and Wade's large bore rifles getting into the fight.

Letting the shotgun dangle by its lanyard from the saddle, I reached for the *Eighty-Six* as Carbine swerved around a charging trike, and unprepared for the sudden movement, I fell from the saddle.

Even as the ground slammed into my side and shoulder with excruciating pain, I held onto the prototype weapon with a death grip. I'd lost it before in a fight, and I wasn't about to let that happen again.

Rolling onto my side, I narrowly missed a large trike foot stomp the ground where I'd been a moment before.

Flinging myself backwards and away from the dinosaur, I jerked the rifle up and fired without aiming.

The bullet missed the ape rider but clipped the trike's shoulder with a small splash of blood.

Bellowing in pain, the dinosaur thrust its black horns at me, digging grooves in the ground as I dodged them. Racking the lever, I jammed the muzzle of the *Eighty-Six* against the trike's skull and pulled the trigger. Bits of flesh and bone splattered against me as the dinosaur fell.

Staggering to my feet, I was almost knocked down by a Shaynee whooping as his pony raced past me. From the glimpse I got of him, it was Runs With Dogs, which made me wonder if he was trying to run me over intentionally.

The ape rider leapt off the dead trike, thrusting an obsidian tipped spear at my face.

Deflecting it with my rifle, I drew my left pistol and fired into his chest at point blank range. The flame that burst from the barrel lit the big monkey's hair on fire as he toppled over.

Pausing, I looked around me for the next target.

It was utter chaos.

Between the dark flames, blossoms of gunfire, burning structures, and the shapes emerging from the partial darkness, I wasn't sure where to go. To my right, Horny Devil was fighting another trike, their large horns and bone shields slamming into each other while Squatting Bull fired an arrow from his trike's back at the other rider.

I didn't want to go that way.

Then, to my left, I saw the gleaming metal railcar of Reydan White in the firelight, parked on the steel rails of his railroad off to the side of the fort.

Without thinking, I ran towards it.

Miraculously, I reached it without being shot, stabbed, or trampled. But there'd been a couple of close calls on the way.

Around the railcar were dead Pinkertons; two of them were shot through with ape arrows and another appeared to have been beaten to death with a stone axe or club. In the darkness, his body was too mushed up to tell which.

Inside the encampment, numerous tents were aflame and several of the small buildings. From what I could tell, it appeared the soldiers had holed up in the buildings and were laying fire out at the apes. But there were limited openings to shoot from, and I saw a lot of uniformed bodies splayed out across the grounds of the fort. Of the short fence on this side of the fort, there was almost nothing still standing. It had been knocked down and trampled by the large trikes, and the few men who tried to use it as cover were lying dead beside the broken rails in the churned ground.

Gritting my teeth, a dangerous thought crossed through my mind that perhaps now was the time to kill Reydan.

If his armored car was here, he was probably here. Most likely inside.

Knowing that Skyla was safe far away from the fight was enough for me to risk turning my back on a battle to end an old feud.

Stepping onto the small porch at the end of the car, I pounded my fist against the metal door while cocking the hammer back on one of the Colts.

To my surprise, the door jerked open almost immediately and the large barrel of a gun was pointed directly at my face.

Behind the pistol and the dark shadow of the man holding it, I could see Reydan White sitting at his desk beside a lit kerosene lantern. The former raider didn't even bother looking up. He just puffed away on a cigar and shuffled some papers between his thick fingers, totally indifferent to the battle raging outside his reinforced armored car.

I took a pair of steps back, waiting for a gun blast to be the last thing I saw.

Instead, the man holding the gun moved forward into the faint fire and moonlight and closed the door behind him with a resounding clang.

Cato.

My former boyhood friend and now Reydan White's loyal protector holstered his pistol. Without a word, he turned, grabbed the steel ladder that led to the roof, and began to climb quickly.

I growled in disgust. So much for my revenge.

An ape arrow splintered against the side of the armored car, pelting me with shards of wood.

Wincing and ducking, I grabbed the ladder and followed the gunman to the top of the car. It wouldn't provide much cover, but at least it'd be off the stinking ground and away from the trikes.

Ahead of me, Cato raced across the roof of the car, then slid on his backside towards the misshapen lump hidden beneath the canvas tarp.

A trike, riderless and riddled with bullet holes, slammed into the side of the armored car, shaking it slightly. Bellowing in pain, the beast raced away and crashed into one of the burning buildings as if blinded. Blasts of gunfire and shouts came from inside the building as the dinosaur knocked a corner of the building down upon itself.

"Shit!" I shouted at the sight, and ducking low to make myself a smaller target, I ran towards Cato.

In front of me, the gunman jerked the tarp off, revealing a fat barreled, boxy looking contraption attached to the top of the railcar. Feeding into the side of the gun was a rectangular box of large cartridges, strapped together with strips of white canvas.

Grabbing the bizarre weapon by a pair of D shaped handles, Cato rotated the entire contraption around, pointed the barrel towards the front of the fort and opened fire.

Unlike the Gatling guns, with their noticeable pop-pop-pop noise as they fired from rotating barrels, this was a continuous stream of gunfire emanating from a single barrel jutting out of the fat circular mechanism. And the strapped together cartridges loaded themselves neatly into the gun.

It was awesome and terrifying to behold as it stitched across ape and dinosaur alike. I'd never seen anything like it.

I wanted one.

"Watch out for the damned Indians! One is riding a trike!" I shouted into his ear as I raised the *Eighty-Six* and began shooting at anything that looked big, hairy, and not of this side.

Cato nodded and began firing in small bursts, quickly mowing down anything near the burning buildings. Then he turned his attention towards those rushing with fire brands trying to burn more of the fort down.

Apes quickly noticed the short bursts of fire and flame bursting from the strange gun atop the railcar, and from the darkness, began to rush towards us.

Shooting the *Eighty-Six* empty at them, I slung it and drew both Peacemakers.

Apes loomed out of the darkness around us, too close for Cato and the fancy gun to hit. I shot anything that came close to us as apes began struggling to climb the smooth sides of the armored car after us. Several climbed the ladder to the top of the railcar, and I shot them off before they made it more than a couple of steps towards us.

Bodies piled up on the ground.

Shaynee braves, including Otto, flitted in and out of sight as they raced their ponies between apes and trikes, shooting, stabbing, bashing, and gleefully killing the hell out of everything. Somehow Cato managed to avoid hitting any of them.

A raptor charged out of the darkness and leapt at the armored passenger car. Metal screeched as its black claws scraped the side below us.

I leaned forward and fired a pair of shots into the little red feathered dinosaur's body.

Not liking that, the horrid beast shrieked and ran out of sight.

With the intense firepower from the strange gun, the battle was quickly over. As the fat-barreled gun fired the last of the cloth belted cartridges, Cato nodded with satisfaction and swiveled the gun back into its previous position.

Grabbing the tarp, he quickly covered the weapon.

"What the hell is that thing?" I asked the notoriously quiet gunman while emptying cartridges out of my pistols to reload.

"Maxim," he replied simply.

"A what?"

"Maxim machine gun." He carefully tucked the tarp back into place, once again turning the strange gun into a misshapen lump on top of the railcar.

"Where do I get one of them?" I asked while shucking empty cartridges out of my pistols and reloading.

He didn't respond. Instead, he chose to walk around me and move towards the ladder at the far end of the armored car.

"Asshole," I muttered under my breath. In the firelit darkness in front of me, one of the braves, Runs With Dogs, pranced his pony to a stop and slid off the back of it. With deft movements, he stalked across the battlefield and began taking scalps from apes he'd killed.

Sighing, I holstered the freshly loaded Peacemakers and followed Cato off the modified and reinforced passenger car.

By the time I leapt from the bottom rung onto the platform, the steel door to the armored car had closed with a loud slam and a lock was thrown from inside. Only the faint scent of cigar smoke was left behind.

Apparently, Cato wanted nothing more to do with me, and it seemed my revenge would have to wait for another day.

***

It was a miracle that no one on my side appeared killed, and by that I meant the Shaynee. It was obvious the soldiers had suffered from the sudden attack in the dead of night. Their torn and mutilated bodies were laid out all over the place, but there were no dead Indians in sight.

I was rather pleased with how the braves had performed.

They'd been reckless of course, riding their ponies between burning buildings, tents, and across the open battlefield in and around Fort York, chasing and killing apes while soldiers were shooting at anything that moved and Cato firing that magnificent Maxim all over the place. But it appeared they'd come out unscathed except for a few minor wounds, nothing that a Shaynee brave couldn't shrug off. And I watched as they took their well-earned scalps.

"Arthur did spectacularly," Wade was telling me. "He kept his cool, and that heavy cartridge rifle of his really did a number on the apes. Rarely did he hit one and it got back up."

"Well, thank you, Mr. Mackin. To be honest though, we were so far away from the battle that it seemed rather unsporting," the writer replied, seemingly embarrassed about his part in the fight.

"Nonsense. Staying safe and picking off the enemy one at a time is a grand way to spend a battle. Unlike Jed and the Indians, who prefer to dash in amongst the fray and risk themselves foolishly, gentlemen such as we prefer a little distance between ourselves and the enemy."

Across the prairie came a woman's shout that friendlies were approaching and not to dare shoot them.

A minute later, Ashley and Skyla rode into sight.

"Looks like we missed quite the fight," Ashley said wryly as she watched soldiers dumping buckets of water on the still raging fires.

"You did. Weren't you supposed to wait for dawn before fetching reinforcements?"

"Psssh. The shooting stopped and we just came to take a peek… promise. You know we couldn't let any of you get sacrificed without having a say in the matter," Ashley retorted with a sly smile as she looked up at Reydan's armored car behind us suspiciously. She pointed with the barrel of her rifle at the canvas tarped lump on the roof. "Let me guess, that's the source of all that noise we heard?"

Skyla slipped from her dappled gray horse and hugged me as I answered, "Good guess, it's something called a Maxim machine gun."

Arthur stroked his mustache thoughtfully. "Machine gun, eh? I'd heard of something like that being developed and tested near London. A gun that can fire without being cranked like a Gatling. Simply squeeze the trigger, and the gun does all the work, even loads itself."

"It was mighty neat to see in action," I said. "Brandthorn had told me that Reydan ordered some sort of fancy British gun a month or so back, but I certainly didn't expect that."

Soldiers began to wander the battlefield, searching for dead and wounded. Men cried out in pain as they were moved into a safe place near us to have aid administered.

"Ladies, gentlemen, if you'll excuse me, I do believe my talents are needed," Arthur said before racing away to the nearest group of wounded.

That made me realize just how handy it would be to have a formally trained doctor with our group. We seemed to run into all sorts of bloody accidents and fights.

While soldiers began to make their way out onto the battlefield, the Indians mounted their ponies and slinked away in the darkness, back towards our makeshift camp on the prairie. Squatting Bull rode his trike by us haughtily, several bloodied chunks of hair hanging from his belt. The young brave looked pleased, and I noted blood on the horns of the trike. It seemed Horny Devil had earned his pay today.

As we watched, soldiers shouted as they found a couple of apes that were still alive.

Even wounded, the uniformed men still had to practically dog pile on top of the hairy savages to pin them down in place and tie ropes around their hands and feet.

Several more soldiers were injured in this as we watched. One had a nasty bite on his shoulder, and the other had his outer thigh sliced open from a broken ape arrow wielded by a particularly angry brown and white mottled ape.

A couple of trikes wandered around, sniffing at corpses and bellowing lightly to each other.

One came near us, a beautiful dark brown triceratops with light yellow streaks running along its body. It could have been Sara's mother for all I knew. Tattered reins dangled from the dinosaur, looped around the beak and horns. I rested a hand against the flanks of the big dinosaur and watched as it nuzzled its beak against a dead ape. This wasn't the first time I'd seen such behavior, the trikes seemed to have a fondness for their masters.

Wade and Ashley stepped closer and looked over the beast. "Be perfect for our show... much better than that wretched three-legged trike

Twin Moons was riding. Jed, do you have a rope? It seems rather docile."

I looked around for my troublesome horse. "It's on Carbine. I don't know where he is. He dumped me from the saddle and bolted."

"He'll turn up, he always does," Skyla smiled. She knew my horse had a penchant for abandoning me and staying alive.

I drew my Bowie knife and cut the torn reins off the trike.

A man with a pair of soldiers trailing him coughed to get our attention as he approached.

One of the soldiers raised a lantern and I realized it was Captain Hawney in front. His uniform was smeared with blood and ash. In one hand, he carried a revolver.

He gestured with the pistol around us, "What do you think of this bullshit?"

"I think the apes just wanted to go home," Skyla replied.

"My fort is destroyed! All because apes wanted to go home?" he shouted angrily. "Hell, we could have just opened the gates for them!"

Skyla pointed at a female ape lying between us with a pair of Shaynee arrows sticking out of her hairy back. One of the arrow shafts had snapped off halfway. "Winter is coming. They don't have warm clothing, they aren't used to this side, and are probably getting hunted down pretty good by everyone looking for a bounty. I bet it has been hard on them to keep all these trikes hidden from us for so long. I think they just wanted to get back to the other side."

Hawney grunted in acceptance of her explanation.

I ran a different colored strip of white hide braided into the trike's pebbled dinosaur leather reins through my fingers. "Looks like they are using deer or antelope hide to repair their equipment." I sniffed the leather. "Ugh, seems they aren't good at tanning either or did a quick job of it."

The Captain turned back towards the shattered and trampled palisade of his fort and watched as soldiers ran back and forth fighting fires that burned the buildings and tents. "Sergeant Gibbons learned some of the ape's language, did he not?"

"I believe he learned a little," I said as the trike stepped away and wandered off. Wade and Ashley watched it go longingly.

"Good. When he arrives with Colonel Carver, we'll have him interrogate the ape survivors."

"Captain…" I hesitated, dreading asking the question.

"Yes, Jed?"

"How many did you lose?"

The tall officer sighed. "Not sure yet. But not as many as we could have. Luckily for us, one of the bounty hunters made it to our fort just minutes before the attack. The apes had caught the others with him, and he escaped and almost killed his horse getting here. He gave the alarm, and we were able to slow the ape advance at the fence momentarily before falling back into the buildings."

"Bounty hunter, huh?" Wade asked curiously.

"That'd be me," came a gruff voice to our right.

From the darkness, a short, balding man approached. He wore a bandoleer of cartridges across his chest. Reaching the dead female ape, he squatted down and swiftly cut her right thumb off with a blood smeared knife. "If the Injuns were smart, they'd take thumbs instead of scalps. Army pays for thumbs."

Recognizing him from the inside of Captain Brandthorn's office many weeks ago, I scowled. "Simon."

He grinned crookedly up at me from where he crouched as he put the severed thumb into a small leather pouch on his belt. "Yes, sir. That's me. Who are you?"

Raising my boot, I lashed outward, the heel smashing into his broad face. The bounty hunter toppled backwards with a cry, blood erupting from his crumpled nose.

Captain Hawney jumped between us. "What the hell, Jed?"

I ignored him and glared at the bounty hunter. "That's for the saloon girl you've been beating on."

"What in the devil are you talking about?" Hawney shouted angrily.

Simon leapt to his feet with the bloody knife held outwards in a makeshift fighting stance.

I drew my right-handed Colt, but kept the barrel pointed at the ground. "Play stupid games, win stupid prizes," I warned.

He snarled as blood dribbled down his unshaven chin.

A dark shape slid behind Simon. A hand grabbed him by his greasy hair while a kick to the back of the leg dropped the bounty hunter to his knees. Simon gasped in surprise as Otto placed the sharpened edge of a knife under his Adam's apple.

"Otto!" Skyla shouted in surprise. "Don't!"

"No, maybe we should let him," Wade said. "Men who beat women should be put down before they can reproduce."

"Agreed," Ashley said as she shifted her rifle to rest against a shoulder.

"I'll not have this!" Hawney screamed, as he raised his pistol to point at the scarred Indian. Behind him, his two soldiers lifted their rifle barrels slightly but hesitated, as though unsure of who to aim at.

"Let him go, Otto. He ain't worth you getting shot over," I said after a moment.

The scarred brave lowered the knife and shoved the bounty hunter away. A thin line of blood showed where the blade had nicked the man's throat.

Hawney slowly lowered his gun, and the men behind him followed suit.

Otto shifted away, moving to stand beside me and Wade.

The bounty hunter touched the back of his free hand to his bleeding nose. "You will all pay for that." Giving us a lingering glare, he turned and stalked away into the darkness.

"You should kill him, Huck Berry." The scarred Shaynee brave looked at me with disdain. "Leaving enemy alive is weak."

I slid the Colt back into its holster, thinking how right my new blood brother probably was.

"He can't just go around killing everyone!" Captain Hawney said angrily. Holstering his pistol, he jabbed a finger into my chest. "Step carefully, Jed. Simon is not under my control, he's a stinking bounty hunter, and I doubt he has many morals."

"Certainly seems like he don't," I mused as I thought of the gap-toothed girl back at the Bucket o' Blood whose life would hopefully be better now, but I doubted it. As long as Simon had money, she'd probably tolerate him.

After Captain Hawney walked away with his escort, one of the Shaynee braves appeared out of the darkness, yanked the intact arrow out of the back of the ape and inspected the shaft and feathered fetching. A moment later, the brave slipped the arrow back into its quiver, then quickly scalped the dead ape. Looking rather pleased, he waved the brown mottled patch of hair and skin at Otto then moved towards the next corpse without a word.

Skyla grabbed my arm. "I don't like Simon," she said with a shudder.

"Yeah. I want you to keep an eye out for him," I said with a bad feeling. "If he comes near you, shoot him, stab him, do whatever. But he's got a reason to hate me now, and he already beats on women."

Wade grabbed Ashley's hand. "I'd tell you to be safe… but you scare me."

She laughed and patted the rifle sling over her shoulder. "I'll take him out if he comes within five hundred yards of me."

"We should go kill him now," Otto suggested again, gesturing with his knife in the direction that the bounty hunter had gone. "No one will see."

"Probably should. But Captain's right. We shouldn't go around killing everyone that crosses us until they give us enough cause."

The scarred Indian shrugged indifferently, and I noticed several new scalps hanging from his belt. Drops of blood had fallen onto his buckskin pant legs from the freshly taken hairs. I gestured at them. "Good job. Looks like we're the heroes for the day."

But an hour later, once Carbine had returned, we and the Shaynee were slipping back into our blankets a mile away from the cliff face, again separated from the soldiers.

The good news was we didn't have to stick around and deal with the aftermath of the battle, instead we could get a bit of well-earned sleep.

The bad news was that I was wrong; we'd lost two Shaynee braves in the fight, and we hadn't even crossed through the Shimmer yet.

***

At mid-morning my group and the Shaynee braves rode up to the smoking remains of the fort and the hundreds of soldiers and Pinkertons waiting to cross through the Shimmer. In the distance, I saw the reporter Parsons and his photographer taking group pictures of the men about to enter Prehistoria near a rebuilt corral now filled with rounded up triceratops in the background.

I sighed. It reminded me of the picture that Skyla and I had taken in Fort York before it fell, the same picture used on the cover of the newspaper for Parsons' article about me.

Leaving everyone behind but Otto, the Indian and I made our way to where Colonel Carver stood with Captain Hawney, surveying the damage to Fort York.

"This is a hell of a mess, Captain," Carver grumbled to Hawney as we approached.

"Yes, sir," he replied. "But it could have been much worse if it hadn't been for Cato; he saved the day with that machine gun contraption of Mr. Whites."

I rolled my eyes, of course Hawney wouldn't give any credit to the Shaynee.

"Indeed, but I hear the Indians helped a good bit as well," Carver glanced at us, his eyes lingering on Otto's fresh scalps. "But the attack was pointless, just the same," the Colonel waved a hand towards the thick pillar of smoke rising from the west where a large mound of ape bodies was being burned. "If these dumb apes had made it through Fort York, they'd have just run into the soldiers and Pinkertons standing guard on the other side. The big monkeys didn't know it, but they never had a chance at getting home alive."

"Not with their numbers at least," I added. "But they still managed to cause a lot of chaos and death."

"Yes, sir. Now imagine if the ape army that took Fort Jipson had attacked us at the same time. We'd have been up the proverbial creek." The Colonel shook his head. "But, with any luck, this should take care of most of the remaining apes on our side."

"It would have been nice if some of those men on the other side had come through to help the fort," I mentioned. It'd been a thought that gnawed at me until I'd fallen asleep last night. I knew there were men on the other side but was surprised they didn't come to help.

Carver frowned at his subordinate. "They tried. The gates were barred shut and apparently no one on this side was willing to risk leaving their shelter to open them."

Captain Hawney had the decency to look embarrassed and not offer up an excuse.

"What's the plan, sir?" I asked of the Colonel.

"Nothing changes. Simply put, first through the Shimmer will be you and the Shaynee. You'll link up with the Shayana scouts on the other side and lead the way, roughly following your escape trail to the forest lining the edge of the eastern side of the canyon. From there, we'll hit them from above with everything we've got. Targeting that damned dragon first, if it's there."

"You are assuming we are able to sneak up on them," I said. "If we can't, they'll be waiting on us."

"Shouldn't be a problem. The Shayana are going to create a diversion with their pterodactyls, a feint really, to draw them away from the entrance and out of their caves into the open. That's when we'll hail lead and damnation down upon them."

"I'm sure you've thought of this, but while we can make it on horseback and on foot just fine, we can't get any cannons or Gatlings in there without cutting a trail. If we start dropping trees for horse teams and wheeled weapons, the apes will know we are coming a long time before we get there."

"We won't be taking Gatlings or cannons, and the men will be on foot," Captain Hawney said.

"Just small arms then?"

"Yes." He waved an arm at the field outside of the smoking Fort where hundreds of men waited. "Lots and lots of small arms. In an elevated position, firing from the cliff face, we should be able to wipe out the apes. As for you and your... braves... after we get close to the canyon, you'll split off with a detachment of men, led by Sergeant

Gibbons, to cover the entrance with the intention that no ape is to escape the canyon alive."

That sounded just dandy. They'd be shooting down from a defendable cliff face while we'd be in the open, trying to stop a stampede of trikes and apes from escaping the killing confines of the canyon.

A thought occurred to me. "Any chance we can borrow Reydan's new gun?" I doubted it, but it'd be mighty nice to have that against a charge of mounted apes.

"The Maxim? No," Colonel Carver answered my question with a disappointed sigh and shake of his head.

Well, that was a shame. It'd have been useful. "Is that its name or type of weapon?" I asked, curious.

The Colonel glanced at the tarped gun on top of the armored car with a frown. "Both. And according to Mr. White, it's the only machine gun on this continent and shall not be used for anything but his personal protection."

"Nice of him to share," I shook my head.

"Actually, he will be. He's told me that he has a dozen more guns under contract with Maxim in Britain. He has made it well known that he intends to arm the Pinkertons with them."

"Pinkertons with machine guns... what could go wrong?" I muttered to myself bitterly.

Hearing me, Captain Hawney spoke up. "The Army will get ours... eventually. We got Winchester Repeaters already, and we'll get some Maxims once the Army gets a shipment. Then we'll wipe the damned apes out."

"Yes, we will," Colonel Carver agreed as he stared at the damaged fort. "Every damn one of them."

I noticed Hawney staring at Otto, his eyes roving over the scarred brave.

The Indian, feeling the attention, turned to face the Captain. "What want, white man?" he asked bluntly.

"Just curious," the Captain pointed at the fresh ape scalps in disgust. "How many scalps have you taken of white folk and soldiers?"

Otto stared at the man, and I could tell the brave was seriously considering answering.

I moved Carbine between the two of them and spoke up before Otto did something that we'd both regret, such as telling the truth. "He's on our side now, as are the rest of the Shaynee."

"Agreed," Colonel Carver said. "Leave it alone, Captain."

"But Colonel," he protested, "these savages-"

Carver spun around and took an aggressive step towards his underling officer. "I will not repeat myself."

"Yes, sir."

"Go see to your wounded," he ordered.

Hawney nodded curtly, then walked away quickly towards the undamaged tents that'd been converted into field hospitals.

"I apologize for his outburst, gentlemen," Carver said to us. "The Captain has been out West for some time and old habits die hard."

Otto grunted in agreement.

**

I rode back to the others with Otto.

Fredrick had joined them and was off to the side, talking excitedly with Arthur about something. As I watched, the famous hunter mimicked firing a rifle and laughed.

I wished I could be that carefree.

"Otto, do you know what we are doing?" I asked the Shaynee.

"Yes. White man risk Shaynee first."

"I'll be with you. And there will be some soldiers with us."

He grunted noncommittedly, then turned his pony and headed towards where the other Shaynee braves waited his instructions.

I guess he figured riding point for the white man was to be expected.

Wade ran a pair of fingers down his goatee. "What's the plan, Jed?"

Patting Carbine's neck, I tried not to think of how we were once again about to cross the Shimmer and into a land of great danger. "It's kind of a simple show. But maybe we can pull it off. Basically, we sneak over there, leading the troops, and let them shoot a bunch of monkeys in the canyon while we try to stop any from escaping out the canyon entrance."

"Just us?" Skyla asked with concern, looking at the rather small group we had of whites and Indians.

"No, there'll be a detachment of soldiers with us to help. Sergeant Gibbons will be leading them."

"Good," Ashley said. "Because it sounds like the Army is kicking over an ant hill and we'll be in the worst position for it."

"You ever do anything like this before, Jed?" Wade asked. "When you were in the Army?"

"No, but fighting the Nez Perce was a lot different than the apes. The apes have killed a whole lot more folks than the Nez Perce could have ever done."

The group was quiet.

Fredrick and Arthur approached us, noticing we were being solemn.

"Everything alright?" the Scot inquired quietly.

"While the Army and Pinkertons have all the fun, we'll be risking our necks with the Indians in the worst possible way," Wade said solemnly.

"Heaven forbid you give a speech, Mr. Mackin, because it's very unrousing so far," Arthur said.

I chuckled.

"Where will you be, Fredrick?" Ashley asked.

The famed hunter scowled in disgust. "Arthur and I have been directed to stay with the officers, Parson, and that photographer fellow."

Ashley smirked. "Have fun with that; Captain Hawney is about as charming as a porcupine."

Fredrick raised an eyebrow. "Is that a jest?"

"Unfortunately not," Arthur replied. "He's rather moody. I know from experience."

"This is getting better and better." Fredrick picked up a discarded ape arrow and snapped it over his knee angrily before tossing it aside. "What about the rest of you?"

"We'll all be with Jed and the Shaynee," Wade said.

"Lucky you. I told them I'd come along for an adventure worth retelling, not to sit on the sidelines with the press and officers," Fredrick groused.

"Just stay alive, there will be plenty more adventure for all of us," I assured him. "After all, no one gets through life unscathed."

***

The Shimmer hadn't changed since I'd discovered it. But the cliff face around it had.

After discovering the apes on the other side, I'd collapsed the mountainside down over the tunnel with dynamite, only to have the ape army dig through a couple of days later. Since then, as Fort York was built around it, the tunnel entrance had been reinforced with thick beams to prevent another collapse and the strange shimmering air you stepped through to the other side was relentlessly studied by scientists.

They couldn't figure it out though. No one could. No one knew where it came from, why it was here, how it existed, or anything else. Any number of theories and possibilities had been offered by scientists of all sorts, but no one could prove anything. One lunatic fringe scientist even suggested another type of human-like creature from one of the stars in the sky created it to test us. He was promptly escorted off the Fort and out of town before his madness could spread.

The Shimmer simply was. It existed, unexplained, yet still connecting two worlds together through a short tunnel in a mountainside.

One side, ours, was as normal as it got. The other side, who knew. We hadn't explored much of it yet, but we had noticed it had the same sun and moon, but the stars were a little different. Yet time seemed to change at the same pace, if it was noon here, it was noon there. Dawn or dusk here, dawn or dusk there.

The biggest difference seemed to be that the other side was almost like a time of ours, trapped in a period of times without mankind. Of dinosaurs, there were different sorts, from multiple prehistoric periods. And then, there was the Shayana.

The Shayana were just as big of a mystery as the Shimmer. Because for the Shayana to exist, that meant there had been multiple Shimmers in our past, allowing for a group of Indians and a group of white English settlers to both enter Prehistoria. And the Shaynee, according to their legends passed down for generations, came from Prehistoria originally… which meant somewhere around here another Shimmer or maybe this one had existed before at some point.

It was all very confusing.

But the scientists were having a field day with it all. Entire books were written on theories, but no one had any proof to justify anything. I tended to just accept it as weird as all get out.

Several soldiers pushed open the fire singed gates that had ape arrows embedded in the logs and my group led the way along the steel rails into the tunnel.

As before, when Carbine's nose touched the dividing line between our two worlds, the air shimmered outwards, flickering like water for a short distance as he moved through. He'd done this repeatedly, but like before, he leapt through as quickly as possible to get it over with. Exiting the Shimmer left an uncomfortable tingle across your body as if someone walked across your grave.

The Indians were funny to watch go through. You could tell they were baffled at the Shimmer, yet they held it together with a steel resolve to look as bored or fearless as possible as they rode through on their ponies. But every one of them shuddered at the tingle and their mounts sure as hell didn't like it, a few going so far as to buck and try to race away before being wrangled back into obedience by their riders. Horny Devil didn't seem to mind so much, and I wondered how many times the trike had already been through the tunnel under ape ownership.

After the Shimmer, Otto and myself led the way, walking on either side of the railroad tracks, followed by the Shaynee braves and then the rest of my little group of white folks.

Reaching the other side of the short tunnel, we stopped.

The beautiful, lush valley that had once sprawled out below the mountainous cliff face was now modernized with railroad tracks cutting along the bluff to the west towards the sea. Massive amounts of dirt had been ripped from the hillside and moved to give a gentle slope to the locomotives as they descended into the valley.

Around us were multiple layers of palisades made of logs from our side with Gatling gun emplacements and cannons pointing outwards in a half circle, defending the tunnel and Shimmer from any unwanted entrance by ape or beast. Some Gatlings were set up in the backs of unhorsed wagons, I assumed to give them quicker response in case of a large attack. This was what Colonel Carver had meant about the apes not being able to get through. Had they fought through Fort York, they'd have stepped out of the frying pan and into the fire.

"Used to be real pretty," Skyla mused as she looked at the empty valley and the wide river that flowed through the bottom of it. In our times coming here before, this valley had been filled with dinosaurs. Now, it stood silent except for the occasional shriek of a pterodactyl in the distance and the puffing of a returning locomotive and rail cars coming back from unloading large amounts of building material to Whitesberg. The new Prehistoria town was a priority and I bet if this area was guarded this heavily, the fledgling town was protected even more so.

"Yeah, stupid civilization," Wade grumbled as he drew his heavy Ballard rifle from its scabbard and rested it across his pommel.

"White man ruin everything," Otto said. Behind him, Runs With Dogs and several other braves within hearing muttered their agreement.

I kept quiet, taking in the empty view and thinking about what lay before us. I hoped like crazy the Shayana had managed to take out all the ape scouts. Or this attack would fail before it began as they rushed from the canyon to meet us. Fighting an army of apes in the middle of a prehistoric forest filled with trees hundreds of feet tall and dozens of feet thick didn't appeal to me any.

"Keep moving, ya filthy Injuns," came a call from behind us followed by coarse laughter.

Turning in my saddle, I saw the column of soldiers beginning to cross over on foot. My group and Colonel Carvers were the only ones who would be mounted for this attack. I knew it chafed the backsides of a lot of soldiers to see Indians on ponies while they walked, but our part of the assault required us to move fast to get into position, and possibly move fast to get back to the main force if we were overwhelmed.

"Let's go," I said before the Shaynee could take offense and scalps.

Leaving the steel rails and ring of protection, we rode down the valley, towards the river and where a small group of Shayana waited.

Henon met us with a pair of decapitated ape heads and a broad grin. The big Shayana raised the heads in greeting as we slowed our horses to a stop.

"Well met, Jedidiah and Skyla. Here are the hairy men's scouts."

"Only two?"

"Hairy men lazy."

"Good job then, Henon." I pointed at Wolverine Wade, Ashley, and Arthur, introducing them, then jerked a thumb at the scarred brave beside me. "This is Otto."

The two men sized each other up and I wondered what they were thinking. For all appearances, Henon looked like a Shaynee. His skin was a deep bronze and he had black hair and dark eyes. It seemed little of his group's English blood ran through his veins.

Otto nodded gruffly and Henon stuck his hand out. After a moment, the Shaynee shook the Shayana's hand, and I supposed history was made as the two groups, separated by the Shimmer for unknown generations, came together once again.

Henon pointed at Squatting Bull sitting astride Horny Devil. "Thou hath tamed a three-horned beast. Well done. Takes great strength to do so."

The young Indian brave grinned at the compliment while his mount eagerly munched on a large purple and green fern.

"Aw, look at Horny Devil," Ashley said. "I bet he's happy to eat his own fodder again."

"Probably tired of our wimpy grass. Look at this, the plants are huge over here," Wade said as his horse nibbled at the tall, thick blades of grass.

Arthur moved his horse closer to get a look at the rest of the Shayana. They were a diverse group of blonde haired, blue eyed, and dark haired, brown eyed sorts, showing off their ancestral diversity in an interesting mix. And like Henon, the others wore a simple garb of leather clothing with steel breastplates, swords on their hips, and a rifle slung over a shoulder. Of the rifles, I saw a mixture of the Winchester Repeaters recovered from our doomed prior expedition, several of their own makeshift black powder guns, and a few single shot Springfields that the Army had given them.

Some of those guns wouldn't be much help in a fight, but their main role here was to help me guide the troops to the canyon and cause a diversion to lure the apes out of their caves before the attack.

A shout arose in warning from the soldiers on the hill behind us, and over the forest came a trio of giant pterodactyls winging into view.

Only Skyla and I in our group had seen this before, and understandably, I saw most of the others' jaws drop. The Shaynee braves drew weapons, and I waved at them to point the rifles away from the pterodactyls and their riders.

"Magnificent," Wolverine Wade whispered.

"Are they friendly?" Ashley asked, her rifle barrel held low but ready to be jerked into a shoulder at a moment's notice. She'd shot an attacking pterodactyl out of the air on her last visit here, so I could understand her hesitancy to relax.

Skyla chuckled, "They're friendly. So long as you aren't a Pinkerton."

The Shayana before us grunted angrily and muttered amongst themselves. They had no love for the so-called detectives.

Landing before us, the large pterodactyls' huge wings beat air on us until they settled down into a crouch on folded wings with clawed hands resting on the ground.

The birds were monstrous, their wingspan easily stretching well over forty feet, and their leathery bodies stood ten feet tall before ending in a yellow head with a large red fin on the back of the skull. Their coloring was yellow above and a mixed green beneath, with a pale whiteness along their bare feet and dark claws. A leather harness with a saddle of sorts rested on the creatures' backs, intertwined amongst the wings, and complete with stirrups.

From the closest prehistoric dinosaur's backside slid a small, lithe man with dark skin and blonde hair pulled back into a ponytail and intertwined with red feathers. A necklace of fangs and gold beads dangled from his neck.

"Chief Thenory," I said in way of greeting and introduction to the others, and he clasped my hand firmly.

"I see thee brought an army. Good," he said, nodding towards the large number of soldiers and Pinkertons exiting the tunnel on the hill above us. He looked over the rest of our group, then noticing Otto, he paused, staring at the scarred Indian mounted on the pony before him. "Well met, I take it thine art our relation?"

Otto looked confused.

"He's asking if you're kin, Otto." I tried to decipher the Chief's words for him. "You and the other Shaynee braves look a lot like some of his people."

"White Chief have yellow hair," the brave replied, obviously confused as to how the Shaynee and Shayana could have anything to do with each other when their Chief was blonde and of a light enough tan to show his true skin color underneath.

"Yeah, I know," I said while Thenory chuckled. "But a lot of them look like Henon. And like you."

The braves looked as confused as their leader.

Runs With Dogs edged his pony closer towards the pterodactyl, either to get a better look or to touch it.

"Don't!" I called to him in warning as he reached out a hand. The short brave glared back at me before reluctantly moving back to the others.

I rolled my eyes. I promised Chief Toko I'd bring back as many of his braves as possible and Runs With Dogs was too good with a rifle to risk losing a hand to a pterodactyl and too damned stupid to realize the risk he was about to take.

"Our Breehas riders art ready, and await the attack," Thenory said with a toothy grin.

"Breehas?" Wade asked.

"That's what the giant pterodactyls are called," Skyla said, pointing towards the closest dinosaur bird. It was the same one that Chief Thenory had ridden. The other two riders stayed mounted and watched the distant forest edge for any threats.

Thenory's Breeha took that moment to let out the screech for what its name came from.

"Ah, I get the name now," the famed wolverine slayer laughed. "What a terrible racket."

"Where art Gibbons?" Chief Thenory asked.

I gestured up the hill towards the column of soldiers making their way towards us. "He's with them."

"Ah, good. He has shown an excellent tongue for the hairy men speech but needs much work."

"Yeah," I grunted, recalling how Sergeant Gibbons had stayed behind with the Shayana to learn the guttural speech from the tribe's young ape slaves. The Chief and I hadn't seen eye to eye on that, and it still bothered me that the Shayana kept ape slaves until they were considered too big, then they threw them off their mountain home. Strangely enough, Gibbons, a black man, didn't seem to care about the slavery so long as they weren't African.

"How's Oscar?" Skyla asked the Chief. She was the only person I knew who knew her former boss, and cared anything for him.

"He is well."

"I can't believe you let him come back," Ashley scowled.

The thought of the fat, lazy, egotistical jackass of a paleontologist who now worked for Reydan White gathering information on valuable resources in Prehistoria that the two of them could exploit was aggravating to us all.

"He helps my people," Thenory said, before touching the gold and tooth necklace that dangled from his neck. "For a rock of no value to us."

Otto spat to the side. "White man love gold. Kill many of each other for it."

"Perhaps they kill all of each other," Squatting Bull snorted in disgust from behind us.

Ignoring the young brave, I looked from Otto to the Shayana Chief. "You know what? Otto needs to visit your home. He'll help you realize Oscar's intentions."

The scarred brave grinned wickedly. "I know how to handle Weak White Man," he said scornfully, referring to Oscar by his given Shaynee name.

"We would be overjoyed," Thenory half bowed to Otto, misunderstanding his intentions. "But now, we prepare for thy attack." Turning on his heel, he stalked over to the big pterodactyl and climbed onto the beast. Strapping himself into the strange saddle that was mounted on the bird's back, he nodded at us. "Until we meet again after the battle."

His bird stretched out its giant wings and flapped several times, rising into the air while pelting us with drafts of wind. Behind him, his escort did the same, rising with their Chieftain until they turned and flew away towards the Shayana mountain home in the distance.

"Astonishing," Wade said, staring after the pterodactyls.

"I want one," Ashley gushed. "Wade, can I have one?"

"Anything for you, dear," he replied, and I knew he was already scheming on how to get one for their show.

Henon had been silent until now, watching the unorganized mass of Pinkertons walking out of the tunnel above us in their dark suits and hats with guns and shiny badges strapped on.

Sighing, he turned to us. "Are thee ready?"

Before I could answer the big Shayana, a rider raced down the hill in our direction.

It was another Lieutenant, one who I'd seen running errands before but never learned his name. He trotted his black horse to a stop beside us. "Captain Hawney says that your horses are to be left here," he said, in a tone that demanded no debate.

"What?" I demanded anyways.

"You and the Indians are to lead the way on foot, and if you encounter anything, back off and wait for the soldiers."

"No," I said bluntly.

"It's okay, Jed, we can-" Skyla started.

"No," Otto repeated me, crossing his arms across his scarred chest.

"You cannot refuse this order," the Lieutenant glared at me, and noticeably tried to ignore the Shaynee braves crowding in a circle around us.

"Can and will," I told him. "We're a civilian attachment and we ride, or we don't go."

Finally looking at the fearsome Indians surrounding him, the young Lieutenant swallowed hard then lowered his voice. "Sir, I'd ask you to reconsider…"

"Jed's right. We aren't prepared to go horseless and traipsing through the forest. We're all wearing riding boots for goodness sake," Ashley pulled a foot from her stirrups and raised it to show the young officer.

Growing annoyed at both the order and the poor officer forced to relay the request, I pushed Carbine closer to the Lieutenant's black horse. "If Captain Hawney has a problem with us riding, tell him that he can take it up with Colonel Carver. But we're riding, his order be damned."

Red faced, the officer whirled his horse around and raced back up the valley to where I assumed Captain Hawney would take the news of our disagreement poorly.

"Good call, Jed," Wade said as we watched the man ride away, kicking his boots against the horse's sides to urge it on faster.

I looked at Skyla, who appeared puzzled by my abrupt refusal of the order.

"I'm not having you and Ashley engaging in an attack that you can't ride away from at the drop of a hat. If things go south, I want the pair of you riding like all get out back here and not stopping until you get through the Shimmer," I explained.

"I'm not leaving Wade. He can't be trusted on his own," Ashley protested with a smirk.

Skyla spoke up angrily, "And I just got you back, I'm never leaving your side again."

Not knowing what to say, I simply winked at her. She was a good woman.

Wolverine Wade just chuckled, shook his head, and checked to make sure his rifle was loaded.

Otto grunted. "Shaynee good fighters on foot or on pony, but rather ride than walk."

I nodded, knowing that was true, but also remembering my promise to the Shaynee Chief to keep as many of his men alive as possible. Having horses would help with that if the attack went badly.

I glanced down at Henon, who had waited uncomfortably during the exchange. While old English was the dominant language of the Shayana, I was sure he still had a hard time following a lot of our newer words. But I figured he got the gist of the conversation and that we had just pissed off someone important.

"Henon. Let's go."

***

Henon stayed with our group while the rest of the Shayana guides were split evenly between the column of soldiers and the Pinkertons behind them. The ones who went with the Pinkertons grumbled a good bit but did as they were told by their big Shayana leader. The ape heads were tossed away for the small green compys to find and gnaw on. Those little whip tailed scavenger dinosaurs were like the buzzards and coyotes of this side.

Leaving the ruined valley and railroad behind, we entered the darkened interior of the forest and its towering trees.

Henon seemed pleased with how the smaller Indians' ponies moved through the forest compared to the larger horses we white folks rode. In return, the braves seemed intrigued by the big Shayana. Otto and Henon whispered back and forth as the Shayana walked beside the scarred brave on his pony. Considering how much the two were smirking and snickering at times, they were getting along just fine.

I wondered if the Shaynee would truly end up trying to settle with the Shayana in their mountain top fortress. The two cultures would probably complement each other well since they shared a common ancestor and some of the same language. But I wondered how the Shaynee Indians would tolerate the English influence into their culture. To a degree they already had allowed it on our side of the Shimmer, and that outside influence had both benefited them and cost them dearly at the same time. We introduced them to horses and guns, along with diseases, firewater, and genocide.

After a moment, I shrugged to myself and shoved those thoughts away to concentrate on the matter at hand. The past was the past, all we could do was move forward.

I knew that we were being sent first because the Shaynee were considered the most expendable. If anyone had to blunt an attack by running headfirst into a bunch of apes, why not the cheap but lethal Indians?

Personally, I'd have sent the Pinkertons first. To me they were the most expendable, and their skills in the forest were pitiful at best. They stumbled along in the very back of the column, cursing and growling, and generally sounding like a herd of jackasses.

Finally, after a couple hours of traveling, my group moved far enough ahead to give us some quiet as we made our way in a large loop, roughly following my escape path, towards the backside of the canyon.

"How far is it, Jed?" Wade asked as he swatted a large prehistoric fly away with the back of his hand.

"At this rate? Another few hours." We were walking our horses to give them a break and so as not to get too far ahead of the men that followed on foot.

"I can't believe you made it through all of this alone… after we left you behind," Skyla said sadly and regretfully.

I gave her a smile. "You did exactly as you should have done, and I'm glad Lieutenant Daniels and Fredrick forced you to go. By the time I came to and crawled out of the cave, this area had been scoured by apes. If you hadn't left me, you'd all have been caught, killed, or sacrificed."

"I know… but I'm still sorry. It must have been terrible," Skyla said.

Glancing up, I saw a flock of small pterodactyls silently sitting in the lower branches of a tree watching us ride below. They reminded me of buzzards waiting for death.

"Only terrible thing about it was not knowing if you were safe," I told her sincerely. It'd occupied my thoughts the entire time I made my way to the Shimmer.

After working our way around and through a particularly dense patch of underbrush, and more than a few of those giant trap plants that snap shut on unsuspecting creatures, Henon held his hand up, and we stopped our horses a dozen paces behind him.

He was staring through a gap in a wall of fern fronds towards bright patches of light trickling through what appeared to be an opening in the forest floor ahead of us. I shifted in the saddle but couldn't see what he was looking at. I placed my right thumb on the hammer of the *Eighty-Six*, preparing to cock it back and fire, just in case.

At Otto's gesture, the Indians behind us fanned out, slowly moving their ponies into a line facing the direction that the Shayana watched. The ponies' feet stamped softly on the grassy undergrowth of the forest floor as they waited impatiently. Horny Devil stayed where he was, rubbing his horns against a narrow tree trunk.

Hesitant about what was going on, I looked at Skyla. She smiled gamely from the back of Smoke.

I gave her a grin before checking on Wade and Ashley a bit further off to my left. The two of them seemed content enough, sitting with their rifles across their saddle pommels, and keeping an eye out for anything that might attack us. They'd never been this far into the interior of Prehistoria, and I could tell they were both excited and wary.

Lastly, I looked at Otto on my right. The scarred Indian was leaning forward to watch the bright points of light that filtered through the undergrowth where Henon was looking. In his hands he held his new Winchester Repeater, decorated with a single red raptor feather dangling from a braided strip of cord.

Henon turned back to us, raised a finger to his lips, then motioned us to come forward.

Tapping my heels to Carbine's side, I walked him beside the big Shayana and stopped. Once our group of two and a half dozen were together again, Henon reached out and pushing aside a thick layer of fern fronds, stepped into the light.

We moved forward after him through the dense growth.

Almost as one, we pulled back on our mounts at the edge of the clearing in shock.

There were six of them.

Massive beasts, twice as tall as a man, with small heads and two rows of large triangular bone plates jutting up along their back from neck to tail. And at the end of the tail were two pairs of long spikes that swished back and forth through tall grass as the dinosaurs ate. Their skin was a mottled mix of green and white streaks, and the bone plates sticking up from their backs were reddish brown and almost a tan along the upper edges. Closest to us were a pair of small ones, about the height of Carbine, a bit greener than the adults but otherwise the same... just smaller.

I looked over at the Shaynee braves.

The Indians were all staring in disbelief. Even the normally stoic Otto's mouth was open, his dark eyes wide, and his knuckles clenched white on his rifle. Henon stood off to the side of us, arms crossed over his chest with a slight smile on his face. That gave me a good feeling that these armored beasts weren't about to notice us and decide to impale or squash some people.

We watched in silence as the lumbering beasts munched on a field of large red and green ferns near the center of the clearing. I'd seen one of these once before, but it was just a skeleton ripped apart and almost completely eaten by scavengers. I recognized the alternating bone plates along the hump shaped back of the dinosaur.

"Stegosaurus," Skyla whispered. "I think. Charles Mannish discovered pieces of them a couple decades ago, but he hypothesized that the armor plates were formed in a single row. This may be a different type, or he may have simply been wrong. He also suggested that they may have a second brain near their hips."

"A second brain?" I whispered back doubtfully.

She shrugged slightly, "I know, I know. Sounds kind of crazy. But the only way to be sure is to cut one open and look."

"Some other time perhaps," Wade said, shifting his grip on his rifle.

"Jed!" Skyla whispered urgently, tugging on my sleeve and pointing.

One of the Shaynee braves had dismounted and was slowly approaching the closest adult stegosaurus from behind.

"What's he doing?" Ashley asked.

"Touching it," Otto replied. "To show his bravery."

"No. No! Get him back. Stegosaurus may be territorial, and we don't know what they'd do to protect their little ones," Skyla whispered frantically to Otto. The brave shrugged off her concern while keeping watch on his man slinking forward through the large ferns.

"It's no use, Skyla," Wade told her. "If it wasn't dangerous, he wouldn't be doing it."

One of the adult stegosaurus' heads snapped up. Grumbling deep from within, the dinosaur adjusted its stance as the others began to take notice that something was off. The two young stegos moved closer to the adults.

"They know he's there," Ashley whispered.

"No, they know we are here," I said as one of the small heads turned to where we sat on the backs of our mounts.

Henon looked very concerned and began to wave at us to back up.

The Shaynee brave was close to the rear end of the largest stego. With a toothy grin towards our position, he gently placed a hand on the hip of the spike tailed dinosaur.

The beast bellowed in surprise and jumped forward slightly, shaking the ground as it landed.

The spiked tail whistled as it twisted to the side and cut through the air, followed by a terrible scream as the bone spikes were driven through the showoff Indian's chest and out his back, folding him in half over the tail.

Ashley gasped and held a hand over her mouth.

"Ouch," Wolverine Wade said with a grimace.

Otto jerked his rifle up, and leaning over in the saddle, I managed to slap it back down before he could fire a shot.

"Don't!" I hissed at him as he glared daggers at me. "If the apes hear shooting, they'll know we are here!"

The entire herd of stegosauruses began to move, stomping flat tall grass and colorful ferns as they began to shift in a circle. The young ones made their way into the center of the herd. With a swipe of its tail against the ground, the adult scraped the Indian off its bloodied tail spikes.

Grumbling, the scarred brave lowered his weapon, and spoke quickly in Shaynee so the other braves wouldn't begin shooting.

Suddenly, Squatting Bull pushed his trike through the brush and into the clearing. With a shake of its black horns, Horny Devil bellowed at the stegos and lumbered its way between us and the plated dinosaurs.

"That's smart," Skyla said. "The stegosauruses probably won't mess with a trike."

"Probably?" Wade whispered back.

Skyla shrugged. "They're both herbivores…"

The stegos seemed to be content with the appearance of a triceratops and began to shuffle off in large steps away from our group's position. After a minute, they were pushing between large trees and ferns and disappearing out of sight, with only the trampled ground and a skewered Indian to show they had ever been here.

Otto slid off his pony and ran around Horny Devil to the downed brave. Touching my heels to Carbine's side, we moved into the clearing after him. The scarred brave was cradling the wounded Shaynee's head in his lap. Blood dribbled from his mouth, and the two puncture marks through his torso were big enough to put my fist through. The fact that he was still alive, made apparent only by the slight rising and falling of his chest and the way his wide eyes darted around as he took in the other braves gathering around him, was a testimony to Shaynee fortitude.

Otto was whispering something to him, something so low that I couldn't make it out from where I sat on Carbine. But whatever the words, they seemed to put the wounded brave at ease as he took a gurgling breath, shuddered, and lay still in Otto's arms.

Another brave slid to the ground, and between him and Otto, they quickly lashed the dead Shaynee onto the back of his pony.

The sound of the approaching soldiers and Pinkertons behind us grew louder and I knew they'd catch up to us within minutes.

"We'd best be moving," Wade warned.

"Sorry about your man," I told the scarred Shaynee leader sincerely. Another brave that I'd failed to keep alive on this trip.

"We go," Otto said, ignoring me and grabbing a fistful of mane before leaping onto his pony's back.

Our group took off at a quick trot, trying to keep ahead of the army as I pointed out to Henon which direction we needed to go. I'd only been this way once, going the opposite way that we were going now, and it was difficult trying to lead based off such little knowledge of the area.

I glanced at Otto as the brave rode silently beside me. "You ready to move your people here, now?"

He frowned, then nodded. I was certain he was thinking about how he would kill one of the stegos to bring honor to himself and his tribe.

"If you think that was something, wait until you see a Tyrannosaurus," I warned the brave.

"Tyranos... rus?" He repeated the strange word, butchering it something awful.

"Yeah," I grunted. "Big, lots of teeth, mean... Let us hope we don't run into one of them. Even with all these men, it'd be almost impossible to kill."

There was a glimmer behind the brave's dark eyes, probably a hint of madness, as I was certain that he was thinking he needed to kill one. He'd have to beat Fredrick to it.

Henon carefully made his way across a wide, shallow stream and we followed him. Small fish-like creatures swam away from our splashing, and I swear I saw something that looked like a giant crawfish that probably weighed as much as my saddle back under an overhanging rock ledge. Whatever it was, Smoke saw it also, and that horse couldn't get out of the water fast enough.

I remembered this stream. I'd hid under several large ferns as a pair of apes watered their trikes here.

We were getting close.

***

An hour later, Henon and Otto managed to kill a pair of ape scouts walking through the woods near the canyon edge. They appeared relaxed and unsuspecting that such a large force was moving towards their canyon.

The killing of them was impressive to watch.

Henon snuck up behind one and hacked about halfway through its neck with his sword while Otto threw his tomahawk into the back of the other ape's skull from about twenty paces. Ashley looked at her bullet holed tomahawk with newfound respect after witnessing that impressive feat.

Best of all, the two different tribesmen did so without alerting the apes in the canyon below.

Henon left us here, going back the way we came to slow down the soldiers and Pinkertons so they wouldn't make a big ruckus as they moved into position along the forested edge looking over the canyon below.

We left the Shaynee braves inside the forest with the horses and lone trike. And then, with Otto, my small group carefully moved into a position overlooking the remains of the fort.

Apes were everywhere, along with many trikes, and judging from the number of cages we saw mounted on large handcarts, a handful of raptors as well.

"No dragon," Ashley whispered from where we lay on the hot rocks. The sun beat on our backsides as we peered over the edge and droplets of sweat splattered onto the rocks beneath us.

"Yeah, I'm not sure if that's good or bad," I muttered back.

"Maybe it died during the fall of the fort?" Wade asked.

"I wouldn't bet on it. It seemed like a tough fire breathing buzzard. We shot the daylights out of it, and it kept flying."

Skyla was quiet as she surveyed below us with my telescope. I hoped the sun wouldn't glint off the glass and give away our position. Last thing we needed was to stir the apes up before anyone was in position to kill them all.

A small stone bounced off my back. Looking behind me, I saw Runs With Dogs beckoning me back to the tree line.

"I think the Army is here. Otto, you good?"

The brave was quiet for several heartbeats before giving a quick nod of his head. "Shaynee take many ape scalps today."

Leaning closer to my blood brother so the ladies wouldn't hear me swear, I lowered my voice. "Damn right you will." I pulled away and began to slide backwards off the rocks. "Let's go, everyone. It's almost show time."

The soldiers and detectives were quieter than before, but still louder than I preferred. The soldiers did well though moving to the edge of the forest above the canyon, and it seemed only half of the Pinkertons would be shooting while the others were held in reserve. Possibly to cover their flank should my small force fail to stem the tide spewing from the entrance once the battle was joined.

As Pinkerton Lead Detective Thompson and Colonel Carver began positioning their forces along the edge, my small party rode away through the forest, along the cliff side but out of sight as it sloped down towards the entrance.

We also took with us two dozen soldiers supposedly handpicked by Captain Hawney for their willingness to let bygones be bygones and work with the Shaynee while being led by Sergeant Gibbons.

But from the distasteful looks on the faces of the soldiers, I knew instantly that was a load of crap. They'd been ordered, not asked. Gibbons was the only one of them who I trusted, and that was just because I knew the burly black Sergeant viewed apes as lesser beings than the Indians in terms of who he regarded with any amount of humanity. But I supposed it didn't matter, considering the looks on the faces of the Indians, they were disgusted to be fighting alongside soldiers as well.

Judging by the sun, we were running low on time to get our group into position before the mounted Shayanas' pterodactyls caused a distraction. And with the added two dozen men on foot slowing us down now, we would be hard pressed to get set up in time. Of course, it's easy to judge a sun wrong, so the natives could begin the diversion at any moment, and we'd be up a creek far away from our position to stop the circling of our forces by a nest of apes kicked over like a beehive.

So, we hurried through the forest, luckily avoiding any more ape scouts, until we reached roughly the narrowest portion of the canyon entrance. The apes had left our palisade in place and from our position in the trees we would have a straight two-hundred-yard shooting range as they came spilling out through the small entrance along the river that flowed through the canyon.

After tying Carbine off while he munched on a withered apple, I peeked through some thick fern leaves and the sight of the former battlefield was gut wrenching.

I had witnessed firsthand the charge of mounted apes against the sharpened stakes embedded along the palisade and the carnage as we fought to keep them from overwhelming our defenses. And I witnessed the dragon belching flame on our Gatling gun and cannon positions, turning men into writhing, screeching, scarecrows of flame as those defenses crumbled.

My eyes found the position of Captain Brandthorn's last stand on the top of the berm, fighting valiantly to give us precious time to flee the canyon. The image of the ape leader's thrown spear piercing through my friend's chest would be forever seared into my memory.

"Goodness…" Wade whispered as he and Ashley moved to see the battlefield. They'd been safely on the other side of the Shimmer, waiting permission to cross when the fall of Fort Jipson took place. I'd described the battle in detail to them, but hearing it was vastly different from seeing the remains of the fight.

The ground was still torn and churned from dinosaur hooves, cannon balls, and thousands of rounds of ammunition unloaded into the mounted trike charge. The front of the palisade was scorched dirt and rock from the dragon's breath. Sharpened stakes that'd been driven in to prevent the sort of charge we faced were jutting out in all sorts of crazy angles depending on how the trikes hit them. Many were smashed down while others were burnt to ashen nubs in the ground.

A massive mound of blackened bones showed where the great number of trike, ape, and human bodies had been pulled out of the canyon and set on fire. I suspected it would be a long time before they were gnawed away by the scavengers of this side. Even from this distance, without the use of my collapsing telescope, I could see dozens of compys bouncing and skittering over the ashen and gristly black bones and skulls, worrying away any leftover pieces of flesh or bone marrow. The little green scavengers moved quickly, their long whip-like tails balancing their small bodies as they nipped at each other and tugged over the remains. Above them, balancing on the bones, was a handful of pterodactyls, looking like plump prehistoric buzzards as they squawked and hopped around on rib cages and skull horns.

"This looks like quite the battle," Wade said.

"It was awful," Skyla admitted. "Worse than Granite Falls in a lot of ways. And the dragon... it was terrifying."

Ashley had my telescope out and was pointing it at the giant mound of burnt bones. "I don't see anything in that pile that doesn't look like man, ape, or trike. Wait... no, that's much too small. Must be a raptor skull." The sharpshooter lowered the brass telescope. "Sorry, Jed. No sign of your dragon."

"Maybe it was too large to be moved from wherever it fell?" Skyla said hopefully.

"Doubt it." I flicked away a rather large centipede that was skittering over some fall leaves beside me, then shuddered in disgust at the thought of the insect crawling over me unknowingly. "My money's on it being alive. Which means we need to keep an eye out."

"Yes, sir." Wade was already looking at the open sky in front of us with a frown on his face.

***

Otto let out the chirp of a small bird from his position, signaling us to pay attention.

A pair of mounted apes were riding into the entrance with some of those giant brown flightless birds thrown over their mount's backs. Skyla had called them Ortho-somethings. Having feasted on a couple while we stayed with the Shayana, I could attest to them being good eating. The pair was a hunting party I assumed and unlikely to be looking for the scouts we killed earlier... I hoped.

We waited for them to ride out of sight into the former fort before giving the signal to Runs With Dogs and Sergeant Gibbons. The soldiers and Shaynee braves began moving to the edge of the forest and taking up positions along the giant prehistoric trees.

Skyla moved behind the same tree I was at, and not for the first time, I questioned all our sanity in allowing her to come. After everything we'd been through, she'd proven herself time and time again to be more than just a paleontologist from a stuffy science building in Washington. But her safety was everything to me, and once again, I was allowing her to put herself in harm's way.

The only difference was this time, I had the blessings of her father. And that, surprisingly, meant a lot to me.

But I really wished we had a few Gatlings, some cannons, or one of those newfangled Maxim machine guns that Reydan had been keeping up his sleeve. As it was, I had a line of Indians to my left, my group and Skyla in the center, then Sergeant Gibbons and his men stretching out to my right. It would have to do. Luckily, everyone was armed with a Repeater... except for Wade with his heavy, long barreled Ballard and Squatting Bull who preferred the traditional Shaynee bow and arrow to a rifle. But they were both pretty good shots, so that'd help.

As it was, Colonel Carver was risking us with our meager firepower to stop the army from being flanked. I'd have felt better if our numbers were doubled, but then, if the Army and Pinkertons did their job, there wouldn't be many apes leaving through the fort entrance.

The sound of Breehas screeching echoed through the canyon to our position.

The diversion had begun.

Wade raised his heavy, octagonal barreled Ballard into position to fire. Likewise, beside him his fiancé did the same with her *One of a Thousand*. Skyla smiled at me, her rifle already in position. Again, I wish she and Ashley had stayed back. But they were just so damn stubborn...

I racked the lever on the *Eighty-Six* and settled in behind the polished black walnut stock.

It was time to pay attention. The Shayanas should be grabbing up unsuspecting apes, flinging them down to their deaths, and essentially kicking over a beehive to get all the apes into the open so our side could reign death and destruction upon them.

And then, even though I was expecting it, the first volley of gunfire caught me by surprise.

It sounded like a hellacious firestorm of blasting gunpowder and cracks of hell letting loose as bullets shot and echoed through the canyon. The sound of roaring apes reached us a moment later. The soldiers and Indians along our line began tucking firearms into shoulders, lining the sights up on the entrance and waiting for the inevitable ape stampede.

The firing continued into the canyon, and I really wished Skyla was in that position instead of this one.

The pair of mounted ape scouts we'd seen earlier came racing back on their trikes, heavy feet thundering as they pounded towards our position.

Over a dozen rifles fired simultaneously.

Both apes fell.

One of the trikes stumbled, then ran after the other, limping and dragging a front leg as they moved away from our position.

Wade loaded another large round into his single shot Ballard with a slight grin. "Pretty sure it was my shot that hit the lead ape."

Ashley scoffed, "No, it was mine." She jacked another round into her rifle's chamber with a wink.

"If you say so, love," Wade smirked.

"I hit trike in..." Otto pointed at his knee.

"The knee? Why'd you do that?" Skyla asked.

"Best way to stop it. Learned at battle of your town."

I grunted and racked another round into the *Eighty-Six's* chamber. "I'll keep that in mind."

More trikes came pouring out of the entrance between the burnt remains of the palisade. It was a mix of mounted and unmounted dinosaurs.

We opened up on them and started dropping bodies.

Several raptors raced between the trikes towards our position, edging ahead of their ape masters and bounding towards us.

I winged one, and I was confident that Wade and Ashley each took another out, before a volley of fire wiped out the others.

Most of the men along our line had risen to a knee, or standing, to shoot over the tall prairie grasses and ferns. The Indians joined in the firing with the soldiers, firing wildly into the herd of trikes. Apes and trikes fell alike during the stampede of horned dinosaurs. Most of the unridden trikes were streaming in front of us, away towards the open prairie. But those that were mounted turned towards our position, riding at us in an attempt to break free and flank the shooters we had on the cliff walls.

From my experience, I knew most of the apes inside the canyon would climb the walls to try and get at their attackers. And I hoped Colonel Carver and his men were ready to repel them. But the ones that we were engaging now were hellbent on hitting our allies up the canyon from their unprotected side.

The same thing had happened when I had first discovered the canyon and interrupted a human sacrifice.

But then it had been just me, Carbine, and my lone rifle.

This time, we had an awful lot of firepower, and we dropped apes almost as quickly as they exited the palisade.

Then our firing became ragged as men began to frantically reload while others continued shooting.

I noticed many of the soldiers still shooting trikes, even after their rider had fallen.

The horned beasts toppled over, bellowing in pain and anger, as bullets punched through their thick pebbled hide. Sergeant Gibbons stood up, in full view, screaming at his men to target the riders and conserve ammunition. He kicked one soldier in the ribs who didn't comply fast enough.

Intentionally, I aimed for the apes, ignoring the triceratops unless they were moving in our direction, and I had no better shot. But for the most part, the dinosaurs seemed eager to move away once their riders fell.

Except for several mounted trikes.

Their riders were smarter, and rode bent over, hidden behind the large bone shields that covered the dinosaurs' necks, and charged right at our line.

The first of the pair, a magnificent horned beast, stumbled and fought to continue charging us as the soldiers poured heavy fire into it. It collapsed, mere yards away from our positions along the tree line.

A split second later the rider jumped from behind the bone shield, racing towards the soldiers, a rough, ugly scream on his black lips and a stone axe raised high.

Before the soldiers could react, the ape was upon them, swinging wildly.

While Gibbons and his men dealt with the ape among them, the second of the trike pair charged the Indian side. The Shaynees rolled aside at Otto's shouted commands, letting the horned beast ride through their lines before twisting about and shooting the ape in the back. The hairy monkey toppled over to the side, riddled with bullets, as his mount bellowed in pain and raced off into the forest.

"Jed!" Skyla shouted, pointing to our right.

I rose to a knee and turned, bringing my *Eighty-Six* to bear on the blood splattered ape still fighting amongst the soldiers. I was worried about hitting the men and held my fire even as the ape nearly decapitated a soldier with a brutal swing of his axe.

Ashley elbowed me aside, leaned forward, and fired her *One of a Thousand.*

The bullet burst through the rampaging ape's skull, spraying blood, brain, and bone.

Gibbons quickly moved to a downed soldier while shouting something at the others that I couldn't quite make out and gesturing towards the sky.

A terrible scream pierced my ears from above and a belch of fire exploded to the right of our position.

Several soldiers were instantly turned into human torches as the wave of heat blasted over us. They ran, screaming as cartridges in their weapons and belts burst from the heat. Two of them only made it a couple of steps before collapsing, the third flailed and rolled, shrieking until Sergeant Gibbons put the man out of his misery with a single shot from his pistol.

The dragon swooped low then flew past the palisade and into the canyon.

Everyone went nuts.

The remaining mounted apes and trikes raced away in the opposite direction, while uniformed soldiers and Shaynee braves ran deeper into the forest behind us. Knowing the dense forest and towering trees were better than nothing against a flying monster, I jerked Skyla upright and shoved her ahead of me.

Once far enough inside, I bent over to catch my breath and looked behind us. Smoldering flames burned the ground; nearby were the three charred remains of soldiers in positions of agony.

"The dragon!" Skyla shouted, panting.

"It can't get us under the trees," I told her, hoping it was true.

"Huck berry!" Otto shouted while riding his pony towards me with Carbine in tow. Somehow, he'd raced back to our mounts, and being in superior shape to me, the scarred brave didn't appear to be out of breath at all.

Without thinking, I slammed the *Eighty-Six* into the scabbard, grabbed the pommel and pulled myself up into the saddle.

"Now what?" I shouted at the brave as rapid firing came from up the canyon among the shriek of the Shayanas' pterodactyl riders.

Without answering, the brave viciously kicked his mount's ribs, sending his pony racing up the canyon edge towards where we'd left my other friends and the main body of our attacking army.

"Damn Indians," I muttered as I twisted Carbine around and gave pursuit. I hoped my blood brother had a good plan.

***

Carbine had almost caught up to Otto when we came crashing through the undergrowth and to the main forces' position.

It was like riding into hell itself.

Everything seemed to be burning.

Grass, trees, men, rock.

Everything.

There were dozens of bodies lying along the canyon edge, some still writhing on flame. Other soldiers and Pinkertons fired at the dragon that was destroying them. As I drew back on the reins and stopped Carbine, I saw a shrieking Pinkerton, his torso and head wreathed with fire, leap off the cliff to his death on the rocks below.

Otto kept riding through the hell like he'd been born into... or perhaps from it.

Leaping his pony over bits of flame and corpses, he raced along the edge of the canyon directly towards where the dragon was flapping its wing as it breathed flame at a mixed group of Pinkertons and soldiers firing around several large boulders.

The massive ape mounted on the back of the dragon tugged on the reins, fanning flame back and forth against the boulders. The unfortunate men who were firing around the edge were instantly aflame.

Otto raced his pony straight at the cliff as I jerked the *Eighty-Six* free and pulled it into my shoulder. If we could kill the dragon's master, we may be able to stop the dragon.

Otto's pony went over the edge.

The scarred brave leapt off his horse at the last moment, screaming Shaynee obscenities, with a decorated tomahawk in one hand and a knife in the other.

And he landed on the dragon.

Sort of.

He hit the dragon's closest flapping wing, stabbed his knife into it to stop him from falling off, then climbed to the top of the fire breathing beast where the ape leader rode.

The ape seemed more shocked than I was.

He barely raised his hands to defend himself before Otto was onto him. Even from the distance I was at, I could see blood splashing from the blades hacking, stabbing, and generally slicing the ape leader apart.

The dragon seemed to realize something was amiss, and twisting around, tried to snap at the stranger on its back.

Otto shoved the dead ape and the corpse tumbled to the canyon floor below. Then the scarred Indian climbed up the dragon's neck and gripping one of the beast's horns, slammed his tomahawk blade into the beast's skull over and over.

The damned thing just didn't seem to want to die. Roaring, it twisted and flailed, slamming into the cliff edge, its large talons gripping the rock and climbing to the top. Otto hung on gamely, at times barely managing to keep a grip on the dragon.

Kicking Carbine's sides, I ran him towards the suicidal Shaynee brave, unsure of how I could help.

With a burst of fire and flame that lit a good forty feet of cliff edge on fire, the dragon twirled around and dropped into the canyon and out of sight.

A moment later there was a thud that shook the ground and another burst of fire that rose into the sky followed by an ear-piercing screech of what I hoped was a dragon giving its death cry.

Carbine skidded to a stop in front of the flames. I could feel the heat from them as smoke rose into the sky from whatever strange burning liquid the dragon had spewed over the rock and grass ledge.

Gunfire was becoming sparse, and apes appeared to be taking advantage of the smoke and chaos to escape into the trees. It seemed the battle was over.

Taking one last glance at the sight of hellish inferno that I was in the middle of, I rode away from the flames and screams of wounded and dying men, back towards where I'd left Skyla.

But my blood brother was gone.

There was no chance he could have survived that fall on the dragon.

And by racing up here, we'd foolishly left my small group with two less men.

The tide had turned, the apes were retreating, and that meant those left alive in the canyon would be pushing out the entrance by Skyla and the others.

Through the smoke, Chief Thenory swooped down to land in a small clearing of burnt grass and charred men. The wings of his breehas sent swirls of smoke spinning across the cliff top. I ignored him as I ran Carbine back into the forest, desperate to get back to my friends.

***

Reaching my old position, the first thing I noticed was the large mound of corpses in front of the trees.

Trikes and apes.

It looked like there'd been a big push after I'd left.

But now, there weren't any more fleeing apes or trikes in sight, and the area was eerily quiet as I approached on Carbine. In the background I could hear a scattering of shots from our forces' positions up the canyon from me. Unfortunately, I wasn't sure if it was firing from guns or cartridges cooking off in the heat of the dragon's flame.

"Skyla! Gibbons!" I called out as I approached.

From behind one of the large horned dinosaur bodies rose the black Sergeant with a big grin on his face. Beside him popped up Skyla, then Wade and Ashley. It appeared that they'd been using the body as cover and firing their rifles over the top of the dead beast.

Before I could dismount, Runs With Dogs stalked over to me from the tree line with several more braves in tow.

"Where Otto?" he demanded.

"Dead. He fell into the canyon."

The brave frowned with an untrusting look in his eyes then turned back to the others. In Shaynee he told his Indian friends, "Huck Berry says he left him to die."

"That's not what I said," I growled back in broken Shaynee as the other braves looked at me threateningly. "I said he fell into canyon. Once you see his body, you'll know how he died. Bravely."

Sergeant Gibbons quickly moved along the line, checking wounded and dead soldiers while we reloaded and waited on whatever survivors of the Army were left from the dragon's attack.

A couple of hours later, I was leaning back against the pebbled hide of the dead trike next to Sergeant Gibbons, watching the Shaynee braves stalking across the small battlefield in front of us.

They were killing the wounded, scalping the dead, and looting anything that looked of value.

A dozen feet away, Ashley lay comfortably behind her *One of a Thousand* rifle under the shade of a relatively small tree for this side, intently watching the Indians do their grisly work.

Still inside the shade and comfort of the massive trees, the soldiers tended to their wounded with Skyla's help. Somehow the Indians managed to come out of this in one piece, with just a few minor wounds. Nothing that they would accept treatment for. Meanwhile, Gibbons and I watched for any more apes to try and sneak out of the canyon and waited for the Army to come find us.

An ape lurched to her feet behind one of the braves on the battlefield, one arm dangling uselessly, the other clutching a heavy stone club. With an angry howl she swung the weapon.

Boom!

Doubling over, the ape dropped in a crumpled heap.

"Nice shot. If your rifle wasn't so pretty, I'd tell you that you need to start keeping count on your stock," Gibbons told the sharpshooter as he lifted his Winchester and showed us a long string of neat little grooves gouged into the side.

"Not my style," Ashley said while racking the lever on her rifle and settling back into position behind the stock.

"Sergeant, I never got the chance to ask. Did you interrogate those ape prisoners from the Fort York attack?" Wade asked as he chewed on a stem of grass.

"Yes, I did."

"You learn anything?"

Gibbons jerked a thumb towards my favorite paleontologist, "Just that Skyla was right. They were cold and wanted to go home."

She gave a slight smile before returning to changing the bandage on one of the soldiers. She was never one for bragging when she was right.

"Were there any others? Or did we kill them all during the attack?"

"Brownie... that's what I called the one who was willing to talk on account of his fur color, he said a handful went over the mountain, looking for warmer lands instead of risking the fight to cross through the tunnel."

"He said all that?" Wade frowned.

"Well, it took a lot of gesturing and small words that I knew to make sense of it," the Sergeant admitted.

"Other side of the mountain, huh?" I thought back to when I first staked claim on the area the tunnel was on. There'd only been one other claim anywhere nearby, and it'd been on the other side of the mountain. A man named J. Johnson.

I hoped the apes didn't catch the man unawares. But something told me for a fella to live that far out there on his own, he had to be a mighty tough hombre.

The braves were positively giddy as they hacked off obsidian arrowheads from thick ape arrows and picked through the dead apes' possessions. Any sort of small weapons made of obsidian was prized and quickly looted. The larger clubs and axes were left behind, too heavy for the lithe Indians to use.

One brave devised a clever method of removing a dead trike's horn by shooting it off with his rifle. Others followed suit, and I quickly had to leave my comfortable spot in the shade to tell them to quit as bullets began ricocheting all over the place, with some zipping uncomfortably close by our position under the trees.

Soon the braves tired of their looting and scalping and returned with their bloody and shiny prizes.

Not long after the last one came back. Captain Hawney and Colonel Carver rode to our position with about fifty men and Fredrick and Arthur tagging along beside Parsons and his photographer. Some of the men had bandages wrapped around their arms and torsos, a few showed visible burn marks on their faces. There was no sign of any Pinkertons.

"Still alive, Jed?" Fredrick called out.

"Still alive!" I shouted back as Skyla gave him a slight wave.

"Is this it, Colonel?" Wade asked as the officer stopped his horse.

"No. The remaining Pinkertons are with the badly wounded."

Sergeant Gibbons moved away from the trike corpse we'd been resting against. "Sir," he saluted his superior.

Colonel Carver returned the salute then glanced at the scorched earth from where the dragon's breath had sprayed fire. He frowned. "Losses, Sergeant?"

"Six, sir. Three from the dragon."

The Colonel sighed and removed his hat before rubbing his eyes wearily. "We thought we were ready for it, Sergeant... but we were not."

"Jed told us what he saw, sir." Gibbons jerked a thumb at the smoke still rising into the air from where the army had ambushed the canyon of apes.

"If it hadn't been for that Indian... I don't know that any of us would still be alive," Captain Hawney said, giving some uncharacteristic praise for the Shaynee.

I looked at Squatting Bull on the back of his trike. He shrugged indifferently at me. Probably because he didn't trust any white man's word.

"Yeah, Captain. Good thing we had horses." I glared at him. "It'd have been a long walk to save you."

The officer had the audacity to look partially embarrassed by giving us such a bullshit order as leaving our mounts behind.

"Did any apes escape?" Colonel Carver inquired, ignoring my angry look at his underling and surveying the piles of dead in front of our position.

"Yes," Sergeant Gibbons growled. "It was a shit show with the sheer number of trikes they had. If any apes rode that direction," he pointed towards the far side of the canyon entrance, "then they got away. But anything that came towards us got smoked."

"Good, let them warn the others what happens to those who cross the US Army," Captain Hawney said firmly.

Fredrick rolled his eyes.

"Arthur, how was your second taste of battle?"

The writer looked sheepish. "I think I missed more than I hit once that dragon attacked."

Fredrick leaned over and slapped Arthur on the shoulder. "He did fine. It was like shooting monkeys in a barrel until that dragon attacked... it was almost unsporting. As if I cared anything about that when it comes to these apes."

"Gentlemen," Colonel Carver called from astride his horse. "Shall we enter the fort?"

"Skyla, hang back," I said as I stepped up into the saddle. Carbine snorted and jerked his head back and forth. "We don't know what we'll find in there."

"I'm staying with you," she protested. Smoke stomped her hooves as if in protest as well.

"Let the rough and rugged men protect us delicate flowers, Skyla," Ashley said as she flipped her braid over a shoulder haughtily.

Wade barked a short laugh, and I felt myself blushing.

"That's not what I-"

"Oh, it's fine, Jed. I'll hang out in back with Ashley."

I looked at Wade helplessly, and he just shrugged before urging his horse onwards.

"Women," I muttered to myself as I followed the others.

A shout came from the front as the column of soldiers stopped abruptly near the scorched palisade.

The line of soldiers moved aside, and a lone figure stalked towards us.

I recognized him at the same time as the Shaynee braves.

With loud whoops of excitement, they kicked their ponies' flanks and rode around the column of soldiers to the front, followed by the heavy thudding of Squatting Bull on the back of Horny Devil. Several soldiers had to leap out of the way to keep from being gored or trampled by the tamed trike.

"Is that who I think it is?" Fredrick asked in awe.

"Otto," Wade whispered in shock.

"I'll be... he's alive." I couldn't help but grin a little. The scarred Shaynee brave was being back slapped by the other whopping, excited Indians while attempting to look as nonchalant as possible. The soldiers all looked impressed as hell at this Indian who'd single handedly taken out a dragon, then walked through a battlefield to meet them at the fort's entrance.

"I reckon that means there isn't anything else left alive in the fort then," Fredrick grumbled while hefting his rifle.

"Most likely not," Wade said in astonishment as the scarred brave approached, nonchalantly walking through the column of soldiers as a proper badass should.

"Huck Berry," he said with a wink.

"Otto. Good to see you alive."

My blood brother shrugged with one shoulder, as if to say, of course I am.

With a wave of Colonel Carver's arm, the soldiers began to move forward again, walking between the slow running river and the palisade, stepping over bodies of scalped apes and around the occasional trike corpse.

With *Eighty-Six* in hand, I rode past the scorched churned palisade and into the canyon with the others as the surviving breehas and their Shayana riders circled overhead.

***

Fort Jipson was gone.

It appeared that everything human had been put to the torch. Mounds of burnt bodies and equipment lay off to the side. Among the piles, I saw the remains of numerous rifles, saddles, tack, and equipment in ashen heaps… along with hundreds of human bones and charred skulls.

The single log house that Reydan had built as his headquarters was destroyed, ripped down and the wood used to fuel the fires that burnt the corpses from the earlier battle. The neat rows of crosses from the small cemetery had been ripped out of the ground and were missing, most likely burned as well. The dozens of neat rows of tents were gone, but it seemed the apes liked the canvas. It was scattered all around the area, and I saw numerous small bags, body coverings, and such made from it on the ape corpses.

The corral was gone, and all the horses and cattle that'd been left behind appeared to have been killed and eaten. I was glad I got Carbine and Smoke out in time. Although I bet Carbine would taste like pure jackass for all his tormenting of me.

But other than the repurposing of our canvas, it was as if the apes wanted to remove any presence of us. It was almost as if our being in their canyon defiled it.

They'd even begun to build a new altar amidst the rubble of the old one Captain Brandthorn had dynamited.

While the Shaynee braves and soldiers checked the dead apes that lay scattered across the canyon floor for any fakers, I walked Carbine to the makeshift altar with my small group, and we stared at the makeshift altar in silence. It wasn't much. Just a few large stones brought together, nothing like the old obsidian altar the apes had before.

Fredrick stepped closer and ran a finger along the top of the rock in the center. "It's been used," he said. "Within a day or so, some of the blood is still tacky."

Several breehas landed nearby. Their riders dismounted and walked our way, and from the familiar stride I could tell which one was Chief Thenory. He and his other pterodactyl riders all gawked at the number of apes that lay strewn about the canyon floor.

Hoof beats made me turn, and Colonel Carver rode to a stop on his brown gelding. He gestured at the altar with the tip of his officer's sword, "I guess we know now why we didn't find any of our men."

My jaw dropped and I looked at him in disbelief. "The apes had prisoners of ours?"

"Yes," Chief Thenory said, looking at the altar in disgust. "We saw a dozen of thine men held captive and one of ours."

Otto snorted in disgust while glaring up at the mounted officer. "Why wait to fight, white man?"

I stepped towards the officer, feeling angry and frustrated at not knowing men had been left behind as I'd made my escape from the fall of the fort. "What the hell, Colonel? We just left them here to be slaughtered at the ape's convenience?"

"We didn't have the men or resources available," Carver snapped back. "If we had, we'd have wiped the damn apes out weeks ago."

"Well, I'm glad you finally got around to it." I gestured across the canyon angrily at all the scattered dead apes, trikes, and occasional raptor.

"What do you want, Jed? An apology for me making a military decision and not consulting you?" the Colonel demanded, a bright crimson creeping along the sides of his neck as he grew impatient with me.

"No, dammit! I just…" I raked a hand back through my hair, frustrated at the thought of having left men behind to be sacrificed for some wicked ape god but also knowing there was nothing I could have done.

"It's not your fault, Jed." Fredrick picked up an empty brass cartridge off the ground. From its location, it had to have been fired during the fall of the fort. He twisted it between his fingers while watching one of the Shaynee braves cut the throat of a wounded ape nearby that weakly grabbed at him. "None of this is."

"I just wish I'd known! I was last in the tunnels, I blew them shut, dooming anyone else still alive in the fort."

Skyla grabbed my arm to stop me from my angry pacing. "Jed! There's nothing you could have done."

I kicked a clod of dirt with the toe of my boot angrily. It didn't make me feel any better.

Colonel Carver looked down from his gelding at me sternly. "Stop thinking of yourself as a hero, Jed. Because there's no such thing as one. You're just a man who keeps winding up in the wrong place at the wrong time and coming out on top. You have to learn that you can't save everyone."

I thought of Brandthorn, of how he fought from the top of the berm to give his men a chance to retreat, eventually dying with an ape spear thrust through his chest. What sacrifice he'd shown... what bravery.

With my eyes, I found the place on the palisade where he'd fallen.

I walked away from the group without a word.

Carver was wrong. Heroes existed.

Captain Brandthorn had been one. Wolverine Wade, Fredrick von Holsack, Ashley James, Skyla Stratten... even Otto were all heroes. Because they did what needed to be done regardless of the cost. They stayed and fought at the Battle of Granite Falls, the fall of Fort Jipson, the rescue of Fort York at the Shimmer, and in Otto's case, even killed a dragon with a tomahawk.

But not me. No. I was just a bad man trying to make good. I certainly didn't consider myself a hero.

I'd made it a dozen rapid steps towards the berm before hearing someone jogging towards me from behind. I looked over my shoulder and saw Skyla catching up.

"You're a hero in my book," she said with a sad smile.

"I'm not. But you're a hero in mine," I replied truthfully as I thought of all she'd been through since arriving at Granite Falls as a naïve paleontologist in search of a dinosaur.

Skyla blushed but said nothing.

We walked in silence until reaching the spot where Captain Brandthorn fell. The ground was churned from the apes climbing over the burn and scorched in places from the dragon's fiery breath. Burnt grass crunched beneath my boots as I looked around the spot. I didn't know what I was looking for, but I just felt compelled to be here.

"He was a good man," Skyla said, recognizing the place we stood.

"Yes."

I sighed.

There was nothing here. No body, no weapons, not even a blood stain. Nothing to show the passing of a great man and friend. "Let's go find Wade and the others… and make sure the Shaynee's aren't cutting the wrong throats."

***

Below the cliffside to where the Pinkertons and soldiers had fired from, was a mound of bodies that lined the edge of the cliff where they'd been shot off. Long, yellow and green feathered arrows speckled the top edge of the cliff like a pin cushion from where apes had fired back at the hundreds of shooters. There were also fallen soldier and Pinkerton bodies mingled in the pile, still smoldering from dragon flame.

We found our Shaynee warriors with Otto by the dragon's corpse.

The scarred brave stood in front of it, gesturing wildly with his tomahawk as he told the Indians of his brave and daring rescue of the helpless white men.

We sat on our horses, watching, while I translated what I could to the others, trying to leave the more offensive parts out for the sake of Ashley and Skyla.

Wade chuckled beside me. "The man has a right to brag. He killed a dragon."

"Lucky him. Meanwhile, I still haven't gotten my Tyrannosaurus," Fredrick complained.

"Stick around long enough, and you'll get your chance," Ashley promised the famed hunter.

"Lookie there," Wade pointed with a jerk of his head. John Parsons was helping his photographer set up his strange camera to take photos of the mounds of dead below the cliff side. "Chronicling the brave victory of man over ape in glorious battle, no doubt," the showman said sarcastically.

"Was it not?" Arthur asked, carrying his long Martini-Henry rifle slung over a shoulder. The Lord Elcho bayonet he had strapped to his waist.

"It was a slaughter, not a battle. The only real fight we had was from that," Fredrick gestured at the giant dragon corpse in front of us. Otto had climbed onto the top of the dead thing and was mimicking tomahawk blows to the bloodied head of the beast. His braves were listening in rapt attention.

"You uh, wipe that sword of yours off on your pants?" I asked, pointing at the blood that had smeared onto Arthur's pants.

The author tilted the bayonet sheath up from his waist to look and sighed. "It'll wash out."

"What did you think of all this?" Ashley asked.

"Terrifying and exhilarating, all at the same time," he gushed.

"Sounds about right," Wade agreed.

"I can't wait to write about it. I've already started a plot outline for a new book based off what I've seen here so far."

"Looking forward to reading it, Arthur," Fredrick told him. "But I've always been more of a non-fiction writer myself."

"Ah yes, but imagination! That's where I'll make my fortune!" Arthur pulled out a small notebook from his shirt pocket and waved it. "I've been taking notes!"

"Then I wish you well in your future endeavors, sir."

"Think Otto will mind if I look at the dragon?" Skyla asked.

"Of course not, you're his blood brother's woman. He wouldn't dare object," Ashley told her with a sly smile.

Skyla's faced blushed a bright crimson and she pulled her hat lower to try and hide it.

Wade and Fredrick chuckled while I just grinned at her.

"Mr. Wolverine! I mean, Wade, Mr. Wade! Sir!" A soldier approached on foot, waving to get the famed Westerner's attention.

"What is it?" Wade called back, chuckling at the excitement of the young man.

"We've found something for your show!"

Ashley and Wade shared an excited look and quickly turned their horses around to follow the soldier. Arthur looked torn between the dragon or the new find, and after a moment's hesitation rode after the sharpshooter and her beau.

"Well, while they're off having their fun, let's get a look at this dragon beast," Fredrick said.

We walked through the group of Shaynee braves as Otto hopped off the corpse and grinned at me broadly before being slapped on the back by his Indians. They were happy all around for once, both at having their leader alive and having defeated such a monstrosity. There would be much pow-wowing and such in the village when they arrived home.

I poked the dragon with the barrel of my *Eighty-Six*. Just to be sure.

It didn't move.

The dead critter was dark green with large, scaled wings, a short neck and long tail. Its head was reptilian, just like in the cave painting we'd found so long ago, and full of jagged teeth. A pair of black horns swept back along its neck, several feet in length. And at the tips of its wings were feet, with black talons.

"Huh, look at that." Skyla pointed at the scales on the underbelly of the beast.

I leaned forward to get a better view.

There were marks in them, deep scratch marks, almost like gouges.

"Are these..." Fredrick paused before gently touching one of the grooves, "from bullets?"

"Bowie, please?" Skyla asked, holding her hand out to me.

I drew the razor-sharp blade from its sheath and handed it to her, grip first. She carried her own blade, an extremely sharp obsidian chipped ape blade, but obsidian wasn't the strongest rock when it came to prying.

With the blade of my Bowie, Skyla slipped it between a pair of scales. Leveraging her body weight against the blade, there was a muffled pop and a ripping sound. A large dark green, almost black, scale came off in her hand.

Then she dislocated another scale and held the pair up for us to see.

One of them had a hole punched through it and the other had a lead-colored inch long gouge in it.

"Theory time," she said, but I was already tracking with where she was going.

"Let me guess, bullet proof?"

"Yes, indeed. I don't know what these scales are made of, but they are ridiculously hard." She smacked one hard with the thick spine on the back of my Bowie's blade. Nothing happened. "If you shoot it close enough, with something high powered enough, you'll get penetration. Otherwise, the bullet is deflected, leaving the dragon unharmed but probably angry."

"Yeah, we've seen them angry all right," Fredrick groused, looking at the cliff face that still smoldered from dragon fire.

I kicked the dead beast where its ribs would be. "That explains how it could soak up so many bullets and keep flying. Most of them weren't doing any damage at the range we were shooting it. Is this monster coming back to the Smithsonian with us?"

My favorite paleontologist looked at the dead dragon sadly. "We don't have any way to move it. What I'd give for my butchers and some wagons." She sighed. "I'll do some quick sketching and a basic autopsy, if you don't mind me keeping your Bowie for a bit. But I know Colonel Carver is wanting us out of here as soon as possible."

"Use it all you need to." I noticed Fredrick looking behind me and turned.

Parsons and his photographer were headed our way.

"Why don't you check on Wade and Ashley? I'll keep the journalist entertained," Fredrick suggested, noticing my grimace as I watched Parsons stumble through a patch of partially eaten ferns.

"Thanks. I owe you one." Winking at Skyla, I grabbed Carbine's reins and slid back into the saddle. Clicking my tongue, I turned him, and he began walking in the direction Wade and his fiancé had gone with the soldiers. It appeared my untrusty steed and myself would be heading towards the back of the canyon.

I found the engaged pair riding with a group of soldiers who were taking turns pulling a pair of the apes' large two wheeled carts. Like the typical carts used to move supplies for the apes. Except these carts had cages on the back of them and a raptor held inside each one.

Wade grinned triumphantly from the back of his horse as I approached. "Two live ones, Jed! These will be a big draw for the show!"

"Well, congratulations. Don't let the little demons eat you or your show's attendees."

Ashley rested her rifle butt against a thigh and pushed her dirty blonde braid over a shoulder. "This is a big deal, Jed."

"How did you catch them?"

Wade waved his hat at the small dinosaurs. "Found 'em caged like this. Their ape handlers were nowhere to be found. I guess we got lucky and popped them before they could release the little beasts on us."

"Thank goodness." I despised raptors. The feathery little bastards were all tooth, claw, and viciousness. Swift, lethal, and ugly.

One of them attacked the side of the cage in a flurry of black claws and loud shrieks. The two soldiers pulling the cart looked back fearfully, afraid it was going to get loose. Another soldier raised his rifle hesitantly, as if unsure whether the dinosaur might get out or not.

"Might want to keep that gun on them. They get out, there'll be hell to pay," I warned.

The soldier nodded, sweat trickling down the side of his face.

I was sure it wasn't just the heat causing that.

***

But it was hot today. We'd been through a long march, a brutal counterattack, and I was ready to get back to the other side of the Shimmer and relax for a bit.

The Indians left the dead apes inside the canyon alone. They hadn't killed any of them and thus felt it wasn't right to mutilate them. But they were rifling through their shit as quickly as possible, picking up any trinkets that seemed of value and snapping off hundreds of obsidian arrow heads and spear points to take back home. Otto seemed content enough with just knocking out a handful of fangs from the dragon with his tomahawk and putting them in a pouch. I was willing to bet the next time we crossed paths he'd be wearing a mighty fine necklace of them.

Shouts went up from the front of the canyon, and soldiers began making their way towards the front to reform into their column. Chief Thenory and his breehas riders were winging up into the sky and flying in the direction of their volcanic home.

It seemed it was time to go.

I went back to Fredrick and Skyla.

She was hurrying to dig through the beast's stomach with Fredrick jotting notes that she dictated to him in her journal. I was glad to see she had the forethought to bring a pair of the leather gloves that went past her elbows to keep the blood and guts off her.

"Time to go."

She pulled out part of a human arm from the stomach, blanched, and dropped it into a gooey pile of stomach bile, pieces of soldiers, and big chunks of what looked like some dinosaur. "Look at this." Reaching into the pile, she pulled out a piece of light green hide wrapped around mangled red flesh. "I think the dragon was off feeding when we attacked."

"That's some bad timing. If it'd been here when we started that attack, it may have saved some lives," Fredrick pointed out as he folded the journal and slipped it into one of the saddle bags on Smoke's back.

"We got lucky with Otto pulling off that loco stunt of his to kill it."

"Yes, we did. Look." Skyla grabbed the gaping wound from the scarred brave's tomahawk on the head of the dragon and pulled it open. He'd managed to hack through the skull and slice open the brain. "If he'd been a little more off to either side, he'd have missed and just made it angrier."

Fredrick peered into the wound. "Lucky little Indian."

"I wouldn't call him little." I rubbed my chin and face where he'd put a beating on me. He carried strength in that lithe body of his.

More shouts came from the canyon entrance, and the few soldiers who were still on the way began to jog. The Shaynee were also moving towards the palisade in a small group, with their warrior hero Otto in the center.

"Let's get out of here. I'd hate to be around when the apes come back," Fredrick warned.

"Agreed."

***

We left the canyon and returned through the forest trail that'd been cut out for resupplying the former fort. On guard as we rode at the front of the army column, we watched for apes and dinosaurs, but saw none. Squatting Bull and Horny Devil led the way, the thought being that if something bothered the trike, it was probably something that needed to be killed.

We went slow due to the walking wounded, and about a dozen were carried out on stretchers made from poles and scrounged canvas tent sheets. And where a single ape could haul one of the rolling cages with a raptor in it, it took two men to drag each along the trail. Wade and Ashley rode beside them, ready to shoot the little critters if they managed to escape, but adamant that they also be protected at all costs. Our Shayana guides had left us after the attack, following their Chief and his pterodactyl riders back home on foot. From what I'd gathered, they were in great spirits about the destruction of an army that'd been camping on what was almost at their doorstep.

"A shame to abandon the fort again," Captain Hawney said, spitting off to the side.

"Fort Jipson is gone. If we keep letting politicians and scientists dictate where our forts go, we'll never conquer this land," Colonel Carver retorted. "But now, Whitesberg..." He whistled. "Mr. White knows what he's doing. For a quartermaster, he's got a tactful mind. He proved that when he chose the location for his town."

I rolled my eyes. Quartermaster, my ass. I don't know what part he played during the actual war, but it certainly wasn't something so peaceful.

"But the Fort, sir, after everything it cost us..." Hawney began.

Carver held up a finger to make a point. "The canyon cost the apes as well. The bullet riddled corpses of their army will serve as a warning to any more apes who try to use it against us. They know it's undefendable and they just suffered a grave defeat, including their leader and his dragon. I expect we won't have any more trouble from them for some time."

Skyla glanced at me, and I shook my head. It wasn't safe to not expect trouble.

Hawney grunted. "Then it was all for nothing. They wiped us out, then we wiped them out, and we're right back to where we started."

"That's defeatism, sir. I'll not have it," Colonel Carver glared at his subordinate.

Ashley spoke up. "Fort Jipson wasn't for nothing."

"No, it was not," Wade said, his eyes never leaving the dangerous forest around us. "We met the Shayana, established an ally and better armed them in the war against the apes."

"Entirely correct," Carver said. "Take note, Captain. The civilians are more optimistic than you."

We passed an overturned carriage. It'd become something of a landmark on this trail, signifying that you were almost to the valley and the Shimmer.

Otto stared at it in amusement. "Only fool white man bring that here. Soft rear means soft hands." He showed me the callouses on his hands. I was glad he didn't show me his riding callouses.

"Well, he was a big Chief," I told him, referring to the Senator who'd been ripped out of it and eaten.

"Dumb Chief."

"No argument from me there." I turned in the saddle to look behind us. The rest of the Shaynee rode in a mass of ponies behind us with no sort of formation. They looked rather excited to be heading home after such a victory.

"You got a big pow wow planned for tonight, Otto?"

He grinned toothily. "Yes. You come. You blood brother now."

"As much as I'd like to party with you, I need to get back to my ranch." I gave him a dirty look. "I gotta make sure your tribe hasn't killed off all my cattle to feast on."

He chuckled and repeated what I said in Shaynee to the others. The way they started smirking and snickering made me worried.

"Otto." Colonel Carver removed his cover and wiped the sweat from the band before placing it back on his head. "Will your Shaynee braves be ready in seven days?"

The scarred Indian grunted an affirmation.

"Seven days?" Skyla asked. "What happens in seven days?"

Captain Hawney chuckled.

"What?" I growled. "I thought the Shaynee were done after this?"

"The Shaynee are done when the US Government says they are done," Carver said as he pulled back on his reins to allow us to pass him.

"Did the Indians not tell you?" Hawney smirked. "Maybe it's the language barrier."

"Tell me what?" I said, starting to grow impatient and more than a little ticked off.

"The Shaynee are going with you to find the axemen."

We looked at Otto in shock. He shrugged with one shoulder as though it were no big deal.

"Otto!" Ashley said. "What deal did Chief Toko come to?"

"Good deal. We fight until we get land."

"No, Otto. That's a shit deal." I sighed and ran a thumb along the allosaurus claw necklace. I'd discovered rubbing it was soothing. Weird, but it worked. "Well, great."

Otto said nothing.

Once we crossed back through the Shimmer, we parted ways. Wade and Ashley loaded their caged raptors onto the train to take back to Cheyenne with Fredrick, and Otto took his braves back to their village to celebrate the battle and honor the fallen. Arthur, meanwhile, decided to come to my ranch at Skyla's request to look at her mother and Charles' healing wounds.

Colonel Carver told me to bring the Shaynee braves to Whitesberg in a week to prepare another expedition.

This time we'd be off to meet the axemen.

***

"Arthur, I appreciate you coming out," I told the Scottish writer and former doctor as we rode along the forest-surrounded wagon trail on the way to my ranch.

"I'm happy to help. My schooling shouldn't be for naught."

"Just the same, thank you," Skyla said as she trotted Smoke alongside Arthur and me. After spending so much time surrounded by others, it felt strange to be alone with just Skyla and the writer. For one thing, there was considerably less war paint on my companions now and they seemed rather pleased with my presence instead of a barely concealed loathing that the Shaynee braves gave off to us whites.

We rode out of the forest trail and into the open fields around my ranch house. Right away, I knew something was amiss.

Bo and another man were working on the barn, putting the final touches on the trim. I hadn't hired anyone, and there were several more horses in the corral then there should have been. No one else was in view.

With an uneasy feeling, I dropped my hand to the butt of my Colt. Skyla noticed and shifted the reins to her left hand while dropping her right into her lap, where it'd be closer to her Merwin-Hulbert pistol should she need it.

"Something wrong?" Arthur asked as he noticed our subtle movements.

"You never know." It was possible that Bo had found help for the ranch, but knowing how busy the man was, I didn't see how he would have time to go find anyone unless they rode to the ranch and asked to be hired. And being a mostly reformed outlaw meant that I didn't trust anyone, especially people who just happened to ride up at an unlikely time when you needed them most.

Our horses only made it several more steps before a man stepped out of the barn doorway. Even at this distance, I could tell by the shape of his shoulders and the way he stood who it was.

"Jed, is that...?" Skyla asked. She'd never met the man, but I'd described him once as being a big fella.

"It is."

"Who?" Arthur asked, thoroughly confused now.

I sighed but kept my hand on the revolver. "My father."

Bo waved at me, but the man he worked with ignored us, continuing to hammer away at a piece of trim around one of the shuttered windows. From behind the barn raced Sara, her little horns swinging from side to side with her head and bone shield as she happily ran to greet us.

Carbine neighed, and side stepped as she ran amongst our horses.

"What in the world... that's a little triceratops!" Arthur practically squealed in delight as he leaned down in the saddle to get a better look at her prancing between our horses.

"That's Sara. We found her abandoned in the ape valley before they turned it into Fort Jipson. She's a good little girl," Skyla said as she smiled down at the bouncing trike. Skyla and Sara were close, with the little trike being more of the paleontologist's than mine.

"Why are you here?" I asked bluntly as we reached my father.

"Long story," he glanced from me to Skyla and Arthur, as if unsure of what else to say in front of them. "Why don't you put away your horses first and rest a spell."

"I reckon I will, since it's my ranch and all," I told him sarcastically while dismounting. Carbine tossed his mane and tail in the air and started walking towards the corral on his own. Muttering to myself, I caught up to him and grabbing the reins, led him in through the gate. You never knew what sort of trick that horse was up to.

"Arthur, I'll handle your mount. You can go on to the house and check on Mrs. Stratten. Just knock before you enter, we've had some troubles recently and they might be a bit guarded." It was a good ploy to get the writer away while I dealt with my father.

"Sure, Jed." He passed his reins off to me and walked to my house.

After Skyla and I removed the horse's riding equipment, I finally turned to face my old man with a frown.

He'd been leaning against one of the corral posts, nonchalantly chewing on a long stem of hay, and waiting patiently as we worked.

"I'll ask you again. Why are you here?"

He looked from me to Skyla, then back. "What does she know?"

"I know all of it," she replied coolly as she rubbed Smoke down with a handful of hay.

Father chuckled lightly, "I very much doubt that, Miss...?"

"Cut the stalling, you know who she is." Carbine snorted, sensing my displeasure, and eyed the big man warily. Knowing my horse, he'd probably give my old man a kick if he had the opportunity.

"Yes, I do. It's my pleasure to make your acquaintance, Miss Stratten. You are every bit as lovely as your mother."

"You can call me Skyla."

"Skyla it is then. You can call me Gene, short for Eugene."

I pointed at the far side of the barn where the unknown man worked beside Bo. "Who is that? I've seen him before." Once we'd gotten close enough, I realized he was the gun hand who had delivered my father's message of peace to me after trying to break me out of jail with dynamite.

"Travis."

"Travis, eh? He got a last name?"

"Not that I know of," Gene admitted with a shrug.

"You just wander around with a man whose last name you don't know?"

"I know he's from Texas. That's enough for me."

"Okay. Why are you and Texas Travis here?"

He spat the hay out of his mouth and frowned. "Gang had a bit of a falling out. You hear about that heist down by Rock Springs? The train getting held up about a week ago?"

"No. But I don't really read the papers any."

"Too bad," he winked, "you're in them an awful lot for a man in hiding."

"I heard about it," Skyla said as she brushed down Smoke. "The bandits took the pay for the railroad."

"The East-West railroad?" I said, my jaw dropping slightly.

"Yes. Why?" My father chuckled. "The owner a friend of yours?"

I laughed bitterly.

"You never told him, did you?" Skyla asked, turning to me in amazement.

"No. Never had the chance."

"Told me what?" Gene demanded, rising off the post to his full and imposing height.

"Reydan White, the owner of the East-West railroad, led the raiders on our old home back in Charleston." I stared at his face, watching for a reaction as I dropped the final kernel of truth from our past in his lap.

"That rotten…" my father shouted before kicking the post he had leaned against a moment ago. He pointed a finger at me, accusingly. "You knew this and didn't tell me?"

"Like I said, I never got the chance. Last time I saw you, you almost blew me up in that jail cell! The time before that, you let some of your gang try to kill me!" Now I was getting angry and stepped into my old man's personal space. "Who are you to be pissed off?"

He grunted and took a step back, raising his hands defensively. "You're right… It's okay, Travis," he called out, looking over my shoulder.

Glancing back, I saw the gunman holding a hammer in one hand and a pistol pointed at me in the other.

"Put that down, or shoot. Either way, you die by the count of three," I warned him as I nodded to Bo. The old ranch hand had his own pistol pointed at the gunman's head from a yard away.

"One."

The gunman didn't move an inch. He just stared down the sights at me, as if calling my hand to see what cards we'd play.

"Two."

"Lower the gun, Travis. We're just sorting out some old issues," Gene said. Without a word, Travis holstered the pistol, and turned back to trying to fit the piece of bottom trim around the barn window as if nothing had happened.

Bo looked frazzled, and after I nodded at him, he holstered his piece and went back to sawing another board to length while side eyeing the gunman working with him.

"Well, aren't you all just a bunch of warm and fuzzies," Skyla said in disgust.

Gene tipped his hat. "Sorry, Skyla. We've all got some temper problems." He stared at me. "Now tell me, why is Reydan White still breathing?"

I sighed and rubbed my temples as I thought of how to explain the past few months to him.

***

"He needs to die, Orville," my father insisted.

"No kidding and don't call me that."

"Okay… Jed. But either you kill him, or I'll do it for you."

"What about Cato?" Skyla asked.

"Cato?" Gene's jaw dropped. "He's alive?"

"Have you heard of the Black Plague?"

For the first time that I could recall, my father looked bewildered. "Yeah, the fast draw gunman that bodyguards Reydan... you're telling me that's Cato?"

"Yup."

"Well, that certainly complicates matters," he admitted reluctantly.

"It shouldn't, he's a jerk," Skyla muttered.

Gene shook his head. "Strange, he was always such a sweet kid."

I laughed without humor. "When I first realized who Reydan was, Cato stopped me from putting a bullet through his skull by threatening to kill Skyla if I did," I explained, greatly simplifying the meeting between the railroad tycoon and myself for the first time since he'd whipped me close to death.

"We raised him better than that," my old man said in disbelief.

"Reydan's been his father for the last twenty years," I spat back.

Putting a hand over his face, my father groaned. "Okay, two things. We need to talk to Cato and kill Reydan."

"Good luck. Reydan's got an army of Pinkertons and an armor-plated personal train car with a Maxim machine gun mounted on top. As for Cato... I already talked to him. He invited me to shoot it out with him."

The door to the house opened and shut. Morgan stepped off the porch and walked towards us.

"Quick, what does he know?" I asked my father.

He shrugged. "Pretty much everything since your darling Skyla told them about me already when you were supposed to have been dead."

I groaned.

"Sorry," Skyla admitted. "I was in mourning."

"Looks like some plotting going on here, Gene," Morgan said as he reached our group and hugged his daughter tightly. "Glad to see you're okay," he whispered to Skyla. She smiled back at him and patted his back.

My father nodded slowly. "A bit. How's Mrs. Elizabeth?"

"Arthur says it looks like a butcher stitched her up, but the wound is uninfected and healing nicely. She will be fine, except for a scar."

"That's good news." I turned and pointed a finger at my old man. "Now I'll ask again, why are you here?"

"Well, Orvil-"

"Jed," Skyla and I both corrected him at the same time.

He shook his head as Skyla and I shared an annoyed look. "Right... Jed. Long story cut short, after we stole Reydan's payroll the gang double crossed me. If it weren't for Travis, I'd have been rolled into a ditch by now. He stayed loyal."

"Maybe it's time you stopped outlawing?" Skyla suggested.

"I'd agree with that observation," Morgan said as he rested a boot on the lower brace of the corral. "Seems like you and Jed have both reached a fork in the road, where you have the option of going straight. Jed's made his choice."

"Can you get Gene a pardon as well?" Skyla asked her father hopefully.

"No. It's going to take all the political pull I've got to secure one for Jed, and the only chance that has on working is that he's a hero of the New West. Gene here, well, he's not got any definitive redeemable qualities that I can plead to his advantage. No offense, sir."

My father snorted and gently pushed Sara away as she nudged her beak against his leg. "None taken. I was good at outlawing and proud of it, I'd hate to turn my back on it just because I was betrayed by men who worked for me."

"What are you going to do then?"

"Kill Reydan, deal with Cato, and kill off my old gang and start fresh."

"Sounds simple enough," I said sarcastically.

"It would be if you had put that devil in the ground by now," he snapped back.

"You're going to kill Mr. White?" Morgan sputtered in shock.

"I thought you said he knew all of it?" I challenged my old man.

"Well, the Reydan White involvement is a new development!" he shouted.

Morgan looked from me to Gene and back, his eyes wide. "He's the son of a sitting Senator, the owner of East-West railroad, and one of the richest men in the country, plus protected by the Black Plague and hundreds of Pinkertons. You can't just shoot him!"

"Can't? Or shouldn't?" Gene replied angrily. "Because either way, I don't care."

'Both!" Morgan shouted.

"Stop! All of you!" Skyla pushed herself between our fathers. "If anyone should kill Reydan, it should be Jed. He's the one who was almost whipped to death. If he hasn't done it yet, then no one should."

I scuffed the toe of my boot in the grass. "Yeah, Skyla, about that... I've been planning on killing him when I get the chance. Actually, I thought I had him during the Fort York attack too, I tried to get to him in his rail car."

She threw up her hands in despair. "My father is trying to get you a pardon. I thought that meant you were leaving outlawing behind!"

"It does, and I did. I've just got one little bit of unfinished business to take care of."

She pointed at me and Gene accusingly, "You two deserve each other!" Spinning on her heel, she stormed away towards the house. "I'm checking on Mother!"

Sara bellowed lightly as if disgusted at us also and trotted after the angry paleontologist.

We were all quiet for a minute. I could tell my dad was embarrassed at Skyla's outburst, and to be frank, so was I. But that didn't mean she wasn't right. Morgan coughed awkwardly then walked over to Bo and began to help him saw window trim pieces to size. In the silence I could hear the shuffling around of the protos moving in the barn behind us.

"Alright. You kill him," I told my father, making up my mind suddenly. "He's all yours."

"You certain? He flayed a lot of your flesh and spilled a lot of your blood with that whip."

"I'm not losing Skyla over him." I'd made up my mind as I stood there watching Smoke play with Carbine and the other horses in the corral. It used to be that I'd give anything to gut the red-bearded bastard, but now, I was feeling rather optimistic about my chances at getting a pardon and having a future with Skyla.

My father grinned at me. "You made the right choice; I like her."

I glanced at the house where a trickle of lazy smoke drifted from the chimney. "I like her too."

***

After agreeing to let my old man kill my mortal enemy, I felt as if a great weight had been lifted off my scarred shoulders and back. For the first time in decades, I could forget about the Union raider who burned my home, killed my neighbors, and mutilated me. It was rather freeing.

While my father and Travis schemed about the best way to handle Cato and kill Reydan, I lounged around the ranch working on odds and ends for the next few days.

The time at the ranch was almost perfect.

I'd made some amends with my father, and he entertained us nightly with grand stories that he told everyone he'd made up on the fly. I knew they usually had a basis in truth often because I'd been involved myself, but my father changed himself from the bad guy to the good and seemed to make the story work. Lots of Robin Hood type stories it seemed. Arthur stayed around, and we practiced shooting rifles almost daily; he was getting quite good with that big cannon of his. Travis kept to himself mostly, talking only to my father and Bo on occasion. He generally stayed busy, but in his free time I noticed him learning how to read with Bo's help. I caught him several times drawing letters and words in the dirt with a stick. The gun slinger would hastily smear them away and walk off nonchalantly. But I made sure I left some of my easier books in the bunkhouse for him to find.

Arthur and Charles really hit it off. The British butler had indeed used an earlier version of Arthur's Martini-Henry rifle, and this morning, they'd gone off hunting for some mule deer to supplement our food supplies with fresh meat.

Skyla and Morgan had taken Elizabeth into town with Bo. It was her first trip away from the ranch since she'd been shot. The matriarch of the Stratten family had thinly concealed contempt for me and was eager to go back to Granite Falls and get a hotel room. Morgan would take her back East the following day. Although I would be willing to bet staying out West would do wonders for her health, she couldn't stand the notion of staying longer than possible.

It sounds bad, but with Elizabeth gone, it was like a gloomy fog had moved away from my ranch. For such a good man, I've no idea how Morgan put up with her like he did.

And then Travis, he was sent into town yesterday by my father, to discretely dig up whatever information he could about Reydan's whereabouts and plans.

That left just me and my old man that morning at the ranch.

The morning when trouble visited me again.

The rider appeared again, as Bo had said he would. Every day for almost a week now, without fail, he'd ride within sight of the ranch, sit for a bit then leave. Only to return again the next. Never at the same time, but slowly, methodically, he'd been keeping watch on my ranch and wanted us to know it while keeping himself unknown.

"There he is, Orville," Father told me, nodding his head towards the open fields in front of the house.

"Don't call me that," I reminded him for the hundredth time.

He ignored me. "He's just sitting out there, watching us. See that? The glimmer of light? He's got a telescope."

I nodded and stood up from the rocking chair. "Well, he ain't the only one. There's one in my chest in the house. If you want, you can watch." I stepped off the porch towards the barn and corral where Carbine waited.

"What are you going to do?" he called after me.

"Whatever I have to. But this mystery shit ends today."

The rider stayed in place as I rode closer. I could tell he was watching me through the glass, and since he'd ridden off every time anyone else approached, he must have been waiting for me.

That was a bad sign. I glanced down at my Colts. They were both riding loose in their holsters and ready for a fast draw.

I sighed. It had been a rather nice morning so far.

The telescope the rider was using lowered, and I recognized the face. Gritting my teeth, I felt my hands clench tighter on the reigns.

Simon.

The damned bounty hunter.

Slowing Carbine to a stop a couple paces away, I stared at him, waiting for the man to speak.

He glared back, and I could see the fading black bruises around his eyes from where I'd smashed his nose in with the heel of my boot.

"Jedidiah Huckleberry Smith…" he said my name slowly with a sneer.

I squinted at him from beneath my hat. "You're on my land. Get off it or be buried here."

He laughed with an almost evil chuckle. "The big heart-eating hero of Granite Falls… you're not going to do nothing. You're a goody goody. A goody little two shoes. A man who sticks up for what's right, whether it's a town under attack or a cheap saloon whore who can't take a punch. You're a sucker for doing what's right. That makes you weak."

I stared at him silently, waiting to see where this was leading.

Nudging his horse, he moved closer to me. Carbine didn't like that, and side stepped away from him.

"I'm going to hurt you, Jed," he snarled.

"That a fact?"

"Yes. See, I've been watching your place for a while now." He dipped his head towards my ranch house. "I know who is here. I know who isn't. I know your hired hands' routine. And I know what you have in that barn. Them little dinosaurs." He grinned wickedly. "I'm going to kill you, but before I do, I'm going to kill your hired hands. I'm going to shoot your cattle. I'm going to burn your barn down with all those dinosaurs in it, and I'm going to find that little lady of yours and-"

My bullet hit him in the throat.

He jerked away from me, his hat falling off his head, and revealing wide shocked eyes. Blood dribbled from his mouth as he coughed weakly.

I held my Colt Peacemaker at waist level, still pointed at him. It was all I could do to retain the rage and fury that'd suddenly boiled up inside me like a roaring fire of righteousness.

Shooting him wasn't enough. I wanted to physically attack him for threatening Skyla. I wanted to rip his heart out like I did that ape and eat it. I wanted him to suffer.

Instead, I sat on Carbine and watched the man slowly topple off his horse and die.

I guess I'd finally grown some self-control.

***

"Who was he?" Father asked as I rode back to the house, leading Simon's horse with its master's body strapped across the saddle.

"An asshole."

He closed the extended telescope and set it down gently on the porch decking. "I thought you weren't big on killing."

"I'm not," I snapped back.

"Then what's the story with him?" He gestured with the telescope at the body strapped to the horse.

"He threatened Skyla."

"Oh." He put his hands on his hips. "What do we do with him?"

"Shovel and shut up. No one needs to ever know."

"What about the horse?" Father looked the mount over. "Good looking beast."

"Once we bury the body, we turn him loose. He'll find his own way. Maybe the Indians get him, maybe a dinosaur, maybe he finds his way home. Either way, we clean our tracks. Nothing tying us to Simon."

"The horse's name is Simon?"

"No. How would I know what the horse's name is?" I jerked a thumb at the corpse. "That's Simon."

"Well. Sounds just like the good old days. Making bad people disappear. We were good at that." He eyeballed me. "Speaking of which, you kill the Sheriff?"

"Yes."

Gene glared angrily. "Well, you did a piss poor job of it. What were you thinking? Taking the risk of walking him out onto the prairie and killing him like that? You could have easily been seen."

"Oh, and I suppose you'd have done it better?"

"He'd have woken up with a slit throat and the world a better place with me walking away clean and no one the wiser. But taking him out in his underwear, while I'm certain that was a fitting means to an end, I raised you better than that."

I jerked the hat off my head and slapped it against my thigh angrily. "Raised me? You raised me better than that? You asshole, you tried to have me killed a month ago! And now you stand there telling me that I didn't kill someone well enough to meet your high standards. Screw you!"

My father jumped forward off the porch, grabbed me by the leg, and pushed me over the side of Carbine.

134

Hitting the packed ground like a sack of potatoes, I swore and leapt to my feet.

The horses were going nuts. Carbine was trying to get away from Simon's horse but was lashed to his saddle. Both weren't happy with the direction things were going between we two humans.

And neither was I.

Throwing caution to the wind, I charged my old man.

Stepping aside, he grabbed me by the waist and added to my momentum, driving me directly into one of the poles holding the porch roof up.

The roof shook and I fell.

This time I didn't bother to get up. I just sat there, sprawled out against the edge of the porch, dirt all over my pants and shirt, and with Carbine watching me in confusion.

"You done?"

I rubbed the spot on my head that'd hit the pole. "Yes, sir," I said begrudgingly.

"Good. Now, if you want to bond or something silly like that, we can do it while we bury that man you shot before Skyla gets back."

"Fine," I sighed. "Shovel is in the barn."

***

By the time Skyla and Bo returned, Simon was buried, his horse run off my land, and what money the bounty hunter had was safely tucked away in my father's pockets.

I guess we were certainly alike in that regard. We didn't mind taking from the dead.

Bo pulled the brake on the wagon and helped Skyla down.

"Any trouble?" I asked.

"No," Bo said, "lots of excitement about Prehistoria being opened to homesteading though. All sorts of schemers in town."

"The bullets you ordered were in too," Skyla gestured at a large sack in the back of the wagon. "We picked them up."

"Oh, good. Might need them." I patted the *Eighty-Six*.

"I guess tomorrow is the big day, right? Back to Prehistoria?" my father asked. He already knew but seemed to be interested in making some small talk with Skyla.

"It is," she smiled at him. "Will you be alright alone here?"

"I've got Bo and Travis to keep me company. And Orv... Jed... has a decent book collection to keep me occupied for a bit."

"What will you do?"

He smiled at her conspiringly. "Ma'am, I am going to kill Reydan and get my adopted son back. I don't know how or when, but soon."

Skyla frowned. "I think you should leave it alone."

I scuffed my boot against the ground in frustration. "Skyla... Reydan sent raiders to kill us all because of what I know about his past. There ain't no making peace with him. And he doesn't deserve a lick of peace anyways."

"Besides," Gene reached out and touched her shoulder. "We have an advantage we'll be taking."

"What's that?" she asked.

"He doesn't know about me or Travis. He'll never see us coming."

"What about Cato?"

"I'll figure out a way to talk some sense into him."

"Well," she looked at him hesitantly. "Good luck, I suppose?"

He surprised her by reaching out and enveloping her in a bear hug. "Thank you. And thank you for watching over Jed."

She hugged him back. "You're welcome," she whispered.

Bo picked up the shovel from where we'd left it resting against the house. He looked at the fresh dirt on it, raised an eyebrow towards us, then walked across the yard and took it into the barn.

"Here comes Arthur and Charles," Father said while pointing towards the wagon trail. "And they've got fresh meat from the looks of things."

"We'll eat good tonight," I said. "And tomorrow... we take the train for Whitesberg."

***

"These damn Indians have been waiting most of the day for you. They keep eyeballing us funny, especially that one on the trike."

"Oh, that's Squatting Bull, he won't bother you. He likes white people," I lied to him as we waited to board the train at Fort York. Even though it was doubted that many apes were left on our side, a large palisade had been hastily erected around the Fort in all directions with several Gatlings mounted at the corners. Just in case.

"Yeah, well..." the soldier looked uncomfortable still. "I'll be glad when they're gone. White and red men don't mix."

"We have been killing the hell out of each other for some time now," Fredrick admitted as he waved at the Shaynees. A few halfheartedly waved back while the others ignored him. The famous hunter smirked. "Yeah, they don't care for us much. But I'd rather fight with them then against 'em."

"Still, Indians riding on a train instead of attacking it? Who ever heard of such a thing!"

I patted the soldier on the back. "I'd worry more about fitting Horny Devil on that flat railcar."

"Yes, sir." He bobbed his head and ran back to help the other soldiers push the trike into place. The triceratops didn't want to get on the train, he was fighting like hell every time Squatting Bull tried to ride him up the ramp onto the specially designed and sturdily reinforced railcar that was supposed to be used to haul Wade's dinosaurs for his show. All the other Shaynee braves were already on the train, leaning out windows and hooting and hollering as the men struggled with Horny Devil.

"We're getting nowhere," Fredrick lamented.

I grabbed the closest soldier, making sure he was a Private. "Where can I find some whiskey?"

"Sir, we're not allowed to have any in the Fort."

"Just the same, I'm paying triple the usual price for a bottle. Ask around for me, would you? Discretely and quickly?"

The Private took off at a jog, and soon we had three full bottles of rot gut whiskey. Holding them under my arms, I walked towards where Horny Devil was bellowing and standing firm as a half dozen soldiers tried pushing and pulling him aboard the flat car.

"You aren't doing what I think you're doing?" Fredrick asked, taking a pair of the bottles from me so I wouldn't drop them.

"Doesn't hurt to try," I shouted at the group sweating in the cool air. "Hey! Hold up there a moment!"

Pulling the cork out of the bottle with my teeth, I poured a bit on my hand and smeared it on the trike's beak.

"What you do, Huck Berry?" Squatting Bull shouted at me.

"Trying something new, cause your way ain't working."

The beast's thick tongue slapped around, tasting the whiskey. The triceratops tail swung back and forth, knocking over a couple of soldiers who were watching me with puzzled looks on their faces.

Tipping the brown bottle up, I slipped the opening into Horny Devil's mouth and let the trike slurp it up as fast as it poured. The bottle drained quickly, and the dinosaur nudged its beak against me for more.

"Well, look at that." I grinned up at the young Shaynee on the back of the trike. "He drinks firewater like an Indian."

Squatting Bull scowled.

I quickly poured the other bottles into the beaked maw of the dinosaur.

"What now?" Fredrick whispered.

"I guess give it some time to get woozy and hope I didn't kill it," I whispered back.

That didn't take too long. After about twenty minutes, the beast let out a horrible belch and started to look a bit glassy eyed.

"Push away, gentlemen!" I called out to the soldiers warming themselves by a small fire. Begrudgingly they got up, and with some gentle coaxing by Squatting Bull, they managed to load the beast into the specialized railcar moments before the trike staggered and lay down.

"Let's hope he wakes up when we get there."

"You ever been to Whitesberg?" Fredrick asked.

"Nope, although from what I hear it's pretty impressive to see. Hey, look who it is."

Skyla was quickly walking in our direction with Fredrick, Charles, and Arthur in tow. She beamed with excitement.

"The horses are loaded," Charles said.

"Carbine give you any trouble?"

Skyla slipped her arm around mine. "Of course not."

Charles nodded at the trike. "Is that beast dead or sleeping?"

"It got a little woozy," Fredrick gave me a wink.

"And was having a hard time standing up," I said with a straight face.

"Why would it…" Skyla noticed the row of brown and clear bottles on the ground, her eyes went wide. "You gave it WHISKEY?!" She shouted, throwing her hands in the air. Charles laughed.

"It worked!" I tried to justify myself.

"Yeah, but we've no idea what it could do…"

"A splendid idea!" Arthur said.

"Good morning, Governor!" Captain Hawney approached us on horseback.

I looked around for Governor Hale, wondering why the Wyoming Governor would be here. "I haven't seen him."

"He's not with us," Skyla said at the same time.

Fredrick blushed from behind his spectacles and called back, "Good morning, Captain."

"What the-" I looked at him in surprise. "YOU'RE the new Governor?"

"That's right," Hawney said with a twisted smile. "You both are talking to the newly appointed Governor of Prehistoria."

"Only until elections can be held," Fredrick added.

Skyla grabbed him by the arm. "Why didn't you tell us?"

"We were busy with the trike!"

"Elections? Are there already that many people in Whitesberg?" Arthur asked curiously.

"Mainly just workers. The town is being built and established first, then we're going to open the area up for homesteading and such."

"What about all the dinosaurs and apes?" Skyla exclaimed.

"With the defeat of the ape army, we can't keep Prehistoria to ourselves. We must allow civilians access to the other side. There are risks, lots and lots of risks that we will be making known to all homesteaders, but we can't hold them back any longer. The petitions to Congress have grown too powerful and numerous, and Reydan White's father is pushing the Senate hard to pass the law. It's all but a done deal."

"That will fill his son's pockets nicely. He has the only railroad to the other side," Charles muttered.

"When?" I asked, looking at Skyla. Her eyes were still wide, and I could tell she was thinking about all the implications.

"Probably a month," Governor Fredrick von Holsak admitted.

"It will be fine. We'll take Prehistoria one way or another," Captain Hawney growled as he kicked over one of the empty whiskey bottles. "Hey! Private! Clean this mess up!" he shouted at the same soldier who I'd asked to find me whiskey.

"I guess you won't be coming with us?" I asked my friend and famed hunter.

"Nonsense. My new title isn't going to keep me from adventuring in an untamed prehistoric land!"

"Governor, I highly recommend that-" Hawney stuttered.

Fredrick cut him off with a wave of his hand. "It's fine, Captain."

"Good on you," Arthur grinned. "The more the merrier on this expedition!"

"Well, let's get loaded before the train leaves without us," Charles said while herding us in the direction of our railcar.

***

I'd never traveled to the west of the valley the Shimmer overlooked so it was all new country for me, and I stayed glued to the passenger car window for much of the ride. The freshly laid train tracks were smooth and even, and I wondered how many people had been eaten to lay them.

Skyla rested her head on my shoulder, watching the outside pass us by slowly as the train burned coal and crept up a particularly steep grade. Being a gentleman, I was sitting by the window with her on the inside to protect her from anything that might try to come in. Being not a fool, I had my rifle sitting upright between my legs and my sawed-off shotgun laying across my lap.

The other passengers were mostly a rough bunch. Loggers from what I could tell, brought in from the towering redwood forests of California to help drop the monstrous trees of Prehistoria and shape them into usefulness. There were a half dozen Pinkertons who appeared to be riding guard duty, and a couple of businessmen in dark suits and hats with carpet bags. Everyone was armed, and for good reason.

Our passenger car showed signs of having traveled this route before. There were jagged rips and tears in the siding from unknown beasts with more than a few fired cartridge shells rolling around underfoot. But there were no signs of blood inside the car, so that was a good omen. Almost as soon as we crossed through the Shimmer about a dozen good-sized pterodactyls landed on the top and rode along for a few miles. That explained the large amounts of poop on the roof and sides and the horrible fish odor that assaulted our nostrils.

We crossed through an opening in the prehistoric forest, full of beautiful flowers, colorful ferns, and a pair of allosauruses with bloodied snouts ripping chunks and strands of flesh off the underside of a bone armored ankylosaurus.

"Beautiful," Skyla murmured. "Maybe a breeding pair? We don't know their social structure yet; I'd love to watch them for a while."

I rubbed the claw hanging from my neck absently as I watched the long-tailed beasts with small horned ridges running from snout to the top of their heads feast. "They look kinda peaceful, considering how vicious they can be."

"Just like people," Fredrick said as he leaned forward to get a better look.

BOOM!

Skyla and I both jumped in surprise as the largest of the pair of dinosaurs twitched, and together they raced away into the safety of the trees.

Charles had risen half out of his seat, nickel plated Schofield in hand, looking around wildly for an enemy to engage.

"Got him," laughed one of the Pinkertons as he racked another cartridge into his rifle's chamber. The badged detective next to him slapped him on the back in congratulations while the one across shrugged. "Yeah, but he ran off. No kill, no point," he thumbed towards the side of the passenger car next to them.

Leaning over, I saw chalked marks on the wall with several crossed out to indicate five.

"Playing games, are we?" I called out to them.

"Jed, leave it be," Skyla whispered while tugging at my arm.

"What's it to you, Newspaper Boy?" the Pinkerton who'd fired the rifle sneered. One of the detectives laughed while the other looked worried. I knew that damned newspaper article about me would lead to trouble and here it was.

"Can't now," I told her. I'd been insulted and this was still the West, even if it was the New West. Honor had to be defended.

"I can put a stop to it," Fredrick said.

"Don't you dare," I told him as I stood and handed the shotgun to Skyla. Charles sat down, but I noticed he kept his pistol at the ready. We'd already had several run ins with Pinkertons, but I knew the Stratten family butler wasn't about to engage in a gun fight with Skyla sitting across from him unless absolutely necessary.

The detective grunted, laid his rifle aside, and got up. Passing his coat and hat to his fellow detectives, he moved to the center of the aisle. Several loggers shifted in their seats to make more room in the middle of the rail car. Loud whispers seemed to fill the room, and you could almost feel the excitement in the air at the prospect of a fist fight in the narrow confines of a train.

The badge on the Pinkerton's hips glimmered in the sunlight streaming through the open windows. I rolled my shoulders to loosen up. This fight would need to be ended as quickly as possible. This was a small space, a fight would be nasty, plus I didn't want to lose.

Facing each other, we raised our fists and stalked down the aisle towards each other.

Arrows whistled through the windows, striking flesh, seats, the floor, and my opponent.

He howled as an obsidian-tipped arrow ripped through his shoulder.

Skyla screamed and I heard both barrels of the shotgun fire behind me.

"Apes!" a Pinkerton cried out while ducking down behind a window.

The loggers sprang into action, and before I could get back to my seat and my rifle, the railcar erupted in a barrage of gunfire.

"Holy shit!" I cried while cringing at the assault on my ears. Fredrick was firing his Winchester out the window so fast that I doubted he was hitting anything.

Grabbing my rifle, I jacked a round in the chamber and leaned towards the window to find a target.

Nothing.

The firing faded off around me.

My front sight weaved back and forth as I moved the barrel around, looking for something to shoot.

"Where's the apes?" Arthur asked in disbelief.

The wounded detective was pressing a bandana around the arrow piercing his shoulder. "They hit us like that sometimes, out of nowhere. Just fire a bunch of arrows and chuck some spears and that's it. We usually don't see them."

"Did you see them, Skyla?" Charles asked.

"I saw one. He was sitting in a tree with a bow." She rubbed her shoulder. "I don't think I hit him though, he was too far away. Jed's shotgun was just what I had my hands on at the time."

Taking the sawed-off shotgun, I wrapped my arm around her shoulder and kissed the top of her head. "You did good."

"Well, looks like the apes saved you from a fight," Charles muttered.

"More like a beating," I whispered to her and Fredrick while breaking open the shotgun and replacing the two fired shells with new ones. "You couldn't see it, but he had some mighty scarred up knuckles and a crooked nose. That detective isn't just an asshole, he's a brawler."

The Brit shook his head, "You'll never learn, Jed."

***

The rest of the ride went without incident, we did see several other dinosaurs, mostly those large flightless brown birds that seemed to be all over the place around here. The detectives left them alone while they tended to their wounded companion.

Then, steaming around a curve, we came upon Whitesberg.

We couldn't see the town at first, just a monstrous wall being built of prehistoric tree trunks. All manner of ropes, rigging, and sweat was being used to maneuver what I guessed was at least twenty-foot-tall trunks into place. The top of them were even chopped to a nearly identical height and ended with a sharpened point.

"Ain't that something?" I leaned out the window to get a better look. The town's wall had a damn portcullis for the train to enter under. Jagged iron points were at the bottom, set to sink into the ground when lowered to prevent the heavy gate from being pushed open with brute force. In the old days of Europe, they used battering rams and fire.

"It's like a castle wall. But made of wood instead of stone," Skyla gushed.

"Look at the top, there's a scaffold of some sort," Fredrick pointed a finger.

Craning my neck to look up through the car window, I could tell he was right. There were people walking along the top of the wall. Not only that, but I could see several openings that had what I assumed were cannon barrels pointing out.

"How'd he get all this built so fast?" I wondered out loud.

A logger behind me leaned forward, close enough I could smell the stench of stale sweat and chewing tobacco. "They've been working around the clock for a couple weeks now. Got about a hundred men working on that wall. Another hundred or so inside starting to put up buildings and such." He spat a glob of brown liquid out the window. "No expense spared. That's what the foremen keep saying. They pay good but work us like dogs day and night. Of course, they lost a lot of men when they first started to see dinosaurs. Now most of the beasts know to stay clear of Whitesberg... the Pinkertons will shoot them up if they see 'em."

"What about apes?" Fredrick asked.

"No. No apes out here by the coast. Don't know why..." The man leaned back, and I took a deep breath of clean air free from his stench. I'd gone a while without bathing before, but never by choice. If this fella slipped into a tub, the water would probably turn to sludge.

The train chugged under the portcullis, and we saw the town. It was big and situated at the top of a hill. For once someone finally took the high ground. I guessed the town was about the size of Granite Falls, but about half encircled with the wall. The portion remaining to be built faced the sandy shores of a sea covered by several Gatlings and cannon emplacements.

"Makes sense," Fredrick nudged me. "By building the other side of the wall first, any attacking forces would have to attack through sand, I'd say that'd be rough on dinosaurs and apes alike. Should slow them down a good bit so you can lay heavy fire into them."

"Quite the tactics for a 'Quartermaster' huh?"

"Reydan said he was a quartermaster?" Arthur asked as he peered out the window in awe.

"Yeah."

"He could have someone advising him who knows what they are doing," Arthur suggested.

"No, he knows what he's doing," I growled. "He's showing the world that he has the power and resources to pull off domesticating Prehistoria. He means to stamp his name on this side forever."

"Not much you can do about that, Jed," Charles muttered as the train began to slow.

I grunted and felt my face twist into something of a sideways smile. I wouldn't be doing something about it, my old man would be. Reydan's days were numbered.

The train rolled into an unloading platform. There was no station yet, just a heavy-duty walkway for unloading cargo and animals with several unevenly spaced canvas sheets spread out overhead to keep the blazing sun off any workers waiting for something to do.

The wounded Pinkerton was first to depart the train, followed by the loggers and businessmen as we collected our bags from beneath the seats and grabbed up our various weapons.

Walking down the aisle behind Skyla, I glanced out the window and saw a familiar face. "Well, look who it is."

Fredrick adjusted the spectacles on his nose and groaned in recognition. "Oscar. How is that little fella still alive? The odds must be against it out here."

"I thought he was with the Shayana stealing gold?" Charles growled dangerously. The Brit hated Oscar, more than any of us it seemed.

The fat, pompous little man was wearing his typical black suit and hat and looking very annoyed as he paced back and forth along the boardwalk.

Stepping down the railcar's steps, Skyla waved at him, and the former paleontologist huffed over. Charles looked disgustingly at the little man.

"It's about time," Oscar pointed at the passenger car behind ours. "I've been standing out here ever since the train came in."

"What is it, Oscar?" I shoved past him, heading towards the cattle car containing our horses. The Shaynee were already off the train and gathered around the car containing Horny Devil. The trike was beginning to show signs of sleeping off a drunk stupor as he shook his horns and bellowed loudly.

"They're waiting!" he practically shouted then gestured toward the few buildings that'd been built already. Around them were a half dozen partially completed in various forms.

"Who is waiting?" Skyla asked as she followed me with Fredrick.

"Colonel Carver and the others!"

I stopped abruptly. "Now? They can't wait until we get our gear and horses situated first?"

"No! It's time. The train was late."

"Fine." I jammed my fingers in my mouth and whistled loudly to get Otto's attention. He trotted over, his decorated rifle bouncing off his back and gleaming in the sunlight.

"Otto, time to talk with the Colonel."

"White man always talk," he sneered and·pounded a fist against his chest. "Shaynee do."

"Well, you can listen to what he has to say or stay here."

"I come."

"Good. Skyla, Fredrick, you ready?"

"I'd rather check on Smoke first, but I guess I am," she said, looking worriedly towards the car containing our horses. There were a few arrows embedded in the side of the car.

Fredrick patted her back. "You all go on. Arthur and I'll get the horses situated and catch up later."

"Yes, the horses should be fine. They were inside cattle cars, unlikely to have been hit by any stray arrows," Arthur ducked, swinging his hat at a rather large, winged insect. "But we'll check on them."

"Alright, Arthur. Appreciate it," Charles said.

Oscar was already walking away at a furious side to side wobble. Stretching my legs out, we hurried to catch up. "Seems a bit lowly work for a prestigious new Governor!" I teased over my shoulder towards the famed hunter making his way to the horse car.

"Shuddup!" Fredrick called back.

***

We ended up waiting on Fredrick anyways, because apparently you can't have an expedition in Prehistoria without the new Governor being in on the planning.

"Where's Arthur?" I asked the hunter as he came into the future 'Turner's Trade and Goods' store. I only knew the name of this building because there was a wooden sign lying across some sawhorses outside being painted blue and white. Turners was only framed without siding, but there was a roof, so we were thankfully out of the sun with a gentle salty breeze blowing in from the ocean to keep us cool.

Fredrick shifted his spectacles on the bridge of his nose and jerked a thumb pointed outside. "Feeding the horses at the stables. Jed, I tell you, Carbine is as sweet of a horse as a man could get. I don't understand why you think he's so terrible."

I ground my teeth in frustration. That damned horse would be the death of me.

"Alright, lady and gentlemen. Here's the plan," Colonel Carver unrolled a map across the hastily built table that looked like it was made from scrap lumber.

I leaned forward to get a better look.

The officer pointed at an area on the map, by the edge of the sea. "The scouts have gone as far as here with no sign of any axemen. Henon tells us it's further down the coast, about two more days by horse. According to the Shayana, there aren't any ape villages west of the Shimmer. Apparently," the officer grinned wickedly, "the axemen keep them away. Whoever these axe people are, be careful. If the apes are afraid of them, they can be a powerful ally... or enemy. Once we make contact, let us keep on their good side if we can."

"How big of a settlement are we talking about?" Charles asked.

"Big," he motioned to where my favorite Shayana was sitting on a bench outside the building, staring in fascination at the vast amount of construction going on around him. "Henon says it's a big circular village, walled the entire way around with several entrances over a big moat, backed up against a river that leads into the ocean. He says it has many houses inside, rounded wood ones, like he'd never seen before. Probably a thousand people or more."

"Interesting," Skyla murmured, tapping her finger against the table.

"What is, Miss Stratten?" Colonel Carver looked up from the map to the paleontologist across from him.

"Well…" she took a deep breath and closed her eyes for a moment before continuing. "We've discovered, basically, American Indians and settlers from old England. Obviously, Prehistoria has multiple entrance points like our Shimmer. Or had them. Other Shimmers that lead to different time periods in our own history. So, these axemen, most likely, are from a civilization in our past."

Carver wiped sweat from his brow with the back of his hand. "Yes… The military has come to the same conclusion."

"So… Vikings?" Fredrick raised an eyebrow from behind his spectacles.

"That's what I've been thinking," I stuck my thumbs in behind my gun belt. "Axes… Men… Vikings seems like the logical conclusion."

"Oh, how fascinating!" Oscar exclaimed, eagerly leaning forward to get a better look at the map.

"Vikin?" Otto tried to pronounce the word.

"Vikings," I corrected him, then explained. "Big fierce warriors. You'll like them. They kill people and take their stuff."

My blood brother grinned. "Shaynee same as Vikin."

"Viking. Vik… Ing. It's, oh never mind," Oscar shook his head in disgust. "Heathens," he mumbled.

Colonel Carver coughed to get our attention back to him. "As I was saying. This will be a quick and easy, relatively speaking, expedition. No apes trying to kill you, just Prehistoria."

"Should we be worried that these axemen haven't tried to contact us yet?"

"Henon says they tend to be distrusting of outsiders and prefer to keep to themselves unless trading."

"What do they trade?" Skyla asked.

"Weapons, tools, fish, and such."

I rubbed the dark stubble on my chin. "Henon coming?"

"Yes."

Fredrick leaned forward over the map. "How many men are going with us?"

"You're it."

"What do you mean… you're it?" I asked, as we all began looking around in bewilderment.

"Mr. White has convinced me that we need to keep our manpower here at Whitesberg to protect it while the defenses are being built," Carver said.

"Excuse me, but what the hell, Colonel?" Fredrick growled. "Seven civilians? Through the most dangerous territory in the world?"

Carver straightened and glared at the Governor. "You'll be fine. There are no apes, it's just a few days, and you're heavily armed."

"Weak White Man not armed," Otto said, pointing at Oscar who scowled back.

I stepped into Oscar's personal space and stared down at him. "Did Reydan tell you about this?"

He had the decency to blush a little, but the former scientist didn't budge an inch. "No. But I'm sure my employer has his reasons. I am valuable to him."

"Sir, what about the Shaynee braves?" Skyla asked.

"They stay here."

"No. Shaynee go with Huck Berry," Otto stated flatly while pointing at me. "We no work with soldiers or pink men."

Carver was silent for a moment before nodding abruptly. "That's fine. Probably save us some trouble anyways. Governor, you are of course more than welcome to stay here and help oversee your territory."

Fredrick straightened, "Nonsense, until settlers are allowed into Prehistoria, my job is moot."

"Very well, sir. I wish you all the best of luck. You leave tomorrow." Colonel Carver nodded abruptly, rolled his map, and walked away.

We all stood silent, looking at each other in amazement while in the background coarse shouts, hammering, and yelling filled the air from the workers around us.

"I feel like we've been summoned, then kicked out into the wilderness," I finally said.

"I believe Reydan is making a move to get rid of you and any undesirables, Jed," Charles said while looking at Skyla worriedly.

"That's my boss you're talking about," Oscar whined. But I could tell from the way his eyes darted about, he was worried. The last expedition we went on, we lost almost everyone and barely escaped with our lives thanks to the Shayana. This time, we'd be on our own.

"It's not too late to back out," I said. "No one is making us do this."

Skyla kicked at a pile of sawdust under the table. I could tell she had something to say but was being mum about it.

"What is it, dear?"

"I want to go. I want to see these axemen, or Vikings, or whoever they may be. I want to see a lost culture, trapped on this side." She looked up, her face set. "And I want to be the first to do it."

Charles frowned at her. I was certain that he was thinking this was not what Skyla's father agreed to when he let his daughter cross the Shimmer, because it's what I was thinking.

I turned to Otto. "You don't have to come. You can take your braves and Horny Devil back home."

"Shaynee must go. Must do as government say, or our peoples' days will be few."

Fredrick shook his head in frustration. "You can come settle when it's open to everyone, I'm Governor and I'll see to that. No need to fight for the white man."

The Shaynee shrugged indifferently. "I go with blood brother. See Vikin. Scalp apes. Get many wives."

"Sounds fun," I admitted.

Skyla slapped my arm with a playful glare.

"Fun except for the multiple wives part I mean…" I felt a blush creep up my neck.

Otto laughed at my embarrassment.

"Sounds like we're all in. Except for Oscar who doesn't have a choice," Fredrick chuckled. "I reckon tomorrow we'll be stepping off on yet another grand adventure. Might as well get some sleep."

***

It was too early to turn in, so while Otto was checking on his braves and mounts, Skyla and I went for a walk with the new Governor to see what this Whitesberg place was all about.

"The lots are pretty expensive since they are limited inside the wall," Fredrick told us. Then he stopped and pointed at a building whose thick wood siding was being hammered on. "Jed, I believe you know Carson Skinner."

"I should say so," I hoisted my *Eighty-Six*. "He gave me this. Why? Are you saying that's his building?"

A man stepped out from the shadows of the doorway, tall and well-built with slicked back hair that was gray and receding. High cheekbones with a mustache and goatee, he cut an imposing figure with a pistol holstered on his right side, the butt turned forward for a calvary draw.

"What do you think?" the man asked as he rested a hand against the unpainted siding.

"I bet it cost you an arm and a leg," I said as we walked towards him.

He shook his head. "That's no joke for a man who survived the War Between the States. I came near to losing a limb myself."

I cringed inwardly as I thought about how he never seemed to have a sense of humor.

Carson Skinner nodded towards Skyla. "Good evening, Miss Stratten. How is the Merwin-Hulbert treating you? I hear it has seen some use."

She patted the pistol on her hip. "It has saved me several times."

"Good, a tool should properly serve its master."

Fredrick tipped his hat towards the sun to get a better look at the building. "Good looking place, Carson. I'd heard you sold your old store and were moving out here."

"I believe this will be a good jumping off place for any settlers. Which means there'll be lots of interest in guns and ammunition." He gave a sly smile. "Of which I'll be ready and willing to sell them at exorbitant prices."

"Who else is buying lots out here?" I asked.

"It's going to be a regular town in here. We've got a bank, a saloon going in over there," he pointed at a roped off lot. "A couple of blacksmiths and wagon builders. Several general stores and trade stores. The usual stuff to start off with. Stables, hotels, etc. Oh, and they are putting in something of a port down there by the water. Ship builders, all that. Seems to be quality establishments, what with the high cost of the lot and all. It keeps the low brows out."

"Reydan's going to make a fortune off this place."

"The man plans on ruling a prehistoric empire."

Skyla glanced at me, and I knew she was thinking of my father's plans to kill him because I certainly was. With any luck, Reydan would be in the ground soon, and his blight removed from Prehistoria and everywhere else before he could strike at me or my friends again. But first, we had to survive his latest attempt to subtly kill us off with this unprotected expedition.

Carson looked out the corner of his eyes at me. "I saw you kill the Mayor of Granite Falls in a shootout."

"You were there?"

"Passing through on my way here. What'd he do to deserve such a death?"

"He sent raiders to my ranch, wounded Skyla's mother, and pissed me off."

He nodded thoughtfully. "I also heard Sheriff Beauford's body was found. Out on the prairie in his pajamas. Executed." His eyes narrowed as he faced me.

I kept my face as stoic as possible. "That ain't much of a shame."

He spat off to the side in disgust. "No. No, it ain't."

"Wait, you don't think that..." Skyla looked from me to Carson, then back again as realization dawned on her. "Jed, did you?"

"He murdered Jim."

She put a finger in my face. "That doesn't mean that you can just kill him!"

Fredrick put his hand on her shoulder and gently drew her backwards. "Skyla, Jed just did what should have been done a long time ago. Beauford was a mad dog that needed to be put down."

"You don't seem surprised," I accused the new Governor while shocked at how calm he was.

"Once I heard his body was found, it wasn't hard to put together. You came through the Shimmer before suppertime but didn't get to your ranch to be attacked by raiders until late that night." He rubbed his thick mustache thoughtfully. "That evening was also the last time anyone saw the Sheriff alive."

"You'd have made a great detective, too bad you're a politician now."

"A man who can think has many options."

Skyla pulled away from the Governor, and it was easy to tell that she was confused and unsure of what to say or do.

Carson watched us, an amused expression on his face. "Sheriff Beauford did deserve it, Skyla. He murdered Jed's friend. And he wasn't the only one that crossed Beauford and wound-up dead under mysterious circumstances. I believe that Jed did the world a favor by getting rid of him."

"Fine, you all defend him." She pointed her finger at me again. "Jedidiah Huckleberry Smith, I love you, even though I greatly disagree with you at times and the risks and actions you take."

"Yes, ma'am."

Fredrick clapped his hands. "Well, now that we got that out of the way... anything else worth looking at before we leave tomorrow, Carson?"

The tall gun salesman jerked a thumb towards the ocean. "Some dead creature washed up this morning; Skyla should find it interesting."

Skyla started walking in that direction before Carson finished talking. "Let's go!" she called over her shoulder excitedly.

I shook Carson's hand. "Good to see you, friend."

"You as well. Good luck on your expedition, keep your powder dry out there, and keep your tracks small. No telling what might decide to hunt you."

"That sounds kind of ominous," I admitted.

He frowned. "Stop using big words; the dumber people think you are, the more of an advantage you have over them."

"Yes, sir."

***

The white sand crunched under our boots while the sun beat down relentlessly. There was no shade. Just a handful of shadows shifting about from small pterodactyls circling overhead and landing to pick at unseen things in the sand. They reminded me of seagulls from the South Carolina coast. Except these little leathery birds were supposed to be extinct and would try to eat you if they could.

Skyla had already reached the dead, bloated creature and stood by a long piece of driftwood near the corpse. There were several Pinkertons standing in the shade of the massive body, and as we walked closer, a familiar shape moved from behind and into the sunlight.

"Oscar," Fredrick muttered angrily.

"I wish something would eat him already."

"That makes two of us."

"What is it, Skyla?" the Governor called out as the smell hit us. It was fishy, meaty, and smelled of rot and decay. The stench reminded me of bad seafood.

"Elasmosaurus!" she shouted happily, pointing.

Squinting, I realized that what I assumed was driftwood, was a ridiculously long neck, stretched out on the sand with a rather small head compared to the rest of it.

"Elasmos...urus," I butchered the pronunciation. "I wish they'd stop with the weird Latin names. They're hard to pronounce."

"Agreed!" Fredrick quickened his step and I stretched out mine to keep up. "Elasmos is good enough for me."

The dead beast had three flippers. The fourth was missing, along with a large circular chunk of its body near the tail. Some sort of giant bite. I wondered what beast could do such damage to a dinosaur of this size.

"So, this is a... Elasmos...ororus?"

"Elasmosaurus," Oscar declared, resting a hand against the bloated corpse. "Skyla is correct. It is a type of plesiosaur that lived during the Cretaceous period. The first fossils were originally discovered in Kansas by Army Surgeon Turner and Army Scout Comstock and gifted to a Mr. Edward Cope at the Academy of Natural Sciences in Philadelphia."

I held my hand up to slow him down. "Several questions. First off, what's a Cretaceous period? Secondly, I've never heard of this Academy before."

"It's a period of time, roughly 80 million years before you were born, and the Academy is something of a colleague and at times, competitor, of the Smithsonian," Oscar said in exasperation.

I rolled my eyes. The man was certainly knowledgeable but would have made a shit teacher with his better than thou personality.

"And it appears that Mr. Cope was right the second time he put the fossils together," Skyla said as she picked up the ridiculously small head on the ridiculously long neck and inspected it. "Originally, he had the tail and head swapped, thinking that it was impossible the creature could have a neck this long. But as you can see, the neck is long while the tail is short."

"I wonder if they are any good eating," Fredrick mused.

"Maybe fresh, but this one stinks to the heavens." I glanced at the Pinkertons. They didn't seem particularly interested in keeping an eye out, I was going to bet that they'd gotten complacent around this fancy town with its lack of savage apes nearby. One was lighting a cigarillo with a match while the other practiced flipping his knife into the side of the dead plesiosaur. Every time the blade was pulled out, there was a slight hissing noise as gases escaped from inside the bloated body and juices squirted out from the slit the blade left. The stench was growing stronger with the stab wounds.

"Barbaric," Oscar turned his nose up at the Pinkertons before he inspected the bite mark. "Skyla, look at this," he carefully reached out with both hands and pushed, then pulled on something out of my sight. After several wiggling attempts, it broke free. He held the object up. It was a large dirty white triangle with a thick pinkish bit of flesh on the bottom edge.

Skyla dropped the head into the sand and came over. Gasping, she reached out and took the triangle from him. It was bigger than her hand. "Carcharias Megladon...that's... that's impossible," she whispered.

"A what? And how?" Fredrick asked, moving closer to get a better look.

"It's a shark, anywhere from fifty to seventy feet long. Mouth big enough to swallow a person." She held the object up. It was a tooth. "With these, all around its mouth."

"What did you mean by impossible?" I asked Skyla.

Oscar shook his head and took the tooth back before answering for her. "Megladons shouldn't exist at the same time as this Elasmosaurus. Best we can tell from dating fossils, they should be millions of years apart from each other."

"Well, they ain't, and we should be millions of years apart from them according to your science," I told him while rolling my eyes. "But here we are, with a giant dead elasmos missing a flipper from an even bigger megladon."

"It's Elasmosaurus," Oscar muttered in annoyance.

"Remind me to keep out of the water." Fredrick looked down the sandy ocean beach towards a pair of pterodactyls screeching at each other. "I can swim, but I'd rather not with those beasts out there."

"Hey, what's that?" The Pinkerton detective jerked his blade out of the corpse and pointed with it towards the water.

Things were moving towards us in the water.

Lots of things judging by the small dark shadows moving under the light blue water.

Lots of things headed straight towards where we stood by the bloated body.

I looked at the sand and saw rivets of bodily juices coming out of the corpse and running into the small waves lapping at the beach.

The Pinkertons had attracted these things…whatever they may be.

I grabbed Skyla's hand and started to pull her back up the beach. "Fredrick," I warned, but the Governor already had his rifle unslung and pulled into his shoulder as he carefully backed up. Oscar quickly moved away as well, following my lead.

The first one climbed out of the water. It had a blueish silver body, the size of a whiskey barrel, moving on three sets of legs, small spikes sticking up around its shell, and a pair of nasty looking pinchers waving in front of multiple sets of eyes in its face.

It was a prehistoric crab of some sort, and it was all ugly.

One of the detectives looked at us backing away and laughed, then drew his pistol and shot the thing. The bullet thumped through its shell and the crab dropped flat. "See? There's nothing to them. Just target practice." He cocked the pistol again.

Several more crabs climbed out of the water, moving quickly towards the corpse, and the two detectives began shooting at them as well.

"There's ah… there's a lot of them, Mr. Todd," Oscar called.

"Naw, if we kill a few the rest will piss off," the Pinkerton I presumed was Todd replied.

But the crabs didn't stop. Six more came out of the water staggered in a ragged bunch. One stopped and looked like it tasted the Elasmos juices from where they trickled along the sand. It died next, with a bullet from Todd, then the others died also as the two detectives emptied their pistols into them.

These six had made it halfway up the shore before they'd all been shot.

"Damn them. They just aren't getting the message." The detective that wasn't Todd holstered his pistol and unslung his rifle. "This ought to scare them off."

Boom!

A crab thrashed, spraying sand in a frenzy as it died. But more kept coming.

We moved further away, with Oscar a dozen paces ahead of us already.

"What the-!" The detectives began to back up, firing their rifles as fast as they could work the actions. But as the crabs rapidly died on the beaches, even more took their place, steadily advancing across the bullet and dead crab pockmarked sand.

As the crabs grew closer, Todd turned to run and tripped.

One of the pinchers grabbed his boot.

BOOM!

Fredrick fired from beside me and missed. He worked the action quickly, slamming the lever and firing immediately again.

The bullet hit the crab holding Todd's boot. But Todd was already scrambling on all fours, his bare foot churning sand as he tried to rise back on his feet.

The other detective grabbed him by the arm to help.

Another crab latched a large pincher claw on Todd's leg.

There was a nasty crunch as the pincher snapped bone.

Blood squirted as the detective screamed in pain.

Todd's fellow Pinkerton flipped his rifle around and began slamming the buttstock on the face of the first crab. Greenish gray goo splattered as the shell around its face broke and crushed inward from the onslaught.

Jerking the *Eighty-Six* off my shoulder, I lined the ivory beaded front sight up on the next closest crab and dropped the hammer on it. The large bullet hit the crustacean with savage efficiency. It was like the crab turned itself inside out.

"Let's go!" I shouted. There were almost two dozen crabs rapidly scuddling across the beach. But the detective trying to pull Todd was having a hard time. The pincher was still holding firm to Todd's broken leg and the weight of the dead crab dragging across the sand was slowing them down.

Jerking the Bowie from its sheath, I ran down the beach towards them. Behind me I could hear the repeated booms as Fredrick shot at the crabs closest to the detectives. He even managed to hit a couple.

Reaching the detectives, I grabbed the pincher and began hacking at what seemed like an elbow joint. Clear fluid sprayed as I broke through the thick outer crust and into the softer tendons.

Desperation drove me to hack faster as Fredrick dropped a crab six feet away.

Any closer and I'd stand a risk of being hit by one of the Governor's bullets.

With a loud grunt and swinging with all my might, the joint severed under the thick blade. Grabbing the screaming detective under the other arm, we dragged him away as the crabs began to swarm over the Elasmosaurus, ripping and tearing off chunks of decaying flesh with pinchers and stuffing the pieces into their mouths.

***

"Thank you for saving my man's life," Detective Thompson said, offering his hand for a shake.

In the partially completed building behind us, I could hear screaming as Todd's leg was being amputated by Arthur. It was a hideous noise, born of extreme pain, and I wished the man would pass out already.

I looked down at the hand and turned to walk away, leaving it unshaken.

"Jed!"

Gritting my teeth, I turned around. The leader of the Pinkertons gave me a half apologetic smile. "I hope you aren't still sore about me drawing a pistol on you that one time. I just didn't want you to do anything foolish."

I hadn't seen the man since the evacuation of Fort Jipson, right after he wiped out an innocent ape village to rescue Fredrick and Oscar. "Don't you ever point a gun at me again," I told him through gritted teeth.

Thompson chuckled and I didn't like the way he was looking at me. It was as if he knew that he'd have to again, and that one of us would end up dead, and he didn't think it would be him.

Puzzled, I walked off to find my friends.

"Jed!" A different voice this time, too squeaky and high pitched to be Thompson's.

Slowing my brisk walk, I waited for a little man to catch up. He had greasy hair, swept off to the side of his skull and plastered down with sweat. "Jed!" The fellow shook my hand vigorously. "It's a pleasure to meet the Heart Eater of Granite Falls."

I gave him a stiff nod, annoyed but curious as to what this man wanted.

"I'm Tinker. A scout for Colonel Carver. I heard you were going to go find the axemen?"

"We are."

"Ah good, yes, well, I'm glad to have caught up with you beforehand. The Colonel thought I could give you some help with finding your way."

"Have you scouted far?"

"About a days' worth. We don't like to spend the night outside of that if we can help it," he gestured towards the wood staked wall behind us.

"We are going further than that." I turned to go.

"Hold on," he grabbed me by my arm and without thinking I jerked it out of his grasp.

"Sorry... sorry." He raised his hands innocently. "I just... there's a place you can camp on your first night that's along your path. It's got a natural corral where your horses, mules, and even that trike will be protected."

I paused. A spot like that would be helpful to know of. "I'm listening."

"I can't help you after that, but I've stayed there a couple times while scouting. There's a stream that runs out of the forest, across the sandy grass and beach and into the ocean. The water can get brackish, but usually it's drinkable."

"How do I find this stream? Just ride along the beach until I see it?"

"No, there are several of them you have to ride through to get there. Keep an eye out for a large pair of rocks with a giant chunk of driftwood lodged between them. There's a stream just on the other side of those rocks, and a decent-sized flat spot behind them that you could stay in. There's also a depression past that with some good grass for picketing mounts out of sight, a bunch of trees and junk are tangled together there, make a good place to put the horses."

"Thanks." I turned to go.

"One more thing; I recommend a fire."

"A fire?"

"Yes, sir," he bobbed his head excitedly. "Since there aren't any apes, we usually build a big fire to keep any curious dinosaurs away."

I felt my brow furrow, that went against what I'd have done. "Does that work?"

"Well..." he shrugged, "I'm still alive."

"Good point. Appreciate it, Tinker."

"Yes, sir. Stay safe!" He excitedly slicked his hair down and quickly walked away.

Strange little fellow, I thought. But it was nice of him to share that bit of information.

***

"Prehistoric crabs… who would have thought?" Charles watched the Shaynee cook several of them over small fires nearby. "Skyla, next time I go where you go. Your father would never forgive me if something happened to you."

"They just wanted the Elasmosaurus, they picked it down to a skeleton within a couple hours. Which is kind of nice, since I get to see a complete skeleton now instead of trying to put together a bunch of fossils in the proper order because they came from the field jumbled up and missing most of them," Skyla said as she sketched the finned ocean beast from memory in one of her journals.

"If that idiot detective hadn't been sticking the corpse with his knife over and over, he probably wouldn't have drawn the crabs and lost his leg," I grunted.

Otto pulled a crab leg off the fire and sucked out the meat and juices from inside.

I felt my upper lip curl; crab meat had never been a favorite of mine.

Looking in our direction, he waved the long leg at me then discarded it by tossing the severed limb over his shoulder.

We white people were a little way off from the Indians and sitting by the corrals watching Carbine and the other horses pester Horny Devil. Strangely enough they seemed to get along, with Horny Devil hopping around and shaking his horns like he was trying to play with the quicker and more nimble beasts of burden. Sir Lancelot, Charles' beautiful Arabian stallion, was even joining in on the play, and usually he was aloof from the others, as though his pedigree prevented him from having fun with more common horses.

"It's just a reminder," Arthur spoke as he scratched his initials into a board with a bent and discarded nail. "A reminder to us all to pay attention. Nowhere here is safe," he waved his arms around us. "Even when we think we are, there's still unknown threats out there."

Fredrick wiped an oiled rag down the length of his rifle barrel. The humidity here was hell on blued steel. "I still believe in shooting first… and often."

"I concur," I told him as I stuck my hand out for the rag. Carson Skinner would never forgive me if I let a spot of rust form on the *Eighty-Six*. There were already entirely too many scratches and dents in the black walnut stock.

Oscar strutted around the corner of a completed building and saw us sitting in the shade by the corral. Ducking his head under a unhung sign that read 'Whitesberg Bank', he quickly walked in our direction.

"Good evening, Skyla… and gentlemen," he said, hesitating slightly as he looked at Charles. The two had a strong distaste for each other. But then, everyone but Skyla seemed to have a distinct distaste for the former paleontologist.

"What is it, Oscar?"

"Oh nothing, I was just cornered by that Reverend from Granite Falls. He was shaking that tattered old book at me and saying my days may be numbered and some foolishness. I practically had to run to get away from him."

"Really? The Reverend is here?" I stood and looked around for my friend. He wasn't in sight. I'd have to find him later.

"You know, Oscar. It is dangerous over here," Skyla warned him with a worried look on her face as though she cared about his future wellbeing after shrugging off this mortal coil.

"Nonsense. I have you all to protect me."

Fredrick racked the lever on his Winchester and glanced into the chamber. "We may be too busy protecting ourselves, Oscar."

Skyla's former boss scoffed, "There's no major threats here. No apes. This is just a meet and greet, and Reydan is very interested in what these axemen may have to offer in form of trade."

"Ah, yes. How can they fill his pocket, that's his natural instinct. Meanwhile, Colonel Carver wants us to build an alliance with these people to fight against the apes."

"Much more noble," Oscar sneered. "I bid you all a goodnight and will see you in the morning."

"Goodnight, Oscar," Skyla said while the rest of us kind of just grunted and gave noncommitted noises. Even Arthur seemed to be put off by the man's demeanor, and he barely knew him.

"Arthur, how's that detective doing?" Skyla asked.

"Todd?" the writer and doctor looked up. "Oh, he'll be alright. He lost a lot of blood, but we managed to get some sugar water in him after he woke up."

"Tough luck," Charles said before ripping a piece of jerky off with his teeth. He waved the remaining bit of dried meat at us all. "Let that be a lesson, complacency kills. Especially when facing the unknown."

"Agreed."

***

Henon led the way out of the fort with the rest of us strung out behind in a loose column with the Shaynee and Horny Devil bringing up the rear.

Pterodactyls circled overhead as we left the safety of Whitesberg and headed into the sandy hills between the ocean shore and prehistoric forest. We had three days of travel ahead of us, so we packed light with only a few mules. Hopefully the mules wouldn't get eaten by the time we got to the axemen village.

It was slow going, but without the ape threat, Henon preferred to lead us through the open space of the sandy hills. I still didn't feel safe though and kept the *Eighty-Six* out and resting across my saddle pommel and an uneasy eye towards both the tree line and the ocean.

Fredrick and Charles apparently felt the same and kept their weapons close at hand, but the difference between those two was that Fredrick's horse carried two rifles and he had a double holster hanging from the saddle that contained a spare pair of spectacles in one pouch and another pistol in the other. He was the sort to stay armed to the teeth.

The Indians seemed indifferent. They laughed, jawed, spoke Shaynee at each other and us, and seemed uncaring of any threat or danger in the area. At first it irritated me, and then I realized they were playing brave with each other. Because at the same time, their hands never strayed far from their decorated rifles and bows.

Still, after watching one of the braves get speared to death by a stego earlier, I was more than a bit annoyed at how casual they were acting.

I pulled back on Carbine's reins, looking behind me to where Otto was. I wanted to have a talk.

Carbine surprised me by bucking, hopping sideways on stiff legs, then hurling me head over heels onto the ground.

"Ugh! You sorry son of a…" I spat sand and glared up at him. It'd been a long time since he'd done anything like that.

He glared back and side stepped, snorting.

The Shaynee braves burst out in laughter as they rode past. Otto shook his head with a frown. Oscar laughed hysterically and kept riding after the others.

"Jed? Are you okay?" My friends slowed down, and Skyla looked at me with concern.

"I'm fine," I growled. "Just my dignity and rear end hurts."

Standing, I stalked over to Carbine and grabbed his reins. Jerking his head towards me angrily, I stared into his brown eyes.

"I don't have time for this shit," I whispered to him. "You do that again, and I will shoot you and ride one of the damned mules."

Carbine snorted and jerked his head away from me. I pulled him back and glared, wondering what was wrong with my horse.

"Horse jealous," Otto grunted.

"Jealous?" Charles chuckled. "Otto's probably got a point there, Jed. Used to be just you and Carbine, now you're always with us. He probably feels like you don't give him enough attention."

I closed my eyes and shook my head, "You've got to be kidding me."

"No joke," Fredrick added. "Horses are particular." He reached behind him into one of his saddle bags and pulled out a couple of dried withered apples and handed them to me. "Try these."

Palming one, I slipped it under Carbine's muzzle, and he took it quickly. The old fruit seemed to brighten his spirits.

"Alright boy, I'll spend some more time with you, okay?" I rubbed his head.

He jerked his head up and down as if in agreement.

"Good. Now can I have a damn ride?" I growled.

He turned a little bit, as though presenting his side for me to mount.

Grabbing the pommel, I hoisted myself up. "Now that my horse's jealous rage is over, can we continue on our quest?"

Skyla winked, "Waiting on you, Heart Eater."

"Who told you that? That's the second time I've been called that," I complained.

"Everyone at Whitesberg was talking about you," Charles said. "Apparently, your legend grows."

Fredrick began to trot his horse after the Shaynees who hadn't stopped moving. "A man can't pick his nickname; he just has to hope he gets a good one."

Charles spun Sir Lancelot around, the Arabian kicking sand with his heels beautifully. "Let's go!" the Brit shouted and rode after the others.

"Great," I muttered to myself as Skyla smiled at me and we followed the others.

Just call me Jedidiah Huckleberry 'Heart Eater' Smith, I thought to myself.

That was a real mouthful.

***

Tinker had been correct.

This place was a pretty good spot to bed down for the night with our small group. The natural corral he'd spoken of was true. A great storm must have hit the shore at some point, twisting trees and debris into a thick mess. With a few hours of work in the setting sun, we managed to chop and pull with rope and horses a place big enough for the horses and mules to fit. A bit uncomfortable, but safe for the night. As for Horny Devil, Squatting Bull rode him into the forest, promising to be back at the first light.

The Shaynee brave said they'd sleep better in the trike's natural environment, with the beast to warn him should anything strange approach.

I didn't want to part with such a valuable warning maker, but we didn't have room in our makeshift corral for the beast. And I certainly didn't want it to stomp on my head while I was sleeping.

It was past dark by the time Otto slipped beside me and squatted down by the fire. Leaning close, the firelight flickered shadows across his face, giving his frown a menacing look.

"Pink men follow."

I almost dropped the cast iron pan holding Skyla's and my dinner into the fire. "Pinkertons are following us?"

The scarred Shaynee brave dipped his head in affirmation. "Runs With Dogs saw them while hunting meat. They wear the gold badges of Pink Men."

Fredrick sat upright from where he rested and cleaned one of his rifles. "Pinkertons? Dammit, Jed! Reydan sent them after us. No wonder he didn't want Colonel Carver to give us a military escort… Much easier to kill us out here and pretend it was Prehistoria that did it."

Skyla grabbed me by the arm, worry across her face.

I looked towards the tree line. "That ain't going to happen."

Oscar snored loudly and rolled over under his blanket, oblivious to the danger headed our way from his employer.

Arthur moved closer to us. "Easy, gentlemen. We don't know that for sure. I haven't even met this Reydan fellow, and he's willing to kill me?"

"Death by association," I patted his back. "Sorry, Arthur. You picked the wrong crowd to hang out with."

"Great," he said glumly while grabbing his leather rifle scabbard and pulling it closer to him.

"How far away?" I asked my blood brother.

"As white man say, maybe hour."

Charles dabbed the corners of his mouth with a handkerchief before setting his partially eaten plate down. "What's the plan, Jed?"

I looked around the moonlit landscape of the beach towards the tree line.

"Kill them and send their heads back to Reydan on a mule."

Skyla gasped and held a hand to her mouth at my savage suggestion. "Jed!"

Frowning, I sighed and rubbed my temples. Women. I'll never understand them.

I decided to compromise.

"Fine. We just kill them."

***

The fires burned bright behind us. We lay in small, shallow depressions hastily dug from the sand facing the trees while the ocean lapped against the shore in the distance behind us. This was the only direction to attack us. The rest of the area flattened out and there was no easy way to approach us which was why we picked it. So that just left the forest.

Skyla squirmed suddenly and swatted at her leg. "Ugh," she whispered. "Something was crawling on me."

"Something... prehistoric?"

"That's not funny."

I chuckled anyways. The tree line was dark, shadowed by the massive trees that towered over everything in Prehistoria. Somewhere out there were the Pinkerton Detectives. We assumed they would attack tonight, before we got too far away from Whitesberg and put them at an unnecessary risk. The problem was, we didn't know when, but this was where the scout had told us to stop for the night. If he knew about this spot, then Reydan's minions probably did as well.

I heard something. A clink. Something metal connecting with metal. The sound was faint, but it was there.

Fredrick gently kicked my boot with his.

He pointed towards the tree line on his and Charles' side.

There.

In the dark underbrush of the trees.

Something moved forward, slowly.

Another shape joined the first. Then another. And another.

The grass clumps and the sand it grew in kept their approach quiet. I counted the shapes moving towards us.

Six.

That didn't make any sense. We numbered almost two dozen. Reydan wouldn't have sent just six men after us. Even with an ambush in the middle of the night, we had a good chance of surviving against that many men.

Arthur's heavy Martini-Henry was resting beside his body, and the writer slid it forward into a firing position.

The Pinkertons approaching us suddenly dropped out of sight. I squinted down the sights of my rifle. It was as if they'd disappeared into the night.

Arthur used his elbows to prop himself up for a better look.

Fredrick jerked him back down as a Gatling gun opened fire from beneath the trees.

Pop! Pop! Pop! Pop!

Fire blossomed from multiple rotating barrels as large bullets cracked overhead and flew towards the large fires that we'd made, splashing holes in the sand.

That certainly wasn't expected.

I pressed my face deeper into the sand and locked eyes with Skyla. Hers were big and wide, and I was sure that even though I was trying to put on a brave face, mine were as well. Being downrange under a Gatling gun is not an experience to be sneered at.

Somewhere behind us, Oscar was screaming in fear and surprise.

I started chuckling even as bullets zipped by dangerously close.

We probably should have told him what we were doing instead of leaving him to sleep. But in our defense, he was already in a protected spot between a rock and a large bit of driftwood. If he didn't raise his head or try to run away, he'd be safe.

And since he was unarmed, he was kind of worthless in a fight anyways.

The Gatling stopped abruptly as ghastly screams came from the trees.

I peeked my head over the mound of sand and rocks that had been scooped in front of our position.

The dumb bastards hadn't thought about what it was like to fight Shaynee braves in the dark aided by Henon.

They'd just met the face of savagery.

The six hidden men rose and charged across the open sand towards our fires. I guess they figured our unknown was better than the horrific screams and frightful cries coming from behind them.

Jerking the *Eighty-Six* to my shoulder, I raised myself on my elbows and pulled the trigger. The firing mechanism broke like a glass rod. Perfection.

The large bullet dropped the man closest to us.

At that, Arthur fired. A man spun to the side, falling to the ground and writhing with a hoarse scream.

Then Fredrick began firing. It wasn't as fast as a Gatling, but he emptied his first rifle in a hurry into the group of men, killing at least one. Then he dropped the rifle, picked up his second, and fired at the remaining men who'd taken shelter behind several large boulders.

"Surrender!" The shout came from the Pinkertons behind the boulders.

"Like hell; you first!" Fredrick shouted back before firing again. A chunk of rock blasted off the closest boulder.

A hoarse cry came from the tree line, painful and long drawn out, it sounded inhuman.

"You hear that?" I called out. "That's the Shaynee cutting noses off your friends. Throw down your weapons or face the same fate!"

Skyla gasped and pulled a hand over her mouth while her other kept the Merwin-Hulbert pistol pointed towards the rocks. "Are they really?" she whispered in horror.

"I dunno. But that scream sounded awful," I whispered back.

"Okay. We give up, as long as you don't let the heathen Injuns have us!"

"Drop your weapons and come out with your hands raised."

Three men stepped out from behind the rocks, their hands raised high and glancing fearfully behind them. Nothing but silence came from the woods. But we all knew Otto and his braves were back there and probably hoping one of the prisoners would make a run for the trees.

"Walk towards us, slowly."

I whispered to Charles and Arthur, "Cover me."

"Yes, sir," the journalist lowered his head slightly, placing his cheek back on the stock of the Martini-Henry and aiming the barrel at the surrendering men. Charles didn't move from where he lay, except to nod his scarred face slightly.

"I'll cover you too, Jed," Fredrick said softly.

"I'd rather you didn't…" I muttered to myself while standing.

"What's that?" he asked.

"Nothing."

Moving quickly, I reached the three men. One of them was Tinker.

"You little weasel," I growled while checking them for any hidden weapons.

The Army scout dipped his head in embarrassment. "Sorry, Jed."

There was a boot knife on one of the Pinkertons. I jerked it out of his boot, tossed it aside, then slugged him in the back of the kidney with my rifle butt. The man went down with a cry of pain. "That's for hiding a knife."

I pointed the rifle barrel at them. "Start walking. Towards the fires."

"But… the others?" the third man asked, jerking his head towards the tree line without moving his raised hands while the other climbed to his feet painfully.

"I wouldn't worry about them anymore, the Shaynee got them. Now, move!"

Tinker and the two Pinkertons stumbled their way across the sand and clumps of grass to our fires. The rest of my group was waiting for them beneath a large tree that'd given us shade in the evening.

"What the hell, Jed?" Oscar screamed at me. His spectacles were missing, and his face and clothing were covered with sand. It was evident the man had tried hiding frantically.

"Shut it, Oscar!" Charles told him while pointing at the badges of the men. "They work for your boss as well, and they didn't let you in on the plan? How blind are you? Reydan doesn't care if you live or die. You've outlived your usefulness to him."

"No! No… that's impossible…. And that doesn't mean you had to leave me by myself…" the former paleontologist grumbled but took a few steps back as I marched the trio in front of the fire.

"Sit." I gestured towards a nearby log.

The three sat and I squatted down in front of them to look them over in the firelight.

Tinker was dressed the same as before, and the two other Pinkertons were wearing their usual black attire with badges on their belts. The one I'd hit in the kidneys glared. He had the wild, feral look of a man who causes trouble and gloats afterwards.

"Arthur, there's some leather strips in my saddle bags. Tie their hands, please."

The writer quickly did as I asked and then moved to stand behind me.

Charles coughed, then nodded his head slightly towards where Skyla stood. The scar along his face gave him an evil look in the firelight.

"Fredrick?" I asked. "Would you be so kind as to take Skyla and Arthur and check on Henon and our Shaynee friends? If anything, just to make sure that Otto and his braves aren't teaching Henon how to scalp."

Fredrick looked baffled but nodded slowly. "Certainly, Jed. But are you sure?"

"Absolutely." I couldn't let Skyla see me like this. I couldn't let her see who I was at times like this, when dark things had to be done for good reason. She wouldn't understand. But Charles would. He'd already seen it once before.

Skyla glanced from me to the trio of men and back again. She looked concerned but didn't say anything. And with a slight smile, she dipped her chin to me, and allowed Fredrick to gently put his arm around her and guide her towards the prehistoric woods behind us. Arthur followed them, his Martini-Henry slung over a shoulder and the Lord Elcho held in hand.

"What…what about me?" Oscar whined.

"I don't much care what you do, Oscar."

He turned and followed the others to the woods.

I waited until they were out of sight before swinging the barrel of the *Eighty-Six* towards Tinker.

"Talk."

He opened his mouth to speak. "Look, Jed. I-"

"Don't you dare!" the kidney punched Pinkerton shouted, shoving the Army scout bodily with his shoulder.

Shifting the barrel, I fired and put a bullet through the man's chest. At this distance, burning gunpowder ignited his shirt from the muzzle blast as he fell backwards without a word. Tinker and the remaining Pinkerton looked scared shitless and had a little blood splattered on them for good measure.

"I said..."

"Talk! Yes, sir. Reydan sent us." Tinker stumbled over his words, trying to get them out fast enough.

"I thought you worked for Colonel Carver."

"I did. I mean, I do. I just... Reydan offered me a lot of money to guide his men." Tinker looked at his feet in embarrassment. "And I knew where you'd be tonight," he said softly.

Charles walked around the men, and poured a little from his canteen onto the dead man's flaming shirt to put it out.

"Charles?" I dipped my head towards where our gear lay.

The Brit nodded slowly and walked over to his saddle and bags.

"What about you?" I pointed the barrel towards the surviving Pinkerton. "You got anything to say for yourself?"

The detective shook his head. He looked scared out of his wits. But I felt no sympathy; I remembered Skyla's face as the would-be ambusher's Gatling fired round after round over our heads with intent to kill us all. She was afraid. Hell, I was afraid too. And Arthur had been behind his mound of rock and sand fearfully saying prayers.

These men tried to kill us.

Charles looked up from where he crouched by his bedroll, twisting something between his hands. "You sure about this, Jed?"

I looked Tinker and then the Pinkerton in the eyes. "Yes."

The Brit stood, a noose in his hands.

"Which one first?"

"No! No! You can't do this," the Pinkerton spoke finally, raising his tied hands together in front of him in a pleading motion.

"Him." I pointed at the detective.

Charles dropped the noose over his head and cinched it tightly around his neck. The other end he hurled over a conveniently thick tree branch. The tree that gave us shade earlier would now give us another use.

"No. No. No. Please?"

I held up my hand and Charles paused.

"What would you have done if one of us had said please? What would you have done if one of us… if Skyla… had begged for her life?" I glared at him. "No. Today you die."

Charles grabbed as high on the rope as he could and jerked with his entire body weight on the end of the rope.

The detective slid backwards off the log, his legs kicking madly, bound hands grasping for the rope.

Again, Charles pulled, dropping his body towards the ground and using his body weight to lift the Pinkerton high enough so just the tips of his boots scraped against the soft sand. The detective convulsed as his body was deprived of air.

After several long minutes ticked by, the body twitched once more then stopped and swung gently from side to side. Charles let go of the rope and the dead Pinkerton collapsed in a heap with a muffled thump.

Tinker had said nothing the entire time, just staring at the ground in front of him. It was as if any flicker of hope was gone, and he'd resigned himself to death.

The Brit wordlessly removed the noose from the corpse and walked towards Tinker.

I held my hand up and Charles stopped, the noose held in both hands about to be dropped over the Scout's head.

"Tinker."

The scout looked up, hopeful.

"I'm giving you a second chance that you do not deserve... Help us find the axemen and we'll take you back to Granite Falls. There you will testify to what Reydan paid you to do."

"Yes, sir!" He nodded his head eagerly and I noted that his greasy slicked over hair had sand stuck in it.

"You won't be armed though. And you'll be bound the entire time. Just because I'm giving you a second chance doesn't mean I trust you one bit."

"You can trust me, Jed! Or not. I just… I won't let you down!" Tinker was wide eyed and seemed to fervently mean it.

"Jed…" Charles started to protest.

Leaving Tinker, I pulled the British butler to the side and out of earshot of the scout.

"What is this?" he asked. "A conscience? I thought you killed everyone who crossed you."

"I need him alive. He's proof that Reydan is a piece of shit. And I don't know about you, but I'm not ready to kill a soldier just yet."

Charles kept his eyes on Tinker's back. "He could do any number of things to hurt us, or Skyla. And you're going to trust that he won't simply because you spared his life?"

"I don't trust him for jack. I'm just using him. If he dies on this trip, so be it. That's his fate. But if he makes it back, I've good use for him."

The Brit nodded slowly and smiled slightly at me, the motion making the side of his scarred face turn upwards hideously. "Say what you want, Jed. But you aren't all bad."

"You can say that if we make it back alive. Besides, my old man is supposed to be taking care of Reydan. With luck, we'll return, and the red-haired bastard will be long dead, and we can let the law take care of Tinker."

Moments later Otto emerged from the darkness, having snuck up on us unseen. "Pink Men dead," he said simply.

I noticed a pair of freshly taken scalps hanging from his belt and jabbed a finger at them. "Don't let Captain Hawney see those, he'll cause all sorts of ruckus."

"Shaynee not fear Cap-tan." Otto lifted his head with pride.

"I know, but it's best to keep the Shaynee on our side than fight against them."

"Those are...you scalped them? The Pinkertons?!" Tinker's jaw dropped and his bound hands began to shake uncontrollably.

Charles stepped in front of the new prisoner. "I take it you've never fought against Indians before?"

"No... I just transferred out here from Massachusetts! We don't have Indians no more!"

The Brit laughed. "Seems you didn't have much schooling then."

"I can write my name!" Tinker protested.

"Shut up," I ordered the scout. "Let's get Skyla and the others and get some of that sleep that these Pinkerton bastards tried to deprive us of."

Otto dipped his head and walked back into the darkness.

Sighing, I looked for a place to put our prisoner for the night.

Coming to a decision, I grinned to myself.

Seemed to me the best place would be between two Shaynee braves with fresh bloodied scalps on their belts. That ought to keep him on good behavior for the night. And tomorrow, well, we'd worry about that when it arrived.

***

"Why aren't we turning around and confronting Reydan?" Arthur asked. The writer had taken great offense at being almost killed by the railroad tycoon's minions.

"Because we're already part of the way, and Skyla would go nuts if she didn't get to make contact with these axemen people." I couldn't tell him about my father's plans and how getting ambushed by these dirtbags didn't change them. I also didn't tell him about how Morgan Stratten was trying to get me a pardon and thought that sucking up to the US Government would help.

"It means that much to her?"

"Yes," Charles replied as he carefully guided Sir Lancelot around a pit in the sand. There was no telling what might live down there. Tinker had already warned us of foot long worm-like things that would burst out of the sand and attach themselves to you and suck your blood until you hacked them off. They sounded like prehistoric leeches, and we were all very anxious to not meet any.

"Well, why are we bringing that?" Arthur jerked a thumb behind him.

Not too far back, under the watchful eye of the Shaynee, Tinker was riding a horse and pulling a wheeled Gatling gun. At first, I couldn't believe that Reydan sent his men with a Gatling. But after riding along the sandy beach with it being wheeled behind a pair of horses, we realized just how easily it could be moved in the firm packed sand.

"You never know, we might have need for a Gatling," Fredrick replied.

"But you trust *him* with the Gatling?" Arthur's eyebrows rose questioningly.

"He can't outrun us on that horse with the gun strapped to it. And the ammunition is on that mule over there," I pointed to the one Runs With Dogs was leading. "So, it's not like he can shoot it either."

"What's that?" Skyla asked, pointing into the distance at a dark shape beached on the sand just out of high tide's reach.

Reaching into a saddle bag, I pulled out my collapsible telescope. Pulling back on the reins, I had Carbine slow to a stop and looked.

My vision kept moving as Carbine slowly took a step forward one at a time, refusing to come to a complete stop no matter how much I pulled back on the reins and swore.

Finally, I gave up and passed my telescope off to Fredrick. "You look."

"It's a boat," the Governor said in awe.

"Think it's the axemen?"

"No. It... it looks like a pirate ship."

Baffled, I stuck my fingers into my mouth and blew a loud whistle to halt the group. Otto and Squatting Bull looked back in disgust, probably thinking we white folks needed another break. Henon just shifted the sword at his waist and sat down in the sand to wait.

I dismounted and Carbine turned his head back towards me to nicker. It was as if he was laughing at me. I swatted his big head and took the telescope from Fredrick. Now, on the firm ground without an obnoxious horse making me bounce, I looked at the dark object in the distance.

Sure enough, it looked like a pirate ship. I didn't know much about boats, but through the lenses I could see that it had two tall masts with tattered sails and everything. It was short in length though, and tall, and looked like it was resting on its side somewhat with its hull exposed.

"What see, Huck Berry?"

I lowered the telescope. Otto had ridden his pony back to where I stood and was looking at the shape curiously.

"Old ship."

"What mean, ship?"

"I mean a boat. The sort that brought us whites to the Americas many years ago."

Otto grunted in disgust. "Maybe this one take whites away?"

Arthur chuckled, until he realized that my blood brother appeared to be only partially kidding.

I shook my head. "More like it brought someone to Prehistoria."

"Let's take a look," Charles said eagerly, reaching out to take the telescope from me.

"Yes, let's!" Oscar agreed, rubbing his thick hands together eagerly. No doubt he was dreaming of treasure and plunder.

"What do you think, Fredrick?" I asked.

"I think the style is a good hundred years old... but judging by the ship's condition, it hasn't been here more than a few weeks," the Governor rubbed his thick mustache thoughtfully. "It doesn't make sense."

"As Ashley says, nothing about this place makes sense," Skyla reminded us. "It may be another civilization, or from a period of time in our past... there's no telling."

"Agreed," Charles said, as he lowered my telescope. "But I do see a bunch of port holes, or whatever they are called, openings for cannons to fire through."

"Think they'll shoot at us?" Oscar asked warily.

"Only one way to find out," Fredrick told him with a grin. "Get your white flag ready, Oscar."

"Harumph," the former paleontologist crossed his arms over his chest.

"Henon!" I called to the Shayana tribesman. He stood, dusted sand off his rear end, and jogged back to us.

Squatting down, I drew an outline of the ship in the sand with the tip of my finger. "You ever see anything like this?"

The big Shayana looked at the dark shape in the distance and raised an eyebrow in curiosity. "Yes. Axemen trade with them."

"You've met them, then?" Skyla asked.

"No. They only trade with axemen. I have seen ship only from a distance, never close."

Fredrick removed his spectacles and wiped a speck of sand off them. "What do they trade?"

"Don't know."

"Well. Let's go see if anyone is home."

***

We rode forward carefully, keeping an eye on the ship for anyone or anything moving on board. There was cargo netting draped over one side, half buried in the sand by the bottom of the hull. But no footprints. Had anyone left the boat, the tracks had been long washed clean by the tide.

"Look at that!" Arthur pointed. There was a buxom woman figurehead carving on the front of the ship, her wooden chest jutting out proudly with her carved hair splayed out on either side.

"The Thirsty Wench," Skyla read from the engraving on the side of the boat. "Charming."

Fredrick grinned, "All in all... not a bad name for a ship."

"What do you think? Pirate? Merchant? Slave ship?" Oscar asked, looking up at the carved figure head.

"I reckon we'll know once we see what's inside," I told him while slipping down off the saddle.

Tying off our horses and trike, we boarded the ship by climbing the frayed and twisted rope netting. Skyla climbed beside me, both of us taking our time while the Shaynee and our Shayana guide raced to the top.

Otto whooped as he climbed over the splintered railing of the ship first and waved with his tomahawk down at us. "Hurry, Huck Berry! Much plunder to be had!" he cried.

"Who taught him the word plunder?" I wondered out loud.

"Must have been Henon. Hey, Jed, what's this?" Skyla paused and pointed at a series of large circles about the size of my hand that appeared to be cut into the sides of the ship in front of our faces. The circles went in streaks, this way and that, ending as abruptly as they began.

"I've no idea."

"Sea… monster," Oscar grunted from below me and I looked down. His face was red with exertion, and he was sweating profusely. His hat had fallen off and lay in the sand below. Without thinking, I pulled mine lower over my brow to keep it on then grabbed for the next horizontal rope piece to pull myself up.

"That makes as much sense as a pirate boat being on the beach in Prehistoria," Fredrick said as he reached the top ahead of us.

"Anything is possible here," I agreed before stopping to look behind us. Carbine was tugging at his picket knot, but the other horses were standing calmly. And most importantly, Horny Devil was laying in the sand with his legs folded under him as if he didn't have a care in the world.

Taking another step on a rope rung, I pulled myself up and found my face inches away from the large open bore of a cannon.

I ducked quickly, startled.

Nothing went boom.

Cautiously, I raised my head and peeked over the edge of the squared opening.

Darkness.

No sound. No light. Just a foul stench coming from inside that made me wonder what we'd find.

Edging around the open port hole, I climbed to the top of the ship and over the strangely crushed and splintered railing. Standing unevenly on the lop-sided deck of the boat, I reached down and helped Skyla carefully over the destroyed edge.

Oscar stuck his hand out, but I ignored it and took in the top of the ship instead. There were numerous dark stains splattered over the deck, I assumed some or most to be blood, but wasn't sure. I didn't know what ship decking was supposed to look like. But what was most fascinating, were the circular cuts continued over the crushed railings and crisscrossed the deck, stairs, and even some were imprinted into the sides of the thick masts that jutted from the middle of the front and back of the ship.

Skyla elbowed me in the side then jerked her chin towards Oscar who was straining to get his bulk over the edge.

Sighing, I reached over, grabbed the back of his coat, and jerked the former paleontologist over the rail and onto the deck where he collapsed in an exhausted and red-faced heap. "Thanks, Jed," he mumbled but I was too busy watching the Indians and Henon excitedly exploring the open deck and looking over the edge at the ocean and sand below.

Shifting the *Eighty-Six* in my hand, I moved with Skyla across the deck to what I assumed was the door to the captain's cabin. Otto was already there, trying to open it. The veins in his neck bulged as he tried to tug the door open. He gave up in a rage and kicked it uselessly.

"Let a white man try it," I told him with a sideways grin.

He scowled as I rested my rifle against the side of the cabin, dug my fingers in around the latch, and braced my right foot against the wall.

Charles gently took Skyla by the elbow and shifted her aside, then drew his nickel-plated Schofield revolver, cocked the hammer back, and nodded at me to give it a try.

With both arms straining, I pulled on the door. The latch creaked under my hands, and I feared it was going to rip off, but finally, slowly, it began to ease open.

Without warning the door swung open freely and dumped me onto my rear end.

Otto jerked his tomahawk from his belt, snarled, and leapt into the darkness as Charles twisted around the doorway with his pistol, trying to find something to shoot at.

There was a horrible screech, some Shaynee swear words being flung about in the darkness, and a god-awful ruckus that ended when Otto abruptly leapt back into the light with a scrawny starved looking cat clutched in his scratched and bleeding arms.

"What the-" Charles lifted the barrel of his gun away as his jaw dropped.

The black and white feline hissed, snarled, and dug its little claws into the scarred chest and nipples of the fierce Shaynee brave, who promptly screamed like a girl and threw the cat halfway across the ship.

True to its nature, the scrappy little beast landed on all fours and scurried up the closest mast and out of reach of any of the other braves who were too busy laughing hysterically at their leader.

Otto's dark skin blushed and he shouted something in Shaynee that was both perverse and insulting.

"That was rather unexpected," Fredrick quipped as we turned back to the cabin and peered inside the open door.

Bits and pieces of broken light shone through cracks in the walls. Charles stepped inside first, his pistol at the ready as he carefully navigated his way around the dark room. A moment later he was out of sight, and several moments after that, light flooded the room as he pushed open a shutter and wedged a stick in to hold the hinged wooden board open.

"Let there be light," Arthur said as we entered the room.

Fredrick coughed immediately and Skyla gagged while I pulled my bandana up over my nose. "That's foul," she said.

"Smells like that cat has been in here for some time." Charles pointed at the small, dried pieces of manure scattered on the planking and the unmade bunk in the corner of the room. "Watch out."

"There." I pointed at the open book that was lying near a rickety overturned table. "That must be the captain's log."

Arthur picked it up and shook it gently before turning it towards the light streaming in through the windows that Charles had opened. "It's near illegible from old water damage, but it's certainly the Thirsty Wench." He flipped through a handful of crinkled pages then paused, "Looks like the last entry is September 4th....1718."

"1718!" Fredrick grabbed the logbook from Arthur's hands and stared at the faded scribbled writing. "This ship is almost 170 years old but looks like it was just sailed a few weeks ago. Impossible! This is... this is astonishing. This ship pre-dates the American War of Independence!"

"You mean the colonial revolution of ingrates?" Charles smirked.

"Hush, you filthy Monarchist. Look here," Fredrick pointed at an entry in the crinkled pages. "They were carrying some sort of livestock. But I can't make out what it was. Bound for some place called Novagant."

"Novagant? Interesting..." Charles mused.

Skyla moved through the room, ignoring the men's banter as she looked over various objects strewn about the place. "This ship is astonishing. It's straight out of the 18th century. The Smithsonian would give anything to have it in their collection."

"No way to take it with us. But we can always gather some odds and ends on the way back to Whitesberg," I told her, my voice muffled behind the red bandana. "The Thirsty Wench looks like it's survived a few storms and lots of tide risings where it lays, I doubt it's going to float away anytime soon."

"Huck Berry." Otto stood at the cabin door beckoning me with his hand to come with him. The scratches on his scarred chest were bright red and looked painful. "You see. Below."

Arthur gently laid the logbook on a clean spot on the bunk, and we left the room, following the Shaynee leader to where Henon stood waiting above a giant hatch that'd been braced open. Oscar leaned against the hatch, a thoughtful look on his face.

"What is it, Henon?"

"Thy Thirsty Wench hauled forth a precious cargo," he pointed down into the opening.

I leaned forward, holding Skyla's arm as she did the same to keep her from falling inside the cargo hold.

"Ugh. That smells worse than the cat cabin," Skyla said as she held the crook of her arm over her face to try and block out the evil stench coming from below.

"What are they?" I asked, peering down into the darkness at the mass of corpses lying amongst piles of manure and puddles of urine. The smell was overwhelming. Even with my bandana on, it took effort to not throw up.

"Ceratopsids," Oscar said. "Of the exact species, I don't know. But judging by their size, they are juveniles, probably rounded up from their parents and brought here for some reason. We should send Tinker down there to bring one of the bodies up so we can study it."

"Why Oscar," I chuckled, glancing at where the traitor sat cross legged in the center of the lopsided deck, "What a noble suggestion."

"Hey, hey now. No, thanks. Send the damned Injuns. That isn't no job for no white man."

I gave the traitor a dark look. "I wasn't asking you, Tinker."

"Why would the crew of the Thirsty Wench have them?" Skyla asked as she kneeled to get a better look into the hold.

"Axemen," Henon said loudly from beside me.

"Were they going to eat them?" Arthur asked, a handkerchief pressed against his nose.

"No. Axemen." Henon pointed off the ship towards the open water as one of the Shaynee braves by the rail let out a surprised shout.

"Vikin! Vikin!" the cries of Shaynee warriors echoed across the Thirsty Wench as Otto's men took cover and prepared their decorated rifles and bows.

I rushed to the edge of the splintered railing and saw a trio of strange ships approaching us on the open water.

Almost in unison, the wide, sleek boats turned and moved along the coast in much shallower water than I would have thought possible. The ships all had a single mast with a furled red sail and many, many oars moving in unison. The sides also carried painted round shields, slung along the entire length of the boat and there was a carving of some sort, standing upright at the front of each that looked vaguely like a dinosaur. I saw dozens of bearded men in helmets standing in the boats staring at us as they glided past the Thirsty Wench's resting place.

Then the ships turned again, this time one boat sliding to the shore to our right and the other two boats landing on our left. The axemen's oars ran them aground at full speed, and it was incredible to see how far up onto the wet sand the ships would go.

Men detached the round shields and leapt from the sides of the boats onto the sand without even getting their leathered boots wet. They avoided our picketed horses and lone trike, which was good. I'd hate to kill a man for taking a horse as half-worthless as Carbine.

"Hold your fire! Don't shoot!" Fredrick shouted.

"Otto! Tell your braves!" I told my blood brother, but he was already yelling in Shaynee at them. Several of them looked like they were ready to start shooting, and although the axemen didn't appear to have any firearms, there were a helluva lot more of them than us.

Otto shoved one of the braves then knocked his rifle barrel down with his hand to drive home his point.

I knew if I tried that it'd start an immediate brawl with the Indians, so I let the scarred Shaynee leader do his own thing with his people. He seemed to have a good eye for which of them were quick to fire as I saw him get after several braves.

The axemen lined up in rows with their painted round shields held before them.

"Whoever they are, they are definitely Vikings," Fredrick exclaimed excitedly.

"Shouldn't they have horned helmets?" I asked, eyeballing the round metal and leather helmets they wore that certainly did not have any horns on them.

Oscar sighed. "Only in children's bedtime stories. Didn't any of you get a decent education?"

From the first row of men on the left side of the Thirsty Wench, one stepped forward, jabbed his spear into the ground, and stared at us from beneath his helmet while his body language suggested he was annoyed.

"Jarl Bjarke waits," Henon said, pointing a finger at the lone axeman.

"Someone should go talk to them," Arthur suggested, looking at me.

"Good job for Jed. He's a charming chap," Charles smirked.

"I'm thinking we send Tinker. If he dies... he dies. No big deal," I argued sarcastically.

"Oh, hell no!" the Army scout shouted in protest, raising his tied hands before him in a pleading manner. "Besides, I'm a prisoner!"

"I'll go!" Skyla exclaimed, pushing her way to the railing, her eyes wide with excitement.

"You'll do no such thing!" I told her. "I will go with Henon."

"Well, I'm going with you," my favorite paleontologist said firmly.

"No," Charles said, moving to stand in her way.

"If they are some sort of Vikings, they respect armed women... to a degree," she protested.

I slung the *Eighty-Six* over my shoulder. "Just the same, me and Henon will go."

"What if Vikin kill you?" Otto asked, his dark eyes showing a glint of humor.

"You'd better kill him back!" I waved a hand at Henon to get his attention. "Let's go."

**

The axemen, who for all reasons appeared to be Vikings, waited patiently as Henon and I climbed down the cargo netting on the ship. With no small effort, I managed to keep myself from falling several times. I've never been the most graceful of men, especially in riding boots on a rope ladder.

Walking away from a beached pirate ship, across the wet sand with a pre-Colonial Indian tribesman by my side and the gentle ocean breeze on my face towards a line of Vikings made me think about how absurd Prehistoria was. And how amazing it was at the same time. A clash of civilizations separated by thousands of miles and hundreds of years, there was no telling who or what we'd discover next.

I tucked away my thoughts and focused on the task at hand.

Oscar and Skyla had discussed Vikings several times during this trip, and I wish I had paid more attention to them. What little I'd gleaned from their talks and recalled from books during my outlaw childhood amounted to Vikings being fierce raiders, brave explorers, and hardy settlers. They were also not the sort to be trifled with. Especially if you were a Christian monk in a monastery full of gold chalices and crosses near the coast. They loved to loot those places.

I stopped a dozen feet away from the lone axeman and not knowing what to do, I gave the man a stiff nod in greeting while wondering if I could draw and shoot him before he could throw that spear of his through my chest.

Henon kept walking and clasped his hand around the man's wrist in greeting.

The bearded face of the Viking broke into a grin, and he slapped the back of the Shayana. Gesturing at me and the ship behind us, the axeman began speaking to Henon.

While they talked, I looked over the two rows of warriors behind them.

Almost all of them had beards, some twisted in braids with bits of colored string in them, others were wild and stuck out haphazardly. Many men had strange markings on their faces and arms. The round shields they carried were all painted with designs that ranged from several colors to intricately detailed paintings. And the men all carried lots, and lots of weapons. Axes, spears, swords, bows and quivers full of arrows... the Vikings were armed for battle.

I wondered if they were hunting after the Thirsty Wench.

Finally, after what seemed like a good ten minutes of conversing, Henon waved at me to come forward.

I crossed the distance between us in several long strides and studied the Viking in front of me.

The axeman was a bit shorter than me, but stout as any man I'd ever seen before. Veins and corded muscles in his bare arms showed the man's strength and he looked like he could choke out a bear in a wrestling match. He wore a shirt of chainmail with a pair of small axes strapped around his waist, and a sword sheathed across his front. His shield had what looked like an oddly shaped hammer painted on the front with lots of detailed twists and weaves of color inside of it.

I couldn't help but think of how good that shield would look hanging on the wall in my ranch house.

The Viking grinned from behind his beard and shook my hand, wrist to wrist, as he did Henon. His grip was strong and sturdy. Then he spoke, and while I thought I understood the occasional word, they sounded strange as though from long before English became a language.

"Jarl Bjarke," the axeman said in way of introduction.

"Jedidiah Huckleberry Smith... you can call me Jed."

"Je-ed," the Viking said, nodding his head in understanding before speaking again.

Henon began to translate. It was noticeable that he'd been around us for a bit and picking up on our lingo, as his language was less Shakespearean and theatrical sounding than before.

"Jarl Bjarke and his axemen seek the Thirsty Wench and beasts inside. They need mounts, like three horns the hairy men and Squatting Bull ride."

"Oh hell, the Vikings ride dinosaurs?!" I blurted out while glancing behind me at the ship. I couldn't wait to tell the others. Prehistoria was just getting better and better.

Bjarke ignored my outburst while Henon rolled his eyes and they both continued.

"Thirsty Wench was due.... Many days ago... Mikah saw ship and brought axemen here."

"Mikah?"

Henon pointed at the first man standing in the row. Tall and imposing with jet black hair, the Viking wore an angry scowl beneath his beard and dark markings around his eyes. He was also missing his left arm from below the elbow. Mikah carried no shield or bow, instead in his lone hand he carried a drawn sword whose naked blade shone in the sun. Several small axes were jammed into the belt around his waist, all turned so that he could grab them with his right hand.

"Huh. Kind of mean looking fellow," I quipped.

"He is… berserker… a mighty warrior."

"Noted. Thenon, tell the Jarl that we come in peace. We didn't attack the Thirsty Wench or kill his trikes. But we do seek his help in fighting against the apes."

The big Shayana native spoke roughly, gesturing at me, the ship and the people lining the railing, and back towards the Jarl's men. Once finished, Bjarke shook his head and chuckled before speaking.

"Bjarke says thy and thine men must fight with them before they help. Thou must prove thyself in battle first."

I patted my twin Colt revolvers in their tooled leather holsters. "Figures. Where are the apes at?" I figured something like this would happen; in Prehistoria it seemed you were only as good as your battle prowess.

The imposing Viking, Jarl, spoke again, roughly this time, just a few words.

"He says not hairy men, but that thou will see."

"Oh, wonderful. Something new." I looked back at the ship behind me. Skyla's black hair was blowing in the ocean breeze. Arthur and Charles stood nearby with rifles in hand and the Governor was peering through my telescope, watching our little meeting. The Shaynee were all over the place, hiding along the upper deck, one had climbed into the crow's nest on top of the mast, and I could see several rifles peeking out from the darkened portholes along the side of the ship. They were ready to brawl if need be. "Is it safe for everyone else to come off the ship?"

Bjarke must have picked up enough of what I was saying to understand as he nodded curtly.

"Henon, is it safe?" I repeated while whispering to the Shayana cautiously; I'd prefer my ally tell me it was safe rather than an unknown Viking of mysterious origins.

"It is."

"Good. Let's get the others."

***

The axemen crawled all over the ship after we left it, looting anything that the Shaynee hadn't already taken. By then Otto and his braves had scoured the entire ship for anything of worth that could be slipped into a waistband or thrown into a leather wrapped pack on their pole sleds they still pulled behind their ponies. I hoped that if the Shaynee had taken anything the Vikings wanted, it wouldn't turn to bloodshed. But it turned out the axemen were truly only there for the now deceased young trikes.

Once it appeared that we'd be staying the night at the Thirsty Wench, we fed and watered our horses and trike, put them together the best we could with a guard, and made ready to spend the night on the beach.

We did this well away from the ocean water as there was no telling what had made those strange circle imprints in the ship, and the sound of the crabs snapping that Pinkerton's leg was still fresh in our minds.

We fetched enough driftwood to throw together a couple of small fires. This time the Shaynee braves didn't bother distancing themselves from us, instead preferring to use the same fires as we inferior whites.

The Vikings, meanwhile, hauled their three long boats with their oddly shallow bottoms past the high tide mark on the shore and used them to create a triangular fort with a large bonfire in the middle. They didn't appear to have any firearms, but plenty of bows and quivers full of arrows were set in positions along the boats.

At first our groups stayed separate, then Squatting Bull managed to strike up a conversation with one of the Vikings over whose claim to a particularly large piece of driftwood was stronger.

After lots of miming with hands and Shaynee and Viking swearings, Otto and Henon finally broke it up and had them throw axes for it.

The axeman won, his small axe beating out the young brave's tomahawk at hitting the knot in the end of the log. The sullen Indian reluctantly retreated, leaving the driftwood prize behind as he picked up smaller pieces scattered across the tide mark.

But that dispute led to several of us being invited over to the Vikings' makeshift fort.

And the Vikings turned out to be big drinkers.

From the bottoms of their boats, they pulled out various carved horns and began drinking some sort of sweet smelling, thick liquid. They seemed pretty upset about the loss of the young trikes in the cargo hold but didn't seem to care much for the missing sailors.

And speaking of which, while I'd been introduced to the axemen, Otto and some of his braves had been sneaking through the holds under the Thirsty Wench's deck and found no living souls or bodies... or pieces of people bodies for that matter. But from the circular imprints all over the ship, it was clear they'd engaged in some sort of battle with a sea dinosaur. Only a couple of cannons still had a charge in them and there were blood stains everywhere. But whatever took the men couldn't work the hatch to get at the ceratops, which was why they starved to death in the darkness of the hold.

As soon as we crossed into the triangle of boats, a horn was thrust into my hand by Mikah, and the axeman gave me a stiff nod before moving back to sit in the sand by a fire. Even after the loss of their ceratops shipment, they were happily singing some sort of coarse Viking song. It was poetic sounding, and I asked Henon what it meant.

"They sing of Valhalla. Where the axemen go after death to fight and feast with their gods forever."

"Well, that sounds kind of nice."

The Shayana chuckled. "Tis an honor to go to Valhalla."

I sipped my drink, almost gagging on the thick mixture. Skyla was staring at the carved horn in my hand, and I passed it to her, assuming she wanted a try. Instead, she held the horn up to the firelight, turning it around, while a wide smile slid across her face. "Jed! Do you recognize this?"

Squinting, I looked closer at the black horn. "No. It just looks like a horn to me, with some sort of fancy carvings."

"Those are runes, a form of Viking writing, but this… this is from a hollowed-out trike horn," she said in awe.

"Doesn't look like any trike I've seen." I raised the curved horn up and inspected it.

"Because it's not from the trikes we've seen so far."

"Well, that's neat," Fredrick took the horn from Skyla and sipped. "Mmm… some sort of mead. No doubt tempered with the honey derived from prehistoric flowers." He took a larger swallow. "I do like it." He held it out to Oscar and Otto to try.

To the former paleontologist's disgust, Otto dipped his finger into the horn, tasted it, then frowned. "Firewater take too many of our people. Even thick sweet firewater bad."

"Oscar?" the new Governor offered.

He shook his head vigorously, obviously displeased at sharing a horn with the finger of the leader of the Shaynee braves.

Fredrick shrugged and took another sip. "More for me then."

"Just give the horn back to Mikah over there when you're done," I said, pointing at the one-armed berserker. "I get the impression he ain't the sort to be messed with."

Henon stepped in front of my small group with Bjarke. The bear of a Viking grinned broadly with crooked teeth and spread his arms open in invitation. It was apparent he'd had more than a couple hornfuls of prehistoric mead by now and was enjoying himself immensely. There was even a drinking horn tucked into a strip of leather at his waist, keeping the mead upright and available.

"Jarl Bjarke welcomes thou and thine companions. He invites ya'll to come and sit with him."

Skyla chuckled at the Shayana's attempt at using our English mixed with his. I had to turn my head slightly to hide my smile.

Following Henon and Bjarke, we moved towards the far side of the fire, where the Viking Jarl had chosen to claim as his space at the tip of the boat triangle. His spear jutted upright from where it'd been thrust into the sand along with a bow and quiver lying on a piece of hide beside it. Even though they were having a good time, the Vikings were prepared for immediate battle should the need arise.

Bjarke threw himself down beside his spear and took a hefty sip from his horn. Unsure of where to place ourselves before a Jarl, we sat in the sand before him. Otto looked a bit put out; he wasn't used to showing honor to anyone except his Chief.

The Viking Jarl swung the drinking horn towards the Thirsty Wench and began speaking.

I found myself listening more intently this time, and realized that with effort, I could make out a few words of what he was saying while Henon translated. They were different, but the meaning was there behind the butchered pronunciation. Skyla and Oscar later told me that at the height of the Viking power, they'd spread over a large portion of Europe, and many of our words came from theirs. It made sense.

"Jarl Bjarke say kraken attack big boat. Carry off sailors to the depths of sea."

"A kraken?" Oscar's brow furrowed.

"Ja," the Viking said, looking somewhat peeved at having been interrupted. I took that to be a yes.

Reaching over to his quiver, Bjarke pulled out an arrow as Henon explained.

"Kraken is a great beast of the sea."

Bjarke drew a boat in the sand with the tip of the arrow. A boat identical to the axemen's with a single mast and sail, and circles for shields attached at the sides. It was an impressive drawing. Then he drew thick tentacles wrapping around the boat and waving into the air around it.

The Shayana continued, "It has many arms. For grabbing and pulling men to their deaths."

"That sounds like a kraken, alright," Fredrick said before taking another drink from the borrowed drinking horn. He burped quietly.

Jarl drew small circles on the tentacles. I sat upright. Those matched the strange markings that were all over the Thirsty Wench. Beneath the ship, he drew what could only be a pair of large eyeballs and a beaked mouth on a giant blob.

"That's what attacked the ship? And all the pirates, or sailors, or whoever is missing?" Skyla asked but looked like she didn't expect a response. Instead, she kept talking, as much to herself as us. "That makes sense. I'm sure there are all sorts of tentacled, prehistoric sea monsters out there. The Thirsty Wench may have been dumping dead ceratops overboard and drawing the beast's attention, or they may have simply had the bad luck to cross its path."

Bjarke viciously stabbed the sketched blob, leaving the arrow sticking upright from the center of the drawing. "Vega!" he cried out in Viking speech.

The Shayana pointed at the kraken drawing. "Vega?" he repeated.

"Ja."

Henon paused, then turned to us, a worried look on his face. "Kill. Jarl Bjarke says kill. He wishes to kill the kraken. With your help."

***

"Oh, hell no!" Oscar sputtered. "This is nuts!"

Otto nodded and patted the decorated buttstock of his rifle. "We help kill. Shaynee strong warriors. Better than Vikin."

I could tell he was still pretty groused about Squatting Bull losing the axe throwing contest earlier and looking for a chance to save face and regain honor for his braves. What better way to do that then to slay a sea monster?

Fredrick was sitting upright, his back stiff and straight. He looked around our small group with an excited look on his face. "An excellent idea. I would love to participate in the death of such a fabulous creature."

"How?" I asked. "The beast attacked a pirate ship and survived. How are we to deal with such a monster?"

Bjarke made a cutting motion with the flat of his hand, silencing us. Jerking his spear from the ground, he shook the weapon at us while drinking another mouthful of mead at the same time. Some of the liquid sloshed out and ran down his beard and onto his tunic. He didn't seem to mind. "Vega!" he screamed, raising the spear overhead.

Around us, drunken Vikings repeated the yell then went back to their mead.

"Oh dear..." Skyla said.

"Doesn't he understand? This kraken could be any manner of prehistoric cephalopod!" Oscar was standing now, obviously agitated. "You know what a cephalopod is, right? Oh of course not, you uneducated fools! It's a giant squid, octopus, cuttlefish, or some such undiscovered ancestor!"

"So... tentacles, right?" Fredrick asked with a bemused smile under his bushy mustache.

"Yes! Tentacles! Big ones, long, with suckers and hooks and all manner of such on them for catching and eating prey!" Oscar was shouting now. Other Vikings were staring, wondering what was going on. Mikah put down his drinking horn and picked up his sword.

"Oscar," Arthur hissed. "You're stirring up the axemen."

"They should be stirred up! We're talking about going after a kraken!" Oscar lowered his voice though, but now it was a loud whisper. "It'll eat us!"

I'd had enough of this and raised my hand to silence him. "Shut it, Oscar. You're not helping." I looked at the Jarl. His amicable demeanor was gone, and now he had an axe in hand and looked as though he were about to leap up and cut the former paleontologist down. Henon was speaking rapidly, translating to the Viking leader.

"Henon. Ask the Jarl if there is any other way to have their help against the hairy men."

The Shayana paused, gave a quick nod, then repeated what I said in whatever sort of old northern tongue the axemen used.

Jarl Bjarke replied with a single word and a frown.

"He sayith nay," Henon translated needlessly. It was obvious. We'd have to fight a sea dinosaur to get their help.

***

"Do we really even need their help? How many apes can there be? We just wiped out an army of them in that canyon," Charles said while feeding a twig into our fire.

"Many, many hairy men," Henon said from where he sat in the sand, sharpening his sword.

It was late and the Vikings had gone to sleep, leaving a handful of them on guard, walking around the boats with armor on and spears held in hand. They did not trust this prehistoric land. Which was probably why they'd managed to thrive here from what I gathered.

We sat around our own fire. Skyla beside me, my new blood brother Otto on the other side, and Fredrick and Charles across the fire. Oscar had gone to sleep, adamant that he'd have no part in what he called a suicide plan thousands of years in the making. But with Henon translating from the Jarl, we'd managed to get a little bit of information of what we may be facing.

Basically, a sea monster.

Oscar had spouted off all sorts of Latin names as Henon described what the Vikings knew of the beast. Apparently, it could be anything from a color changing cuttlefish to a giant tentacled squid or even some sort of octopus. He wasn't a lot of help, but from the Vikings we learned that the beast did not have a shell. That was good, I wasn't sure how well my *Eighty-Six's* .45-70s would do through water and a prehistoric shell. They had a hard enough time penetrating the bone shield of a trike.

"Alright," I said. "We don't have much of a choice, so we'll use the Thirsty Wench to store any gear we don't need. Just take weapons and ammunition."

"I hope their boats can carry everyone," Skyla said.

"Not everyone. Because you're not coming," I told her.

"Jed, don't you-"

"He's right, Skyla," Charles said, not meeting Skyla's eyes. "Jed and I discussed this already. You and I, along with a few of the Shaynee, will stay behind on the Thirsty Wench to look after the mounts."

"No!" She stood and placed her hands on her hips. "Jedidiah Huckleberry Smith. Don't you dare leave me behind while you risk your life."

I stood almost as quickly as her. "Skyla. We need someone to watch the horses and trike. I don't want Carbine or Smoke to get eaten while we're out on the water. It may take us a few days to stir this thing up, and that's a lot of time for something to come eat our horses."

"Well, there isn't much Charles, myself, and a few braves can do about it!"

"You'll have the Gatling. We'll hoist it onto the Wench tomorrow morning and set it up. That should be enough to deter any hungry dinosaurs. Except maybe a Tyrannosaur."

She looked around the fire angrily. "And you all are fine with this?"

"Skyla," Fredrick ran a cotton patch through one of his rifle's barrels then peered up at her. "We need someone to stay behind. And we need Jed, he's too well armed and too good of a shot to leave behind. And we all want you to be safe... and you will be."

Otto pounded a fist on his scarred chest. "Maybe-wife of blood brother will be protected by Shayana like she maybe-wife of Chief Toko. No harm will come to you."

"See? The Indians will watch over you." I grinned at her lopsidedly, knowing that I'd won this argument.

Skyla stepped around the fire, coming close to me. "Maybe-wife, huh?" She whispered in a conspiring manner.

I felt my face get hot and it wasn't from the fire. "Well... you know... Otto, he just, ah..."

She thumped me in the chest. "Hush. Okay, I'll stay on the ship. But you be safe out there with the Vikings."

"Yes, ma'am."

Arthur spoke up from where he sat sharpening his Lord Elcho. "I think we all need to be prepared to go to edged weapons. Because, well, tentacles and such."

"Agreed," Fredrick snicked the lever shut on his Winchester. "We'll shoot for the body of the beast as much as we can, but with water and in boats, it will most likely come down to blades."

"Do you even carry a blade?" I asked in a teasing manner. I'd never seen him use one.

The new Governor scoffed. "Of course. Sometimes a man must cut his way out of things. But... that being said, I'd prefer something with more reach. I think I'll borrow one of the Shaynee or Viking spears for tomorrow's hunt."

"I'm still confused on how you are going to get this kraken to come to you," Skyla said as she sat back down.

"I've got a few sticks of dynamite in my saddle bags. Tempted to try that and see if we can stir it up. Jarl Bjarke is confident of where it lives, he said his ancestor fought one and they believed it lived in a deep underwater cave by some little island of rocks."

"How'd they lure it out?"

"Blood. They collected buckets of blood and poured them into the water to get the beast to come to them. Apparently, it took a while, all sorts of creatures showed up first. Including what sounds like one of those megalodon shark things that ate our long necked Elasmosaurus friend."

"Then what?" Arthur asked. He hadn't been with us when we'd talked to the Jarl.

"Then they stabbed and hacked it to death. Losing most of their men in the process. But it was considered worth it, the kraken had been scaring off much of the sea critters that the axemen eat and causing a famine in the area."

Skyla looked worried.

"It'll be different this time." I patted the disassembled and partially cleaned Colts on the blanket in front of me to reassure her. "We've something Bjarke's ancestors didn't. Gunpowder."

"And lots of it," Fredrick added.

***

The next morning, I stood in the middle of a Viking longship trying to get a feel for my sea legs while Tinker threw up his breakfast over the side. I wasn't about to leave the traitor behind with Skyla, although the Shaynee would have probably kept him in line. But I figure the man was expendable. While I wasn't ready to execute him, I was willing to accept another swinging blade. Or in his case, a borrowed axe. I didn't trust the man with any guns, and we'd made it clear that if he tried anything, the Vikings would kill him and drink mead out of his skull.

Fredrick wore an excited expression on his face and kept his head on a swivel as he looked around the three boats for any sign of sea beasts worthy of slaying while Arthur kneeled beside him with rifle in hand and the massive Lord Elcho bayonet strapped to his waist.

Henon and Oscar waited back at the Thirsty Wench with Skyla and Charles. The Shayana tribesman had no dog in this fight and the cowardly former paleontologist would have just been a waste of space. I did wish we had Charles though, or even Squatting Bull, but the Shaynee brave refused to leave Horny Devil.

Otto was with me though along with several of his braves. The normally stoic native had a grin on his face as the sea breeze blew through his black hair. He'd never been out on such a vast body of water before, just the occasional lake or river. I thought it would have bothered him and the other Shaynees, but they took it in stride. Although more than one had joined Tinker in throwing up over the side.

The axemen that lined our boat rowed in unison with long thin bladed oars, their swords and axes lying beside where they sat and ready to be grasped in a moment. We stood in the Jarl's boat, leading the way for the other two as they rowed towards the rocks that lined the far beaches edge. The other boats were led by Mikah and Geir. The one-armed berserker stood at the front of his longboat, beside a figurehead of a horned ceratops carved into the bow. The other Viking, Geir, was a little man with lots of strange markings inked into his skin. Henon warned me he was quick with his blade and temper.

I touched the allosaurus claw hanging from my neck, rubbing the smooth surface as I watched the water for any signs of giant tentacles reaching out to grab at us.

We were about to step in some serious shit. Once again, I found myself pondering on the direction of my life and the poor decisions that I'd made that led myself into this position. Immediately, I thought of Skyla waiting for me back at the Thirsty Wench; I suppose my life hadn't turned out so bad. But it'd really suck if this was where I was to meet my end.

As sight of the Thirsty Wench faded away, we approached the rock island where the Jarl's Viking ancestors had made their stand against the previous kraken.

Jarl Bjarke pointed at it with his spear and shouted a throaty cry that the other axemen repeated several times.

They were anxious for battle and Valhalla.

As for me... I looked down at the *Eighty-Six*. It was tied tightly to the longboat with thin braided cord provided by one of the Vikings. There was enough slack that I could shoulder and shoot with it, but if I were to drop it overboard in any chaotic battle it wouldn't be lost. The thought of dropping it into the salty water made me shudder. Carson Skinner would skin me alive if I lost the prototype rifle.

Arthur saw me shiver and must have thought it was my nerves. "No worries, Jed. We're as ready as we'll be for the beasty."

"I like the plan," Fredrick checked the knots on his braided cords. He had two rifles tied to the boat. "Simple is best."

"It ain't much of a plan. It's shooting, hacking, and slashing. That's all."

"We'll be fine," the Governor patted the stick of dynamite he had tucked into his belt with a wink from behind his spectacles. I had a stick tucked into mine as well. But Otto had two. Unbeknownst to Skyla, we'd all agreed if the beast swallowed us, we were going to do our best to light the dynamite from inside and go out in style. Arthur refused his stick, citing his belief that he'd be able to cut his way out with his fancy bayonet. Otto claimed his stick and tied it to the other. The Shaynee leader thought it would be a fine way to go out.

I looked over the side as the boat was rowed over a massive dark patch below, showing a sudden change in the depth of the ground under the water.

It looked like the sort of giant hole a kraken would lurk in.

Jarl Bjarke shouted something, and the Vikings slowed the boat by turning their paddles against the water, then stowing the oars inside. The other two boats followed suit, gliding silently across the large patch of deep water as the axemen, Indians, and we Westerners watched over the edge for a glimpse of the giant beast.

Thirty minutes later, we were all getting bored.

We hoped that by crossing over the kraken's home that we'd draw its attention. But so far, it was quiet except for the occasional screech of a distant pterodactyl.

I pushed the toe of my boot against Tinker's backside to get the traitor's attention. "Care to go for a swim?"

"No, sir!" he practically shouted, jumping upright and clinging to his borrowed axe.

Fredrick leaned over the side, looking down into the water in disgust.

"Well," he pulled the stick of dynamite from his belt and fished a match out of a pocket. "We don't have all day for this." Striking the match, he touched the small flame to the gunpowder filled fuse and lit the stick.

"Wait! Won't the water put it out?" Arthur asked.

"No." The Governor jerked a painted shield out of the rack on the side of the boat, tossed it onto the water and dropped the dynamite onto the floating chunk of wood and gave the shield a push. It moved several feet away then began to slowly move back towards us with the small lapping waves.

"Damn. Jarl! Best start rowing!" He grabbed an oar from a startled Viking and thrust it back out into the water. "Pull dammit! Or die!"

Jarl shouted at the axemen and they grabbed the oars, slipped them back into the water, and began to pull. Fredrick's frantic pulling and shouting spurred the men to row faster, and soon we were well away from the floating dynamite.

KABOOM!

Water sprayed in every direction. Even as far away as we were, it rained down on us. I swore as I thought about how wet my weapons were getting.

Fredrick dropped the oar, leapt up, grabbed his rifle and propped a foot on the edge of the boat. "That should do it, lads!" he cried.

Vikings grabbed spears and axes and nocked arrows to bows. They were ready and shouting in their coarse language at each other joyously as though the thought of battle excited them.

All three boats were floating around each other, within a good hundred feet of each other and circling where we'd blown the dynamite.

A bluish green suckered tentacle burst through the water beside Mikah's boat.

The tip rose a hundred feet into the air. The tentacle was thick and pulsing as though some massive heart was beating blood through the limb. The whitish suckers on the underside flared and closed, grasping at nothing.

"Ohhh shit," I whispered in awe.

The one-armed berserker gave a ferocious battle cry and swung his sword towards the tentacle, slicing halfway through it and shocking us all out of our bewilderment.

Arrows were loosened.

In a moment, a couple dozen arrows pierced the suckered tentacle.

It slapped down, narrowly missing Geir's boat and rocking ours with large waves.

Tinker fell overboard with a cry.

Arthur rushed over to help, and I grabbed his shirt to stop him. "Leave him! We need your Elcho!" More tentacles were rising from the water, searching for us as they twisted around and grasped with their suckers. One began to curl around our longboat.

Jarl brought his mighty axe down on it swiftly, severing several feet from the limb. Watery blood squirted wildly as the tentacle thrashed back and forth. Axemen charged it, excited to have something to attack.

They hacked and slashed with swords and axes. One of them, a mighty inked fellow with a great beard, managed to run his spear all the way through the limb right before the tentacle was jerked back into the water, the axeman with it, still holding onto his spear and shouting angrily.

It was unbelievable how many tentacles were rising out of the water and grasping at us.

It was chaos.

Absolute chaos.

Arthur swung his brutal Lord Elcho and nearly sliced a two-foot-thick tentacle in half. The top portion fell over, dangling uselessly as the suckers grasped an oar and jerked it out of its holder and into the water.

As for me?

I was dodging tentacles and keeping my *Eighty-Six* aimed at the large roundish mass growing as it approached the surface under us.

"Help me!" Tinker cried from the water as a suckered tentacle wrapped around his leg and pulled him away from the boat.

Shifting the barrel, I lined the sights up and fired into the tentacle. The bullet hit and punched through.

It didn't do anything.

Tinker was jerked under the surface, and I watched as he was pulled out of sight towards the ever-growing dark creature rising beneath us.

Another axeman was jerked into the air by a tentacle. This greenish blue limb wasn't wrapped around him. Instead, its suckers were stuck to him. He thrashed and twisted about wildly, swinging his axe against the beast's limb that crossed his chest from shoulder to hip.

"Here it comes!" Fredrick shouted.

I felt the boat lurch sideways. A wave of water slapped over the side and sloshed around our feet. The *Eighty-Six* slipped from my grasp and over the side as I grabbed the side of the boat to steady myself. The rifle splashed and in a moment the line was taut as the weapon sunk.

The mighty sea beast came up from the depths of the dark ocean between the three of our longboats.

The monster consisted of two massive eyes that swiveled in different directions as they took us in. Above its head was a giant sack, perched high, bulbous and almost comical. It was certainly some sort of a prehistoric octopus. I remembered seeing a small one wash up on the shore near Charleston as a boy. It scared me then, and this one scared me now.

Mikah hurled a spear and it buried itself into the squishy side of the monster with no result. The berserker roared angrily.

Beside me, Jarl hacked at a tentacle pulling an axeman overboard.

Two quick slashes and the severed piece flopped around as the axeman began cutting the suckers off his skin with a knife from his leather laced boot.

Otto and Fredrick rapid fired their rifles into the gooey bulb on top of the octopus' head. They quickly emptied the guns, and Fredrick used the stock of his to bat away a tentacle seeking to pull another one of us into a watery grave.

The thrashing octopus was sending waves pushing our boats further away from the beast, leaving us cutting and hacking hopelessly at the suckered tentacles.

I was knocked off my feet as a Shaynee brave was jerked out of the boat. Screaming, the last glance I had of him was letting go of his bow and stabbing at the tentacle with an arrow snapped in half as he was dragged out of sight.

"This is bullshit!" Fredrick shouted as he swung a Viking sword. He connected and a slight cut opened in the tentacle. Some nasty looking watery blood oozed out before it slammed down on the boat, cracking one of the shields stacked along the side.

"I agree!" Arthur screamed as he fired a pistol one handed towards the mighty sea creature's head, or body, or whatever the hell was near its twin eyes.

"The eyes! The eyes!" I yelled back while pulling myself up. We needed to blind the slimy suckered bastard. There was a discarded Viking axe sliding on the boat deck within reach and I grabbed it. My Bowie knife was a mighty blade against a man but wasn't squat against a prehistoric kraken.

Otto repeated my yell in Shaynee, and several braves began flinging arrows at the beast's closest eye. At this moment, I really wished that Squatting Bull was with us instead of sulking with his trike. The Shaynee kid was a spectacular shot with a bow and arrow.

An axeman caught on to what we were doing and began shouting in his rough Northman talk. Within seconds anyone on our boat that wasn't fending off tentacles were throwing spears and shooting arrows at the eye. Which was about five people. The damn tentacles were everywhere.

"Look at that!" Arthur shouted, as he ducked an oozing severed tentacle nub and slipped another round into the chamber of his Martini-Henry rifle. I could tell he desperately wanted to get back to shooting. He pointed with his trigger finger.

Mikah's boat was moving.

Not away from the monster.

But towards it.

And at the very front by the carved prow was the berserker, a spear tucked under his arm like a medieval knight racing to slay a dragon.

"Whoa shit!" Otto cried in his Shaynee-accented English.

I laughed and dodged as a tentacle slammed down, cracking the upper edging of the boat and knocking a pair of shields off. The hilarity of the situation and Otto didn't escape me.

But the inked one-armed berserker wasn't in a laughing mood as his longboat rammed into the flat side of the octopus and he drove the iron tipped spear through the center of the kraken's eye with a heroic battle cry worthy of the dead kings of Valhalla.

The axemen on Mikah's boat leapt off and onto the webbing of the octopus. Several fell and slipped on the slimy goo, sliding off into the water while others began stabbing deep with their weapons to keep themselves from falling.

"Hey! Is that Tinker?" Fredrick shouted as the tentacles attacking us withdrew and the prehistoric sea beast fought against the axemen on its back.

One of the tentacles had the traitorous scout in its suckered grip and was waving him back and forth like a bat trying to dislodge Vikings who were thrusting, hacking, stabbing, and generally going all out frenzied on the back of the beast.

"Certainly is," Arthur cried while lining his sights up on the second remaining eye. He pulled the trigger and the kraken flinched slightly as it punched through the eye and into something important in the bulbous mass behind it.

The tentacle holding Tinker snapped like a whip and hurled the traitorous soldier against the side of a longboat. He went limp and sunk from sight.

I realized the water around us was turning a blackish blue from the oozing blood and leaking juices of the sea dinosaur.

Our longboat lunged forward as Vikings slipped behind the oars and began rowing like mad towards the kraken. Geir's boat was doing the same thing. And I noticed that the Vikings in both the boats were eyeballing each other more than the mighty suckered octopus before us. They were racing each other to see who could get to kill the wounded creature first and it was apparent that Mikah's crew was well ahead in the game.

Fredrick whooped with excitement as he pulled one of his rifles out of the water by its braided cord. Salt water streamed out as he shook the barrel upside down.

Otto had a tomahawk in one hand and a short knife in his other. He was perched like a cat aboard the front of the ship, ready to leap into the fray as soon as we were close enough.

Quickly grabbing the cord that was, hopefully, still tied to my rifle, I felt immense relief when I felt the heavy drag in my hands of the *Eighty-Six*. Quickly reeling it in, I thought of how I'd make sure to never mention this to Carson Skinner should I survive the finality of this fight.

The gun was soaked. I laid it reverently down on the boat's deck, hoping that the thick layer of oil I'd put on it would keep it from pitting until I could clean it.

And that I'd survive long enough to clean it.

But this part of the battle would be up close and gooey, and something primal deep inside compelled me to use the axe to finish this monstrosity off.

The underside of our boat slammed between two exceptionally large tentacles, barely beating Geir's boat. One of the massive tentacles lashed out. With a horrific crack, our mast snapped in half. I felt the heavy thud through my feet as it crashed down to the decking on the boat just before leaping off onto the slippery beast.

Blueish black blood or ink was leaking everywhere. The sea was a churning froth of tentacles. And the back of the beast was covered with men hacking, slashing, stabbing and generally going to town on the sea monster.

Swinging the axe, I gave a rebel yell and slammed the edge of the axe into the soft side of the octopus. Half the blade sunk in.

Using the weapon's shaft, I pulled myself forward, my booted feet slipping as I crawled on hands and knees towards the bulbous mass on its head that seemed like a heart or brain or something important.

The entire blasted sea creature thing was slipperier than hog snot.

But we were killing it. Slowly, and chaotically, we were taking our toll on the beast.

Drawing my right-hand Colt, I emptied the entire cylinder into the remaining eye. The bullets seemed to disappear in the gelatinous mass without doing any damage. Holstering the gun, I crawled closer.

Somewhere behind that eye had to be a brain.

Otto had the same idea. With a Shaynee battle cry, he threw a feathered lance. Half the length of the spear disappeared into the eye, and it seemed to do something. The eyeball stopped moving around and the creature began to thrash even more frantically beneath us.

Unsure of what to do with myself, I began hacking at the side of the great bulb on top of the head. Eventually I had to hit something important, and it was what a bunch of Vikings were doing. Maybe they knew something I didn't.

Geir moved forward, slipping and sliding, while using a pair of axes to hack and pull his way towards the dead eye.

Reaching it, he lunged forward, grabbed the shaft of Otto's spear sticking out, and began pushing with all his might to drive it forward. His leather booted feet kept slipping out from under him, causing him to drop to his knees, then surge forward again as he gained some small purchase on the slippery beast.

Arthur moved forward, falling several times until he got to the axemen. Together they put their weight on the shaft and something inside the giant kraken gave way beneath their combined strength.

The spear suddenly shifted forward, sending both the axeman and the doctor flying forward. The pair of men sunk into the gooey dead eyeball up to their forearms.

The beast stopped thrashing beneath us. Tentacles dropped. The kraken began floating with the gentle lapping sea waves instead of making the great frothing waves that had threatened to swamp our boats earlier.

"Whoa," Fredrick appeared next to me with a gore-covered axe resting over his shoulder. He was splattered with bluish black blood all over.

Looking down I realized I was too.

In fact, all of us were.

Mikah gave a throaty shout of victory, thrusting his sword high overhead. Axemen all around us joined in the cry, followed by the Shaynee with their warlike battle cries, and finally us white men, just shouting woohoo.

***

The mighty kraken had been slain.

But not without losses.

Fredrick lost one of his rifles. Otto lost several of his braves. And the Vikings lost Jarl Bjarke when the mast of our longboat snapped and crushed his chest in.

The mood was a solemn one as the axemen rowed their broken longships back to the Thirsty Wench.

While they rowed, we modern day men immediately set about cleaning our guns in the leaking, battered boat. It was an exercise in futility until we could completely break them down to their tiniest bits, but better than letting the salt water begin their hideous work of rusting our weapons. With some urging, Otto and his remaining men began the same with theirs. Their Winchesters were a gift from the US Government, one unlikely to occur again anytime soon. I hoped the Shaynee understood the value of them.

The axeman who seemed to take over the leadership of our boats was named Asger. I noticed him repeatedly eyeballing the other two ships and their leaders.

"I think we're in for some sort of power struggle among the axemen," Fredrick groused as he wiped an oil rag down the barrel of his lone remaining rifle. He was pretty bent out of shape over the loss of his other Winchester still.

"Looks like it. What you think, Asger, Geir, and Mikah?" I whispered back.

"Seems like. Only one can be the Jarl."

"How be?" Otto asked.

"Don't know. But I got a feeling we will find out soon enough," I pointed with the cleaning rod towards the shore. "There's our ship."

Everything looked fine on the Thirsty Wench. I could see Skyla's black hair blowing in the sea breeze as she waved. Beside her stood the tall soldierly form of Charles, and then the shorter, portly Oscar.

I waved back to let her know that I still lived.

"There will be a thing," Asger said out of the blue as he turned to us, a wry smile crossing his bearded face.

We looked at the axemen in shock.

"You speak our language," Fredrick said accusingly.

"Some. I learned from Shayana and the men of the ship," he pointed towards where the Thirsty Wench and my beloved waited.

"What do you mean by 'there will be a thing'?" I asked, my curiosity overcoming my surprise.

"A thing. A meeting. To determine who shall lead."

"You lead?" Otto asked.

"Doubtful, my lithe friend."

The scarred brave glared at him dangerously.

I held out a hand to keep my blood brother from going to war. "Let it be, Otto. It's not an insult."

Asger twisted the braids of his beard thoughtfully. "No insult. Thou fought valiantly, Otto. Worthy of Valhalla."

"Who else speaks our language?" Fredrick asked, looking around suspiciously.

"Myself. Mikah. Several others. We would deal with men of the ship when they come to trade."

I racked the lever on the *Eighty-Six* and sighed. It still felt like there was grit or something in the action. "Did the Jarl?"

"No, he did not. Yet, he asked that we listened to thou in silence."

"Clever."

"Bjarke was good Jarl. A good warrior too. And will go to Valhalla to feast and fight forever."

***

Skyla and the others climbed down from the Thirsty Wench and rushed across the shore to meet us. She threw arms around me and kissed my stubbled cheek.

"Survived again, eh Jed?" She hugged me tight.

"Again," I agreed. "I'm making a habit of it."

"Who'd we lose?"

"Jarl Bjarke, a bunch of Vikings, and a couple Shaynee. Oh, and Tinker. No big loss with him."

She turned to Otto. "I'm sorry."

The scarred Shaynee grunted. "They fought and died honorably. Except for Wind Blows. He drowned."

"What now?" Charles asked as he looked at the Vikings.

"I guess we'll go to their village. They have a funeral planned for Bjarke… and then they decide who the new leader will be."

"Politics," grumbled Fredrick. "Been there, done that, and managed to not get stabbed in the back too deeply."

Asger crossed the wet sand to us with several axemen. He grinned at us from under his blonde beard while spreading his arms as though he had good news. "We shall walk thou to our home. You will bring thy mounts, and all are welcome."

Oscar had approached unseen, the soft sand muffling his footsteps. "Oh, lucky us," he muttered.

"Hush, Oscar. They may have something of value for you to loot or steal for your boss."

"Humph," the former paleontologist crossed his arms over his belly. "I quit Reydan's employ after he tried to kill me with you."

"About time you came around," Charles glared at the short man.

"Now I'm in this for myself."

"You always were."

Around us the axemen were loading their longboats with crap looted from the Thirsty Wench. The Shaynee looked on jealously as the Vikings were able to take much more than the Indian braves were able to carry on their pole sleds. In Geir's boat I noticed a large tentacle was stowed along the center, the suckers curled in on themselves in death. Proof of the defeat of the kraken.

Asger jammed the butt end of his spear into the soft sand. "Pack and let us be on our way. In two days we will reach Novagant, in time for Jarl Bjarke's funeral." He stared at us from under bushy eyebrows. "That is not something I wish to miss."

"We won't slow you down any," I told him sincerely. Being mounted had its privileges.

"You should left horses at home. They don't live long here," Asger said.

"You have some?" I said in surprise. We hadn't seen any sign of horses in Prehistoria yet.

"Our fathers' fathers did. They are gone now."

"What's Novagant?" Oscar interrupted before I could ask more.

"Our home."

"Jed," Charles pointed back towards the Thirsty Wench. "What should we do with the Gatling?"

I thought quickly. Bringing it with us could prove useful, but to what end? Asger had assured us it'd be a quick and safe ride to their home free of any apes. The only real threat was a dinosaur and setting the Gatling up would be a pain in the thick of a fight against a prehistoric lizard.

"Leave it on the ship," I said, making up my mind. "We'll protect it from the weather and such the best we can, but for now, let's leave it. Might come in handy on the way back."

"Works for me. Hey! Fredrick!" the Brit called out to the Governor who was overseeing the buttoning up of the ship. "He says leave it!"

Fredrick waved back that he understood and closed another one of the cannon portholes with Henon's help. Skyla had insisted that we protect the Thirsty Wench as much as possible for research purposes later. That meant closing all the hatches, portholes, and whatever else would allow rain and weather to blow inside. The ship itself was wedged pretty good on the shore, and we didn't think that'd it float away, but just in case we used some of the thick ropes on the boat to stake it down the best we could.

Asger picked up his spear and pointed it to the ship.

"Captain Darby be happy to see you take care of boat. He was fond of it."

"So that's the Captain's name… Do you think he's still alive?" Charles asked.

The Viking shook his head from side to side. "No. He not leave boat if still living."

"Was that his cat in the cabin?" Skyla asked.

"Prince George? Yes."

I laughed. "The cat's name is Prince George?"

"We should bring him with us," Skyla said, with one of those faces that I had a hard time saying no to.

"Good luck catching him," I told her sincerely. Prince George seemed damned near feral.

"I'll get Henon to help me."

"Prince George may not want to come."

"Nonsense. We'll take care of him."

Two hours later, as we left the Thirsty Wench behind, Skyla finally admitted, with scratches on her hands and arms, that Prince George did not want to be taken care of.

***

We made the ride in two days, with the Vikings walking on foot in front of us carrying gear on their backs in small bundles. They traveled light, basically a bunch of weapons, a bedroll, and some food. Plus mead. Where that came from, I've no idea. But they managed to pass some around nightly while toasting the heavens, the stars, their gods, and their deceased Jarl.

Otto strictly forbade any of his braves from taking part in the drinking. He'd seen too many of the nearby tribes weakened by drunkenness to allow a single Shaynee under his leadership to follow that path. Fredrick and Arthur, however, enjoyed it for them all.

Our first glimpse of Novagant was from a distance when we first reached their furthest fields.

The Viking town was on a high crest of land, safe from any heavy storms that would slam waves against the coast.

Pulling my collapsible telescope from my saddle bags once again, I slowed Carbine to a stop along the beaten path and peered through the brass tube.

"What do you see, Jed?" the Governor asked.

"Well, Fredrick, it's a fortress. Looks like a moat was dug around the entire place, and the dirt was thrown up to make some sort of palisade."

"Yeah. Looks like water from the ocean feeds into it and that's how they keep it filled. But I'd reckon that means the moat is at the mercy of the tides."

"Still," Charles gently rubbed the scar on his face. "An impressive defensive measure against attacking apes or dinosaurs."

"It has worked well for us," Asger agreed as he dropped his pack and rolled his shoulders stiffly.

"Is no one going to mention the dinosaurs in front of us?" Oscar exclaimed, looking around in bewilderment. "Look at them!"

"They are magnificent," Fredrick drawled.

"Wade would be jealous," Charles grinned.

In the fields before us, there were dozens of axemen, axewomen, and I reckoned, axechildren, along with at least ten ceratopsids working the lush green fields before us.

Unlike the trikes that the apes and Squatting Bull rode, these horned beasts were of several varieties. Some had multiple spikes sticking out of their bone shields behind their heads, while others had two long horns on the tops of their heads but only a small bump above their beaks. Others had triangular shaped bone shields with a pair of holes in them.

Oscar was rattling off Latin names, but I was too busy staring at Skyla's face. It was lit up, like a child at Christmas.

"Jed..." she whispered in awe. "They are so beautiful."

Not as beautiful as you, I thought to myself. Then forced myself to look away and observe the axemen's culture. Like the apes and the Shayana, the axemen were raising similar plants. And in some fields, it appeared to be the rapid wound healing flowers that we'd encountered before, but never on such a large scale.

"Seems the pirates of the Thirsty Wench was rounding up all sorts of ceratopsids," Charles mused while an axeman rode past us on the back of a strange red and black streaked five horned trike. The Viking waved at Asger and the others, giving us only an uninterested look before riding on.

Judging by his reaction, Geir and Mikah had already returned by boat and told them of our coming.

"They must have been capturing them from somewhere and bringing them here to sell to the axemen," Charles said.

"Across the ocean... I must go and see them all!" Oscar squealed in delight.

"I thought you were here to loot and take advantage of the indigenous peoples," I told him.

"Nonsense, Jed. Paleontology is still my passion." He peered at me. "And don't act like you know what indigenous means."

I snickered and pulled my hat lower. I knew a lot of words, and a bunch of my lesser used ones applied to him. He just didn't know it.

"Let us go," Asger said before continuing to lead with Henon down the well beaten path.

It was apparent he expected the rest of us to follow, so I slipped the telescope back into the saddle bag and touched heels to Carbine's flanks. My least favorite horse quickly leapt forward, making me almost fall out of the seat, before settling into a comfortable pace behind the Vikings and Shayana tribesmen.

"He appears to be in a hurry!" Charles laughed while urging Sir Lancelot after us.

"Probably knows something we don't."

"Grain," Otto said, pointing at one of the fields a little way off.

I followed his line of sight and noticed what looked like sheaves of barley being cut and stacked.

"Been a while since our horses have had any of that," I told my blood brother.

He shrugged and slapped the neck of his mount. "Pony eat grass. No need grain."

"Yeah, that's why you Indians end up eating your horses in the winter."

Otto glared at me for a moment then barked a laugh. "Ha! Pony good eating."

Skyla blanched.

Carbine moved aside as Arthur's horse pushed between Smoke and him. The writer was excited. "A new civilization! This is fantastic. I can't wait to tell them of this back home."

"It is impressive," I said while pulling Carbine's reins to the side to keep him from jostling Arthur's horse in revenge. Like me, he wasn't a fan of being touched without permission. "I wonder how they ended up here."

"Probably same as the Shayana, a Shimmer was open somewhere at some time," Skyla said while fanning herself with her hat. The sun was baking us along the coast, and we all missed the shade of the towering forest.

"I reckon we'll find out soon enough." Giving Carbine enough slack in the reins, he quickly trotted in front of Arthur's horse. I shook my head at him. What a horse.

***

We rode over the moat on a heavily reinforced wooden bridge. Carbine's hooves clomped against the thick boards, and I leaned over in the saddle to get a better look at the water below.

There were... things in the murky water below.

As for what, I couldn't tell. But some sort of prehistoric sea life was moving around; I saw several splashes from creatures moving beneath the surface and shuddered.

On the other side of the bridge was a pair of earthen ramparts, most likely using the dirt removed from the moat. But these manmade obstacles were faced with wood. There were very few gaps between the boards, making the entire mound look like it was made of planked lumber.

"Why reinforce a dirt mound?" Arthur asked.

"Clever," Fredrick pointed at the flat boards pressed into the dirt palisade. "Make it harder to climb than dirt."

"While the apes are trying to claw their way up the slick boards, the axemen are on top firing arrows into their faces." Charles nodded sagely. "Simple, but effective."

"Makes the defenses we had at Fort Jipson look pitiful... except for the Gatlings and cannons," I admitted. It was impressive. Along the top of the rampart was a couple of lines of sharpened stakes, tight enough to be a hinderance to someone trying to move through them, but plenty of room to fire an arrow through at any attackers.

An axeman trotted over to where we were as we worked our way inside the dirt ramparts to the center of the village. He waved at Asger and shouted something in... axeman? Viking? Northman? I don't know. Whatever their language was.

Asger waved before removing his pack and dropping it to the ground. "There has been a Thing."

I glanced sideways at Fredrick. Geir or Mikah. There was no doubt as to both axemen's bravery and battle prowess, but which would be better to lead? My gut instinct said Mikah. Geir appeared to want nothing to do with us, while the one-armed berserker was both curious and cordial in his interactions with us.

"Great!" Oscar harrumphed and his shoulders slumped forward in dejection. "We missed the Thing!"

"Thou would not have attended. It was for us alone. You are not one of us," Asger said before asking the other Viking something in their dialect.

The man said a few things, then turned and wandered off. Apparently unintrigued with our little group.

"You're killing us with the suspense," Fredrick told our Viking guide. "Who is it?"

"He said Mikah is now Jarl. There will be a funeral tonight for Jarl Bjarke. Then a feast."

"Mikah be good Jarl," Henon said.

"Oooh a feast and a funeral! That sounds interesting." Oscar's spirits were visibly lifting.

"In the meanwhile, I shall show you around," Asger said. "And show you where you are to stay."

***

Novagant was mighty impressive. And wonderfully laid out, I thought.

After the earthen ramparts, there were rows of wooden houses neatly aligned with thatched roofs. Past that, another rampart. This one, smaller, in a circle. Two roads crossed entirely through the second layer of defenses in a neat X. These wide roads gave traders, workers, and everyone else plenty of room to walk through while going about their duties. But it was noticeable that no trikes were allowed here. Everything of weight was being moved in man pulled carts.

In the intersection of the crisscrossing roads, was a great long house made of vertical planks. This was the only building we saw with overlapping wood shingles. It was a Great House according to Henon and it was here we were told we would be invited to partake in the funeral feast.

There was a lot to take in, and we received numerous stares at our strange clothing, dress, and weaponry. The Shaynees themselves were especially intriguing to the axemen as they sauntered about, occasionally being yelled at by Otto for lingering or looking too longingly at various trinkets and tools. And more than one Viking stared at Skyla as she walked through the place at my side.

I couldn't blame them. She could be covered in cow manure and still be beautiful.

Overall, I found Novagant to be a rather fascinating place. All the others agreed, and even the normally reserved Shaynee leader was visibly impressed. But I could also tell Otto was getting irritated with keeping his braves in line.

Thankfully, we were soon herded out past the moat and to the coastal shore where a large crowd gathered around a long boat.

The sun was beginning to set over the giant trees to the west, drawing long shadows from the Novagant fortress on the hill.

Skyla held my hand and we watched from off to the side of the crowd as Jarl Bjarke's body was carefully carried and placed into the longship by the new Jarl along with Geir and Asger. They reverently laid him down in the center, surrounded by piles of foods, weapons, and mead. His axe and painted shield, they placed in his hands.

His mount, a beautiful dual horned trike, had been slain and somehow, miraculously I thought, loaded into the boat as well.

The mast of the ship was unfurled and billowed slightly from the gentle breeze blowing towards the sea. Only the ropes tied to stakes kept the boat from slipping away from the shore.

Otto grunted his approval. "Fine way meet ancestors."

"Agreed. Bury me with my guns," Fredrick said wistfully.

I chuckled dryly, "Doubt they make a coffin big enough for your gun collection."

"Won't need a coffin at the rate I'm losing them," the Governor growled.

Asger stood by the loaded funeral ship with Geir and Mikah. The new Jarl watched respectfully as his predecessor was prepared to travel to Valhalla. Behind them were hundreds of axemen, women, and children who had gathered to watch. A low murmur hummed through the crowd as they whispered and waited as bundles of dried ferns, grasses, and sticks were carefully placed and tucked into the bottom of the ship.

Finally, with the last Viking off the boat, Jarl Mikah gestured towards the ropes, and the lines were quickly severed.

The ship began to slowly sail away from the shore.

When the longboat was about a hundred yards away, Mikah nodded at Geir.

The short Viking notched an arrow in the string of his bow, then waited as the grease and cloth wrapped shaft was lit from a torch.

Once the flame was burning brightly and appeared in no danger of going out, Geir drew the arrow back and aimed into the sky.

There was silence as the Vikings held their collective breath in anticipation.

The arrow was released.

It flew, burning brightly, and landed into the unfurled sail.

The cloth burst into flame spectacularly.

"Whoa!" Oscar said, his jaw dropping. "I didn't expect that."

"Must have soaked it in something flammable," Skyla said, stating the obvious.

Asger moved away from the others and stood by us, watching the flames grow as bits of flaming cloth fell into the boat and lit the bundles around the dead Jarl.

"We burn him in a moment, and he goes at once to Paradise," the Viking warrior said reverently.

"It is good," Otto said, shifting the rifle in his hand.

"Well, if the Shaynee approves, you know it's barbaric," Oscar said, rolling his eyes.

Otto jerked the tomahawk out from his belt and swung it, stopping the blade below the former paleontologist's Adam's apple. "Shut hole, Weak White Man."

Runs With Dogs and the other braves began to press into a circle, intent on watching the former paleontologist be killed.

"Easy Otto." I gently touched the tomahawk handle and eased the blade away while beads of sweat dripped down Oscar's reddened face.

Asger grinned. "No, this good. Best funerals have fights."

"Not our way, Asger," Fredrick said while removing his spectacles to rub the glass clean with a scrap of cloth. "But I do like your thinking."

At that moment, a fight broke out to our left. One axeman shoved another, and before you knew it, everyone was punching each other in the face and scrambling about in the dirt. The women were grabbing their children and pulling them back away from the fray, scolding them if they lingered too long to watch.

"Oh, look. A brawl!" Arthur exclaimed in excitement.

Asger roared mightily and ran over to a trio of axemen. For a moment, I thought he was going to break it up, but then he bashed a couple of heads together while laughing.

I grabbed Skyla's elbow and began to pull her away. "Time to go, darling."

She frowned but let me move her along. "I just want to watch! Their culture is fascinating."

"We can watch from a distance. Safely."

Oscar quickly followed us, while Fredrick stayed on the shore with a grin under his bushy mustache. Otto beckoned at me to follow him.

"No, this ain't no blood brother stuff," I called out to the scarred brave as he eagerly waved the other warrior braves forward.

He shrugged, shouted something in Shaynee, and ran into the melee, leaping onto the back of the nearest Viking and knocking him to the ground.

"Don't kill anyone!" I shouted after him.

"I hope Otto doesn't get hurt," Skyla said.

"He'll be fine. He's as tough as he looks. Before we leave tomorrow, they'll probably be asking him to stay."

An hour later the large crowd of men were backslapping and grinning as they entered the Great House. It appeared while they'd been brawling, the rest of the townsfolk had been putting the finishing touches on a massive feast.

"Is that a..." Oscar began, pushing his way between Skyla and myself to get a better look.

"An ankylosaurus," Skyla finished as her jaw dropped.

The bone armor plated dinosaur had been killed, processed, cooked, then the meat put back inside the giant shell that'd been overturned between two long tables that were rapidly filling with loud and boisterous axemen. Steam rose off it from the heat of the fire that burned underneath, the smoke snaking overhead and out the roof through a circular hole in the center of the Great House.

"How barbaric!" Oscar muttered.

"Shut hole, Weak White Man," I told him, while grinning at Otto. The Indian had a bruise on his forehead that appeared to be coloring darker as I watched. That was from Mikah, the pair of them had gone at it for quite a bit. Go figure the Shaynee leader would pick the axemen leader to brawl with.

"Harrumph." Oscar picked a seat at the end of the closest table. There looked like plenty of room for all of us and the Shaynee braves. "Do you know how much one of those dinosaurs would be worth on the other side of the Shimmer? Especially to someone like Wolverine Wade? And here we are eating it."

The Governor sat opposite Oscar. "Money isn't everything. Sometimes an experience is worth more than a chest full of gold."

"Not if it's a previously extinct species."

"Oscar. Just shut up and eat. Enjoy yourself," I told him in disgust as I waited for Skyla to sit first. Sliding my legs under the table I sat on the long bench and stared at the portly former paleontologist. "Reydan almost had you killed. Now here you are, literally eating a feast for a king. I say you should savor the moment."

"Agreed!" Arthur tried to sit, but the Lord Elcho strapped to his side wouldn't let him. He fought with the massive bayonet for a moment before managing to make it work and getting his legs under the table.

Before us were plates, bowls, and mugs all made of wood and showing some use already.

"I think mine's cracked," Oscar complained while holding his plate to the firelight from the rows of lit torches mounted in the walls.

"Probably on some axeman's skull," Skyla muttered.

"And where are the utensils?" he said, placing the plate back down in disgust.

I leaned forward and looked further down the table. Past the Shaynee braves who were more out of place then we whites, I saw Vikings pulling forks and small knives from their garments.

"I reckon we should have brought some."

A loud shout rose from the far side of the Great House, and the room began to quiet down. The women serving the food moved back along the walls, and the men put down their mugs and turned to face where new Jarl Mikah stood.

Asger quickly moved down to our table. "Tell thy men to quiet," he told Otto.

The brave hissed at them to shut up, and they stopped making a ruckus while looking rather confused at everything going on.

Jarl Mikah began speaking, loudly enough for us all to hear in the quiet of the giant room.

Behind us, Asger translated the best he could.

"Jarl say how great Jarl Bjarke was. How brave, noble, selfless. He was good man. A good leader. Mikah now thanking us for placing trust in him to lead. That he will lead us to new greatness and new conquests."

Asger paused as Mikah raised his sword overhead, the naked blade gleaming by firelight and shouted.

Around us the axemen began pounding their mugs on the table, sloshing mead everywhere while roaring their approval. Asger joined the others, shouting loud enough to make the Shaynee braves jump.

"What did he say, Asger?" Skyla asked once it began to calm down and the men had turned back to their food and drink.

"He say, we finally cross sea."

"What does that mean?" Fredrick peered at the axeman from behind his spectacles.

"We cross sea, build settlement. Conquer what we find. Gain glory."

***

The next morning, we rode away from Novagant with Henon leading the way on foot.

Mikah was there to see us off as we crossed the bridge over the moat. The axeman was sporting a black eye and looked like he could barely stand from drinking so much last night. There was no sign of Geir, but a few other axemen had managed to survive both the funeral and feast and watched us go from on top of the ramparts.

I slowed Carbine down as Horny Devil's heavy feet shook the bridge as he crossed it after me.

"Jarl," I nodded at the one-armed berserker leader, afraid to do much more than that as my stomach still felt like it was going to burst from the massive meal last night.

He reached out and grasped my arm in his and gave it a quick shake with a nod.

"Jarl Mikah. Be seeing you around, I suppose," Fredrick told the Viking.

"Yes, I may come visit this... Whitesberg..." He gestured towards one of the pistols strapped to the Governor's horse. "I would trade for one of these, very much."

"Next time I head this way, I'll bring you one and teach you how to use it."

I coughed to hide my chuckle at the thought of Fredrick teaching anyone how to shoot.

The axeman grinned happily, then burped and wiped his mouth with the back of his hand.

"Thank you for the hospitality," Skyla said as she rode by with Otto, who gave Mikah a begrudging nod of an equal.

"Where's Asger?" I asked the Jarl. I'd expected him to be here to see us off, but he may have gotten into a bit of trouble last night.

Mikah pointed in the direction Henon was taking everyone, out past the moat, and into the fields.

There came Asger, mounted on a beautiful red and black streaked ceratopsid. This spectacular mount put both Horny Devil and Sara to shame in terms of beauty. It had two spikes rising vertically off its bone shield, and several smaller ones fanning out along the sides. There was only a single black horn on its face, above its beak, and streaks of light red rose from both sides past its dark eyes and swirling on the bone shield itself.

It was gorgeous.

"Heaven help us if Wade sees that one," Fredrick chuckled. "I bet he'd trade his Ballard rifle for it."

"I'm half tempted to trade my *Eighty-Six*!"

Jarl chuckled, gave us a little wave, then walked back past the ramparts into Novagant. His gait had a slight wobble to it, and you could tell the effects of the mead hadn't worn off yet.

"Well, the Jarl doesn't say much," Oscar said as we watched Mikah go. "But he's a frightening fellow."

"Keep that in mind if you try to weasel them out of any resources," Charles said in disgust.

"Why, I'd do no such thing. No, sir. I'm here to trade. It's not my fault they, like the Shayanna, don't know the value of what they have. Why, sometimes it's like trading with an infant."

"You're a beacon of morality, Oscar," Fredrick told the portly former paleontologist.

He sniffed, as if offended. "After this unfortunate business with Reydan White has come to an end with his attempted murder of me, I do believe I'm in business for myself now. And I intend to do well."

Henon stopped as Asger approached on his ceratopsid and I rode to the front of the column of Shaynee with Otto.

"Good morning," I told the Viking.

He grunted in reply, squinting at us from beneath his helmet as if the morning light hurt his eyes. Which it probably did. His mount stamped its large feet and stepped towards Horny Devil.

Squatting Bull eyeballed the other trike warily, and the two dinosaurs flared their nostrils and sniffed at each other.

"Nice mount. It got a name?"

"Sleipnir."

"Sleep near?" Otto laughed. "Funny name."

"Sleipnir," Asger growled in correction. "Twas the name of Odin's favored horse. Name good enough for him, good enough for me," he patted the side of the trike underneath him.

'Well, what are you and Sleipnir up to this fine morning?" I asked.

"We travel with thou. As commanded by Jarl Mikah." The Viking shrugged, then patted the bow and axes strapped to his mount. "I see this Whitesberg with my eyes and tell Jarl of it when I return."

"Good," Otto grunted. "More weapons."

"Yeah. Welcome to the group, Asger." Turning my head over my shoulder, I looked at the line of Shaynee braves on their ponies and the white people on their horses at the back of the group. "Let's go!" I shouted then touched heels to Carbine's flanks.

Tomorrow would wait for no one. And I was anxious to get to Whitesberg.

I wanted to see if my old man had killed Reydan yet.

***

The first day and second day, Asger mainly kept to himself. He was moody, and I figured it was the mead withdrawal. But by the third day, he was back to his normal self, cracking Viking jokes about dying in battle gloriously and telling stories of battling apes.

His mount, Sleipnir, seemed to prefer the company of Horny Devil over the smaller horses and ponies. And often Asger rode beside Squatting Bull, no doubt filling the young brave's simple head full of all sorts of strange axeman notions.

"Trip is almost over, Arthur," I rode Carbine beside the Scottish writer.

"Yes," he said thoughtfully. "Shame, it's been quite the adventure."

"We still got a way to go," I told him as we rode over a pair of giant dinosaur tracks stamped into the wet sand. I pointed at the three toed track that was over two feet wide. "If you want more adventure, we could always see what these lead to."

He chuckled. "I've seen things over here that men have never even dreamed of. I can't wait to write about them."

We were moving closer to the forest. A large patch of thick, stinking mud oozed from the edge of the coastline, forcing us to ride along a small strip of sand and grass beside the tree line.

The sun was blazing down on us. The nasty mud to our right stunk to the heavens as though filled with the rotting remains of dead things. I glanced back at Skyla. She and Charles were riding side by side and seeing me turn in the saddle, she waved back happily.

We were almost to Whitesberg. Probably several more hours and we'd be able to see the modern-day fortress looming over its prehistoric surroundings.

Oscar looked back in his saddle at Arthur and me, then did a double take.

"Hey, Jed?"

"What, Oscar?"

He raised a finger, pointing behind us. "I do believe something is bothering the ceratopsids-"

The monstrous beast that had waited silently and patiently in the trees beside our path lunged forward, snapping smaller trees like twigs, parting undergrowth under its massive weight, and clamping its jaws over Oscar's torso with incredible force.

Skyla screamed in shock from behind me.

Arthur shouted from beside me.

I froze in shock.

Before Oscar's horse could move, a large three toed foot stomped down on it, crushing it beneath the muscular leg of the beast.

With a twist of its massive head, the tyrannosaur ripped the upper half of Oscar off.

The bottom half of him lay still mounted in the saddle of the quivering dead horse under the dinosaur's foot, beside the former paleontologist's foolish looking top hat.

"Oh no… not Oscar," Arthur mumbled in shock.

Asger raced past us on Sleipnir, jerking free his long-handled battle axe from where it was strapped to the side of his mount and screaming a Viking war cry. Behind him came Horny Devil with Squatting Bull notching an arrow to his bow.

Not one to be left out of a party, Fredrick and I jerked our rifles to our shoulders and pulled the triggers at almost the same time.

BOOM! BOOM!

The tyrannosaurus jerked its head to the side from the bullets, then swiveled back to watch the charging pair of trikes.

Stomping its feet to the side, the monster dinosaur turned and roared a challenge. Bits of Oscar's flesh and clothing hung from between his bloodied teeth.

Sleipnir bellowed back and shifted to the right as Horny Devil ran to the left.

Squatting Bull drew back his bow in one swift movement and released. The arrow sunk a third of its length into the chest of the beast, right above the weak, pathetic looking arms.

It did nothing.

Around us raced the other Shaynees, led by my blood brother, firing rifles and whooping like banshees.

I racked another round into the chamber of the *Eighty-Six* and shouted, "Looks like you'll finally get your chance, Fredrick!"

"Not if the damned Indians kill it first!" the Governor cried back as he kicked heels to his mount.

I kicked mine against Carbine's sides, and he bucked, jack knifing front and rear ends.

Hitting the ground like a sack of angry potatoes, I cursed him while spitting sand as he ran away. "Carbine! You asshole!"

Charles had grabbed Skyla's reins and was leading her away from the Tyrannosaurus. Even from this distance, I could tell she was furious when she drew the obsidian bladed knife from her belt and slashed the taunt reins.

In a flash, Smoke whirled and was headed back towards us.

I waved at her to get away as the beast roared again and snapped at Sleipnir. The trike shifted its upper horns around in time to poke the tyrannosaurus in the face and open a long gash along its chin.

The giant dinosaur bellowed again.

It was angry now.

That was enough for Skyla's dapple-gray mare to now turn and run away with my angry paleontologist bouncing on the back and Charles chasing her.

Rolling over, I grabbed the *Eighty-Six* from where it'd fallen and pulled it to me. The prototype weapon was covered in sand. Cursing Carbine again, I smacked my hand against it to try and clear some off.

Horny Devil and Sleipnir were side by side now.

Both trikes shook horns at the monstrous beast in front of them, and one of their riders was slinging arrows while the other shook his battle axe and slung axeman insults.

The Shaynees were riding circles around the trio of dinosaurs on their ponies, which were obviously braver than Carbine and Smoke, and firing rifles upwards at the towering dinosaur.

Horny Devil stepped forward, jerking his horns from side to side in a slashing motion.

The Tyrannosaurus lunged forward.

Squatting Bull threw himself backwards as the dinosaur closed its massive jaws on the Indian trike's bone shield.

Dropping his bow, the young brave slammed a tomahawk down onto the top of the beast's snout.

The angry dinosaur pulled away, breaking off a piece of the trike's shield and ripping the tomahawk from the Indian's hands.

Looking comical, it waved its useless hands while shaking its head in an effort to remove the bladed weapon from its face.

Arthur had slid off his mount, taken up residence behind a large clump of sand, and was letting out the horribly loud occasional boom as he fired his single shot Martini-Henry rifle from the prone position.

Fredrick, meanwhile, determined to not be outdone by the Shaynees, was fighting his horse to keep it close to the tyrannosaurus as he rapid fired his Winchester.

Emptying the rifle, he slung it away.

Reaching at the empty scabbard that should have contained his second rifle, the Governor swore, drew a pistol, and began firing as fast as he could work the trigger.

The massive dinosaur lunged to the side, narrowly missing Sleipnir's horns and clamping its jaws over a brave and his pony.

The Shaynee brave's scream was short, brief, and barely heard over the symphony of over a dozen guns blasting away.

Bullets didn't seem to be working. Nor did arrows.

But I pulled the trigger on the *Eighty-Six* again anyways.

We didn't have shit else to use.

Rearing backwards, the tyrannosaurus roared in pain and anger.

Sleipnir struck.

The red and black trike moved forward quicker than I'd have thought possible for a dinosaur of its size and thrust upwards with its horns.

Both upper black horns on its bone shield entered the monster dinosaur's guts.

With a savage twist and shake of its head, great slits were ripped across the beast's belly.

At the same time, Asger swung his long-handled axe blade into what I assumed was the lower kneecap of the two-legged dinosaur. The blade sunk deep, and the handle wrenched out of the Viking's hands when the tyrannosaur toppled over.

Loops of intestines pulled out of the belly of the dinosaur, twisted around the trike's blood smeared horns.

Not to be outdone, Fredrick forced his horse closer and fired shot after shot from his second pistol into the beast's open mouth as it bellowed in agony and pain.

The tyrannosaur kicked, trembled, and writhed as it died.

Shaynee braves began whooping, the Governor fired a shot into the air, and Arthur and I stood from where we'd been laying prone in relative safety.

"Well, there we go," Arthur grumbled as he knocked sand from the front of his shirt. "Fredrick wanted a tyrannosaurus, and one came to us."

Charles and Skyla rode their mounts back to us. Slowing Sir Lancelot, Charles slid out of the saddle and reached for the tattered remains of Smoke's reins.

Chagrined looking, Skyla handed them over to the British butler who tisked at the cut she had given the strips of leather. "Skyla..." he sighed. "I was trying to protect you."

Patting Smoke's white and gray ringed coat, she smiled out of the side of her mouth. "Just seeing if you could keep up, old man."

"Old man? Hmmph. Now I have to fix these reins."

Skyla looked at the dead dinosaur and the group around it. "Oh, and Oscar. Poor Oscar."

"Not so poor," I said. "He went quick, that's better than most. And to be honest, if we had to lose a man today, he's the one I'd chose. That makes it kind of a win-win situation."

"Jed, you're terrible."

"Yes, ma'am," I agreed, ducking my head to pretend to be sorry somewhat.

"Lady, gentleman, shall we go look at the dinosaur?" Arthur asked.

Charles looked up from Smoke's cut reins in his hands. "Absolutely."

After tying off their mounts and giving me grief over Carbine once again abandoning me, I walked over to where the Shaynee braves, Asger of the axemen, and the new Governor of Prehistoria were triumphantly walking around their giant kill with the others. Skyla, of course, had managed to stow away a small dissection kit in her saddle bags for just such an occasion and looked very excited to start slicing and dicing.

"Impressive kill."

My blood brother grinned wickedly, pleased in his part of the beast's death.

"I do believe I got the final shot into it," Fredrick said hopefully.

"Well, this will have to do. Because I don't want to face another one," I told him.

Asger slid off his trike, patted the beast, and nodded at me. His face was pale, and dripping sweat that I was certain wasn't from just the heat. The axeman was shook.

"Toothed One," he said, pointing at the corpse.

"That's what you call them?" Skyla asked as she gently touched the tyrannosaurus head. There were lots of small holes in it from our bullets.

"Yes."

A low bellow came from the other side of the corpse.

Squatting Bull rode Horny Devil around, and the green and yellow streaked trike looked a mess. Long tooth marks were gouged into his bone shield and about half of it had been snapped off. The young Shaynee brave looked worried.

"Oh no." Skyla left the tyrannosaur and moved to the wounded trike. She gently touched the jagged edge of the broken bone shield as the trike bellowed softly.

"He will heal," Asger said while grabbing his embedded axe by the handle. Placing his foot against the carcass, veins in his forehead popped and his face turned red as he struggled to free it.

Angrily, the axeman let go of the handle and tugged a smaller axe out of his belt.

"Horny Devil heal?" Squatting Bull repeated hopefully.

"Yes. I see worse wounds before." Asger began hacking at the surrounding flesh around his large axe's blade with the smaller one. Bits and pieces of hide and flesh flew as he worked to free the weapon.

Fredrick sighed. "Shame Parson's photographer isn't here. This would make one helluva picture." The Governor moved closer to the beast's open mouth and peered inside. "Oh look, I see part of Oscar in there," he chuckled darkly.

Arthur looked like he was going to be sick.

***

We rode through the portcullis of Whitesberg like conquering heroes as Colonel Carver and Captain Hawney watched from the top of the wall.

They looked down on us, but I could tell that Colonel Carver was grinning from ear to ear while the Captain wore a frown that I was certain had something to do with us still being alive.

I wish I'd interrogated Tinker more and gotten every ounce of information out of that little traitorous scout before his demise. He may not have known much, but now I wondered who to trust and who was under Reydan's employ.

A thought made me smile; perhaps Reydan was already dead.

Skyla mistook my grin for enthusiasm at returning successfully with a real-life Viking and another tamed trike with us. Plus, the saddle bag full of teeth that Fredrick brought back from the tyrannosaurus was a nice bonus.

"Feels good, doesn't it, Jed?" she asked me as she waved to the officers above us.

"Surviving always feels good," I told her. Then my grin faltered and turned into an angry scowl.

Reydan White was standing inside the portcullis with Pinkerton Detective Thompson at his side, and Cato on the other.

Worse, the evil bastard was smiling broadly.

That wasn't good.

Otto let out a Shaynee cry and kicked his pony savagely. The mount bounded forward, and the other braves followed suit, quickly surrounding the railroad tycoon and his two cohorts.

In a flash, Cato had both pistols out of their holsters and pointed at the scarred Shaynee warrior. Thompson stood still; his hands held outwards at waist height and away from his weapons. Reydan merely chuckled, but shifted his silver handled cane from one hand to the other anxiously.

"Jed! What is this shit?" Captain Hawney shouted down. "Tell your savages to back away!"

My blood brother raised a string of relatively fresh Pinkerton scalps overhead and shook them at the officer while shouting in Shaynee.

Charles reached over and snatched Skyla's reins away from her. Tugging on Smoke, he rode Sir Lancelot off to the side and the pair of them away from any potential gunfire.

"What's he saying, Jed?" Fredrick drawled, his rifle still resting over the scabbard and the barrel conveniently pointed at the two closest detectives that were manning the gate.

"A while back, Hawney asked Otto how many white scalps he's taken. He's telling him."

"What's the meaning of this, Mr. Smith?" Colonel Carver shouted as he quickly descended the stairs from the wall and to the ground beside us. Six soldiers followed him, their rifles held at the ready with anxious looks on their young faces.

"The meaning is that red bearded bastard over there sent his men to kill us, along with a scout of yours named Tinker."

Carver stopped in front of me, looking from the angry Shaynee warriors to those still beside me. He stared past us for a moment at Asger mounted on his impressive red and black trike, then turned to the armed men behind him.

"Gentlemen, if the Indians attack, kill them all. But until then, let us discuss this further."

As one, the soldiers pointed their rifles towards the braves.

Otto growled and tucked the scalps away, before jerking a tomahawk from his belt. My blood brother was angry, and that was a worrisome thing. Especially when he was near to someone he wanted to kill.

I held my hands up slowly. "Otto. Take your braves out of the fort."

"No, Huck Berry. We kill white men before they kill us." He glared down at Cato, as if daring the black gunman to pull the triggers on his guns.

"I was told to keep the Shaynee braves alive, by your Chief. I haven't done that well, Otto. But let me do it now." I pointed a finger at the smirking railroad tycoon. "He will die, you have my word. But not now."

"No! He die now!"

"No, dammit! He not die now. We tell Colonel Carver what happened and let him hang Reydan."

"Hang?" Otto looked back at me. There was confusion etched on his bronze face.

"Yes, with rope, from tree," I tried to explain.

"Yes, I know this thing. This hang. It is dishonorable death." The scarred brave looked down at trio of men circled by his braves. "It is good for him."

"Good, now have your braves wait outside the fort with Asger and Squatting Bull."

Otto shouted in Shaynee and the braves lowered their rifles then rode past me in single file, streaming out past the portcullis to where the pair of trikes waited. The leader of the Shaynee was last; he slowed as he passed me and Fredrick. "Hang. Good death for those with no honor."

Fredrick nodded. "Yes, it is, Otto."

"Then feed to crabs."

I chuckled.

"Alright, Jed. The situation has been de-escalated. Now what is this all about?" Colonel Carver said as he watched the Shaynees regroup around the mounted trikes.

Cato twirled his guns and holstered them as Reydan stepped forward.

"Isn't it obvious, Colonel? Mr. Smith's continued assault on my character knows no limits. He is given to these outlandish claims of nefarious doings by me that are simply not true. And now he has the Indians believing him."

"I was there, Reydan," Fredrick said. "Are you discounting the views of the new Governor of Prehistoria? Am I fabricating these truths that I have seen with my own eyes?"

"Oh, we do not doubt you, Governor," Captain Hawney said while wiping sweat from his brow. "But Detective Thompson had already warned us that a group of his men had stolen a Gatling and snuck off with it. We believe they intended to follow you and trade it to the axemen." He pointed behind us at Sleipnir. "Most likely for one of those beasts."

I raked my sweaty hair back in frustration. This wasn't going how we'd anticipated. Reydan had days after his men failed to return to devise a plan to excuse their behavior. He'd outplayed us.

"That is correct," Carver said. "And this Tinker, Reydan's men were nice enough to tell us that he'd vanished with them. No doubt his purpose was to guide them to the axemen."

The Colonel squinted up at the sun for a moment before fixating his stare on Fredrick and myself. "Now. Tell me what happened to the Pinkertons and Tinker. Because, from what I'm gathering and saw that scarred Shaynee brave waving around, you killed them."

The new Governor swore and spat on the ground angrily.

Carbine felt my mood shift, and he shook himself beneath me. I could feel his muscles tense as he prepared himself to move. Reaching forward, I caressed the side of his neck. "Easy boy," I said while thinking quickly.

Things hadn't gone at all as expected. But we had one last ace up our sleeves.

Asger.

I called out the Viking's name, and he rode his black and red streaked trike beside us. Carbine stamped his hooves and moved aside, angry at how close the axeman had put Sleipnir to us.

"Colonel Carver, this is Asger." I didn't bother introducing the other men facing us. Carver was the one I needed to convince. He seemed like the only one who wasn't under Reydan's control.

"Asger," the Colonel nodded while warily eyeing the trike. The horned beast turned its head and stared at the group in front of us with one dark eye, as though wondering if they were friend or foe.

Foe.

Definitely foe, I thought to myself.

Asger rested the handle of his axe against his thigh and nodded haughtily.

"Asger speaks our language, and can tell you of Tinker, who we captured after the Pinkertons attacked us."

The axeman grunted. "Twas little man. Bound in rope and deceitful."

"And where is he?" Reydan asked, gesturing with his hands. "I don't see him with you."

"Kraken killed him."

"The what?" Captain Hawney demanded.

"Kraken. Sea monster. Giant tentacled dinosaur of the ocean. Whatever you want to call it. We killed it," Fredrick grinned. "Actually, Arthur and another of the axemen gave the final blow, but we all did our part in weakening the monstrous beast. It was a magnificent battle."

"And how did this kraken kill him?" Hawney asked. "I recall Tinker. He was a small man, but a survivor. That's why he was so good as a scout."

"Well...ah... actually we didn't trust to leave him behind, so we took him out with us to fight the Kraken and it... smashed him against the side of a boat." Now I just felt stupid.

Reydan guffawed incredulously. Even Cato's eye twitched in what I assumed was a small measure of amusement from the notoriously silent gun hand.

Colonel Carver held his hand up as Thompson bent over and horse laughed while slapping his knee. "Quiet, everyone."

The railroad tycoon quieted down, and I growled in frustration.

"Let's see. The Pinkertons attacked you, for some unknown reason? And you captured Tinker, after your Shaynee braves scalped the detectives. Then you... went into battle against a giant sea monster... where Tinker was eaten. Thus the entire party of deserters and thieves who stole a Gatling gun to trade to the axemen was obliterated and cannot attest to any of their desires or nefarious purposes... correct?" Carver looked at me skeptically.

I glared at Reydan.

I was so frustrated that all I could think of was how I wanted to draw and start shooting the people in front of me.

Cato shook his head slightly and I realized my right hand was trembling above the butt of my Colt Peacemaker while the left hand was white knuckled around Carbine's reins.

Fredrick shifted in his saddle, his face turning dark and dangerous beneath his spectacles. "Are you calling me a liar, Colonel?"

"Absolutely not. But I have to ask, did you personally hear Tinker's confession?"

The Governor sighed. "No... I did not."

"You trusted your friend. There is nothing wrong with that, except Mr. Smith is obviously blinded by his hatred for Mr. White." Colonel Carver looked down his nose at me. "I recommend you reconsider your friendship with this man."

"Hey, now-" I started.

"Enough!" Colonel Carver shouted. "Enough, Mr. Smith! I'll hear no more of your ridiculous accusations towards Mr. White! You and the Shaynee have fulfilled your portion of the agreement. You may return across the Shimmer and the Shaynee may bring their tribe over if they so desire. That is all." Turning on his heel, Carver waved at his ensemble to follow him as he stalked away.

"It'd actually be appreciated if they did," Captain Hawney grinned before going. "If they get eaten, it's that many less heathens to deal with back home."

Fredrick frowned after them.

Reydan White stared at me. "Jed. I do believe things will come to a head between us one of these days."

"Your days are numbered," I growled down at him while wondering why my father hadn't killed him yet.

"Others have tried and failed," he said ominously.

"Mr. White," Fredrick tilted his head slightly. "You didn't ask about Oscar."

"Yes," the tycoon looked around. "Where is he?"

"Eaten."

"Shame. But luckily, I have another paleontologist arriving in a week."

"That's rather... fortuitous of you," I drawled.

"Why, Mr. Smith. That's a big word for a nobody."

"I aim to impress."

Reydan hesitated, looking at me for a moment warily as though realizing perhaps he had underestimated me, before turning quickly to his gun hand. "Cato, let's go."

As Fredrick and I watched them walk away, the thought occurred to me to just shoot the man in the back and be done with it. But for that, I'd certainly be hanged by Colonel Carver, and there was still that chance of a pardon and a life with Skyla.

I mentally kicked myself for not turning around as soon as we had captured Tinker and before Reydan could work his evil magic on the narrative.

"Jed..." Fredrick started.

"What?"

"As Governor of Prehistoria, my office will be here in Whitesberg. I'll keep an eye on Reydan. If I can catch him up to no good, I will."

"Thanks Fredrick, I appreciate that. I suppose you'll be staying then?"

"Yes, sir. It's my job."

***

We ended up staying the night in Whitesberg waiting on the train, and with Asger's help, Otto and I debriefed our little expedition to Colonel Carver by lantern light. The Viking laughed when he saw how barely filled out the officer's map was, and quickly helped him pinpoint several areas of interest and use.

"Hairy men have village, here... and here."

"Not anymore. Pinkertons wiped them out," Hawney winked. "Sent a dozen ape slaves to the Shayana afterwards. They were most appreciative of the free labor."

"Pinkertons doing your dirty work for you?" I asked in disgust.

"They do as they are told."

"Novagant, here," the bearded axeman said, jabbing a stubby finger against the paper and ignoring our bickering.

"Novagant..." Colonel Carver said, rubbing his chin thoughtfully while Captain Hawney marked the spot Asger pointed out with a small x. "Would your people and this new Jarl of yours be interested in campaigning against the apes?"

"Campaigning?" the Viking asked, with an eyebrow raised in curiosity.

"Yes, fighting together against the apes."

He laughed loudly and shook his head. "No. We no need help against hairy men. Hairy men leave us be."

Hawney glanced up from the map in confusion. "Why do they leave you be?"

Asger patted the handle of one of the axes strapped to his waist. "We kill them."

Carver rubbed his eyes wearily.

I was leaning against a rough sawn post in the back of the room, watching all this unfold with amusement. This was civilized men trying to play modern politics with brutally efficient warriors.

Otto noticed my slight smile. "What funny, Huck Berry?"

The group heard the scarred Shaynee speak and turned to face us.

"What is it, Jed?" Hawney asked in disdain.

"Asger. Will you kill the apes for us if they pay you?"

The Viking's eyes lit up eagerly. "Pay what?"

I shrugged. "That's between you and Colonel Carver. But I'd reckon weapons, tools, whatever you'd like."

Asger nodded towards the Colonel's holstered pistol. "I like that."

Carver pulled the pistol out, looked at it for a moment, then gently slid it across the table to the Viking. "Consider it a gift and the beginnings of a long friendship against the apes."

The axeman grinned, picked it up, and pulled the trigger.

BOOM.

A hole punched through the map, through the table, and nearly through Hawney's foot.

The room was dead silent. You could have heard a pin drop.

Carver coughed and gently reached out to take the pistol from the Viking. "We will, of course, teach you how to use firearms."

Red crept around Asger's bearded face as the axeman flushed with embarrassment.

Otto chuckled as we turned to leave the room.

"Where are you two going?" Carver asked as he shucked the empty cartridge from the pistol.

"The Shaynee and I did our parts. We found the axemen and brought Asger back here to negotiate for the coming war against the apes. I figure we're good. Until you or that smooth talking Lieutenant Daniels talks Skyla or me into helping again. But right now," I glanced at my blood brother, "we're done."

Turning, we walked out the framed doorway and into the partially graveled street.

***

The others were waiting down by the stables with the Shaynee braves, so Otto and I headed that direction.

We walked by Carson's store, which was almost finished except for some glass behind the iron caged bars that covered the window. I was looking up, admiring the new Liberty Arms sign, when the gun salesman called to us from inside the store.

Slowing down, Otto and I moved onto the boardwalk as Carson walked out of the building. He took in the scarred Indian in a careful, studious look, then gave him a nod as if to signal that the brave was *alright*.

"Gentlemen. What are you up to this fine evening?"

Glancing at the mostly completed walls around the town, I noted the dozen or so Pinkertons and soldiers manning the scaffolding along the spiked top. "Trying to stay alive."

"How's that?"

"Reydan wants me dead, and his Pinkertons want all of us dead probably."

"Yes, word has gotten around that you killed and scalped a bunch of their friends."

I gave the Shaynee beside me a sideways glance. "The scalping wasn't my idea."

Otto shrugged uncaringly.

"I take it you're worried that Reydan will stir up the detectives to come after you with lit torches and pitchforks tonight?"

"The thought crossed my mind."

"What are you going to do about it?"

"Sleep lightly down in the stables with the rest of my party and all the Shaynees. We can defend ourselves well from there."

"You're more than welcome to come stay at the store. It's a good deal sturdier than the stables."

I glanced at the thick siding and iron bar covered windows. "I can see that. But I reckon there's still a chance that if Colonel Carver is here, Reydan will play nice and try to kill me some other time. Besides, I'd like to stay close to our mounts in case we have to make a run for it."

Carson scuffed a boot on the rough sawn boards of the boardwalk while looking down the street. A pair of detectives were walking along with a dozen or so construction workers. "Of course… if Carver were to get killed in the chaos, Captain Hawney would be in charge."

"You're just a jar full of peaches, aren't you?"

He chuckled.

"We go?" Otto asked, obviously impatient.

"Yeah, Otto. We go. Need to get back to the others before they come looking for us."

"Shaynee no look for Otto. Know Otto take care of self." He patted his decorated rifle slung over his shoulder for emphasis.

"Before you go, I've got something for you, Jed. It was a good thing we crossed paths, saved me from tracking you down. Besides, it might come in handy tonight."

"Please tell me it's the Maxim machine gun that is mounted on Reydan's armored railcar?" I felt myself getting excited.

"No. Sorry. Even I can't get those things yet. And trust me, I've been trying." He grinned conspiringly, "But I do have something you'll like. Be back in a minute."

I watched him go inside the store while Otto sighed and sat down on the boardwalk with his back to the building and his eyes on the street for any threats.

I was too excited to think about anything other than what Carson might have for me. He always had the best weapons and equipment. He'd given me my *Eighty-Six* and second Colt Peacemaker, which certainly elevated my gunslinger status up a notch.

Hoping it might be another Gatling and regretting leaving the one we had on the Thirsty Wench, I felt myself frown when the gun salesman stepped out of the store with a small square package wrapped in paper and tied with string.

"Uh. This doesn't look like a gun," I admitted as I took the package. There was a little bit of weight to it, but it was still fairly light. Holding it up to my ear, I shook it. Nothing jingled inside.

"It's something Skyla had me cook up for you. You should wait to open it with her."

"Skyla?" I guffawed. "What in the world…."

Twisting his mustache, he winked. "You've a keeper there, son. Don't mess it up."

"I get her if Huck Berry dies," Otto insisted from where he sat.

"All the more reason to stay alive." I flipped the package over, looking at it. There was no telling what it might be.

Giving up on guessing, I stuck my hand out.

Carson shook it firmly.

"Thank you, for everything."

"Keep your powder dry, and I'll be seeing you."

"Yes, sir."

***

Reaching the stable with the mystery package under my arm, Otto peeled off to sit with the other braves while I went looking for Skyla.

Charles and Asger directed me towards the back of the stables, where a lone lit lantern dangled from a hook.

I found her there, sitting on a bucket. She was sharpening a pencil with her chipped obsidian ape blade. Beside her rested a leatherbound notebook.

I stepped near and waited for her to notice me.

"Oh, hey Jed." She smiled. "Just trying to get some details in the drawing of that Tyrannosaurus before I forget them."

"Take your time. We've got the rest of the evening off," I grinned.

She saw the package under my arm and gestured with her pencil. "What's that?"

"This?" I raised the wrapped package into the light and lifted an eyebrow. "I've no idea. Carson said it was from you?"

She squealed in excitement and set her blade and pencil down. "Open it! Open it!"

"Okay, calm down. I will." Her enthusiasm was infectious, and I wondered what in Prehistoria she could possibly be so excited about. Pulling a bucket over to her, I sat and began to untie the strings.

After struggling with them for a minute, I finally pulled out my Bowie and cut through the infernal knot.

The paper fell aside, revealing a black leather vest. "Don't bad guys wear these?" I teased Skyla.

Laughing, she picked it up. "I didn't pick the color. But they certainly don't wear one like this..." Peeling back one side of the leather, she showed me dark green dragon scales sewn inside.

My jaw dropped. "This... this will stop bullets!"

"Shhhh!" she said, waving at me to lower my voice. "No one knows except Carson. And I suppose whoever sewed it together, but they wouldn't know the scales could stop most bullets."

"Skyla... I... this is a magnificent gift."

She shoved me gently. "Yes, it is. Especially if it keeps you alive. Now put it on!"

Standing, I slipped my arms through the vest and pulled it over my back. It felt like it'd been tailor fitted to my body. Reaching down, I felt for the butts of the Colt Peacemakers. The vest didn't get in the way. Perfect.

"I can't wait to get shot at!" I hissed at her excitedly.

"Oh, stop. And knowing you, you'll probably get shot at soon enough. Hopefully, not tonight!"

"Hopefully!"

Wrapping her up in my arms, I kissed her firmly. "Thank you, Skyla. You are truly the greatest woman alive."

Grinning, she kissed me back.

***

Asger woke me with the handle end of his axe.

My eyes popped open immediately, and my hand reached for the sawed-off shotgun on my blanket before I realized we weren't being shot at or burned out of the stables. I relaxed for a moment, my eyes adjusting to the darkness inside the stables.

"Jed."

"Yeah?"

The Viking pointed towards the front of the stable. There was a glimmer of light coming from over the spiked wall around Whitesberg.

It looked like we'd survived the night.

"How are the animals?" I asked while quietly slipping out of my blanket.

"Horses and ponies good. Sleipnir good. Horny Devil... still hurt."

"Yeah, getting bitten by a Toothed One will do that to you." I stood and arched my back to stretch out a few stiff muscles. "Losing some bone shield is still better than what happened to Oscar."

The axeman nodded, then shuffled off to wake the others.

I went to the horse stall next to mine. Skyla was lying on a mound of straw with a blanket wrapped tightly around her. Within reach was her gun belt with the Herbert-Melvin pistol and sacrificial trike horned ape knife.

She was learning.

Dropping to a knee, I gently shook her by the shoulder.

"Skyla. Wake up," I said softly.

Her eyes fluttered, then opened, taking me in leaning above her. She grinned. "Nice vest."

I smiled back. "Some pretty girl gave it to me."

She shook her head at the tease and faked a frown. "Whatever keeps you alive."

"Yes, ma'am. You ready to go home?"

She stood, grabbed her gun belt and quickly buckled it about her waist. "The sooner the better."

Holding hands, we walked to the front of the corral. Charles was forking some hay to Sir Lancelot and tipped his hat at us. "Nice vest, Jed."

"Thank you, Skyla got it for me."

"It suits you. Makes you look much more distinguished... but in kind of a bad guy way. It being black leather and all."

I grinned. "It definitely suits me then."

Reaching the open doorway of the stables, I was baffled to see the Reverend sitting next to the corral with his shotgun across his lap and reading his tattered Bible.

"Morning, Jedidiah." He tipped his black hat. "And you as well, Ms. Stratten."

"Good morning." I looked around at the small groups of workers moving towards their assigned buildings and such to get the day going. There were probably four dozen of them wandering around, and another half dozen detectives sitting around the boardwalk jawing in front of the partially completed saloon. The place wasn't even finished yet and was getting customers. "What are you doing out here, Reverend?"

"Just keeping the peace."

"You and Old Bessy?" I gestured at the scripture inscribed shotgun.

"It does dissuade some folks to not bother others."

I chuckled. "That it does. Thank you."

He folded his good book, stood and shouldered the shotgun. "Looks like my work is done here for now. I'll be seeing you, Jedidiah." He tipped his hat. "Ms. Stratten."

"Thank you, Reverend," she replied with a smile.

"Anytime." Turning, he walked down the street, humming a hymn.

"Kind of mysterious fellow, isn't he?" I told her.

"Yes... very strange."

We watched the man of faith walk away, greeting various workers by name and others with a nod of his head.

***

An hour later, we watched Asger leave Whitesberg as he rode back to Novagant on Sleipnir.

Horny Devil bellowed softly after the red and black trike, as though sad to see the big dinosaur leave. Or it could have been from the lingering pain of having half his bone shield bitten off.

The axeman promised to tell the Jarl of our victory over the Toothed One and said he'd make sure to embellish the battle in telling so it wouldn't appear too easy.

"I'm going to miss him," I told Skyla. "He was an interesting man and a great fighter. And he told some great bedtime stories."

Skyla laughed, "Think we will see him, or Jarl Mikah again?"

"The way our fate and Prehistoria's seems to keep intertwining, probably so. Especially with your father pushing me to be a do-gooder for the Army."

Fredrick moved beside Skyla and gave the pair of us a wide toothy grin. "Ready to get Horny Devil drunk again?"

Groaning, Skyla slapped his arm playfully. "A bunch of cowboys and Indians playing with a dinosaur... like children."

I looked at her in fake shock. "What sort of child has three bottles of whiskey?"

Chuckling, Fredrick removed his hat and wiped sweat off the band. Even this early in the morning, it was hot.

"Are you certain it's safe to stay behind?" Skyla asked Fredrick worriedly.

"Probably not. But I've got Carson setting my office up with plenty of hidden guns... That I hopefully will not need."

"Keep them loaded. Just in case." I shook Fredrick's hand. "I reckon we'll see you at Wade and Ashley's wedding?"

"Wouldn't miss it for the world."

"Take care until then."

"You two as well."

The train whistled as it approached Whitesberg, a signal for the giant portcullis on that side of the wall to begin lifting. "Let's get everything and everyone loaded up." Skyla and I began walking towards the station.

"Don't forget to count all the little Indians!" Fredrick called after us.

A few hours later, we rode the train through the Shimmer to Fort York. They'd repaired it a good bit since we'd left. Even though it probably wasn't needed, the small fence they previously had had been rebuilt with a much more solid one, complete with sharpened stakes to slow a cavalry charge.

Disembarking, we rounded up our mounts, got wobbly Horny Devil off his special rail car, and said goodbye to the Shaynee braves for now.

Otto clasped my arm in his. "You all come to village. Eat, drink, fight. Just like Vikin."

"Can't Otto, got a ranch to attend to. That's if the Shaynee left me any cows."

"You blood brother! Your cows... our cows... same."

I frowned and the scarred brave laughed.

A light glinted off the back of the train. I faced it and found myself gritting my teeth. Reydan's armored car was attached at the back. For what purpose the tycoon was coming back to this side, I couldn't guess.

Most likely to finish me off.

"Not today, Jed," Arthur called as he slid into the saddle of his horse. The Scot was watching me stare at the railcar.

I dipped my head at him. "Yeah, not today."

"Today, we live. Today, we celebrate. We worry about tomorrow, tomorrow."

"Sounds like a plan," Skyla told him as she walked over to us. She had her coat on and was carrying mine underneath her arm; we'd stashed them at Fort York before leaving for Prehistoria.

Thank goodness. It was freezing on this side.

Pulling the heavy coat on over my black, dragon scale vest helped immediately to cut the wind that was blowing over the plains towards the mountain range the Shimmer was inside.

Waving at Arthur as he rode off with the Shaynee braves for whatever big pow-wow they'd have in their village tonight, I winked at Skyla. "Let's go home."

"Absolutely!"

***

My ranch was as we'd left it. Except for a trio of envelopes resting on the table.

One was addressed to Skyla, and the other, me. I was a bit put off that it hadn't been stamped with the royal seal of the Smithsonian in wax. At least, I figured he'd have one, being the Regent and all.

"What does yours say?" Skyla asked. From outside, Sara bellowed pitifully; the little trike couldn't fit through the door anymore and was not happy about that.

I skimmed the neatly folded paper. Morgan's handwriting was small and a bit sloppy, as though from a man who was accustomed to writing often and quickly.

"Seems like your father is making some headway in my pardon. He's called in a few favors and such. What about yours?"

"It's from Mother. She's venting about how horrible this place is and how excited she is to be back east."

"Well, she did come west only to get shot."

Skyla nodded absently while reading the rest of the letter. "She's feeling much better though, and once again demands that I return home as soon as I read this." She picked up the envelope from the table and looked inside. "Oh, she even bought me a train ticket. But there's just one, so she doesn't want you to come with me."

"That's nice. But what's that?" I pointed to what looked like her father's handwriting on the back of the letter.

She turned it over and gulped. "Father says he's proud of me." She smiled slightly, then sniffed. "That means a lot to me."

I drew her close, encircling her shoulders with my arms. "As it should. You've done many great things, and many more to come."

"Will we ever have peace, Jed? With Reydan White trying to kill you?"

"Nah." I folded Morgan's letter, slipped it back in the envelope, then tossed it into the fireplace where it was quickly consumed by flames. I couldn't risk anyone else reading that, if they heard I was up for a pardon, they'd be curious about my past. "But once my old man kills him, things should settle down."

"Speaking of which," she pointed at the third envelope. I'd avoided it because it had Orville written across the front in my father's neat script.

He and Texas Travis had both been missing when we returned. Bo told me they'd packed up and ridden off a couple of days ago without saying so much as a goodbye or thank you.

I took it Bo was a bit sore about that.

Using my Bowie, I slit the back of the envelope open and pulled out the folded piece of paper. The message was brief.

"If we fail, it's on you to make it right.
Love, Father."

Skyla gently took the letter from me and read it. "Gene's really going to do it, isn't he?"

"Yeah," I said softly.

"Good."

***

Two days later, on the morning of Wade and Ashley's wedding, they struck.

The sun was coming up over the eastern pasture and I was saddling Carbine when the bullet struck me in the back.

Pain shot through my kidneys and knocked the air out of me as I crumpled.

Faintly, I heard the lone boom of a rifle from the tree line as I lay gasping and curled in a ball on the trampled dirt.

Grabbing the lower rail of the fence, I pulled myself to a kneeling position as tears streamed down my face from the pain.

Carbine whinnied and nudged his head against me. The *Eighty-Six* was tucked into the scabbard and far from my grasp. But I had my pistols.

Gritting my teeth, I turned to face the trees and the unknown shooter.

A row of horsemen charged. A dozen of them, all wearing black. Faint flashes of light came from the badges on their hips.

Pinkertons.

Rifles and pistols boomed from the riders. Bullets hit around me, spraying me with splinters from the rail.

Carbine trotted for the safety of the far side of the corral.

I couldn't blame him.

Drawing my right pistol, I could only watch as Bo burst out of the bunkhouse with rifle in hand and was immediately cut down. He twisted towards me, his face in shock and his white undershirt splattered with blood from multiple bullets.

I emptied the pistol at the riders.

One fell.

Another bullet hit me from the unseen rifleman... this time in the side.

I pitched forward on my face. My body wanted to scream at the pain, but there was no air in my lungs.

Toppling over, I struggled to breathe while grasping for my other Peacemaker.

228

The riders reached me. One stopped while the others kept firing at the house where Skyla and Charles were beginning to fire back. Hooves pounded the ground around me, threatening to trample me to death.

Dismounting, a lone Pinkerton kicked me over with his boot. The Colt fell, unfired, from my numb fingers.

Laying on my back, I looked up at him helplessly while wishing I could rip the face off his skull.

Detective Thompson smiled back down at me.

"Nothing personal, Jed."

Raising his pistol, he fired.

***

To be continued.

Erik Testerman is a veteran grunt of the glorious Marine Corps, a 'faster than he is accurate' competitive shooter, and an admirer of fine arms and armaments out of his financial reach. He lives in the mountains of North Carolina with his lovely wife, two rambunctious children, and a slobbery English Mastiff.

To learn more about Erik Testerman or to follow his exploits as he navigates the world of the written word, visit http://GunPowderAndInk.blog or on his Facebook page at http://www.facebook.com/AuthorErikTesterman

CHECK OUT OTHER GREAT DINOSAUR BOOKS

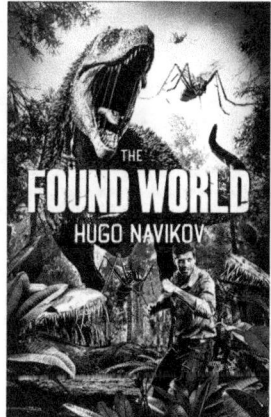

THE FOUND WORLD
by **Hugo Navikov**

A powerful global cabal wants adventurer Brett Russell to retrieve a superweapon stolen by the scientist who built it. To entice him to travel underneath one of the most dangerous volcanoes on Earth to find the scientist, this shadowy organization will pay him the only thing he cares about: information that will allow him to avenge his family's murder.

But before he can get paid, he and his team must enter an underground hellscape of killer plants, giant insects, terrifying dinosaurs, and an army of other predators never previously seen by man.

At the end of this journey awaits a revelation that could alter the fate of mankind ... if they can make it back from this horrifying found world.

HOUSE OF THE GODS
by **Davide Mana**

High above the steamy jungle of the Amazon basin, rise the flat plateaus known as the Tepui, the House of the Gods. Lost worlds of unknown beauty, a naturalistic wonder, each an ecology onto itself, shunned by the local tribes for centuries. The House of the Gods was not made for men.

But now, the crew and passengers of a small charter plane are about to find what was hidden for sixty million years.

Lost on an island in the clouds 10.000 feet above the jungle, surrounded by dinosaurs, hunted by mysterious mercenaries, the survivors of Sligo Air flight 001 will quickly learn the only rule of life on Earth: Extinction.

SEVEREDPRESS

facebook.com/severedpress
twitter.com/severedpress

CHECK OUT OTHER GREAT DINOSAUR BOOKS

PRIMORDIA
by **Greig Beck**

Ben Cartwright, former soldier, home to mourn the loss of his father stumbles upon cryptic letters from the past between the author, Arthur Conan Doyle and his great, great grandfather who vanished while exploring the Amazon jungle in 1908.

Amazingly, these letters lead Ben to believe that his ancestor's expedition was the basis for Doyle's fantastical tale of a lost world inhabited by long extinct creatures. As Ben digs some more he finds clues to the whereabouts of a lost notebook that might contain a map to a place that is home to creatures that would rewrite everything known about history, biology and evolution.

But other parties now know about the notebook, and will do anything to obtain it. For Ben and his friends, it becomes a race against time and against ruthless rivals.

In the remotest corners of Venezuela, along winding river trails known only to lost tribes, and through near impenetrable jungle, Ben and his novice team find a forbidden place more terrifying and dangerous than anything they could ever have imagined.

PANGAEA EXILES
by **Jeff Brackett**

Tried and convicted for his crimes, Sean Barrow is sent into temporal exile—banished to a time so far before recorded history that there is no chance that he, or any other criminal sent back, has any chance of altering history.

Now Sean must find a way to survive more than 200 million years in the past, in a world populated by monstrous creatures that would rend him limb from limb if they got the chance. And that's just his fellow prisoners.

The dinosaurs are almost as bad.